D0608519

Reckoning

Scottsdale Series, Book 1

Rivercourt Reads

ISBN: 978-1-9162473-1-4

1

France, 22nd May 1940

"I think he had rather serious intentions towards us, Sergeant." Head cocked, Lieutenant Arthur Scottsdale gazed down at the body that lay spreadeagled before them. Sergeant Grant glanced at his Lieutenant and back to the German. Deciding a response was not required, he chose to remain silent. The dead man represented the end of the enemy's advance party and his inexplicable decision to charge had met with its inevitable end; he'd been cut down.

As his exhausted men were chivvied into moving out again, Scottsdale paused to take a sip of blood warm water, gazing out over the fields slumbering in the sunshine. The mournful lowing of cattle that hadn't been milked drifted towards him; their owners had fled. It was a landscape that felt timeless, yet modernity had come, violently, to this world. A babble of French voices and crying children filled the air. It reminded him of summer holidays and the murmur that accompanied large crowds relaxing at the beach. That was before everything changed and now it was the sound of thousands of refugees crawling along with their possessions loaded on carts, horses and wheelbarrows. Cooking pots, mattresses, clothes, chairs, tables, pictures, tools, pets, all snatched up from the approaching chaos. Heads bowed, they trudged towards the coast and an illusion of safety. Scottsdale saw a great frightened line, a dark stain upon the farmland, families mixed up, an occasional soldier intermingled, and in the background was black smoke and the thunder of guns.

He shook his head in frustration. Only a week ago he and the rest of the 2nd Battalion, The Essex Regiment, had marched into Belgium to finally face the German army. Everywhere they went, smiling people had offered their praise, their food and their thanks; it had been all Scottsdale could do to keep his men sober. The cynics among the men observed sourly that they only gave free food and drink to the condemned, but it didn't dent Scottsdale's determination. His initial nerves had given way to excitement at the prospect of impending action and the cheering civilians had been a validation, that what they were doing was right. Yet those same people now fled, sometimes so quickly their meals lay cooling on the table and the British Expeditionary Force was running with them.

Taking off his helmet he wiped away the trickle of sweat that snaked down his cheek. Standing a shade over six foot-tall, his uniform sat slightly awkwardly on his lean frame. Where once he had taken such care to avoid the slightest blemish, his battledress was now ingrained with dirt. The dust was everywhere, accentuating an angular face that framed a pair of alert brown eyes. He automatically swept his dark brown hair back before replacing his helmet. In his early days in the mess a senior officer had advised him to use brylcreem – "much smarter, old boy" – but he had refused, instinctively distrustful of being told to conform; they would take him to him as he was, not a version of himself presented for their benefit.

Shifting on his swollen feet, he pressed a hand into the dull ache that had made a permanent home in the small of his back. His busy mind noted this in a detached manner, focused only on the need to reform with battalion; to somehow get out of this mess and get home alive. As he pondered their next move, some of the refugees slowed, heads turning to the sky. His instinctive irritation was swiftly replaced by a stab of fear as he heard the first screams. People began throwing themselves into ditches and fleeing into the surrounding fields. Scottsdale found the dark spec coming impossibly fast out of the blue sky. The grating whine of the Messerschmitt Bf 109 liquid-cooled, inverted-V12 aero engines grew bolder as it swept in, the deep chatter of its dual synchronized machine guns sparking panic. Here and there a soldier defiantly, pointlessly, raised a rifle to fire back but Scottsdale was helpless as he saw a family found by the fire, their brief cries cut off by a sudden, bloody death. He closed his eyes and cursed. He was no longer excited.

***

Gathering his platoon together, Scottsdale spoke urgently. In the chaos on the roads they'd lost touch with the rest of the battalion, but a harassed dispatch rider had finally given him directions.

"Grab a drink," he began. "We're heading for Meurchin where we'll get further orders. What we need now is speed – anything you don't need, drop. We have to get back to battalion. And if I find anyone looting, I promise I will take you out and shoot you myself," he growled. There was a muted chuckle from the men and Scottsdale glared at them. "I mean it. If you get left behind to become breakfast for a panzer so be it, but I have to tell the Army why. And I hate dealing with the paperwork." In truth, his concern for private property had been steadily eroding under the twin pressures of German attack and spares supplies, but he was concerned that someone could get left behind in the chaos. He felt the responsibility of getting his men home keenly and knowing his soldiers, at the first opportunity they'd be scavenging.

"We leave in five minutes," he continued. "Sergeant Grant?"

Grant materialised next to him. "Yes, sir."

"Check equipment and rations and see if you can get anything useful from this mess," he said gesturing to the variety of abandoned equipment that littered the area.

Sergeant Grant turned his steady gaze on the platoon, who shifted before him. "Right you lot. You heard the officer. Wilkins, Marsh, go and have a look at that pile. Rest of you, check your water. Anyone short, come to me. And make sure your weapons are clean and ready. I'll be checking."

The men looked back expectantly. "That means now," Grant barked, and the men dispersed quickly. Safely out of earshot, the grumbling of tired men rippled through the summer air.

"Bloody Frogs," Private Wilkins muttered. Ever reliable for the pessimism of his opinions, his expectations of war and of foreigners had been satisfactorily fulfilled since their arrival. "We've barely seen any fucking Germans and all we keep doing is retreating; never any good relying on the bleeding French – no wonder we're on our tod marching back."

"And bugger all to eat either," Private Marsh groused as he settled the Bren gun over his shoulder.

"Pipe down the both of you," Corporal Davenport interjected cheerily. "It may never happen."

Marsh snorted. "I think you'll find it already has, Corp," he observed.

Scottsdale ignored them and consulted his map. "Let's go," he ordered, and they struck off from the main road. The long grass brushed their legs and the sounds of refugees and engines momentarily faded. He idly picked a piece of grass and snapped it in half while even the usual coarse conversation of the platoon quietened. Scottsdale followed the path of a butterfly that merrily pranced ahead of them before turning to glance back at the men. Exhaustion was etched on their faces and he instinctively straightened his aching back. He was anxious to lead by example and not only that, but to lead well. Grimacing, he recalled the cavalier attitude of some of the officers, who blithely dismissed the men as little more than sacrificial lambs destined for death. Scottsdale had forced himself to calm his impulsive anger at their attitude and now shook his head to clear the memory, turning instead to their current plight.

Wild rumours were circulating and only snatches of reliable information had trickled down, but it was clear that something was terribly wrong. Having travelled briskly into Belgium, the 2nd Essex spent an unnerving few days in reserve on the outskirts of Brussels. The volume of refugees was ominous, but more sobering was the bombardment of the city. Scottsdale had watched in some fascination as tracer fire arced lazily into the night sky, but the accompanying drumbeat of falling bombs was more sinister, as were the results. So great was the glare from the burning city, the battalion motor transport didn't have to use their headlights as they travelled through the night. His unease was made worse by their constant retreat; all their briefings had focused on the need to move forward and fight in Belgium, yet over the last week they had been marching steadily back to France. This was not, however, to be viewed as a retreat, as Scottsdale had found out during a recent briefing. "It's not a retreat, it's a withdrawal," the brigade Intelligence Officer had corrected him sternly.

"Can't say it makes much difference when you're being shot at by the Luftwaffe, sir," Scottsdale remarked.

"Don't be impertinent, Scottsdale. We're withdrawing and that's how you shall describe it."

The traditional beginning of a British Army campaign, Scottsdale thought; the strategic withdrawal.

They'd barely been able to snatch a few hours of sleep as they fell back, the towns they passed - Aspelare, Zottegem, Bellegem Boos and Seclin - blurring into one long sleep deprived march. Several times they'd been strafed and bombed as they struggled along the congested roads. It was Scottsdale's first taste of enemy action and it had been both exhilarating and terrifying. Vivid images stuck in his mind; the foreleg of a cart horse neatly sliced off by shrapnel, its shrieks of agony as shocking as the cries of wounded soldiers; an unmarked nun sitting on the kerb, stone dead, clasping a frightened, crying, six-year old girl in her arms. Men and transport lost contact and limped in each evening. Among it all, groups of French soldiers drifted back in a disorganised mass, surly and many throwing away their equipment. A panicked undercurrent was palpable among both soldiers and civilians, and he'd worked hard to ensure their own unit cohesion remained as they struggled to stay in touch with the battalion. He could scarcely believe more men hadn't been lost.

A shout interrupted his reverie and he breathed a sigh of relief. As the gentle sun of the evening warmed them they had at last found the outposts of battalion. Sore and weary they moved through the lines, the inevitable taunts and catcalls of the early arrivals following them. Scottsdale went to report to Major Carter who had established his headquarters in a large manor house. He had taken over the battalion a few days into the German offensive after the colonel in charge had been invalided out. In stark contrast to most, Carter was virtually immaculate.

"Scottsdale. You're late," he boomed. A head shorter than Scottsdale, his squat frame bristled as he stared at Scottsdale. "Where the bloody hell have you been? You look bloody awful."

Scottsdale threw a tired salute. "We were held up by the refugees, sir. The Royal Army Service Corps directed us off the main road but we ended up even worse off." He paused. "The Germans are strafing the columns, sir."

"Yes, I heard, disgusting behaviour," Carter growled. "Causing chaos, Scottsdale, absolute chaos and I can't abide it!" As the Major spoke, Scottsdale couldn't help but think that Carter was actually enjoying himself. He radiated a bullish energy, but his concern for the men under his command was genuine and well known.

"Well?" Carter's voice cut into Scottsdale's ruminations and he realised he'd been staring at his commanding officer without speaking. "You're staring at me like a particularly backward child," Carter continued.

"Er, yes, sir," Scottsdale said lamely.

"Are you addled, Scottsdale? Have you contracted some particularly virulent strain of VD? No? Well, now that you've finally deigned to join us, you're to rejoin Captain Revie and C Company on the canal. The Germans are bloody everywhere, and we expect contact shortly."

Scottsdale couldn't conceal his astonishment. "The Germans are already here, sir?" Rumours had filtered through about how far the Germans had penetrated, but if they were being thrown into a defensive line here the situation was far worse than he'd thought.

"Yes, you pea brained fart, they're already here. That's why we're guarding it!" Carter rubbed his hands together. "We and the rest of 25 Brigade are now part of what the great high chiefs have dubbed the 'canal line'; which is essentially scraping together anyone who can walk and throwing them along a line of canals running all the way from here to the coast. The Germans have gotten loose to our south, like a fox among French chickens. They've turned our flank and reached the coast at Abbeville already."

Scottsdale gaped. "Christ, sir."

"He has nothing to with it, just the usual mix of complacency, incompetence and a determined enemy. Ironic really when you consider the signal circulated by General Gort yesterday."

Intrigued as to what the commander of the BEF was saying, Scottsdale picked up the piece of paper Carter slid towards him and began reading. "'News from the south reassuring. We stand and fight. Tell your men.'" Scottsdale looked up. "That's an interesting way of interpreting 'reassuring', sir."

"Indeed, Scottsdale! In less than two weeks they've punched a hole through the French and reached the sea, all the while chuckling their Teutonic heads off as our army waltzed into Belgium; hence why we've been falling back so fast. They've cut us off from the rest of France and there's bloody Panzers everywhere."

"It doesn't seem possible they've made it so far, so fast, sir," Scottsdale said, shaking his head. "There's so much defeatism and panic out there. I can't understand why they don't seem able to stand and fight. This is their country for God's sake."

"I tend to agree," said Carter grimly. "But they're badly led and being sat behind a bloody great fortification does tend to dent your optimism when the enemy simply drives round you. Nevertheless, our Tank Brigade counter attacked at Arras yesterday and although they ran into Rommel's Panzers and were beaten back, by all account we gave them a bloody nose." He eyed Scottsdale speculatively. "Do you know what 'Gott Mit Uns' means?"

"I believe it's 'God is With Us', sir," Scottsdale opined.

"Very good, Scottsdale," Carter said in mock amazement. "Apparently you weren't just gazing at your teacher's titties during school. Yes, the Germans wear it on their belt buckles and I'm sure they're currently thinking He is indeed. But when they get here, the good Lord above will have nothing to do with it. Herr Hitler has had his fun. We hold the canal."

"Yes, sir. Standing our ground will be a relief."

"Good. We've been allotted a front of about four miles to hold and you'll find C Company down at Pont-a-Vendin, a mile south of here. We're to guard it while the engineers blow the bridges. Understood?"

"Yes, sir."

"Good. Now bugger off." As Scottsdale turned to leave Carter stopped him. "Glad to have you back, Arthur."

"Glad to be back, sir," Scottsdale replied meaningfully.

Scottsdale gathered the men and set off for Pont-a-Vendin, a sleepy town that huddled in the crook of the elbow created by the Deule canal turning south then east. Sending Sergeant Grant to find the rest of C Company, Scottsdale took in the feverish activity around him. Barges were being dragged into the middle of the canal and burned, their furious owners remonstrating with the Royal Engineers. Scottsdale sympathised – the barges were their livelihoods – but they had to be destroyed lest they afford the Germans a means to cross. Streams of refugees continued to appear, desperate to get across the canal ahead of the advancing German columns, but Scottsdale felt a degree of confidence; the canal was a significant obstacle. Around him emplacements were being constructed, rifle pits dug, and houses fortified. Food and ammunition were stockpiled. A Bren gunner on watch carefully wiped the glistening barrel of his gun with a rag while his mate puffed a cigarette. Sergeants were bellowing instructions and obscenities with Sergeant Grant's growl rising above the din.

"No, Pendle, not like that! If the Germans don't kill you – which would be a fucking miracle – then I will! Move!" The sound was reassuringly familiar, and Scottsdale allowed himself a brief grimace of satisfaction as he went to find company headquarters and report.

There he ran into Lieutenant McDonald, universally known as Jock despite his innate Englishness. "Ah, there you are, Scottsdale," McDonald said. "Was wondering if Jerry had you. How are you getting on?"

From the distance came the rumble of artillery fire. Scottsdale sat down wearily. "Don't look now, Jock, but I think we're being followed."

2

The day dawned to the crash of bridges being blown. The men watched in glee, but Scottsdale did not join in. Blowing the bridges meant they could expect contact soon and the dwindling flow of refugees, always a sign the enemy was close, reinforced his apprehension. An eerie silence hung over the position until the ominous rumble of diesel engines drifted across the canal, materialising into a motorcycle combination that raced towards them. A few well aimed shots from the Boys anti-tank rifle chased it off but the men now knew the assault was imminent. Occasional artillery began to hit the town, keeping the men's nerves on edge. Each man knew that this soft summer day could be his last and Scottsdale, too, could keenly feel the grip of his anxiety, which coalesced in a hard knot in his gut. He breathed deeply, determined to project confidence.

Straightening his tall frame, he inspected their positions, stopping here and there to talk quietly to the men. They were nervous, that was clear, but he was satisfied they were ready. Stooping into a bunker, he found several of his platoon sitting and smoking. Gesturing for them to stay seated, he looked round. A bench cut back into the wall had been covered in blankets and acted as a makeshift bed, while a variety of postcards and pictures dotted the walls. Several empty crates were being used as table, cards from an earlier game scattered across the surface. Clearing some space among the scattered kit and mess tins, Scottsdale sat down. "Looks like you've settled in, gentlemen," he remarked.

"All the comforts of home, sir," Davenport replied. "I can think of a few things that are lacking, sir," Wilkins said sourly.

"Plenty of brass to be had if you know where," Pendle replied.

Wilkins rolled his eyes. "Is that all you can think about? I'm talking about food."

"Well I'm glad that it's food that's on your mind," Scottsdale said cheerfully. "The MD says there's a particularly virulent strain of VD doing the rounds that, ah, shrivels your equipment."

There were a few uncomfortable looks which Scottsdale affected not to notice. "Well, at least we're not digging ditches, sir," Grant said, filling the silence.

"That was awful," Pendle agreed. "It was so cold." Scottsdale thought back to their arrival in September last year, when they'd largely been used for pioneering work, creating anti-tank obstacles, unloading ships and repairing roads. The bitter winter had made it even worse. Being assigned to the 25th Infantry Brigade had been a relief; if nothing else, being attached to a fighting unit meant proper training and less manual work. "Silver linings I think it's fair to say," he agreed. "Anyway, we'll be here for a bit," he said, "so make yourselves as comfortable as you can. I'll see if we can get some more food down here. Is there anything else you need?"

"Well, my boots are killing me, sir," Marsh said. "They're too tight."

"Don't mind him, sir," Grant replied. "Always been a few bob short of a pound haven't you, Private? The army doesn't issue boots that don't fit; your feet are the wrong size."

As the laughter died down, Scottsdale stood, satisfied the men were holding up. "You did well today; they'll be more of it to come I'm sure, so make sure you get as much rest as you can."

Scottsdale and Grant moved outside. "They seem to be holding out well," Scottsdale remarked, offering Grant a cigarette.

"So far, yes, sir. They're trying not to think about the lads who aren't there."

"Probably for the best."

"In my experience it is, sir. It's not something you get used to, but it does get easier."

Scottsdale paused. He sensed that Grant was talking to him as much he was about the men and he was grateful. "Makes sense, Sergeant. Isn't it terrible it gets easier."

"Maybe, sir, but it must, otherwise we can't do our jobs."

"And an important job it is too, Sergeant." Scottsdale thought of the fighters strafing the refugees; of the indiscriminate destruction of the towns and villages they had passed, the dead dogs and shattered buildings. "We can't lose."

"Can't see that happening, sir."

"Glad you're so confident, Sergeant."

Grant shrugged. "Long way to go yet, but we aren't beat yet, sir, and there's always the channel."

"Thank god for the channel," Scottsdale agreed. "For now, keep an eye on them. Let me know if there's anyone you want me to talk to."

Grant hesitated. Scottsdale knew he was struggling with the idea of confiding in an officer about one of the men; usually they would take care of this themselves, but Scottsdale hoped – and needed if he was to lead the kind of unit he wanted – they would trust him. "What's on your mind, Sergeant," he asked.

Grant looked back at Scottsdale, seeming to weight up his officer. Finally, he spoke. "He won't thank you for asking, but Marsh has been hit hard by Stevenson's death." Scottsdale thought back. Private Stevenson, Marsh's previous loader on the Bren gun, had been hit by a mortar round early in the week and they'd found out he had died of his wounds on their return.

"I'll talk to him," Scottsdale said. "Thank you, Sergeant."

"Thank you, sir," Grant replied and stooped back into the dugout. Scottsdale gnawed his lip. With a deep breath, he walked towards their outposts, finding his way to the Bren position. There he found Marsh staring fixedly out towards the enemy over the barrel of his machine gun.

"Private," Scottsdale said, sliding in alongside. "All quiet?"

"Not a mouse stirring, sir," Marsh replied woodenly. "It's been a tough week," Scottsdale ventured. "But the battalion did well."

"Yes, sir," Marsh replied. "We just all didn't make it though, did we?" In the gloom his voice was tinged with bitterness.

Scottsdale groped for the right words; he felt every casualty keenly, but he had to make sure those that remained were functioning as best they could. "No, we didn't all make it," he agreed. "But they died well."

"And what does that mean, sir?" Marsh asked with a trace of scorn.

"It means we save more by holding the Germans back. And that gives their death meaning; it matters."

"I guess you're right, sir."

"I am right," Scottsdale replied forcefully. "And before this is over there's a good chance more of us won't make it; so let's just make sure we take as many of the bastards with us we can, eh?"

"That I can agree with, sir," Marsh said grimly. "I want to hurt the bastards if I'm honest."

"You'll have plenty of chances, Private," Scottsdale replied. "Just don't do anything stupid – and follow my orders."

"Fair enough, sir," Marsh said.

Satisfied, Scottsdale moved off. He was winding through their position when a shout went up as a small reconnaissance plane appeared overhead. Several of the men raised their rifles, a practice Major Carter actively encouraged. "Remember, lads. Take them like a high pheasant," he bellowed. "Give them plenty of lead – five pounds to any man who brings one down. I've paid out ten already!"

The men grinned and opened a highly ineffective fire on the aircraft which disdainfully refused to alter course before turning and heading back to the safety of the German lines.

"Have you really paid out ten pounds already, sir?" asked Scottsdale.

"Of course not, Scottsdale. May as well be spitting at it for all the good it will do. Excellent for morale though which we'll need shortly." He gazed across the canal. "That plane means the party's about to start," he added softly.

At midday the bombers came. They were Dornier 17s from Kampfgeschwader 76 and the throaty hum of their engines rose steadily to a penetrating whine as they crabbed into view. The men waited nervously, mouths dry, hands clenching and unclenching on rifle stocks. A few prayed while others took refuge in their hate, girding themselves to repel the assault. Scottsdale reflected that his tremulous anticipation of action now seemed absurd, childlike; now he knew the taint of fear. Looking round he caught sight of Pendle, eyes wide, his lips moving in an inaudible prayer and tried to reassure him. "Steady, lads, we're safe enough here," he called out. "The RAF will be amongst that lot!"

Amongst the heavier drone of the bombers, Scottsdale picked out the higher pitched snarl of fighters, the rattle of their machine guns a welcome relief. Above them an uneven clash played out. Outnumbered and low on fuel, the RAF Hurricanes fell on the enemy bombers desperately. Yet protecting their flock swarmed the German fighters and, while several bombers were damaged, the majority lumbered forward and straightened out for the bombing run, leaping slightly as their payload wobbled clumsily towards Pont-a-Vendin.

On the ground, the blasts blended into one continuous concussion. Desperately making themselves as small as possible, the men huddled under cover as the town darkened under a layer of dirty smoke. Houses were set ablaze, shattered masonry flung across the roads. One bomb landed in the canal, lifting a great sheen of water over the forward positions. Men prayed. Scottsdale forced himself to look out in case the enemy infantry was on the move. Raising his head, he saw a stick of bombs falling obliquely across his front, exploding like dominos until the final geyser erupted near the company forward trenches. Popping back up, he glimpsed a body lying in the road. It had been blown clean out of a slit trench. The dead eyes momentarily held him spellbound until the patter of shrapnel compelled him to duck back into cover. As he did so, a soldier staggered in, running to where Scottsdale sheltered.

"Report to Captain Revie, sir!"

Scottsdale nodded, gut tightening at the thought of leaving shelter. Company HQ was further back in the town and he sprinted down the road at full pelt. He was turning a corner when an invisible hand picked him up and flung him to the side. Sitting up groggily, he remembered the old soldier's saying – you didn't have to worry about the ones you could hear, it was the one you didn't that get you. Touching his forehead, he looked at the red finger, before dragging himself to his feet. As he steadied himself with a hand on the nearest house, he glanced inside the shattered window and stared in disbelief. Lieutenant Berry, one of the officers who had spoken so witheringly of the men, was hunkered down, flinching at every explosion.

Scottsdale's anger surged. "Berry! What the hell are you doing?"

Berry looked up with a startled expression. "I'm – I'm on my way back to my platoon," he stammered.

Scottsdale regarded him with loathing. "Well, get on with it then," he snarled. "The men need you down there!"

Berry nodded and climbed slowly to his feet. Scottsdale felt an overpowering urge to go inside and drag him out, but the whine of an aircraft engine reminded him of his exposed position. With a final look at Berry, he ran down the street at a half crouch until he found Company HQ and threw himself through the door.

Inside, it was remarkably calm. Men were shouting as reports came in of casualties suffered and damage sustained but the machinery of an army unit was functioning. Scottsdale felt a tug on his arm and came face to face with Captain Revie, his company commander.

"Arthur, what's the situation with your section?"

"I'm sorry, sir, I can't hear a bloody thing – what was that?"

"What's the situation with your section?" Revie shouted.

"Oh – one killed and there are several more with light wounds, sir."

"Ok, get yourself bandaged up. Brigade have been on.

They're attacking all along the canal with tanks and infantry."

"Yes, sir. Some of the defences need repairing."

"Then see to it but we have to hold. We can't let them gain a bridgehead. Make sure the men understand."

"Got it, sir, we'll hold," Scottsdale replied grimly.

A shuddering crash broke off their conversation, both men involuntarily ducking as a layer of dust trickled down from the ceiling. Captain Revie coughed as Scottsdale sat down in the corner to have his wound tended to by a medical orderly.

"Come on," he urged the medic. The idea of his men being without him made him uneasy and he was eager to get back.

Captain Revie cocked his head, moving to the door and peering out. "Bastards have finished I think," he said. "Best get back to your lot."

"Yes, sir," Scottsdale agreed, thanking the orderly and darting outside, cautiously scanning the sky. He wound his way back to the canal through a pall of dust and smoke, noting how it had gone from overwhelming noise to relative peace so quickly. He also marvelled again at the sense of relief and exhilaration that coursed through him, lending him speed as he darted through the deserted streets.

The eerie silence continued. Eyes raised cautiously to windows and parapets; friends checked on each other and accepted with grim nods the news of men hurt or worse. There was no time to grieve for them now. Scottsdale ran along their section of trench, houses and rifle pits, crouching low and calling out.

"Steady, lads; watch for infantry; keep your heads low; watch for snipers." Men nodded, and NCOs gave hushed reports. Everyone waited for the next move, dreading the sight of infantry and tanks flooding towards them but the Luftwaffe wasn't finished.

There is beauty in war. A Spitfire swooping low as the sun sparkles on its canopy is beautiful; a destroyer carving through the ocean at thirty knots is beautiful. A Stuka attack is never beautiful. It is calculated, brutal and ruthless. High in the sky, dark pinpoints appeared as the first wave of these supremely efficient machines circled. They were Ju87Bs from Stukageschwader 2 and they flicked their inverted gull wings over for their near vertical dive on the British position. Their targets were points of resistance, headquarters and supply dumps.

"Oh Christ, oh Christ," Private Marsh mumbled, burying his head in his arms.

"Just fucking hit them," Private Pendle exhorted through gritted teeth.

The pop-pop of the British anti-aircraft weapons was overwhelmed by the banshee wailing from the Jericho trumpets fixed to each Stuka as they dived through the sparse clouds. Puffs of flak left dirty smears in the sky and one machine was hit, a ball of flame erupting from its wounded wing. The pilot fought to maintain control, but the aircraft rolled over and plunged shrieking to earth. At the last moment the remaining Stukas pulled up, pilots heaving on the controls, to disgorge their 250kg bombs with pinpoint accuracy. Scottsdale flinched as a house nearby was hit, fire eagerly starting to engulf the structure. To his horror, a soldier staggered outside, flames licking up his back, before running forward and hurling himself into the canal.

Time and again the Stukas came, falling on them with impunity. The town wilted under the assault, houses toppling forward, fires raging and all the while the men cowering, helplessly waiting for it to finish. A voice rang out, summing up the helplessness they felt. "Where the fuck are the RAF?" Scottsdale grimaced; the enemy had control of the sky and the infantry were suffering.

Finally, the wave of Stukas withdrew, leaving pillars of smoke rising from the battered town and Scottsdale moved through their position, his face smudged by smoke. "Be ready for the infantry!" he shouted urgently. "Whatever happens, we can't let them establish a bridgehead!"

As if on cue, machine gun fire cut through the air. German tanks had approached the canal and were targeting the forward positions. High explosive shells detonated amongst them, but it was the sight of the German infantry swarming down towards the canal, dragging rubber dinghies and anything that could float with them, that caused Scottsdale to draw in his breath.

"Open fire!" he roared. Boats emerged from the curtain of smoke that drifted across the canal from the burning houses. They were met with a storm of fire; rifles, Bren guns and the company mortars all hammered towards them. Face set in grim determination, Private Marsh waited as Howells, his loader, swiftly changed over the magazine on the Bren.

"Come on, Tommy," he urged, "They're almost on top of us!" Howells slapped Marsh's shoulder to indicate the Bren was ready, and Marsh snapped out several short bursts, teeth clenched, absorbing the impact of the gun against his heavy frame. One of the dinghies was disgorging German assault troops when the Bren found it, ripping the boat and its occupants into bloody ruin.

Sheer weight of numbers drove the enemy on. The pall of smoke from the burning buildings and tank-fired smoke shells shrouded the shore, allowing enough infantry to establish a foothold on the British side of the canal, pushing back the forward defences in a series of desperate clashes. Depleted and outnumbered the British fought back. A German jumped into a trench and was immediately hit by a burst of fire that spun him around. His comrades came on, shouting in fear and desperation, the stench of cordite, blood and shit mixing in the air. Grenades exploded inside houses with a flat crack, and rifles spat as the enemy advanced, clearing out the forward rifle pits and machine gun nests.

Marsh cursed as several Germans appeared on their flank, having worked their way around the gun position. Abandoning the Bren, he and Howells spun round and charged at the oncoming enemy. With a clash the sides met. A young German private slipped and could only look up in despair as Howells, face involuntarily fixed in a savage snarl, thrust his bayonet into the man's chest. His howl of triumph was immediately cut short as the next German shot him in the face, snapping Howells' head back in a mist of blood. Looking down from his position, Scottsdale felt a surge of anger rising in him.

"Bastards," he breathed. "Bastards." He felt vicious and a need to inflict misery on those who had begun this. Damn these people, damn this war. They had to pay for what they were doing; they had to pay, and they would do so now. He felt a thrill of anticipation, feeding on the energy and anger that flowed through him. Summoning the remaining men of his platoon to him, he spoke loudly over the din.

"This is it. We clear out the bridgehead!" he exhorted. "We kill the bastards!" The men were grimly silent. Each was filthy, blackened by smoke and, in many cases, blood seeped from fresh wounds. Taking a deep breath Scottsdale shouted, "Essex! Advance!"

With a roar, they plunged into the melee. Scottsdale could hear the man behind him repeating over and over, "Oh sweet Jesus, oh sweet Jesus," as they closed on the enemy. Grenades flew back and forth, and Scottsdale was briefly blinded by the flash of a rifle discharging next to him. Men were using every means of assault. A German NCO relentlessly battered a private with the end of his rifle before Pendle embedded an entrenching tool in the man's neck. Both sides were spitting curses, striking out at every opportunity. Seeing a German take aim, Scottsdale swiftly bought his rifle to bear, shooting the man once, twice. Sensing movement ahead, he craned his head and roared in savage triumph, a flood of anger and joy surging through him; the enemy were falling back.

"They're retreating!" he shouted. "Drive them into the river!"

Their spirit broken, the Germans fled, scrambling back into the boats and frantically paddling back across the canal. Their tanks provided a curtain of covering fire, forcing Scottsdale and his men to ground where they continued to snipe at the fleeing infantry. One man was hit as he attempted to climb into a dinghy but stumbled forward and raised himself to his feet, limping on, only to be knocked down again. He stayed down this time, blood swirling away in the current.

***

Scottsdale headed back to his billet, walking slowly and enjoying the fading warmth of another mild evening. After the action earlier that day, he had been busy compiling casualty reports, getting their stretch of the canal defence's repaired and waiting nervously in case the Germans came again. Despite further artillery, it seemed the enemy had paused, and he took the opportunity after a final round of their position, to head back. Lowering himself gratefully onto an old ammunition box that acted as a makeshift chair outside the cottage, he lit a cigarette and inhaled deeply. Nature had laid on glorious days of sun and blue skies and the Germans were taking full advantage. Scottsdale shook his head just as McDonald ambled into view.

"As bad as that?" McDonald asked.

"Hello, Jock," Scottsdale said smiling. "Just the usual, I'm afraid."

"And on such a bonny day as this."

"You know you're not actually Scottish, don't you?"

"Indeed, but in fairness I feel you give me little recourse. Although it's damned odd; one of my ancestors was disembowelled at Culloden."

"How unfortunate."

"Well, yes, let's hope it works out better for us, but it does seem that we're in a spot of bother. In fact, it made me think of Shakespeare earlier."

"Why on God's green earth were you thinking about Shakespeare?"

"Henry V," McDonald said. Seeing Scottsdale's gesture of incomprehension, he continued.

"If we are marked to die, we are enough
To do our country loss; and if to live,
The fewer men, the greater the share of honour."

Scottsdale leant back, then looked back to McDonald. They both began to laugh, long and hard. Scottsdale wiped his eyes. "Christ, Jock," he said. "Madness isn't it." Even as their casualties mounted, he was being reminded of another French field where hundreds of years before men had fought and died. It was endless. He shook off the thought, afraid of melancholy, but his mind ran to the engagement earlier that day. Shivering, he recalled just how profound his fear had been when the enemy had flooded across the canal towards them, how helpless he'd felt as the Stukas had swooped down on them. Yet he'd also felt a burning rage as his men were cut down, an urgent need to avenge their deaths; and when the enemy broke, fierce joy, the exultant counterpoint to his fear. The euphoria that swept through him was intoxicating. He reasoned that it enabled him to operate, that for those short, chaotic minutes, he was a more effective leader; but he couldn't help but be troubled at taking any kind of pleasure amongst that horror, not least when men were dying around him, sometimes because of his orders. Wearily, he ran a hand over the rough stubble on his chin.

Reckoning

The enemy would come for them again tomorrow and they would have to be ready. He shook his head, mind as exhausted as his body, knowing that the sleep would be hard to find that night.

3

Dawn revealed their battered positions. Men stirred and spat, stretching stiff bodies. Occasional artillery fire had intruded throughout the night, keeping many awake. The detritus of battle lay scattered all around. A corpse bumped gently alongside wrecked dinghies at the edge of the canal, while dirty smoke leaked from still smouldering buildings. In the distance gunfire rumbled. Scottsdale could sense the malaise in his men and was determined to keep them busy. He firmly believed that idleness led to introspection and that was dangerous, in himself as much as the men. Brooding would do no good at all and so he summoned Sergeant Grant. Grant announced himself with a rap on the doorpost and stooped inside. He moved deliberately and straightened up. His bulky frame and carefully blank expression mastered by generations of NCOs gave a comforting air of solidity. Scottsdale had once seen him lift a cart almost single handed to clear a road blockage. Older than most of the platoon, he was one of the longer serving members who formed the backbone of the battalion. Grant's actions under fire had merely confirmed Scottsdale's first impressions - reliable, hard and not to be crossed. He was an excellent platoon sergeant and Scottsdale hoped with his help to mould the men into a highly effective fighting force.

"Come in, Sergeant," he said. "Orders for this morning. We need to make sure we're ready for any more assaults, so get the men moving. Repairs to the trenches and houses. Send Marsh to the quartermaster to see if he can scrounge some more rations and pick up some ammunition. I'll be inspecting at 1000."

"Yes, sir."

Scottsdale sensed the split second of hesitation in Grant's reply. "Speak your mind, Sergeant."

"The lads have taken a bit of a battering, sir. Perhaps light duties may be in order."

"I understand, but I want them busy. Hanging around won't help and we need this place ship shape."

"Very well, sir. I'll see to it." Grant saluted and left. Gazing out over their positions, Scottsdale could see Grant briefing the corporals and the inevitable mechanisms of army discipline kicking in as orders were passed down the chain. Taking his own advice, he took out a chart of northern France and began studying it. He was tapping his teeth meditatively with a pencil when there was a tap at the door.

"Lieutenant Scottsdale?" asked a runner. "You're to report to Brigade HQ at 1600, sir. A car will meet you."

Scottsdale shared a glance with McDonald. "Understood, thank you."

"I wonder what that's all about," McDonald asked as the man left. "Word of warning though. Nothing good comes of a summons such as this, mark my words!"

Scottsdale smiled wryly, but nonetheless he was intrigued. As the hours ticked by, he kept returning to the news, worrying at it like a sore tooth. Yet he had no real clue and realising there was no profit in speculation, he buried himself in the minutiae of platoon life, inspecting the positions, compiling casualty reports and trying every trick he'd learnt to find more rations. Blessedly, the front remained quiet with the only excitement provided by an occasional artillery round and an overzealous German patrol that was driven off just after lunch.

Finally, the clock ticked round towards 1600 and, with a final glance back, Scottsdale was driven the short distance to Brigade HQ. It was a hive of activity. Messengers bustled around, a stream of people flowing in and out, the darker shades of occasional navy uniforms mixing with the lighter blue of the RAF and, above all, the khaki of the army; Scottsdale hadn't seen so much red braid since his passing out parade. An unceasing peel of ringing telephones echoed around the entrance hall. He was led by a corporal to the very far end of the building and ascended some stairs. Here everything was quieter, less conspicuous. He felt instinctively wary as the corporal stopped and rapped on a door.

"Come," sounded a voice, and Scottsdale entered a small, richly furnished study. Neat rows of books filled the bookcases that covered two walls. Scottsdale's eye was drawn to a picture of a young man dressed in military uniform propped on a side table; it looked like it was from the last century. The blinds had been drawn over the sole window and a hushed light from several banker's lamps settled over the room. Three comfortable looking chairs were arraigned in front of a broad desk and standing behind it, pipe in hand, was a civilian in a shabby suit. He was entirely non-descript, of average height and sparse hair, except for a pair of grey eyes that observed Scottsdale over a wry smile. Major Carter sat to one side, his face twisted in irritation. On the other side sat a young woman, back straight and hands neatly folded in her lap. She was nearer Scottsdale in age and stared calmly back, inclining her brown curls in greeting as he approached the desk.

The silence lingered until, as he methodically filled his pipe, the man said, "Perhaps you'd be so kind as to introduce us, Major?"

"Lieutenant Scottsdale, this is Mr Griffin," Carter answered brusquely. "He works for the War Office and has something to discuss with us."

"Obliged to you, Major," Griffin said laconically. This," he added gesturing across the desk, "is Margaret Beaufort. As the Major has so kindly said, we work for the War Office. Specifically, Section D, but I doubt you'll have heard of us; or I should hope you haven't."

"New one to me, sir," Scottsdale assured him.

"You don't have to call me, 'sir,' Lieutenant. Had enough of that in the last war. One of the reasons I ended up in my current employment I dare say." He peered at Beaufort quizzically. "What's your excuse?"

"I don't believe you gave me much choice as I recall."

"Nonsense. That doesn't sound like me at all."

Beaufort turned to Scottsdale. "Mr Griffin is a man used to getting his way, Lieutenant."

"I do find it's usually in everyone's best interests," Griffin said.

"But I can help if you need me to," she added, ignoring Griffin.

"Appreciated, Miss Beaufort." Scottsdale replied.

"Shall we return to the matter at hand?" Carter cut in.

Griffin smiled amiably. "Good idea, Major. Now what we are about to discuss is top secret and I'll have you hung from the nearest tree if you repeat it without my authorisation. Clear?" he said, pointing his pipe at Scottsdale.

"There's no need to threaten him, Griffin," Carter growled.

"My dear Major, I don't doubt it, but it still needs to be said," Griffin replied easily, but it was belied by the flint hard stare of his eyes. "All manner of terrible things will happen if this information leaks, isn't that right, Miss Beaufort?"

"Various government acts would be breached, sanctions would have to be imposed. Technically, an act of treason I believe."

"So worth making sure we're clear, you see." "Crystal clear," Scottsdale replied tersely.

"Capital. Now, this is a war unlike any other, Scottsdale," Griffin continued. "We thought the last war was the war to end all wars, but really it was the crack in the dam that has led us here. When victory became so important that poison gas was used, that was the moment that the old ideals of war – chivalry, honour, all that claptrap – died. And with it grew the idea that anything is permissible, no matter how barbarous, as long as you win."

"It would be a fair observation that the implications have not been truly appreciated by our military establishment," Beaufort added delicately.

"As ever you rescue me with your diplomatic language," Griffin said. "Most of the military and political class have abjectly failed to grasp what this has meant and how to respond."

"They're always last to understand what's really going on," Carter said derisively.

"Precisely, my dear Major. They can't understand the world has changed, largely because they don't want to. We face a new threat, the likes of which has never been faced before. It's a threat that anyone with a modicum of foresight should have been able to anticipate. Alas, my warnings fell on fallow ground." Griffin vigorously puffed to reignite his pipe before continuing. "The intent and aim of the Nazis is the subjugation of Europe and the world to their ideals. Everything is secondary to this end – decency, morals, people. All suborned to the quest for total victory. Nothing else matters. To defeat this we, too, must fight differently. Fortunately, there were some amongst us who recognised this and did some time ago." He shrugged in a self-deprecating manner that made clear he was one of them.

"Which is where Section D comes in," Beaufort took up. "We were set up before the war and our remit is as simple as it is broad – how to make the best use of sabotage, propaganda and other irregular means to weaken our enemy. We sit in the Secret Intelligence Service, but we focus on sabotage and other clandestine operations as opposed to just intelligence gathering." She gave a small smile. "In fact, we modelled ourselves on the very terrorist groups that the government was trying to destroy. A popular move as I'm sure you can imagine."

"Yes, in fact someone quipped we were the 'Ministry of Ungentlemanly Warfare' which they imagined was an objection. But I actually found it quite an apt description."

Scottsdale couldn't repress a smile. "Sounds interesting, Mr Griffin."

"Oh, it is, Lieutenant and I'm glad you think so," Griffin replied, refilling his pipe. "But why, I suspect you are wondering, are we telling you all this?"

"I am mildly curious, yes."

Griffin chuckled. "Then allow me to enlighten you. The situation here, as I'm sure you're astute enough to see, is a mess. The Germans have managed more in the last few weeks than they did in the whole of the last shooting match. The question is, what can we salvage?" He smiled broadly at

Scottsdale. "Which is where you come in Lieutenant."

Scottsdale raised an eyebrow. "Really?"

"Really, Lieutenant. You see, we have the chance, in this room, to affect the outcome of the war. Playing for high stakes, Mr Scottsdale! So listen carefully. This campaign is lost, but that's a battle lost, not the war, despite what some would have you believe. And there's another, equally important battle, that's been raging for a decade – the technological war. You see, war breeds innovation. Air power has expanded more in twenty years than two hundred because of war. Look at the tank! New designs, new engines, new weapons – all driven by an explosion in new technology, all capable of tipping the scales in our favour. It's a race we cannot afford to lose. Any advantage could be crucial."

"And your job is to help us win this race?"

"I have many jobs right now, my boy, but none more important than what I'm about to brief you on. We've been in a race to develop RDF – that's Range and Detection Finding, or 'Radar' to our American cousins, who must insist on calling it something else, of course."

"Yes, I know of it," Carter said.

"Indeed, but we are a long way off realising its potential," Beaufort replied. "RDF is something we've been very interested in for a long time. Simply put, it gives us knowledge; it lets us see where we are blind. 'The bomber will always get through' – remember that claim?" Scottsdale and Carter nodded, recalling the then Prime Minister Stanley Baldwin's widely accepted statement before the war. "RDF can invalidate that claim. It can detect the enemy wherever they may be, in the dark, in the fog. It can guide our weapons and see under the waves. The enemy cannot hide."

"Think of the applications," Griffin interjected with relish. "Vector our fighters onto their bombers in the blackest of nights. Guide our navy to the waiting U-Boats. Artillery directed with unmatched precision to where it is needed most. The possibilities are endless."

"Making the invisible, visible," Scottsdale added.

"Precisely," Beaufort said. "But the absolutely critical thing here is to make equipment small enough to fit into an aircraft or a ship, yet still retain the power needed to do the job. That's been the drive; power and size, and it's bedevilled all of our research. We've been in a race with the Germans and the French, working with our people from the University of Birmingham, recently made a breakthrough that could be crucial. In fact, we believe they've got the final piece of the jigsaw."

27

Griffin fixed Scottsdale with a hard stare. "That breakthrough is currently residing in a briefcase in the possession of two French scientists, Maurice Favelle and Helene Dubois," he said gravely. "Section D has been tasked with recovering them and this briefcase – and I want you to go and get them for me."

***

In the deep silence that followed, all eyes were on Scottsdale; his heart was thumping. "I'm to go and fetch them?" he asked.

"That's right, Lieutenant. Tonight, in fact. Our people are either too far away or dead and we're out of time. Major Carter," he said inclining his head, "has kindly agreed to release you and a section of your rascals to assist us."

Carter cleared his throat. "This is a dangerous piece of work, Scottsdale. Mr Griffin has the authority but give me the word and I can fight this."

Griffin tried to interject but Carter cut him off sharply. "I understand the importance of RDF, Griffin, but you're asking my men to clean up your mess, not to mention depriving me of one of my officers. This scientist should have been found long ago. My men are dead on their feet and deserve the chance to get home so they can fight again. And if we know how important this man is, one assumes the Germans may too?"

Griffin inclined his head. "I can assure you that this is not the scenario we had planned for, Major. People have died to keep these scientists identity and location secret," he said matter-of-factly. "So yes, the Germans will be pursuing them, but we must take the risk of using Lieutenant Scottsdale simply because it is a gamble so very worth taking."

"A gamble we hope the Lieutenant is willing to take?" Beaufort enquired.

Scottsdale stared back. The logical side to his brain was telling him to run and run far; they were gambling his life. But he already knew what he would do; he could feel a pulse of excitement. Instead of answering the question, he addressed Major Carter.

"This retreat has been a nightmare, sir. I'm sick of it. And now I've got the chance to make a difference and that's what we're here for isn't it?" He shrugged. "Besides, if I say no, presumably some poor bastard will have to go in my place and that wouldn't feel right."

"You understand the risk you're taking? If we fall back, we can't wait for you."

"I understand, sir."

Carter nodded in understanding. Despite his frustration it is ultimately what he would have expected. Scottsdale turned to Griffin and spoke clearly. "I'm happy to help."

"Capital, Scottsdale, never doubted it," he said with a smile.

"What resources will I have?" Scottsdale enquired.

"You can have your pick of the litter," Carter replied. "One section and anything else you need."

Griffin was leafing through a file. "How's your French nowadays, Scottsdale? Says here you speak it well enough."

"A little rusty but serviceable. I spent time in France before the war."

"Then your presence here is quite the happy coincidence wouldn't you say?"

"Truly."

"Ask Miss Beaufort if you need any help with the lingo. She speaks it like a native."

"Yes, I did wonder," Scottsdale said. "Beaufort is a French name isn't it?"

"It is. My mother was from the Ile De Re, a little island off the coast of La Rochelle."

"So you know France well?"

"I believe it was one of my qualifying criteria," she answered.

"One of your many talents," Griffin quipped, prompting an eye roll from Beaufort. She turned back to Scottsdale.

"As for our scientists, our information is that Fauvelle speaks little English but Dubois speaks it well, so we don't anticipate any communication issues."

Griffin took out a map and spread it out on the desk, gesturing for them to gather round. Placing a finger on it, he continued. "Our latest intelligence has them holed up just outside Lens, about seven miles south of here. An inconsequential place called Montigny-en-Gohelle. There's a small church on the outskirts and we've agreed to rendezvous there in the early hours of tomorrow morning."

"What intelligence do we have on the enemy dispositions?" Scottsdale asked.

"Not a great deal frankly. Lens is their base of operations in this region. This here," he said, placing a finger opposite the canal, "is Annay. The Germans haven't bothered to garrison it yet and most of its people fled after the assault yesterday. Courrieres further east has been used as a forward base so I would recommend avoiding it. Thus far I've no reports of any enemy movement in Montigny-en-Gohelle itself."

"So we don't really know what we'll be facing then."

"Welcome to the life of Section D," Griffin replied straightening up. "Happily, our dastardly foe seems to be consolidating along the canal line. No idea why, we're incredibly vulnerable but the bulk of their offensive operations have halted. Which is all to the good and gives us a chance. But even so, the most we'll hold for is forty-eight hours before we fall back again. Assuming they don't attack in the meantime, of course."

"The bastards never do what you want for long," Carter warned.

"Indeed, they don't. So we must move quickly. We want you over there tonight and have them safely back in our lines by dawn. A quick in and out job is the ticket."

"You make it sound almost straightforward," Scottsdale said.

"War never is, is it? But such is life. Get there, find these Frogs and get them out of there. And if you don't think you can, make damn sure you destroy what they bring with them. It cannot fall into enemy hands." He paused, puffing away on the pipe, examining Scottsdale. "To be honest, I'd prefer you to shoot the scientists than leave them to be captured but I've been persuaded that may be problematic."

"You're thinking of asking me to shoot two unarmed French civilians?" Scottsdale replied, his anger bubbling up at the idea.

"A new kind of war remember," Beaufort said evenly.

"Bloody outrage, Griffin," Carter said. "There's no way -"

"I know, I know, Major," Griffin interrupted, holding his hands up placatingly. "Which is why I'm not suggesting he do so, much as that is the best thing, frankly, to do." He turned back to Scottsdale. "Just make sure whatever is in that briefcase is destroyed if you can't get them out. Clear?" "Crystal," Scottsdale replied stiffly.

"We do have one final party trick to offer, however, if you find yourselves in trouble. Beaufort here has a little present."

"This," Beaufort said, holding up a signal gun, "is to be used should you find yourself in need of assistance – but only if you have the scientists or at least their cargo. It's a distress flare – if we see that we have arranged for a covering artillery barrage on that position."

"Best to be moving away from that position once you used it," Griffin offered.

"Distress flare. Moving away. Understood."

Griffin smiled. "That's the spirit. I've no need to tell you how dangerous this is. I'm sure that's something you've been well used to recently."

"Reason I joined," Scottsdale said. Major Carter's head snapped up at the hint of impertinence while a small smile played on Griffin's face as he studied Scottsdale.

"You'll do Scottsdale," Griffin said as he and Beaufort stood up, buttoning their coats. "Good luck. Bring me back those scientists and you'll have my gratitude. And more to the point, you'll have helped us win this war."

4

Emerging into the fading warmth of the afternoon, Scottsdale puffed his cheeks and exhaled. A competing barrage of emotions assailed him. He was digesting the situation when Major Carter appeared, his face serious.

"Listen to me, Scottsdale. This is a balls up. Griffin should have had these scientists in the bag weeks ago and it's you who could pay the price. So if you're going over there, I want you to be sensible, do you understand?"

"I hope I wouldn't be otherwise, sir," Scottsdale answered curiously.

"I mean it. I'm not disputing this RDF stuff is important but right now, we need all the fighting men we can muster. Remember, we're going to be defending England soon. So no heroics; go and have a look and then get out of there."

Scottsdale hesitated. "I won't take any unnecessary chances, sir," he said neutrally.

Carter gave him a long stare. "You've always been a recalcitrant sort, Scottsdale. It's what I like about you. But don't go gallivanting off after these scientists. It's not worth it. Clear?"

"Yes, sir," Scottsdale replied. In truth, he would only really know what he would do when he was there, but he felt strongly that the mission was important, and he would do whatever he could to make it a success.

Carter clapped Scottsdale on the shoulder. "Good. You're no use to me dead. I'll see you tomorrow." With that, he snapped a salute and disappeared inside.

Scottsdale spent the few minutes of the bumpy ride back to the company deep in thought. Major Carter clearly wanted him to perform a cursory search and return safely. However, Griffin's mission excited him, there was no doubting that and he had to remind himself that being asked to go behind the enemy line was, to say the least, ill advised.

Arriving back at Pont-a-Vendin, he ran into Sergeant Grant, who had been patiently waiting for his return. Before Grant could begin the process of gently interrogating his officer, Scottsdale spoke.

"Ah, Grant, just the man. I want Pendle, Wilkins, Marsh, Davenport, White, Levingston, Dalton and McManus."

"I'll have to check with the medical officer on Taffy, sir. He copped some shrapnel yesterday."

"Taffy?"

"Levingston, sir."

"Is he Welsh? I thought he was from Basildon?"

"He is, sir, but he never shut up about his dog." Grant shrugged. "A Welsh terrier."

"I see. Well if he's fit, include him, if not get someone else. We'll need extra ammunition and rations. Two days' worth but whatever we can find, grab it."

"Marsh can go look, sir. He has a nose for food."

"Good."

"Going on patrol are we, sir?" Grant prompted.

"Not quite. We've been given a job to do, a very important one."

"I see, sir."

"A couple of French scientists have holed up not far from here. What they know could, potentially, alter the course of the war and we've been told to go and fetch them."

"And where would they be, sir?"

"In a church about six miles that way," Scottsdale said pointing across the canal.

"Must be important people," Grant said carefully. "Seeing as how there's an awful lot of Germans between us and them, sir."

Scottsdale chuckled. "Yes, it had crossed my mind, Sergeant. However, it is what it is. So get the men round and let's get busy."

Scottsdale relayed the gist of the mission to the men, who shared a few looks at the prospect. Looking at their wary faces, he spoke urgently. "Listen, I for one am sick of falling back and being nothing more than target practice for the bloody Luftwaffe." The sentiment was met with a few murmurs of agreement. "I'm not going to say this will be a doddle, but you know what?"

"Don't join if you can't take a joke?" Pendle asked.

"Precisely, Private Pendle." When the chuckles died down, Scottsdale continued seriously. "This is our chance to make a difference, to do something that can help us win the war. And that sounds good to me. Kick-off is 2200. In the meantime, rest, eat and then we meet at the forward posts. And one final thing. Can everyone swim?"

Among the quizzical looks were grunts of assent. They would be crossing various canals and there was always the chance they'd have to swim. Scottsdale gave a small shudder. Since nearly drowning as a boy, he had a healthy fear of water and was determined to avoid getting in it. He was equally determined this would not become known to the men.

"Good. Now off with you and I'll see you later."

The men started wandering back to their pitches. "Join the army they said," Wilkins grumbled as he checked the breech of his rifle. "See the world they said. And here we are rescuing a Frenchie with half the bleeding German army on our arses. I'd rather be walking the dog in the rain in Chelmsford!"

"Cut it out, Wilkins," Grant growled.

Scottsdale paced as he waited for dusk. Now the decision was made, he was eager to begin, scanning the other side of the canal and referring to his map. An open plain sloped gently up towards thick woods. A narrow track split the woods, disappearing into the shadows; that was their aiming point. Restlessly, he kept moving and McDonald observed his behaviour with a frown.

"You're like a cat on a hot tin roof, Arthur. It's making me nervous."

"Sorry, Jock, just need a piss," Scottsdale said half-heartedly and forced himself to sit.

"What did they want anyway?"

Scottsdale hesitated, Griffin's warning in his mind. "They needed someone for a patrol, and Joe Soap here has been volunteered," he shrugged.

"And never a better man for the job," McDonald replied with a sympathetic smile.

Finally, the appointed hour arrived. Scottsdale checked the men over. Each had blackened their faces and strapped down any equipment. Marsh was swishing a cosh around. "This should do some damage," he said with satisfaction.

"Careful, you're gonna hit one of us with that thing," Wilkins said, raising an arm.

"Better get out of my way then."

"Give it a rest, Swampy," Davenport ordered.

Marsh rolled his eyes but returned the cosh to his pack. Catching Scottsdale's gaze, he shrugged. "Never know when this will come in handy, sir,"

Scottsdale nodded. Although not official equipment, each man had over the weeks purloined various items for their own use. If it worked for them, he wasn't going to stop it. There were also two small wooden boats between them. They were grim faced but under the tension Scottsdale sensed an eagerness too.

"This is it," he said tightly. "Quick and quiet. Let's get over there, grab the French and get the hell out of there."

He was the first out, threading a way through the forward positions until he reached the canal, its surface black in the faint moonlight. Briefly, the group halted, straining to pick out any threat. A low thrum of gunfire rumbled in the distance but otherwise all was still. Satisfied, Scottsdale turned to Grant. "Bring the boats," he whispered, and the men slithered down the bank, Private White cursing softly as his foot slid into the icy water at the bottom. Ignoring the evidence of the previous day's assault, they splashed gently across the canal. The makeshift paddle in Scottsdale's hand was slippery with sweat despite the cool evening breeze. There had been no sign of any German activity, but he couldn't help but imagine the enemy lying in wait for them. For just a moment he felt a pang of sympathy for the enemy infantry who'd assaulted them the day before.

There was a palpable sense of relief as their craft bumped into the opposite bank. Sergeant Grant was out first, steadying the prow with one hand and helping the rest of the men out. Scottsdale took the lead, moving cautiously forward. The woods that overlooked Pont-a-Vendin loomed ahead and their first task was to get there safely.

"On to the woods," he hissed. Watching the bent figures scurry forward, his adrenalin surged, and he couldn't help but grin in the darkness. It felt good to be striking back rather than scuttling back in retreat again. He glanced up and gave silent thanks for the clouds that sheltered them from the moonlight. The section flitted forward behind him, dark shadows showing up briefly as they ghosted across the canal towpath. Scottsdale caught the ragged breathing of men geed up with adrenalin as they jogged behind him.

A harsh fizzing cut through the air; to their right a flare exploded, casting its lurid white glare towards them. Like puppets whose strings had been cut, the men collapsed, burying their faces into the ground. The dense odour of mud and grass filled Scottsdale's mouth as he waited and waited, eyes closed, for the light to fade, praying they hadn't been seen. Interminable seconds passed until he cautiously raised his head, fervently welcoming the relative silence of their small strip of land.

Rising to his feet, Scottsdale motioned the section on and they worked their way slightly uphill, crouching low. The woods beckoned. He could just make out the start of the path he'd seen earlier but it felt too exposed, so he was planning to work his way through the woods instead. In front of him the trees reached out, in welcome or warning it was hard to tell, yet easy enough to imagine the German infantry waiting inside to cut them down. Scottsdale held his breath until, with a final rush, they reached the woods. He placed a hand on the comforting stolidity of the nearest tree trunk and breathed out, heart thumping. The section closed around him, forming a defensive semi-circle and he raised a hand for silence, listening intently. Very faintly, he could hear German voices and a pulse of fear and adrenalin coursed through him.

"Total noise discipline now," he whispered. "Not a sound."

Tentatively, they crept into the woods, gently moving aside the overhanging branches. They moved as stealthily as they could, treading with great care, but every crack of broken twig, every leaf that crunched underfoot, laid another level of stress on them. A small animal was startled out of its nocturnal hiding place and took off, crashing through the undergrowth. They instinctively froze before breathing out and continuing their progress, silently until Private Dalton stumbled, falling to the ground with an oath.

Scottsdale glared at him. "Careful," he hissed, and Dalton held up his hands apologetically.

They inched forward, clammy palms gripping rifle stocks tightly. Scottsdale glanced back to see the men in single file behind him; their eyes were so white against their blackened faces that he had to swallow the urge to order them to look down. Every shape and shadow in the half-light became a threat, every groan and creak of the trees the warning sound of an enemy. They strained to listen, threading a path between the trees, urgently peering into the darkness. As he moved carefully around a tree Scottsdale heard a rustling. His first thought was that it just another animal. But the noise continued, and he froze.

Holding a hand up, he sank to the ground, the section following suit. The sound grew stronger and unmistakably this was not a natural sound, this was the sound of a person. A German. Scottsdale gritted his teeth, all of them silently saying the same prayer. Not here, not here, just keep going. In the darkness a clearer shape emerged, and Scottsdale felt the gall rise as he recognised the unmistakable outline of a German helmet. The soldier was moving obliquely across their position, rifle slung. Another sound emerged, and it took Scottsdale a moment to place it; the man was whistling. Scottsdale listened, for some reason recalling games of hide and seek from his youth. How many times had he hidden in a place just like this? How frightened he'd been when he got lost and how relieved to hear his brother's voice calling out for him.

The soldier stopped, and Scottsdale's heart sank. He watched intently, barely blinking, before recognising the unmistakable sound of a man relieving himself. He had to stop himself from giggling at the thought of the section being inadvertently pissed on.

Closing his eyes, he focused, urging the solider to leave now his business had been concluded.

Yet the solider stayed. Selecting a tree stump a matter of yards away, he lit a cigarette, the pungent smell of tobacco wafting back to them. Behind his shoulder, Scottsdale thought furiously. Time was slipping away. Every second the sentry was there, the chances of discovery increased. What if others were on their way to join him? Or the man decided to stay there? He closed his eyes and in that moment the decision was made for him – the roar of aircraft was starting to build overhead. The time was now. Inch by inch he slid back to Sergeant Grant.

"We can't wait," he breathed in Grant's ear. "We have to get rid of him." Grant moved nodded imperceptibly and turned to whisper to Private McManus.

McManus was a taciturn Irishman. He spoke rarely but when he did it was always measured and always listened to. Not a great deal was known about his past although Scottsdale had heard whispers of poaching. What he did know was that McManus came from the border county of Monaghan and his home was the woods and the fields. He had the lithe figure of a hunter and yard by yard he now stalked the German sentry. Every nerve in Scottsdale's body was taut as McManus crept closer, stopping frequently, patiently waiting for his quarry to relax, for his thoughts to drift back to Saxony, to that girl he'd left behind and everything he'd do when the war was over. Patience was what led to the kill. Let the man's mind wander as every second death crept closer.

McManus had edged to within a couple of feet when the soldier glanced up at the planes roaring overhead and, in that moment, McManus struck, uncoiling smoothly to lunge forward. Scottsdale watched in appalled fascination as the bayonet buried itself in the man's neck. The German went rigid, hands clawing at his neck, panic shining from his eyes. He half stood, choking, trying to speak, as the tang of urine drifted out. McManus covered the man's mouth to stifle his cries until, as the struggles grew fainter, he withdrew the blade. The soldier sank to earth, feet jerking as his life drained away.

They were utterly still, waiting to see if the man's muffled cries had raised an alarm. Seconds ticked away but no sound came save the rustle of leaves and the heavy breathing of men.

"Well done, McManus," Scottsdale whispered with feeling. McManus nodded, wiping the blade on the grass. "Cover the body, quickly now." As they dragged the body deeper into the undergrowth, Scottsdale glanced down. The man's face was soft, absent of threat. It was a face like theirs, not the face of the enemy they'd seen on newsreels goose stepping past blazing buildings across Europe. Put a British uniform on him and he could have walked into the battalion mess.

Shrugging off the thought, Scottsdale beckoned to the section and set off again. The man's absence was sure to be noted but hopefully not until morning. If before, he hoped the Germans would see it as the revenge of a rogue Frenchman or a retreating Tommy – which was more likely than a group of British soldiers heading south, away from safety. Either way, there was nothing to do but to press on and they continued forward, using an animal trail to make better time. As the map promised, they soon reached a wide clearing. A dilapidated farmhouse sat in its midst and Scottsdale held his hand up for silence. Scottsdale spent several minutes with Grant observing until satisfied by the stillness.

"Who's the fastest man here?" he asked.

Grant glanced at the group. His eyes alighted on Pendle, whippet thin and breathing evenly. "Pendle, sir," he replied and beckoned Pendle over. Taking just a second longer than Grant would have preferred, Pendle scuttled over and knelt beside Scottsdale.

Taking him by the shoulder Scottsdale gave his orders. "We need to check those ruined buildings, make sure they are clear. Wait for the cloud to cover the moonlight, then run like hell."

Pendle looked up and the faint grin could be seen. "Can't wait, sir."

Scottsdale smiled. Pendle was a rogue but a likeable one and vicious in a fight. "Right, on my say so." He scanned the sky for the right moment and as the clouds came to claim the moon, squeezed Pendle's shoulder, "Go!"

Pendle sped off into the gloom before reaching the farmhouse and disappearing. Scottsdale waited, biting his lip, until a low whistle reached them, signalling it was safe to continue. The men hustled across to the first building, a ramshackle shed whose rotting wooden door offered little resistance. Reconvening inside, the air dank and musty with the smell of animals, Scottsdale squatted and gestured for the men to gather round.

"Right," he said in a low voice. "We're going to skirt Annay and go cross country to the church. All being well, it will take an hour but stay close to each other. Understood?"

The men nodded. "If anyone gets lost I'll have their balls," Grant growled.

Scottsdale led the party into open country. Annay was to their right and it remained blessedly quiet. He'd been worried how he would navigate but the sky was lit with the frequent flash of guns. It was like a thunderstorm; a flickering sky then counting – one, two, three – until the thunder reached you. Was it the same with guns? Someone, not far from them, was dying in the night, afraid and bleeding. Or perhaps one moment there, smoking a cigarette, the next nothing, just whatever was next after this life, a life snuffed out by an artillery shell.

Scottsdale scanned the farmland constantly, but the darkness was a comfort even if an occasional curse sounded as a man stumbled. The farmers had started to harvest the winter wheat before the armies came and half-cut stalks brushed against their shins. Occasionally checking their bearing, Scottsdale set a steady pace, pausing only as they crossed a major road.

"This is the road to Lens," he whispered as they reached the field adjacent to the road. "If there's any Jerries about, this is the road they'll be on."

Carefully, they checked for any traffic, listening for the tell-tale sound of engines before scurrying across. The night was calm, the weather still. Scottsdale had the strangest sensation that everyone, on both sides, was holding their breath, regrouping and waiting for the signal to rejoin for the final battle. He shivered.

His apprehension increased as they came to the next obstacle. It was a small canal, but they'd left behind their boats. The surface was velvet, barely a ripple disturbing the surface. As they scrambled down, Grant instructed the men to tie their belongings up and plug their rifles but paused as he noticed his Lieutenant's odd behaviour. Scottsdale was jogging further down the canal, peering into darkness.

Grant shook his head. "There is no accounting for the officer class," he muttered and was about to remove his boots when he heard a slight shout and saw Scottsdale hurrying back.

"Hang on, lads," Grant said, turning to Scottsdale. "Found it," Scottsdale whispered excitedly.

Grant stared blankly back. "Found what, sir?"

"A barge! We can float it over to the far bank." Scottsdale realised he was being slightly over exuberant. "We may need it for the civilians," he offered.

Grant nodded. "Right lads, you heard the Lieutenant. In the barge." They trotted down to where it lay. The long shape lay low in the water, it's snub nose evident in the moonlight. *Le Heureux* was painted on its side.

A soft Irish whisper sounded next to Scottsdale's ear. "'The Lucky,' eh, sir. Good choice."

Scottsdale jumped. "Good God," he said. McManus had materialised next to him. Scottsdale looked at him curiously. "Do you speak French?"

McManus smiled slowly. "Ah, no, sir but the nuns were mad keen on it and a few words stuck," he replied and moved past to leap onto the deck. Scottsdale looked after him, shook his head and joined the rest of the men. They cast off and in moments floated over to the other side, disembarking and tying up the barge.

Scottsdale gazed around. A smattering of young trees dotted the bank, beyond which flat farmland led to Montigny-en-Gohelle. The village was divided by a road, with the bulk on the southern side. Their goal was the smaller, northern quarter where the church lay. Before setting out, he gathered the men.

"The French will be waiting for us at the church. There are no reports of German units, but we take no chances," he warned. "So keep your eyes and ears ready. Questions?"

The men shook their heads and Scottsdale led them on, their progress lit by the soft moonlight. As they moved into another field, Scottsdale caught the scent of something sickly sweet that threatened to clog the nose.

"What the hell is that," Dalton muttered.

"There's your answer," Grant said and pointed. Several mounds revealed themselves to be the carcasses of cattle. They had been disembowelled by stray artillery fire.

"Awful," Davenport commented. As a farmer, he knew the loss would be cruelly felt.

Gingerly, the section picked their way past the rotting corpses and ghosted towards the village which now appeared in front of them. Creeping forward, the dark shapes of houses crowded down on them. They spread out on either side of the street, moving in short rushes. At every creak they froze, heads ceaselessly turning. Very faintly a light showed here and there inside shuttered homes. Slowly they crept on until there, at last, lay their target.

It was a compact and elegant Gothic church. The nave was flanked at either end with smaller side chapels. A series of flying buttresses provided support and atop the roof sat an ornately carved stone cross. Half a dozen stained glass windows lined the side at regular intervals. At the north end of the building was the steeple. It sat on a rectangular base and several high windows pointed to a dwelling space in the tower.

Scottsdale waved the men down as they reached the graveyard. His breath fogged in the dim light. In the distance a dog barked. The church lay inert. Rising to his feet, he led them forward, feet crunching on the gravel. In the moonlight he could make out an occasional inscription on the gravestones; Maurice Durand lies here, aged 14. Beside him his loving mother, Amelie. Some of the ancient headstones were crumbling but the paths were neatly swept, and the graves carefully tended. Fresh flowers lay on a recent grave and Scottsdale wondered if the war had already reached this tiny village.

Sturdy crescent shaped doors greeted them at the church entrance. Taking hold of the large drop ring handle, Scottsdale slowly twisted the handle and pushed open the door. He grimaced as the hinges squeaked before turning to hurry the men inside. The interior was lit by the faint gleam of a few scattered candles but was otherwise dark. The smell of incense and old wood lingered in the air. Like all churches it was still and quiet, even the war felt further away for a moment. Scottsdale trailed his fingers over the rough wood of the pews as they walked slowly down the aisle.

The creak of an opening door startled them, and they raised their weapons. However, to their relief they saw a priest striding towards them. Scottsdale was about to call out, but the man pushed back his cowl and began to hiss at them in a torrent of angry French; evidently, they'd been mistaken for Germans. As the priest paused to draw breath, Scottsdale hurried to interject.

"English father, we're English," he managed to get in. The priest stopped in mid flow and came forward. Holding up a lantern, he peered at Scottsdale's face and uniform before moving it aside and taking in the section. He breathed out and spoke in relief.

"Praise God, that you have come."

5

The priest was a head shorter than Scottsdale but unmistakably solidly built. His frame filled the robes of his office tightly. A wide smile lit up his craggy face, a pair of wild eyebrows rising in tandem. "To think I thought you were Germans!" he said. "I was on the verge of committing an ungodly act!" He shrugged impressively. "A man of God I may be, but I am a man first."

Grant and the men had been following the exchange uncomprehendingly. "Glad he's calmed down, sir," he remarked. "Thought he was going to wake the Germans."

"And the dead," muttered Marsh.

"I am Lieutenant Scottsdale, 2nd Essex and these are my men," Scottsdale addressed the priest.

"And I am Benedict Curzones, at your service. Yours and God's, of course."

"Of course," Scottsdale agreed. He came straight to the point. "We've information that two refugees are hiding here Father. A Dr Fauvelle and Miss Dubois. Have you seen them?"

The priest smiled. "They're upstairs. I can take you to them now."

Scottsdale sighed in relief and turned to Grant. "The French are upstairs. Post a watch at the end of the graveyard. I want to be ready to go immediately."

They hurried down the aisle, Scottsdale glancing at two great windows either end of the transept that depicted a half-remembered biblical scene. The church narrowed as they reached the chancel, an altar table bestriding the width of the church. In front, a smaller offertory table was set up, a variety of cups and plates spread out on its surface. Curzones squeezed past the altar table and Scottsdale saw that they were now in the bottom of the tower. He followed Curzones up a staircase, ascending gradually, the stone worn smooth by centuries of pious men.

An unexpectedly cosy living space greeted them, narrow windows offering a view over the surrounding countryside. Bookshelves lined the walls, beautifully crafted wood inlaid with heraldic and religious creatures, each teeming with ancient looking tomes alongside modern publications, all jumbled up and haphazardly squeezed into place. Scattered candles cast a soft light on the antique tapestries which warmed the room; scenes of hunting and war were woven into them, reflecting the history of the lord who'd commissioned the church to guard his family's souls for perpetuity.

Scottsdale, however, took none of this in. His attention was riveted to the people who waited for him. A man and a woman stood in front of him. The man was blinking from behind smudged glasses and he carried himself tentatively. He was crammed into an ill-fitting suit, but he also held tightly onto a battered suitcase. Scottsdale noted all of this automatically as well as the interesting fact that the suitcase had strong metal locks on it.

Beside him stood a woman, back straight and arms folded defensively across her chest. Tucking a strand of auburn hair behind her ear impatiently, she stared back boldly. Taller than her companion, a dark overcoat swathed her figure. Her eyes, richly brown, were set in a sharply defined face. It was not a face of purely conventional beauty, rather she held herself with a fierceness and energy Scottsdale found captivating immediately.

The man stepped forward. "Please allow me to introduce myself," he said formally. "I am Maurice Fauvelle, research director at the *La Compagnie Générale de Télégraphie*. This is my research partner and niece, Helene Dubois."

Scottsdale shifted his gaze to shake the outstretched hand of Helene. He was struck again by her eyes.

"A pleasure, Monsieur," she said without a hint of warmth.

"The pleasure is mine, Mademoiselle," Scottsdale replied formally. For a moment, they stared at each other. Scottsdale's heart was beating harder than the exertion of the stairway allowed.

"I am here on behalf of Mr Griffin," he addressed them, feeling his French returning like a once well used muscle. "He's asked me to escort you to British lines. We must leave as soon as possible. As you can imagine, it isn't safe here."

"We have little reason to imagine, Lieutenant," Helene interjected. "We've witnessed the desecration of our country while we have been pursued for what we know." She radiated an unbridled anger. "What maintains us is that our knowledge can go some way to avenging our humiliation."

Fauvelle clasped her arm. "Helene is quite correct," he said to Scottsdale. "We are being hunted. Mr Griffin is not the only one aware of the value of our knowledge! We should have been taken weeks ago as I requested," he said in agitation. "A man we once knew, Rademacher, is helping the Germans. And I fear the man who hid us in Cambrai has fallen into their hands. It is surely only a matter of time before they come. I beg you to move quickly."

Scottsdale gnawed his lip at the news. Fauvelle was right. "We leave at once. Please gather your belongings."

He was interrupted by the clatter of boots on the stairs. They turned as Sergeant Grant appeared, looking around until he saw Scottsdale. "Problem, sir. Jerries."

"Strength?"

"Couple of platoons, sir. Had a civilian with them as well."

Helene swore, and Fauvelle closed his eyes in despair. It was the confirmation Scottsdale feared. "The Germans are looking for them too. This must be them." His mind was turning, assessing the options. Could they get out in time before the Germans arrived? He had only moments to decide.

"They'll be here in minutes I reckon, sir," Grant prompted.

"Is there anywhere we can hide, Father?" Scottsdale asked Curzones.

"Yes. Alas, we've often had cause to hide here," he smiled sadly. "There's a cellar under the altar and we also have this." He moved one of the tapestries aside to reveal what looked like the stone wall. However, sliding his hand over the stone he twisted a small knob unobtrusively jutting out of the wall. The wall slid aside to reveal a small space where, at a squeeze, two people could stand.

Scottsdale pondered. It made sense to use the priest hole but now he had the scientists he instinctively wanted to keep them with him.

"Monsieur Fauvelle and Mademoiselle Dubois, please come with me."

"But Lieutenant, surely we should hide here?" Helene protested.

"This isn't the time for debate, Mademoiselle," he said harshly. "Do as I say. We'll hide in the cellar and wait for the Germans to leave." They hurried downstairs, marching down the nave to the offertory table. Following Curzones' instructions Scottsdale moved aside the table and lifted the rug to reveal a trapdoor. One by one they descended into the dark cellar, Curzones passing down a candle before dragging the table back with a squeal.

As Curzones smoothed down his robes, the front door of the church was pushed forcefully open and a group of German soldiers entered, led by an SS officer. The German stalked down the aisle, ignoring Curzones' remonstrations, simply gripping him by the arm and dragging him to a pew at the front of the church.

"Sit down, Father." He towered over the priest. "I am Hauptsturmführer Schiller. You are harbouring fugitives and I want them. Now," he demanded in impeccable French.

"How dare you defile our holy church!" Curzones protested. "How dare -" His protest was cut short by the backhanded swing of Schiller's hand across his face.

"How dare I? I dare what I damn well please in this place, Father," Schiller spat. "You are the old world. The National Socialists are the new world and we know all about the church, Father."

Curzones summoned his defiance. "You don't know God."

"Oh, we do. Allow me to enlighten you." He drew back his arm. "The church is corrupt," he snarled and brought his hand across Curzones face once more.

"It is weak." Again, the flash of the gloved hand.

"It is sick." The thud of the blow echoed in the church.

Schiller paused and wiped the specks of blood off his uniform. Curzones slumped in the pew.

"Bastard," Scottsdale breathed as they listened. Besides him Helene had a hand over her mouth, eyes wide in indignation. Scottsdale could hear Griffin's parting words – nothing was more important than the secrets the scientists carried. Nothing. Griffin would gladly sacrifice a provincial priest if it meant keeping the final piece of the jigsaw of RDF from falling into German hands. Nevertheless, Curzones' plight burned into him. Hearing a man of God being assaulted within his own church was shocking. Even worse, that suffering was being endured to protect him. He sensed Helene watching him.

"We must do something, Lieutenant," she whispered fiercely.

"Trust me, I want to, but you and your uncle are more important. We have to endure this," he replied urgently. The greater good, he thought silently.

"Nothing is worth this," she snapped and began to rise.

"Wait, please, Mademoiselle," Scottsdale said, laying a restraining hand on her arm. Fauvelle, too, reached out to stop her. "He is doing this to protect you."

Reluctantly, Helene shook them off and sat down, burying her head in her hands. Scottsdale felt a great wall of guilt and anger rising in him. Anger at the Germans and guilt for the good man enduring hell to protect them. And anger at Griffin. His gamble was in jeopardy. They were trapped in the church, they were being hunted and only the courage of a priest stood between their discovery and death.

***

Schiller unslung his machine gun and placed it on the pew as he paced in front of Curzones. His richly black boots, muddy from his journey, left small footprints as he circled, examining the art work and windows. The grey-green colouring of his uniform was darkly shadowed in the dimly lit church. Around the snugly fitted collar were the symbols and flashes of his rank and denotation as a member of the Schutzstaffel. The death's head badge stared out from his peaked cap.

"We National Socialists like to look to antiquity, Father," he continued in a calmer voice. "It was a truly blessed time. Do you know why? Because it did not know two of the great scourges of the modern world. Christianity and syphilis. Both send men mad, Father, make them weak. Tell me, what use is something that tells us to forgive our enemies?"

Curzones was breathing heavily. "You have no idea of the power of God. Or the power of France!" he spat defiantly. "Your soul is in God's keeping and God willing it will be with Him soon."

"Bravo Father! I do so admire a little bit of fortitude. Perhaps if the clergy swapped places with the army things might be a little different, eh?" he smiled. "Yet here I find myself in France, victorious." He withdrew a silver case from his pocket and took out a cigarette. Idly he tapped it on the case. "But where exactly do I find myself?" he continued softly. "Not at the front line. Not where the fighting is fiercest, where I should be. No; I am here instead, talking to you." Schiller stopped tapping. "And I think you know why, Father."

"I know only that you are an evil man."

"I know Fauvelle and Dubois came here. Where are they?"

"The only people here are here us and God."

Schiller turned. "Scharführer Schultz!" he barked. "Turn this place upside down." The man hurried off and soon the crack of splintering wood echoed in the church. Schiller perched himself alongside Curzones, smoking, looking up as Schultz returned.

"No sign, Herr Hauptsturmführer," he said crisply. "I did find a priest's hole, but it was empty. Shall I search the grounds?"

Schiller nodded. "Yes. And put a cordon around the village. Quickly."

The German sergeant snapped out an order and the bulk of the men disappeared outside. They were passed by a tall man who carefully stepped into the church. He walked slowly down the aisle, admiring the windows and carvings of gargoyles that adorned the central pillars. Taking off his fedora, his cream trench coat flapped open to reveal smart grey trousers and fashionable shoes. He glanced at the priest with a wrinkle of distaste. "Was this really necessary, Hauptsturmführer Schiller?"

"If you want your erstwhile colleagues, then yes, it is, Doktor Rademacher," Schiller replied shortly.

Rademacher held up his hands placatingly, a small gold ring on his little finger twinkling in the candlelight. It was inscribed with a swastika. "Whatever is necessary, yes I know. Is there any sign of them?"

"Not yet. Although the Father here is not quite finished assisting us."

Rademacher eyed Curzones dispassionately. "I've always been fascinated by your belief, Father. To have such unwavering faith in the face of all the available evidence. It's childlike." He paused and said reflectively, "Or perhaps you do waver? After all, what is faith unless it is tested?"

Curzones was mumbling a prayer, head bowed. "Yes, speak to your God, Father," Rademacher said, patting him on the shoulder. "You will be tested soon enough." He turned to Schiller. "We need to find them. The information they have could be of the utmost importance. However," he added, holding up a finger. "I want them unharmed if possible. They are of considerably less value to me dead."

"I understand, Herr Doktor," Schiller replied. "You will have them."

Schiller turned back to Curzones and eyed him speculatively. Taking a final drag of his cigarette, he threw it to the floor, grinding it out with his boot. He snapped an order and the guards picked the priest up under each arm. Schiller looked around, eyes alighting on the offertory table.

"There," he indicated the table. "Put him on there." Curzones was laid out on the table, head turning frantically from side to side. One guard held him down by the shoulders as Schiller loomed over.

"Now listen to me, Father," he Schiller said. "You know what I need. Tell me and this will all be over."

"I cannot tell you what I do not know!" Curzones pleaded.

"Where are Fauvelle and Dubois?"

"Who? I do not know these people!"

"When did they arrive and where did they go?" Schiller continued implacably.

"Please, you must believe -" He stopped as Schiller stood back and snapped another order. The guards lifted Curzones up, turning the table onto its head until it was vertical. Seizing Curzones, they backed him against the table and tied his wrists around the leg poles. The priest hung there, grimacing as Schiller approached.

"Tell me what I need to know," Schiller urged.

"Please Monsieur, I do not -" At the first word of denial Schiller indicated with his hand and one of the guards stepped forward and launched a savage punch into Curzones' midriff. With a whoosh Curzones expelled his breath and writhed against the restraints, coughing roughly as he fought for air.

"Where are they?" Curzones could only moan in reply and Schiller indicated again. This time Curzones' face snapped back against the table with an audible thud as the solider struck him across the face. He hung there with blood seeping down his face, breath coming in ragged gasps.

"Once more, Father. When did they arrive and where did they go?

"No, please, I...I...," Curzones slumped, unable to go on.

The wet thud of flesh being struck echoed again. Curzones hung forward, blood dripping from his face onto the tiles below.

"They came here, Father," Schiller continued remorselessly. "I know they did. A man suffered greatly to give me that information, suffered much more than you do now. Where are they?" Schiller cupped Curzones' face and lifted it up to meet his eyes. "Where?"

Curzones gulped in air. "Please." He closed his eyes and Schiller let his head drop onto his chest. Once more Schiller nodded and once more the solider struck.

"Ok, Ok," Curzones gasped. "Yes, they came here."

"Finally, we're getting somewhere," Schiller observed, wiping his hands on a handkerchief. "And now?"

"They left but I don't know where they went, I swear."

"I don't believe that. How long ago were they here?"

"I beg of you, please, no!" Curzones voice rose as the soldier struck him again.

In the cellar Scottsdale flinched. His mind seethed. Although he told himself to act dispassionately, his anger was bubbling up.

And it was becoming apparent that Curzones might well break, revealing their position. Regardless, he was damned if he was going to have a priest's death on his conscience. Relief washed over him as he made the decision.

"He won't last long," he addressed the group in a whisper. "And if he talks then we're in here like rats in a barrel. Is there definitely no other way out of here?"

"None, sir," Grant said. "The only way out is the way we came in."

They both eyed the opening above. An idea was forming in Scottsdale's mind. The hatch swung out into the church. If a strong man could swing it open, another could burst out from the top step. It would be a risk but one he felt he had no choice but to take.

"When I give the order, Grant, open that hatch out as fast as you can. Put everything you have behind it and keep going when it opens. I'll be right behind you."

Grant moved into position and Scottsdale checked his pistol. He gave Grant the signal, who launched himself at the trapdoor. Legs pumping, he kept going, the trapdoor flying open. Scottsdale was right behind him, rising above the sill with pistol cocked. Only yards away, the Germans stared in shock. One guard ran for the rifle he had set aside as he beat Curzones. The second guard was quicker, but Scottsdale's first shot took him high in the chest. The other guard died as he turned his rifle towards Scottsdale.

He swivelled back towards the aisle, but the others had already fled, Schiller scooping up his machine gun as he did so. Scottsdale was forced to duck as Schiller loosed off a wild burst in their direction and, as he cautiously lifted his head up, the front door closed with a bang. Straightening up, he moved into the open, followed by the rest of the group.

"Sergeant. Check the front and bolt the doors," he ordered. Behind him, Helene quickly crossed over to Curzones.

"Give them a hand," Scottsdale ordered, and McManus and Dalton gently righted the table, removing the bonds holding Curzones in place. Helene leant over him, stroking his head and whispering softly. She turned to Scottsdale.

"We need water and bandages, please." McManus collected their water bottles and the squad first aid pack and handed them to Helene, who favoured him with a warm smile. She gently tended the priest's wounds before straightening and coming to Scottsdale. "He is in pain, but the wounds are superficial thankfully." She paused. "And thank you for doing that, Monsieur."

Scottsdale gazed back, unsettled by the praise. "I didn't do it to save him - I had to act, he was going to give us away," he said brusquely. "Besides, I should have stepped in sooner. I wish I'd -"

Helene stopped him with a hand on his arm. "I understand why you didn't, Lieutenant. Of all the awful things war does, it is the choices it forces us to make that are often the hardest to bear."

Scottsdale nodded, very aware of her touch but also her perception. There was rarely a simple choice in war and he smiled at her gratefully. She smiled back, her face much softer now, before turning back to Curzones. Scottsdale forced his mind back to practicalities. Grant had bolted the door and they'd begun to build a barricade, using the altar table, chairs and other furniture they'd found.

"Levingston, Davenport, upstairs, extinguish any lights and take up positions in the windows. Shout down if you see any movement."

Scottsdale wondered what Schiller's next move would be. He looked around. The church was relatively defensible. It had been built with the need for security as well as form. The main entrance was solidly defended and the walls stout. Nonetheless, the basic problem remained. They were trapped and outnumbered. If Schiller made an all-out attack it was inevitable that he would break through.

He was still mulling this over when a shout came from above and clatter of boots from the tower announced the arrival of Levingston.

"There's a Jerry coming, sir," he reported. "Carrying a white flag."

Grant turned to Scottsdale. "Orders, sir?"

Scottsdale grimaced. "Looks like they want to talk. So let's hear what the bastard has to say for himself."

53

6

Scottsdale examined the German officer who made a small bow before him. It felt like a test. How to maintain the politeness that a truce demanded while understanding just what kind of man was before him. Beaufort's warning, however, warmed him. This was a new kind of war. New rules. The concept gave him confidence and curbed, slightly, his anger. The man would be treated with the dignity his behaviour demanded.

"Hauptsturmführer Manfred Schiller," the officer snapped out. The click as his heels came together set Scottsdale's teeth on edge.

"Lieutenant Scottsdale," he replied tonelessly. "What do you want?"

Schiller smiled at the brusque tone. "I can only assume we're here for the same reason, Lieutenant," he said. "The scientists, yes?"

Scottsdale looked ostentatiously around. Fauvelle and Dubois were still hidden in the cellar. "I don't see any scientists here."

Schiller sighed. "Let's not make this difficult, Lieutenant."

"Difficult, Captain? This isn't difficult. You're not making any sense."

"Don't play games with me," Schiller warned, voice rising. "Where are Fauvelle and Dubois?"

"Now I will admit we have got a little lost," Scottsdale continued, ignoring the question. "I blame my sergeant.

Never could read a map right isn't that right, Sergeant Grant?"

"Always struggled in school, sir," Grant affirmed.

"And now we're just making our way home, Captain," Scottsdale continued. "Best to let us get on, unless you want to join the two gentlemen you left behind."

"I suggest you reflect on whether your death is a price worth paying for your pride," Schiller snapped.

Sensing Schiller's irritation rising, Scottsdale looked round. "Can anyone else hear a sparrow farting?"

"Your position is hopeless," Schiller interjected. "You are surrounded. Release them to me and I will allow you and your men to leave. That is my offer."

Scottsdale pretended to weigh the offer as Schiller waited. It was, relatively speaking, a good one. He couldn't see an escape short of fighting their way through a superior enemy force. Yet the thought of ceding to the demand, of handing over the civilians to this barbarous man, was an affront. Not after what the man had put Father Curzones through. And, though his mind shied from the thought, not after meeting Helene Dubois.

"Let's assume I agree with you; that these phantom scientists do exist, and our situation is hopeless. And let's assume that I believe your offer, that I could go home, report they had been captured and no one would be any the wiser." Schiller was still, waiting for Scottsdale to finish.

"But there's a problem," Scottsdale continued tightly, shrugging on his rising anger like a favourite autumn coat. Anger at their position, anger at what he had witnessed, anger at the arrogance of the man before him.

"And what is that, Lieutenant?" Schiller asked.

"The problem," Scottsdale said slowly, "is you're a bastard and a bully. I don't like bastards," he spat, "and I don't like bullies. I don't like people who torture innocent men. And I don't like being told what to do."

Schiller blinked. The threat of violence was coming off Scottsdale like a stench. "Fine words, Lieutenant," he said grimly. "But you simply sign your own death warrant. I will burn this place to the ground if I must."

"You do whatever you feel you need to do, Captain," Scottsdale said witheringly. "But we're going home."

"Going home?" Schiller snorted. "Pride and stupidity only end one way, Lieutenant. And I must say your understanding of parley does you a disservice."

"I beg your pardon," Scottsdale replied in disbelief.

"I would have expected a greater level of respect from a British officer towards a superior officer, even if we are enemies today."

"You're an even greater cretin that I imagined if you believe you deserve any respect."

"This is clearly a waste of time. You and your men will shortly be of no concern to me or the war." Schiller made a short bow and turning around, stalked out.

"He seemed upset, didn't he?" Grant smiled mirthlessly.

"He'll be even more upset when I put a bullet up his arse," Scottsdale growled. It had felt good to vent but it also served a wider purpose; he wanted the man angry. Angry men didn't think straight, and Scottsdale hoped to provoke Schiller into a rash assault. It would give Scottsdale's men a greater chance to perhaps inflict enough damage that they could escape. He wondered what the German's first move would be.

The answer was the distinctive rattle of a Maschinengewehr 34 recoil-operated air-cooled machine gun. Almost at once it was followed by the tinkling of shattering glass as the gun raked the windows.

"Christ," Pendle muttered as he dived for cover, the rest of the section following suit.

"Return fire!" Scottsdale bellowed and then shouted to the civilians. "Into the cellar, quickly," and they scurried off. However, turning around he saw that the section was hesitating under the weight of fire, so he moved to the nearest window, elbowing McManus out of the way. "Return fire dammit!" he roared and leaned round to fire into the gloom, almost immediately hearing the answering snap of bullets zipping past and slapping into the thick walls.

Sergeant Grant took up the cry and followed suit, urging the men to open fire. They were arraigned at the windows facing the graveyard and the high ceilings amplified the crash of their rifles, only to be overshadowed by the rapid rattle of the Bren, which rang out before coming to an abrupt halt.

"Bloody hell!" Marsh cursed as he leaned back. "I can't get purchase!"

He was a big man, but the Bren bucked when not mounted properly and it was simply an unequal duel with the well sited MG. Shifting his line of fire, the MG operator snapped out short bursts to cover the infantry cautiously advancing through the graveyard. Pendle waited for the focus to shift from his window, before spinning out to fire, forcing the nearest Germans to ground. An occasional tracer bullet seared inside the darkened church, the interior lit up by the muzzle flashes of the rifles. The section strained to pick out the indistinct figures of the enemy leapfrogging through the gravestones in the moonlight. Pendle lobbed a grenade and although it fell short, it briefly illuminated the most advanced infantry. An NCO had half risen to exhort his men and it was his misfortune was to do so as McManus sighted along his rifle. Gently breathing out, he squeezed the trigger and the German slumped forward over a gravestone, weapon falling from his nerveless fingers before he was dragged back by his comrades. McManus ducked back, swiftly changing the ten-round box magazine on his Lee Enfield rifle.

From the tower, Levingston was sniping at the shapes moving through the headstones. The narrow windows, originally designed to offer protection from siege, hampered his ability to track the infantry. Hearing the rattle of the machine gun ring out, he sought out the gunner, desperately trying to bring his rifle to bear.

"Come on, move," he muttered but the gunner was well covered by a large tomb and Levingston was forced back by a flurry of fire as he tried to find the target.

Beneath him, Scottsdale looked around as he reloaded. The church shook under the assault. Chips of stone ricocheted wickedly around as the ancient walls were pockmarked by fire. Crisp night air from the shattered windows stirred the soup of dirty smoke that hung inside. The dull thud of twin explosions sounded, followed moments later by more grey smoke, as German grenades landed short. All the while, a constant stream of bullets zipped through the air, scarring the stone columns. Scottsdale coughed as the tang of cordite hit the back of his throat. He banged his thigh in frustration, unable to see a way out. The enemy had superior numbers and he knew what would happen next. They would close until grenades could be launched through the windows. Then the infantry would swarm in and overwhelm them. The problem was he saw no way to stop this happening.

Risking a glance outside, he caught the unmistakable sight of German helmets drawing the noose as they closed. A cry sounded, and he saw Wilkins stagger back from a window, blood running out from under the hand clapped to his face. A splinter had raked his cheek and he swore before picking up his rifle again. Beside him, Pendle kept trying to stand but the volume of fire forced him back. Another grenade bounced off the window and exploded, sending wicked scraps of iron towards them. Looking around, Scottsdale decided they had only one choice left.

"Everyone back! Back to the end of the church!" Moving down the windows he tapped each man and moved them back. The transept acted like a person's shoulders – beyond was the narrower neck leading to the chancel and the tower. They would turn it into a redoubt. "Sergeant, tell Levingston and Davenport to come and join us," Scottsdale ordered. "The rest of you, get this over." They heaved the long altar table onto its side, throwing chairs and anything else around it to build the barricade. The offertory table was righted and added, Marsh finding a proper purchase on it for the Bren.

Grimly, their small band waited, watching as their previous positions continued to be pummelled. Scottsdale saw several dark shapes carve through the smoke to drop into the church. "Down!" Scottsdale shouted and moments later a series of cacophonous explosions ripped through the church. The gunfire resumed its battering, plastering the windows, the whine of molten lead buzzing around the church. A wave of cordite and smoke washed over their barricade.

"Everyone be ready," he warned as the volume of fire slackened, the Germans realising that the British fire had ceased. The section's faces were blackened, and they licked dry lips as they waited for the Germans to make their move. "Sergeant, what's the situation with ammunition?"

"Enough small arms but we're running low on grenades, sir," Grant replied.

Scottsdale grimaced. "When they come in, we open up, you hear? Everything we have. If we do enough damage, they'll back off." His words sounded hollow even to him and he felt his despair. Should they surrender? And if so, how was he going to get to the scientists and destroy that briefcase?

Before he had time to consider, a violent hissing bought him back to the church and he saw several smoke grenades fizzing in the aisle, emitting a thick white cloud that hungrily crept out into the empty spaces.

"Be ready!" Scottsdale warned. A cross current of air dispersed some of the smoke and he caught sight of dark shapes at the windows. He had no need to give the order – rifles spat out, the hammering of the Bren reverberating shockingly off the walls. The first German soldiers had the benefit of surprise, but the men behind were exposed. One clambered through, only to be hit as he landed. Another crumpled under the hail of fire but more came behind, joining those who had found cover at the back of the church. One man ran to the door and began dismantling the barricade. He was struck, slumped down but another wrenched it open and more Germans streamed in. Scottsdale glimpsed the outline of the MG-34 and desperately tried to target the gunner but the man slid into cover even as Scottsdale had to duck back under the weight of fire.

As he reloaded, a shout went up and the barricade shook as a grenade detonated. More grenades were traded, shattering the pews to send wicked shards of wood flickering through the gloom. At the end of the line, Private White reeled back, clawing at the ragged gaps in his throat. He collapsed, feet beating a tattoo as his lifeblood squirted through his fingers. Beside him, Pendle slipped in the blood and cursed viciously as he tried hopelessly to stem the bleeding. The Bren was overheating, smoke curling from its barrel and increasingly their fire was interrupted as the weight of German fire pressed down. A shudder went through them as the MG joined in, screaming its hate towards them, forcing them all to cower as their barricade started to disintegrate. Bullets whined overhead, another concussion swept over them. The harsh bark of German commands signalled the closing noose of the enemy infantry, creeping towards them in the shadows.

It was hopeless. Scottsdale's mind desperately sought an escape, but there was none. They could retreat up to the tower but without ammunition it would only prolong the inevitable. Grant ducked and came to him. "We can't hold them, sir!"

Scottsdale stared back. He felt sick. Griffin had gambled them to rescue the scientists. Now the gamble had failed, Scottsdale's men were dying, and the scientists would soon be in German hands.

***

In the briefest of pauses as the machine gunner reloaded, Scottsdale took his chance. "Enough! Enough!" he shouted and waved the torn altar cloth above his head. A few rifle shots rang out until, with a harsh command, the firing stopped. Scottsdale turned to the section.

"Now's not the time for more us to die," he said grimly and with a clatter laid down his rifle. The men followed suit and Scottsdale cautiously rose, hands above his head. He half expected the thud of a bullet. "It's over," he shouted bitterly. "We surrender."

From behind one of the pews, Schiller straightened up and begin snapping out orders. Several soldiers immediately came forward, weapons levelled and herded the British group together, searching them thoroughly. Scottsdale heard a growl as Marsh took exception to being relived of some letters, but Grant laid a warning hand on his arm and the section subsided sullenly.

A squat solider approached Scottsdale and gestured with his rifle. Reluctantly, Scottsdale walked down the aisle towards Schiller, who stood, hands on hips facing him. Scottsdale felt a great weariness descend; his body ached, and his mouth was bone dry. For the first time he felt the blood that ran down his arm to drip off his fingers onto the flagstones below.

"You're a fool, Lieutenant," Schiller began. "Pointless defiance and for what?"

Scottsdale summoned his energy. "I told you. I don't like bullies."

"Bravo. But this little adventure is over, for both of us. What little time there is left in this war, you will spend in a prisoner of war camp. I wouldn't worry though," he added with a wintry smile. "I'm sure it'll all be over by Christmas."

Looking past Scottsdale, Schiller smiled as he saw the trapdoor. "I assume this is where our guests are, yes?" he asked with a smile and snapped his fingers. Two of his men approached, carefully raising the entrance with weapons raised. They spoke into the cellar, beckoning with their rifles, and moments later Fauvelle, Helene and Curzones emerged and were bought forward to Schiller. Scottsdale caught Helene's eye and could only offer an apology with a mute shrug.

"Herr Fauvelle, Fraulein Dubois," Schiller said, giving a short bow. "I would say it is a pleasure to meet you, but you've caused me a great inconvenience. As for you, Father, I trust you now realise the futility of resisting us."

Fauvelle and Helene stiffened but not because of Schiller's scathing tone. They were looking intently beyond him to where Rademacher stalked down the aisle, hands behind his back. He carefully stepped over the body of a soldier, his nose wrinkling in distaste, before coming to a halt.

"Georges, Helene. I am pleased to see you again," he said formally. "This was unnecessary," he continued in mild reproof, "and it is over. But it represents the chance of a new beginning, a chance to harness your abilities in the name of a greater good, to advance the cause of science."

"I would rather slit my own throat than work with you," Helene flashed. Fauvelle laid a restraining hand on her arm. "You have blood on your hands."

Rademacher shook his head. "You will learn, child, that life is not so simple as you make it. For now, I will take that thank you, Herr Fauvelle." Rademacher reached out for the case that Fauvelle still gripped tightly. Sensing his split second of hesitation, Schiller unholstered his pistol and pointed it at Helene. Fauvelle held up his spare hand at once and offered over the suitcase to Rademacher who swept aside the detritus on the offertory table and laid out the suitcase. "The key, Herr Fauvelle," he ordered. Fauvelle slipped the key into Rademacher's outstretched hand and the German undid the clasps with a crisp click. Slowly, he opened the case and for the first time Scottsdale sensed emotion as Rademacher breathed out deeply.

"You have what you need, Herr Doktor?" Schiller enquired.

Rademacher nodded. "I do indeed. I must get this back to Germany for further study." He looked up, eyes glinting. "This is the prize," he breathed as he reverentially flicked through a set of documents. "The cavity magnetron blueprints. This is a great moment," Rademacher whispered. "With this we find ourselves once again at the crest of a scientific wave. You are looking at what could prove to be the most valuable piece of the puzzle in developing *Funkmessgerät*."

Scottsdale gave Helene a quizzical look. "Radar," she supplied dully, and Scottsdale thought back to the conversation with Griffin and how this one piece of technology could alter the course of the war.

Rademacher gently closed the suitcase. "We need to organise their transportation to Berlin as soon as is practical." "I need to offload these prisoners first," Schiller replied. "We're not far from the division HQ we resupplied at yesterday. We can return there, drop the prisoners and find you an escort for your trip back to Berlin."

"Excellent," Rademacher said as Scottsdale's section were roped together with the disconsolate scientists. Schiller began to follow but turned and stalked back towards Curzones.

"Get up," he snapped. Curzones rose to his feet. "You will also come with us. We need to ensure you won't be part of any further anti-German activities."

"He's innocent in this, Captain," Scottsdale said angrily. "He was simply giving strangers shelter when we appeared."

Schiller spun round. "Spare me your drivel, Lieutenant. He was aiding the enemy; and we won't tolerate that." He snapped his finger and a guard advanced on them. Scottsdale gave Curzones his arm as the soldier prodded him painfully in the back with his rifle.

Reckoning

He bit down on his anger and slowly followed Schiller out, glass and wood crunching under foot. The faintest rays of early morning light cut shafts through the dust and smoke. Levingston coughed. Their clothes were stained, each was bleeding, and they left behind them a dead man and a mission failed. And now they marched to prison.

7

They squatted down outside the church as dawn emerged, several guards watching over them. Scottsdale fought an overwhelming urge to sleep. The light of the burgeoning sun played across the grime-encrusted lines of his face. Closing his eyes, he listened to the twittering of the early morning forager; it took him back to early mornings in Essex cycling to the village store to earn his keep. A slight smile crossed his face at the thought of the kindly Mr Hawthorne gently berating him as he larked about. War then had been a dark cloud on the horizon; it didn't seem possible that after the horror of the Great War there'd ever be young British men – boys really – fighting in France again.

Yet even then Scottsdale was fascinated by the stories of conflict and empire, devouring tales of the mass battles of the Western Front. To the not quite formed mind of a boy, it sounded glamourous and exciting. A clash of civilisations, of good against those dreadful Huns. And those soldiers! Marching briskly down the street, strong and clear-eyed in their smart uniforms. "There go the Pompadours," Mr Hawthorne would say admiringly. What a name! And now he was a Pompadour, a solider of the Essex Regiment, and the sleepy village life he'd led was a mirage that he couldn't quite believe had ever existed.

The cough of a motor interrupted his reverie and he glanced round. The men were sprawled out as they waited, their exhaustion compounded by the graves they had been forced to dig after being led from the church. Now more than ever, he had to stay alert. They would need him, be it in a prisoner of war camp or some factory deep inside the Reich. He imagined life in Germany with awful fascination – a Nazi world, a world where he was never free but a prisoner, representing not just a country but an empire and a world order brought low.

He frowned. No, that couldn't be right. He wasn't like some, like Lieutenant Berry, who believed that by virtue of his Englishness he was superior. That delusion had died in the fields of the Somme and the mud of Ypres. Yet even with the recent German successes it was still inconceivable to him that Britain would be ultimately overwhelmed. The fury of the Reich, the level of blind certainty in its destiny and its unquestioning belief in conquest and military expansion – it was incomprehensible that something so vile would not be defeated. They had to find the will and the means to win this fight.

His mind flickered to the thought of escape, feeding a fresh surge of energy. Catching Grant's eye, he nodded slightly. He'd need Grant too, to keep the men alert, to avoid yielding to the crushing force of inertia and numb acceptance. They remained tantalisingly close to the British lines and a short, forced march could see them free. If they succeeded, he would be welcomed. Any men were valuable in the desperate fight to come.

His gaze travelled to the French civilians who sat together disconsolately. Helene had an arm around Fauvelle while Curzones was staring at the floor, rosary beads clacking through his fingers. Could he abandon them to their fate? They'd shown genuine bravery and it had been his job to free them, a job he had singularly failed at. And then there was Helene Dubois. She was mesmerising in her passion and insight, chameleon-like with her emotions, moving from rage to tenderness so swiftly. He was drawn to her instinctively.

Yet he had to make sure she didn't cloud his judgement. He sighed. He cherished the idea of leading well, but also of fulfilling his duty to the country. What if he had the choice of abandoning the civilians to enable the soldiers to escape? Could he bring himself to do that?

He rubbed his jaw and as he did the stern words of his mother came back to him. One day he'd returned home, triumphantly clutching a five pound note he'd found. To his dismay, his mother had made him take it to the local bobby to hand in. He still remembered her words as she'd squatted down in front of his unhappy face.

"Being good is doing the right thing; especially when no one's watching," she'd said seriously. "A clever man once wrote that. Do you understand?" It had guided him ever since and he felt calmer. He would do what was right.

A sharp kick on his boot jolted him back to the present and he looked up in irritation at the bored face of the German guard. "*Beweg dich*," the guard barked, gesturing at a waiting truck.

Scottsdale smiled back. "A cup of tea would be lovely, thank you," he replied without moving. The guard looked uncertain as several of the men chuckled. Sensing he was being mocked, he pointed his rifle in Scottsdale's face and repeated his order louder.

"Ah, in the truck? Speak clearer next time will you." Scottsdale turned to the section. "Come on, lads, time to move." The men insisted on lifting Father Curzones, wincing in pain, into the back and fought to offer Helene an arm, but she merely smiled, climbing nimbly up before turning to offer Fauvelle a hand. Scottsdale was last to board, catching Father Curzones' eye and smiling in what he hoped was a reassuring manner.

As they jolted along, Scottsdale gazed at the church spire receding into the distance. It had been a beacon but had only led to death and defeat. He'd failed and worse, one of his men had died in that failure. Gazing into the sky, he thought of Private White and the letter he would write to the man's family. Hadn't he recently had a daughter? Scottsdale had a vague recollection of White proudly showing off after the girl had been born. He would check, ask Grant. They'd buried him in the graveyard, and Father Curzones had said a prayer over White and the Germans they'd laid alongside. Marsh had protested bitterly at burying White next to the German dead but Father Curzones had quietened him. Scottsdale hoped that being buried in a church would be of some comfort to the man's family. He wouldn't mention the Germans buried alongside.

Swinging off the main road, the truck bumped down a rough track before coming to a shuddering halt. Scottsdale was thrown forward, instinctively reaching out to steady himself, ending with his hand clasped on Helene's arm. Braced firmly against the struts, she raised an eyebrow.

"I'm very sorry," Scottsdale said, reddening slightly. "But thank you."

"You are most welcome, Lieutenant," Helene said with a smile.

"Add bad driving to the list of things I hate about the Nazis."

"A long list I'm sure."

Scottsdale hesitated. It felt like everyone was listening closely to their conversation. He sensed that Helene wouldn't care a jot, but Scottsdale felt constrained. "Growing by the day," he offered with a small smile.

He was rescued as the truck trundled forward again. Helene and Scottsdale shared a wince at the screech of grinding gears before watching the familiar red and white pole being lowered across the road behind them. They had arrived at the local German headquarters and Scottsdale straightened, eager to take in any detail of their prison but their truck almost immediately slowed to a halt and their guard jumped to the ground, beckoning for them to follow.

Scottsdale leapt down first and came to a standstill. A charming chateau lay before them. The truck had stopped at the edge of a moat, its motionless surface dotted with clusters of water lilies. A small guardhouse overlooked the stone bridge that pointed, arrow straight, into the chateau. Dense woodland encompassed most of the perimeter although to his left Scottsdale could see several squat buildings. Judging by the uniforms drying in the sunshine and a variety of bikes, cars and trucks parked alongside, these had been converted to a barracks.

The guards barked a command and they were herded across the bridge towards the main gate. Their truck trundled off around the moat towards the barracks. Scottsdale examined the chateau. Lofty, narrow windows dotted the front, inaccessible to anyone reaching the base of the walls. The distinctive gap-toothed shape of the crenelated outer wall spoke of a history of siege. He caught a glimpse of a German helmet as a sentry walked his route. Ivy spread out across the sun washed stone and at each corner a turret jutted upwards. Where once a baronial banner may have flown, now the red Nazi flag fluttered gently in the breeze.

As they approached, the arched gates swung open. Seeing Sergeant Grant ahead, Scottsdale hurried forward. Coming alongside, he touched Grant's arm. "Sergeant," he muttered. "Tell the men to be ready. I want to get out of here and tonight may be our only chance. And keep an eye out. Understood?"

Grant kept his eyes front as he replied. "Understood, sir. Looks a tough nut to crack,"

"Well, my mother always told me nothing worth doing is easy and my mother was always right," Scottsdale replied.

"Hard to argue, sir," Grant said.

"Impossible in fact," Scottsdale affirmed.

As they passed into the shadowed courtyard, Scottsdale looked round with interest. There were buildings on three sides. To their left lay the chateau's major structure. Several stories high, its grey stone was faded from years baking in the sun. Large, ornate windows were set across the middle floor and smaller windows studded the top floor.

Opposite it was a similar sized building and linking the two was a squatter building along the far wall. A bored looking sentry smoked as he took his shift. It was a peaceful scene but marred by the grey uniforms and occasional barked command in German.

One of their guards stopped to scoop up a mouthful of water from a small fountain that burbled away in the centre of the courtyard. Several bicycles were stacked alongside, probably for messengers Scottsdale imagined. A few trees were scattered in the corner nearest the gate and an Alsatian growled as it cocked its leg in the shadows. Scottsdale's attention was drawn by the clatter of boots on cobblestones which announced the arrival of Schiller. He strode forward purposively, full of energy, barely looking as if he'd spent the night in battle. With a triumphant smile, he made a small bow.

"Welcome to the Chateau du Pirou. This will be your home until we can make the necessary arrangements for your onward transportation. A fine place to spend some time, wouldn't you agree?" He chuckled happily, voice deep with satisfaction. "We are quite pressed for space, however, so

Lieutenant, you will be sharing with the civilians." Scottsdale regarded him sourly. "And my men?"

"Will be taken to our cellar," Schiller replied. "The kind of place they've become accustomed to recently, eh?" He laughed. "Excellent. And I also insist that you join me for dinner later this evening. We have ample supplies and the adjutant's chef is a miracle worker."

"I'd rather starve than eat with you," Helene said scathingly and spat at Schiller's feet.

Schiller's bonhomie evaporated instantly. He leant close to Helene who recoiled slightly. "Be very, very careful, Mademoiselle. I have only so much patience."

He stood back and barked an order in German. The section was led off and Scottsdale felt a peculiar sense of loss as they disappeared. Prodded by the guard, he was taken into the main building with the civilians. Ascending the stone stairs to the first floor, he glanced to the right. This was the main hall, a long, high room. A dining table dominated the room, illuminated by shafts of light flooding through the high windows. Moving up another level, they entered a narrow corridor with regularly spaced stout wooden doors. Led to the far end, their guard herded them inside a small room. It contained two beds, a desk and a solitary chair; above the desk was a small barred window. The locking bar set in place and they turned to face each other.

After a brief silence, Helene spoke. "So - what do we do now?"

***

With a groan Father Curzones lowered himself down onto one of the beds and reclined with an arm across his face, still puffy from Schiller's interrogation. Scottsdale squatted by the side of the bed.

"Father," he said hesitantly. "Thank you for what you did in the church, for your bravery." He struggled to find the right words. "I'm so sorry for what happened, I never thought they'd treat you like that."

Curzones waved a hand. "Please, Lieutenant, do not berate yourself; you're not responsible for that man's barbarity." He coughed softly. "He was so *cold*. And there was nothing you could have done to stop it. In fact, I may very well owe you my life; I'm not sure he would have stopped regardless of what I said." He rested his hand on Scottsdale's arm and gave it a gentle squeeze before closing his eyes.

"Thank you, Father."

"We need to get him bandages and water," Helene said briskly.

Scottsdale nodded. Seeing nothing useful in the room, he turned to the door and banged on it. "Guard!" He paused but there was no reply. Feeling a surge of irritation - at the guard, at the situation and at the feeling of general futility - he hammered the door again. "Guard!" he hollered. He turned back to the room. "They're ignoring me!"

Helene stood up and began beating the door too, sharing a small grin with Scottsdale as they let out the pent up emotion of the last few hours in a cathartic drumbeat. "Guard! Open the bloody door!"

Finally, a German shout sounded, and the door opened slowly, the point of the sentry's rifle nosing inside. Scottsdale and Helene stepped back with their hands raised. Helene gestured to Curzones. "Water," she said, mimicking drinking. Unable to find the word for bandage she picked up the sheet and tore a strip off, winding it round her arm and pointing at Curzones. The guard's face cleared, and he nodded before backing away and closing the door.

"Let's see what that brings," Helene said.

A few moments later the guard returned with a pitcher of water and some rough bandages. "Thank you," Scottsdale said while Helene dabbed at Curzones' face, talking softly. Scottsdale shook his head. "I will make him pay for this, I promise you," he said fiercely.

"And how do you intend to do that, Lieutenant?" Helene retorted. "We're locked up and Mr Griffin's ridiculous plan has failed. Sending a handful of men to find us? We should have been found long ago."

Scottsdale stiffened. "We still have tonight," he said angrily. "And I would remind you that one of my men died in that ridiculous plan, trying to save you."

Helene stopped tending to Curzones and bowed her head. "I cannot tell you how sorry I am for that man's death," she sighed. "What was his name? White, yes?"

Scottsdale nodded. "Private Norman White."

"Norman White. His name will live me for the rest of my life; I won't forget him," she promised, and Scottsdale believed her.

"Thank you," he said.

"It is just so frustrating, we were so close!" she continued. "A few more hours and we'd be free. To come so close and fail, to watch Rademacher carry off our work – I can hardly bear it." Fauvelle squeezed her arm and she smiled at him with affection. Turning to Scottsdale, she continued in calmer voice. "Did you dream when you were young, Lieutenant? I did. Since I was this high," she said, holding her hand up above the ground, "all I ever wanted was to be a scientist like my father. I'd go and visit him and Maurice and I adored it. It felt like we were trying to solve a giant puzzle, and if we only worked hard enough, we would succeed."

"It sounds exciting," Scottsdale said.

"It was! To a young girl expected to play with dolls and cook and clean, it was adventure, it was an escape." Helene breathed deeply. "One day, yes, fall in love, get married and have children, but I wanted more than washing and making dinner and looking after babies. There was a whole world out there and those times in the lab were wonderful. I'm sure I was a nuisance to you both, Uncle!"

"You were a terror," Fauvelle chuckled. "Always wiring up something and setting it on fire. But we saw your potential. Concepts, ideas; you picked them up so quickly. It made Jean and me so proud."

Helene smiled appreciatively. Where Scottsdale would have been embarrassed by praise, she accepted it gracefully and he admired her for it. "We were a team. If something doesn't work, try another way. If that doesn't work, try a third. It was so liberating! And I was so fortunate that my family encouraged me."

Scottsdale thought back to home, to the old boys' club that permeated everyday life. "I imagine you needed that support," he observed.

"Truly. Those grey beards at the university only saw women as cooks and cleaners, and this after the brilliance of Marie Curie!" Her indignation radiated, and Scottsdale warmed to it. "I was going to pursue the path I wanted, not the path some relic thought appropriate for me."

"It would have been dangerous to oppose you I imagine," Scottsdale said.

"Yes, I suppose I have always been headstrong," she said, returning his smile. "Which I got from my father; I never felt closer to him than at the lab. Do you remember what he was like when he was close to a discovery?"

"Completely absorbed," Fauvelle replied. "He talked of nothing else. It infuriated my sister," Fauvelle replied.

"I'd be away for weeks, but when I came back he'd be right where I left him, buried among the chaos of his lab. As soon as I came in, he'd be explaining his latest theory."

"And this was when you first came across Rademacher?" Scottsdale asked tentatively.

Helene's face darkened. "Yes. Papa met Rademacher at a conference. They shared an interest in pulse-modulation" – she glanced at Scottsdale's blank expression before continuing – "one of its applications is detecting the range of objects – so RDF." She shivered. "For a while they collaborated, and Rademacher used to visit us occasionally, but they increasingly argued." She turned to Fauvelle. "Do you remember what he said about universities?"

Fauvelle nodded grimly. "He'd start quoting that insane rector from Freiburg University. 'The duty of students as well as professors is to serve the people under the triple form of labour service, military service and scientific service,'" he mimicked in a pompous voice. "Nonsense." "And Papa wasn't well," Helene explained. "He never recovered fully from being gassed in the last war. The prospect of more horror haunted him, but Rademacher wanted to use science to further his own ambitions. He pestered Papa, insisting they research together but he was just trying to take the knowledge back to the Nazis. It placed an intolerable strain on Papa, not least because Rademacher used his influence from Germany to threaten our funding."

"What happened to your father?" Scottsdale asked softly.

She paused. "He died last year. Partly I think from his wounds, but also of a broken heart. Seeing the world descending into madness again and seeing science twisted to support the Nazis. Einstein was Jewish for god's sake! Madness. Papa couldn't cope. I think the fight went out of him."

"His death was a tragedy," Fauvelle said. "My sister never recovered and when she died I took Helene in and we continued our research."

Scottsdale sat back. They were remarkable people, he thought. Hunted by Schiller and betrayed by Rademacher. No wonder their anger was so fierce.

Helene composed herself. "So you see, this really is the world to us. And so I will be eternally grateful to your men for trying to help us when no one else would."

Scottsdale nodded. "Thank you, Mademoiselle."

"Helene, please," she said gently. Scottsdale stared back and could only nod. She was powerfully different from anyone he had met before, weathered and shaped by a world in tumult, but refusing to let society shape her life. How different from the perfectly respectable girls he'd met at the dances back home. With them, he felt he already knew what the next thirty years of life held. Helene was wilder, and he was only just beginning to get to know her. His stomach knotted at the idea of losing her so quickly but also at the fear that his experiences couldn't match the depth of her life. He was fascinated but quite appalled at himself. Captive in France, his mission a failure and he was daydreaming about a French girl. He had to focus and find a way out of there for the section.

He stood up determinedly. "Bugger if this is the end of it," he said. "You asked earlier, 'what now'. What now is simple – we find a way to get out of here."

8

Evening stole in and found Scottsdale deep in thought. An oppressive heat had risen throughout the day. Gazing out of the window, he watched dark clouds building to the west. They rolled forward in ever increasing waves, struggling to contain the rain within that threatened to spill out. Even the incessant rumble of gunfire was smothered by the low-lying blanket. Distant pyres of smoke rose to meet it, some black and muscular, others grey and dirty.

He closed his eyes, absentmindedly wiping away the sweat from his face. Helene and Curzones had succumbed to the heat and slept fitfully; Fauvelle sat at the desk, eyes closed. Their paltry lunch had long been consumed and Scottsdale's stomach rumbled. The wearisome hours had been spent turning over various schemes for escape and trying to stay alert. His attempts to find a weakness in the window bars had proven fruitless.

As Scottsdale turned, Helene stirred. He caught the momentary confusion in her eyes as it took her a split second to recall where they were; and why they were here. She lay back with a sigh.

"It's so hot," she said, fanning herself.

"It'll break soon," Scottsdale replied, handing her a glass of water.

She sipped gratefully. "Thank you. And I hope you are right, I feel so unclean," she added, pushing back her hair.

"I think you've a way to go before you get to really unclean," Scottsdale replied with a smile, indicating his battered uniform.

"Yes, you are a mess, Lieutenant. Not what I was expecting of a British Army officer."

"Ah, well I have to ask what you were expecting?"

"Hmm, let me see," Helene said in mock seriousness. She began ticking points off her fingers. "Pompous, naturally. An air of superiority completely unearned. Most likely a terrible moustache. Oh, and completed stupid, of course."

"Of course."

"Yet here you are; French speaking, filthy and not even a hint of a moustache."

"I can only apologise." Scottsdale bowed ironically. "They select the most expendable for this kind of mission, you see. Which is usually the least well dressed in the mess."

"Perfectly understandable, Lieutenant. I know the importance of fashion."

"Sadly, fashion and I have never been the easiest of dance partners."

Helene laughed. "Perhaps one day we shall dance properly then, Lieutenant."

"You say that now; I'm not sure you'd say the same when you see my two left feet."

Helene peered down at Scottsdale's feet. "Yes, I can see the odd shape. Clearly it will be a challenge."

"But I guess you're the kind of person who likes a challenge."

"Truly," Helene said, but her face darkened quickly. "I think the idea of a dance is going to be a challenge now, Lieutenant."

"We'll just have to keep trying," Scottsdale said firmly. "As my mother used to say, if at first you don't succeed -"

"Try, try again," Helene finished, smiling a little. She stood up and went to check on Father Curzones. Fauvelle opened his eyes and stretched, yawning.

"What time is it?" he asked.

Scottsdale consulted his watch. "Coming up to eight o'clock." For a moment, his mind wandered back to the battalion. Perhaps even now, Major Carter and Griffin were writing them off and preparing to withdraw. He shook off the thought. There was nothing he could do about that, only what he could do about their current situation. Which, he reflected, didn't feel like a great deal.

They turned as the locking bar was removed. The door swung open to reveal their guard, rifle raised. "*Kom*," he said gruffly, and

Helene gently shook Father Curzones awake. Their little group trooped down the corridor, guards stationed in front and behind them. Glancing into the courtyard below, Scottsdale saw a couple of officers laughing as they smoked. An Alsatian eagerly jumped at them until quietened with a sharp word. They descended to the main hall and there, seated at the table, was Schiller.

He rose and held out his hands in welcome, the ancient wooden floor creaking as they moved towards the long dining table. Scottsdale looked up at the banners that hung from the rafters, trying to recall his schoolboy Latin and decipher some of the mottos. The table dominated the room, illuminated by several candelabra. A sideboard held assorted silver platters and glasses. Every available window was open, but it was still stiflingly hot. The rumble of thunder drifted in. There were six place settings, with Schiller holding court at the top.

"Thank you for joining me," he began. "A chance to pause amongst all this unpleasantness, don't you think? Tonight, we shall look to the future."

Scottsdale stared back; Schiller's blithe welcome threatened to ignite his anger. Warily, he pulled back his chair and sat, the others following suit. A steward decanted red wine; Scottsdale swallowed as it splashed into his glass. The image of White's blood spreading over the flagstones was fresh in his mind.

Raising his glass, Schiller made a toast. "To peace!" Seeing the surprised looks, he chuckled. "Why such surprise? Peace is necessary, at least between us. It's only the gross betrayal of 1918 that has led us here. Once that wrong has been righted, we can move forward together." He paused as the steward placed bowls of soup in front of them. Scottsdale took in the faint smell of mint; he'd always hated pea soup.

In the strained silence Father Curzones raised his glass. "Peace is always to be desired," he said cautiously. "So, to peace it is." Following his example, the others half heartedly raised their glasses and sipped.

Schiller inclined his head to Curzones. "But only between us, Father. To the east lies the Communist threat, while we must continue the fight against the Jews. Only once they have been destroyed can a new world order begin."

Scottsdale couldn't help but interject. "You're obsessed by order."

"If I am, it is because I know what life is like without it. Imagine watching society crumble around you, while people suffer. And not the wealthy; no, it was people like me and my family who bore the brunt, barely enough money to put food on the table, savings wiped out, communists attacking people in the streets. So yes, I talk of order, because order and discipline and pride saved our country."

"And that justifies the invasions, the hatred of Jews, the savagery - you tortured a priest for pity's sake!"

Schiller shook his head. "You can't see it so simply! Torture is inefficient, I'll grant you, but sometimes a blunt tool is required. And what I do, *must* be done, for the sake of the future."

"But the things you're doing, they're unconscionable."

Schiller leant back and puffed out his cheeks. "You know it takes a certain kind of courage to subjugate yourself to a greater good." He gestured to Father Curzones. "Was beating the priest, right? Regardless of what I think of religion, in abstract, in the act itself - no, it isn't. But in a wider context? That's a different question. Germany must win this war and to that end I would do it again and again."

"Morality isn't relative, Captain," Father Curzones said with mild reproof. "I fear for your soul if you can't see that."

Schiller snorted. "What is moral - or rather, what is permissible - is simply, finally, a question of power. If you have the power, then everything is permissible. That is the lesson of history."

"That is simply what you tell yourself to justify your actions," Curzones replied. "It is wrong in every sense."

"To further my goal, to hasten the end of this war, I would torture every priest between here and London," Schiller replied vehemently. "Every time we destroy a city or hurt someone, it's a warning and prevents others from needless resistance. Don't you see why it's necessary?"

Scottsdale struggled to find the words to puncture the man's certainty. "What you describe is a license for evil. In your world, anything, any act, no matter how awful, can be justified. That is a truth that cannot be avoided and that is why you will lose this war."

"Spoken from a viewpoint where struggle and chaos and death don't stalk your life every day. Answer me this. Would you kill to save your family? To prevent their death you must commit a horrible act – do you? Of course you act. You must. And so must we. Yes, sometimes terrible things will be done but history will judge us knowing we had no choice. That we faced an existential threat and had to act. And part of that is we had to do terrible things. But necessary things."

"You can tell yourself whatever you want, but history will judge as you are, not as you imagine," Helene replied forcefully. "We are defined by what we do in life. And there are some things that are simply wrong, no matter what justification you claim. When this is over, when your fantasies are ashes and the Nazis are no more, history will damn you, you deluded ass."

Schiller chuckled. "History is written by the victors, don't forget that," he said and raised his glass in salute. Scottsdale grimaced, and the silence stretched as they each considered the truth of that statement. Finally, Schiller spoke again. "But this is no time for politics! Tell me about life in England, Lieutenant. I've always imagined it's much like Germany."

Scottsdale looked round, his irritation building. Biting back the remark that England was nothing like Nazi Germany, he took a deep breath. Moving the conversation on seemed wise and so he began to speak, at first hesitantly, of his life; of bike rides meandering through country lanes, of village fetes and bonfire night; of trips to the beach, plunging into the freezing sea; the sense of community that sustained so many people, the importance of where you were from. What had once felt stultifying now assumed an aching melancholy. And he realised he wasn't really speaking to Schiller at all; his audience was Helene. He wanted her to understand his world and how he'd ended up in the British Army.

"I'd always found history fascinating, so I joined the cadet force at school," he shrugged. "Field trips and map exercise and drills – it was so much more interesting than the idea of working in the local bank or whatever. I was young and bored. The army was an escape from a world that seemed so small," he said. "That awful moment when you think I'm just like everyone else, my life is going to run and run and be just the same." He sighed. "The things I've seen now, it sometimes feels stupid."

"Not at all," Helene replied. "We're all guilty of that, of trying to escape the path set out for us. Even if I sometimes wish I was I was back in that life sometimes!"

"Maybe we should have stuck it out?"

"Never! We were right to try even if we have ended up here."

Scottsdale raised an eyebrow. "Yes, I can think of better places we could have ended up."

Helene smiled back, but Schiller interrupted. "The military isn't an escape," he said frowning. "This world you describe is so...quaint. I knew a world where the cost of a loaf of bread doubled, tripled just in the time it took to queue up. Life wasn't soft, it wasn't clean," he added with venom. "Everywhere was disorder. Our country was occupied and broken up, the wealth ripped from the soil to feed the hate of our enemies. No," he shook his head, "life was not easy. We were lost until the Fuhrer appeared. People like me are like Germany today – forged in hardship into the spear point of a new world." He observed Scottsdale coolly. "Maybe that's why you are losing. You have become weak and now is the time for Germany to assume the mantle of leader of the civilised world."

The man's arrogance was insufferable. "What of America? They won't stand by as this happens."

"America won't intervene," Schiller said scornfully. "They're weak and their culture, of jazz and easy women, rots them from within. Even if they joined the war, what can they do? That world is as rotten as the old and needs sweeping away."

"The only certainty is that one day you'll lose," Helen said.

Schiller snorted. "We shall see. For you it is academic – if you'll forgive me my little joke." He smiled. "Doktor Rademacher has confirmed that you will be taken to Berlin to work for him. An exciting moment for you both, eh?"

Fauvelle blanched, and Helene looked with loathing at Schiller.

"An escort will be arriving tomorrow," Schiller continued. "I suggest you sleep well as we will be keeping you very busy during your stay with us." He looked up as the door to the hall was opened and there, on cue, was Rademacher. He stalked towards the table.

"Ah, Herr Doktor. Welcome," Schiller said, reverting to German. "I was just informing your colleagues of the plan for them. I take it all is in order?"

"Thank you, Hauptsturmführer Schiller. The arrangements have been made, yes." He turned to the civilians, switching to French. "Monsieur Fauvelle, Mademoiselle Dubois, you shall accompany me back to Berlin. You will be working with my best team and have all the facilities you require. Should you wish -"

Fauvelle was already shaking his head. "Can you really believe we would work with you after all this?" he gestured helplessly. "What kind of people would we be? No, no. We cannot."

Rademacher's head jerked back slightly, mildly affronted. "You will have ample time to reconsider. Regardless, there has been a small change of plan. We shall leave during the night, not tomorrow. There is not a moment to lose and I have already arranged for transportation to a nearby airfield where we will fly on to Berlin. As soon as I have notification the plane is ready, we shall leave. Please gather your possessions."

Schiller snapped an order to the guards and Scottsdale stared helplessly as Fauvelle and Helene were hustled out of the dining room. Helene looked back, her arm gripped by the guard. It couldn't end like this; years in a POW camp stretching ahead. They had to find a way out of here.

Left alone with Scottsdale and Curzones, Schiller poured himself another glass. "I imagine you are interested in news of the front, Lieutenant?" he asked.

Despite himself, Scottsdale's interest quickened. On such news could hinge their fate. He nodded. "I would hear of it, yes," he said guardedly.

"I'm afraid it is not good news for you," Schiller replied with a smile. "Calais and Boulogne are invested and will soon fall. Your famous tank corps counter attacked near Arras but has been beaten back, although it does sound like it gave Rommel a fright!" Schiller laughed. "I doubt it will be long before we break through. What I would give to be there. That's where I should be, not hunting clerks.

You're a soldier, Lieutenant, I'm sure you understand. The need to fight, to prove yourself against a worthy adversary. That is honour."

"And where does torture feature in your notions of honour?"

Schiller sighed in frustration. "I'm supposed to let the priest go even though I know he's helping my enemy? Don't be so naïve. War is about winning. I must admit though," he mused, "I really didn't expect it to be so quick. Whether we turn south, or we make peace, it's clear that this war has been won."

Scottsdale flinched. He was dizzy, wearied by his efforts and the rough wine. A peal of thunder echoed in the dining hall. Briefly he closed his eyes, fighting the desire to give in. There was still hope. If they could only get out of the chateau, they weren't far from the British lines. That was what he had to focus on. He opened his eyes to see Father Curzones watching him with concern and forced a short smile.

"Life never goes the way you think it will, Captain, let alone war," Scottsdale said. "Remember that. Maybe it won't be as easy as you think."

Schiller gave him an amused look. "Not this time, Lieutenant. This is history being made and nothing, nothing at all, can stop us." He raised his glass and drained the last remnants of his wine. Scottsdale looked at Curzones who shook his head helplessly. The war seemed over, they were captive, and Schiller's laughter rang in their ears.

***

"I'm going to have to hurt you, Father," Scottsdale muttered as they were being led back to their cell.

Curzones looked at him. "I'm sorry?"

"Forgive me, but this is probably going to hurt." Their hellish dinner had dragged on, Schiller continuing to harangue them, drinking more and more. Scottsdale and Curzones had endured. Around them, the chateau hunkered down as the storm grew and the night drew in. Thunder growled overhead, and the dining room was lit by flashes of lightning. Schiller raved, his voice rising to be heard over the rain that poured down. Like the sun-baked earth, Scottsdale and Curzones soaked up the German's ranting. Sweat glistened on Schiller's brow until finally he gestured and was helped from the room.

It left Scottsdale and Curzones with a solitary guard. Scottsdale knew this was their chance, before they were securely locked in again. That meant striking now and Father Curzones would have to suffer. He threw out an arm as he stood up, swaying exaggeratedly to give the impression he was deep in drink.

"Bloody Germans. Good drinking though!" he said, slurring his words. Throwing his head back he laughed, and the guard smiled in sympathy at the apparently drunk Englishman.

As they turned into the corridor at the top of the stairs, Scottsdale staggered and put an arm round Father Curzones. The guard was just turning the corner behind them when Scottsdale exploded into life. Seizing Curzones by the lapels, he swung the priest round and shoved him towards the astonished guard, who barely had time to react before the sizeable weight of Father Curzones crashed into him. With a strangled shout, they dropped to the ground, Curzones landing on top of the guard. Scottsdale came over the top immediately and seizing the guard's head, smashed it against the stone floor. The guard flopped back while they remained frozen, waiting to see if they had raised an alarm.

After a moment, Father Curzones coughed. "Perhaps you could move, Lieutenant?"

Scottsdale realised that he was crushing Curzones into the unconscious German and shifted. "Sorry, Father," he said apologetically. "All ok?"

"Yes, just about thank you, Lieutenant," Curzones replied wincing. "I'm glad you didn't tell me you were planning that."

Scottsdale grinned. "You're made of stern stuff, Father! Now, give me a hand. We need to get this chap out of sight." Taking hold of a leg each, they dragged the lifeless form down the corridor. Reaching their erstwhile cell, Scottsdale rummaged in the guard's pockets and produced a key. With a triumphant smile they opened the door and dragged the guard inside. A welcoming silence enveloped them.

"Now what?" Curzones asked.

"I'm not sure to be perfectly honest," Scottsdale replied. "But it's a start. First things first, let's get him secure."

They tied up the guard with ripped bedsheets and leftover bandages, before Curzones fashioned a gag to force between the man's lips. Dropping the inert form onto one of the beds, they leant back, smiling at each other. Father Curzones seemed renewed by the disposal of the sentry. "As a man of God I should not rejoice, but as a man with all my weakness I salute you," he said.

"Yes, that did feel good, I must confess."

He now had several decisions to make. His military imperative was clear – if he could, free the men and get them back to British lines; if he could not, make his own way back. His mind, however, lingered on the French civilians. Where were they now? Could they be found?

"Are we going to find your men?" Curzones asked.

"Yes." Alone he stood a better chance of slipping back to British lines, but he wouldn't abandon the men to captivity without trying to free them. "And it will have to be now.

Hopefully our friend here was on duty all night – if he isn't noticed until morning then we have half a chance."

He regarded Curzones. What should he do with priest? Curzones was implicit in their escape and he feared for the priest if he was left behind. Could they take him with them or would he fatally slow them down?

Curzones smiled as if reading Scottsdale's mind. "I must go back to my flock," he said.

Scottsdale smiled back. "I'm not sure that's wise, Father," he said gently. "For now, at least, I would ask you to come with us."

"Very well," Curzones replied reluctantly. "Until we know how this ends, I will stay with you."

Scottsdale nodded and looked out of the window. On his side was surprise and now, it seemed, the weather. The thunderstorm that had been building was lashing the chateau, a steady drumbeat of rain hammering the walls. He thought back to Schiller's mocking comments. The section was in the cellar under the building opposite. How to move about the chateau without arousing suspicion? Frowning, he turned to see Curzones checking the unconscious German. His face cleared. He had an idea which would give them a chance. It was a slim one, but it was the best one he had.

"I'm afraid I'm going to have to take you prisoner again, Father."

9

The German uniform was an uncomfortably tight fit. Their struggles to strip it from the prostrate guard had threatened to bring him round, prompting Scottsdale to clout him again. That problem could be solved by killing the guard, but Scottsdale dismissed the idea. Killing in combat was one thing, slicing the throat of an unconscious guard quite another.

Finally, they tugged the uniform free and Scottsdale struggled into it. Handing his own uniform to Curzones, he tugged at the unfamiliar *feldbluse* of an ordinary German soldier. Curzones gave him an ironic salute.

"This doesn't feel right," Scottsdale grumbled.

"It doesn't look right either," Curzones replied dryly.

Opening the door, Scottsdale checked outside before turning to Curzones. "After you," he said and followed Curzones into the corridor. Several lights provided a dim glow, but all was quiet. Scottsdale was pleased that he could barely make out the other side of the chateau through the driving rain. He wanted the sentries wet and miserable.

As they trod softly downstairs, they came to the main hall. With a lurch of alarm, Scottsdale realised Curzones was going inside. "Father," he hissed, but Curzones darted over to the table, quickly pocketing some bread and cheese that had been left out.

"You will need this later, Lieutenant," he explained.

"Thank you, Father," Scottsdale replied gratefully, and they continued to the ground floor, the patter of rain growing with each step. Pausing under the arched doorway, Scottsdale gazed intently out through the curtain of rain, searching for any sign of life. The entrance to the building opposite was a darker shape in the gloom.

For a long minute they stood still until, satisfied, Scottsdale turned to Curzones.

"You go first, Father, and I'll be a step behind. Just act like you're a tired, frightened priest being taken back to his cell and no one will suspect a thing."

"No acting required, Lieutenant," Curzones replied.

"We'll be fine," Scottsdale replied. His heart was thudding as the moment of exposure approached and not just with fear; he was moving, his enemy was sleeping, and he had a chance again. "Ready?" Curzones nodded and stepped out into the rain.

Scottsdale unslung his rifle and followed into the heavy, enveloping deluge. Fat raindrops bounced off the unfamiliar helmet and soon they were both soaked, the rain burrowing under their clothes. The only mercy was that it wasn't freezing cold and the courtyard was sheltered from the wind. Restraining the impulse to run, Scottsdale splashed along behind Curzones. A growl of thunder echoed around them, followed moments later by a bright flash of lightning. He glanced at the fountain as they passed, the water dancing crazily under the onslaught. Alongside it a truck was parked and beyond he could see a muted light leaking out under a door; he prayed it didn't open. Instead, he concentrated on the hunched shape of Curzones in front of him.

They were closing on the far side when Curzones stumbled and fell. Scottsdale hurried forward. "Come on, Father, onwards and upwards," he said, grabbing Curzones who uttered a particularly colourful oath as he stood up.

"Occasionally I fail to find equanimity in the face of adversity," he said sheepishly, looked down at his hand. "In this case, dog shit."

"Enough to cause anyone to lose faith, Father. But can we get moving before a German decides to look us up."

In another few yards they had reached shelter, pausing to shake off the rain which pooled around their feet as Scottsdale looked around. To their left was a sturdy wooden door which he ignored. In front of them were the stairs and he took the first few steps up, peering upwards. A faint light filtered down and he guessed it led to living quarters. Softly, he stepped back down to the landing and moved to the stairs that led down.

"The cellar will be down here," he said. "Follow me." Carefully, they descended the first flight, before turning back on themselves. At the bottom, Scottsdale could see a corridor leading off to their right and very carefully he approached the corner, sliding off his helmet to rest his head against the cold stone of the wall. He peered around the corner and flinched; at the end of the corridor was a guard.

Slowly withdrawing, he beckoned to Curzones and they retraced their steps. "There's a sentry at the end of the corridor," Scottsdale said quietly. "We're going to come back down these stairs, making a racket and I'm going to prod you down towards him, ok? I want him to think you're another prisoner and I want you to argue with me."

"Argue? About what?"

"Whatever you want, Father. That I'm an English heathen if you like. I just want him focused on you. All I need is to get close to him," Scottsdale said.

They clattered back down the stairs, making no attempt to conceal their arrival. Turning into the corridor, Scottsdale pushed Curzones forward in front of him. "Now, Father," he hissed, giving him an encouraging prod with the rifle. Curzones gave a small yelp and started babbling in French, looking back over his shoulder as though pleading with Scottsdale. The somnolent guard was fully awake now and had risen from his chair. He was puzzled rather than alarmed, the familiar uniform dulling his suspicions. Scottsdale had used up his few words of German and so prodded Curzones again, laughing loudly as the priest yelped again. The guard chuckled at the sight, too, shaking his head. "*Wie gehts?*" he asked but before Scottsdale had a chance to reply, the guard's attention was caught by a pair of hands wrapped around the bars of the viewing pane of the cell next to him. Snapping at the unknown person, the guard banged on the bars with his rifle and it was then that Scottsdale struck.

"Now, Father!" Swinging Curzones sharply aside, Scottsdale rushed at the astonished guard who was still turning when

Scottsdale's rifle crashed into his stomach. Immediately, the guard slumped over, the breath driven from him and Scottsdale reversed the rifle and drove the butt into the side of the man's head. The guard dropped, and the only sound was Scottsdale's heavy breathing and Curzones struggling back to his feet.

"You were quite enthusiastic there, Lieutenant," Curzones said.

"My apologies Father, just getting into the spirit," Scottsdale replied. Leaning down, he checked the guard was unconscious. As he straightened, he came level with the viewing pane of the cell and found himself looking into the sombre face of Sergeant Grant.

"Hello, Sergeant."

"Hello, sir. Pleased to see you," Grant replied. "Very pleased."

"First time for everything."

Grant looked back with a ghost of a smile. "Terrible times, sir."

Scottsdale laughed and returned to the prostrate form of the guard. "Let's get you out of there then." Rummaging around, he produced the key and unlocked the door. The men spilled into the corridor, beaming.

Pendle came last and shuffled out with a wide smile. "Thought you might have forgotten us, sir," he said.

"I do try, Private," Scottsdale replied. "But the army in their infinite wisdom have entrusted me with your care so sadly I have no choice. Anyway, that was the easy part; now we just need to break out of here, avoid the German army and get home. And we need to do it now."

"Don't join if you can't take a joke, eh, sir," Davenport said.

"Truly," Scottsdale replied. "Or to put it another way, ours is not to reason why."

The men looked at him blankly. "What does that mean then, sir?" Pendle asked.

"It means you shoot when I say shoot, you march when I say march; and you shut up when I shut up. Got it?"

"Yes, sir."

"Good. Now shut up, Private." He grinned, surveying the men with affection, genuinely contented to have them back. Where once he'd found motivation in notions of duty, more and more it was for these men that he fought. "Thankfully, we have some advantages. Everyone's asleep and it's blowing a gale outside. And it's only short march back home." His mind was whirring. In truth he had no idea how they would escape, but he wanted to instil confidence in the section.

A soft cough sounded and they all turned to the cell opposite. Scottsdale looked inside. A pair of brown eyes stared steadily back. "Please, Monsieur," a deep voice said and gestured at the door. Scottsdale briefly considered. Another person to look after was not ideal. However, abandoning him to his fate was equally unpalatable. Taking out the keys, he unlocked the door and stepped back. A middle-aged man with a lined face and imperious nose strode out, drawing himself up to his considerable height.

"My grateful thanks," he said formally. "Louis Beauchene, at your service."

"Lieutenant Scottsdale, 2nd Essex Regiment. Why are you here?"

Beauchene glanced around before answering, frowning slightly in what may have been disapproval at the soldiers' dishevelled appearance. "I am here because I refuse to work for the Boche. When they arrived, they naturally asked me to assist them, but I would never do so." "Naturally?" Scottsdale prompted.

"I am the steward here."

Scottsdale nodded. It would make sense for the Germans to keep the existing staff. "You refused?"

"Of course." Beauchene was affronted by the idea. "I fought in the last war and it wasn't to end up serving Germans their dinner. My family has worked here for centuries and I prefer the company of a cell to working for them."

"I understand, Monsieur. Now, where are we? How far from Pont-a-Vendin?"

Beauchene pursed his lips. "We're just outside Noyelles; on foot, you're a couple of hours away." He paused as he caught sight of Father Curzones and nodded respectfully. "Father," he said and Curzones replied, interrogating him in fast French.

As they spoke, Scottsdale's mind drifted, considering their position. They were already pushing their luck, but he needed it to hold a little longer. Long enough to find a way past the guards and into the darkness. His mind shied a little at the realisation that this would also mean never seeing Helene again. Thankfully, Father Curzones interrupted this train of thought. His conversation with Beauchene had become increasingly animated and now he tugged at Scottsdale's arm.

"*Capitaine!* You must hear this!"

Noting drily that he'd been promoted, Scottsdale turned to face the Frenchmen. "Well?"

"There is a way out of here that isn't through the main gate."

Scottsdale's pulse quickened. "Where?"

"When the chateau was built, it was designed to withstand siege. A safe supply of water was essential. One of my forebears built a channel from the moat under the walls.

It serves a well in the kitchens."

"But surely this entrance was blocked off?"

"Of course," Beauchene replied. "The channel is protected by a set of iron bars. But over the years it would get blocked by all kinds of rubbish that flowed in from the river; branches, mud, even the odd dead animal. It was up to the children of the staff to unblock it. Usually we could clear it from the outside but sometimes it had to be done from the inside. So one of my predecessors had rungs built into the well. We'd go down and clear out all the mess."

"Go on."

"As you can imagine we were always trying to get out of our chores and we found that the bars were wearing loose. With a little work we managed to prise one out, leaving a gap big enough to get through."

"You see, Monsieur, God provides!" Father Curzones said happily.

"Sometimes, Father, sometimes He does," Scottsdale replied cautiously. "How big is this opening?" he asked.

Beauchene shrugged. "The opening is tight, but it can be passed."

"You're sure?"

"I know this chateau inside out so, yes, I am sure."

"Excellent. Thank you, Monsieur, I am grateful," Scottsdale said fervently. He turned to the section and quickly replayed the gist of the conversation. "It will mean getting wet but it's our best chance." A ripple of excitement spread through the men.

Grant cleared his throat. "What about our weapons, sir? The guards passed them off into a room upstairs. Didn't see much when they opened the door but looked like a storeroom to me."

Scottsdale nodded. They would almost certainly be needing them before the night was over. "Come on then, weapons first. Grant, Marsh, with me. The rest of you stay here."

Scottsdale led them upstairs cautiously. All was still except for the pattering of rain. Back at ground level, Scottsdale opened the door they'd passed earlier, a musty smell wafting over them. A variety of wooden boxes were stacked around the room, the German eagle and gothic script stamped on their sides. In the corner were several tall shapes, covered by pale white sheets, that Scottsdale surmised was the art collection of the previous owners. Grant touched Scottsdale's arm and pointed towards a bundle on top of one of the stacks. Carefully, he reached up and laid the bundle down, opening it to reveal their weapons. He grinned wolfishly as he picked up his rifle.

The crack of breaking wood sounded, and Scottsdale turned to see Marsh bending over another box. "What have you got there?"

"Though we could liberate something useful, sir," Marsh said and showed Scottsdale the box. It was filled with the unmistakable potato masher shape of German grenades.

"Good thinking, Marsh," he whispered. The arch scrounger had his uses. "Let's see what else we can find."

They quickly opened more boxes. Some contained ammunition or uniforms, but it was Grant who whistled as he examined a box near the back. He held up what looked like an oversized can of tinned food. It was a steel cylinder about six inches high with a small rod protruding from the top.

"This little bastard is an anti-personnel mine, sir," Grant said.

"Perfect. Take as many as we can carry, you never know when that will come in handy," Scottsdale replied. Marsh and Grant quickly stuffed the grenades and mines in a sack and followed

Tim Oliver

Scottsdale back down to the cellar. The men greeted their weapons as lost friends, their confidence returning as they were reunited. Their own supply of grenades was virtually exhausted, but with the German replacements they had enough and there was enough small arms ammunition to serve. The men quickly inspected their rifles and loaded. The click of magazines slotting home echoed in the small space.

Scottsdale turned to Beauchene. "Where are the kitchens?"

"Behind the dining room in the north west corner," Beauchene replied.

Scottsdale pictured the layout of the chateau. He was sure there would be a sentry above the main house, much as the one he'd observed as they'd entered. Which gave them a problem. Even in the downpour a large group splashing across the moat would surely be seen, so they would have to deal with the sentry. Checking his watch, he saw that it had slipped into the early hours. Whatever they did, they needed to do it fast. He spoke to the section.

"Let's go and find this well. Move quickly and quietly, ok? If anyone so much as farts too loud, they'll hear about it." Scottsdale turned but the men didn't move. He looked at them impatiently, about to snap at them to get moving when Grant coughed.

"Uniform, sir?" he said.

Scottsdale looked down at the German uniform. "Thank you, Sergeant," he said stiffly as Curzones handed him his own uniform. Mildly embarrassed, he swiftly undressed. Feeling more comfortable back in his own uniform, he took a deep breath.

"Let's get out of here."

10

They numbered twelve and as Scottsdale peered into the gloom he welcomed the prayer Father Curzones was uttering behind him. The rain pounded down, but he heard a quiet cough behind him; Sergeant Grant was at his elbow.

"Miserable evening," he remarked.

"Just what we need, sir," Grant replied. "Are we going straight across?"

Scottsdale had just been debating the same question. "Moving twelve of us, rather than two, is risky. Not only because of the sentries on the upper walkway, but also in case anyone appears. The sentries should be looking out at least." Grant leant out. "We can skirt the edges, sir," he suggested. "Stick to the shadows past the gate and work our way back to the main house?"

Scottsdale nodded. "Agreed. Tell the men to get ready. I'll go first, you bring up the rear and the French in the middle. Go."

He stepped out into the rain, immediately turning left. With one hand on the wall to guide him, he moved quickly. The rain mixed with sweat down his back; it was a sticky evening. Behind him the scuffed sounds of men moving reached him. At the end of the building they found welcome cover amongst several old trees. They paused, Scottsdale scanning the courtyard. Sensing no threat, he waved them on and at the southern wall they turned toward the main gate. It loomed out of the darkness and Scottsdale rested his hand on the dark wood, briefly considering if it was possible to scale it. But he dared not linger and scaling a sheer wall with the French in tow was not practical. They scurried on, making themselves as small as possible. Scottsdale tensed, awaiting the shout of a sentry and the glare of a spotlight. Heavy breathing behind told him of the adrenalin among the section. He blinked the rain out of his eyes until, emerging from the curtain of rain, he finally saw the main house. With a final rush, they scrambled over to the entrance Scottsdale and Curzones had left earlier.

Scottsdale held his hands up for quiet. "Total silence now. Upstairs is the dining room and the kitchens. I need a volunteer to help me take care of the sentry upstairs."

There was a brief pause before Marsh pushed forward. "I'll do it, sir."

"Good. Rest of you follow Mr Beauchene while Private Marsh and I go and check the roof."

"Maybe I should go with Marsh, sir?" Grant asked.

"Stay with the men, Sergeant. If something goes wrong, you're in charge." He hesitated with his next words. "If the whole garrison turns out, look after the men. Nothing stupid."

At the first-floor landing, Scottsdale stood aside with Marsh and waved the men into the dining room. "Show them the kitchens," he whispered to Beauchene, "and a good place to stay hidden."

"I will, don't worry," Beauchene said and ghosted past. Scottsdale and Marsh crept upstairs silently, straining to hear anything. Save for the storm, it remained still. Cautiously, they passed the corridor where Scottsdale's cell had been earlier. The lights cast a weak glow down its length. Scottsdale glanced back to Marsh and continued higher, the whistling of wind growing stronger, warm gusts washing over them. Scottsdale's gut tightened as they inched upward. Marsh's stolid frame gave him comfort; he would need his strength.

It grew lighter as they gingerly climbed the last few steps to the turret. Scottsdale had a momentary chill that the sentry might be sheltering there, but it was empty. They quickly crouched down, hidden in the shadowed recess. Driving gusts of warm rain blew in, the moaning of wind echoing around the confined space. Scottsdale gestured for Marsh to wait and carefully inched to the walkway entrance; he had a sudden recollection of childhood history lessons – the walkway was called a *chemin de ronde*. He strained to see into the darkness. Between the cloud covering the moon and the rain, the visibility was limited, and it took him a moment to identify the darker patch on the walkway that was moving. It was coming towards them, quickly. Pulling back into cover, he breathed in the scent of bird shit, wet grass and warm rain.

Leaning close to Marsh, he spoke softly. "Sentry's coming; twenty feet and closing. When he turns, take him."

Marsh nodded, pulling the cosh out of his pack. Scottsdale had always sensed a certain coarseness in Marsh and the death of Private Stevenson had added an edge to him. Now he waited, and Scottsdale consciously tried to relax his taut muscles. Marsh's timing would have to be perfect. He pictured the sentry, walking faster than normal in this weather, thinking of bed. Up and down on his shift, marking time in this safe billet; glancing at the flashes of guns on the horizon, thinking of women and ale. He'd already be instinctively turning as he closed on the turret, hefting the rifle onto his shoulder more securely. Scottsdale realised he was holding his breath and only exhaled as Marsh rose to his feet and glided out into the rain.

His timing was right. Scottsdale glimpsed the guard only yards away. Yet whether it was a sixth sense or Marsh's boots scuffing the stone, the sentry turned. Scottsdale was already cursing as Marsh swung the cosh, the sentry blanching in shock as Marsh's snarling face came at him. Instinctively, the sentry threw up an arm and diverted the cosh, shouting as he tried to unsling his rifle. Yet Marsh's momentum carried him forward and he now enclosed the sentry in a bear hug as a flash of lightning lit the grappling figures. Drawing back his head, Marsh threw it forward, breaking the sentry's nose with a meaty crunch. They both staggered back to the parapet, but the sentry was still shouting, and fear was coursing through Scottsdale. He closed up and seized the man's rifle, wrenching it out of his grip. "Over the side! Push him over the side!" he shouted to Marsh. Leaning down, he grabbed the man's leg, but the boot was slippery in the rain and the sentry was writhing. Finally, he managed to find purchase, lifting the man up as Marsh heaved him backwards. The sentry bucked wildly as he began to topple over the parapet. With a final shove, they tipped him over the edge, his scream rapidly fading as he plunged headfirst to earth.

They leant out, looking down. The sentry lay crumpled on the thin strip of bank between the chateau wall and the moat. "Jesus," Marsh said panting. "Sir," he added.

Scottsdale held up his hand for silence, waiting to hear if the sentry's struggles had given them away. He offered silent thanks the garrison block was on the other side of the chateau. Dread fear of lights turning on, dogs barking, and the shout of German coursed through him. The seconds ticked by, seconds of wonderful silence, and his galloping heartbeat gradually eased. The storm was their saviour. It deadened the noise and the rain wrapped an arm around them that nothing could penetrate. Only blind luck had sent the sentry onto the narrow bank and not into the moat, but Scottsdale felt they were due. He looked at Marsh who was still breathing quickly. Marsh had been forthright in standing up to the challenge and once again Scottsdale marvelled at what these ordinary men were capable of.

Marsh cleared his throat, and Scottsdale realised he was staring; Marsh was shifting uncomfortably under his gaze. Hoping that Marsh thought he was plotting their next move and not ruminating over the surprising capability of the ordinary British soldier, Scottsdale nodded curtly. "Well done, Marsh. Back to the others."

They crept back downstairs and into the dining room. The air hung heavy as the steady patter of rain drifted in through the windows. Scottsdale touched a hand on the back of the dining room chair to guide him, straining to see in the darkness. Suddenly, the roar of an engine starting up ripped through the room. Scottsdale and Marsh flung themselves to the floor while the engine ticked over. At the end of the dining room a shape detached itself and moved towards them, materialising into Sergeant Grant.

"Hello, Sergeant," Scottsdale whispered. "Where is everyone?"

"Through here, sir. Mr Beauchene has everyone stowed away waiting for you."

"Good. Now we just need to know what the hell that is."

"Been as quiet as a church mouse until now."

"Ok, wait here. I'm going to have a look."

Reckoning

Scottsdale crawled to the window. He hadn't wanted to say anything in front of Grant, but in the back of his mind was the conversation at dinner. Rademacher had said that he and the scientists would be flying out during the night. Perhaps this was them; and if so, perhaps there would be a chance to intervene. Logically it was a forlorn hope, but the prospect of a rescue had a seductive appeal.

Hauling himself up, he stood to one side of the window and looked out. Two lines of rain were picked out in the headlights of a truck; a dark shape was visible in the cab. His eyes were drawn to movement as a door opened, spilling a faint light into the courtyard. Scottsdale stared intently as several figures emerged, hunched over under the rain's onslaught. Two of them were unmistakably soldiers, rifles slung over their shoulders as they struggled forward with a wooden crate between them. Behind them, he thought he recognised the measured tread of Rademacher. Scottsdale fixed his eyes on the final pair. One of the soldiers flicked on a torch and he involuntarily clenched his fist. In the faint beam he was sure that it was the scientists and he felt a fierce rush of energy. Some critical military secrets were in that truck; and Helene Dubois.

He sank to the floor. Everything depended on where this airfield was. Swiftly, he crawled into the kitchen where he found Sergeant Grant looking at him quizzically. But his gaze travelled over Grant and settled on Beauchene, a man who knew the local area. Scottsdale ignored the voice that said the idea of a rescue was madness; that if it wasn't for Helene he'd go home. First, he'd see if it was possible. Only then would he consider if it was sensible.

***

"Is there an airfield near here?" Scottsdale demanded.
"Yes, up near Sancourt," Beauchene replied.
"Where's that?"
"About ten kilometres, give or take."
"How do you get there?"

"By car? Go back through the village, turn right and you'll meet them main road. Follow it to the river and it's not far on the other side."

"So you have to go back on yourself from here?"

"Yes. The main road is on the other side of the woods, but obviously you can't reach it from here other than on foot."

Scottsdale felt a surge of hope. "And how far is the road directly from here? Through the woods?"

Beauchene looked at Curzones who could only shrug. "Not far at all. There's an old path that goes through the woods, probably no more than a kilometre or so."

Scottsdale struggled to control his breathing, forcing himself to think rationally. Grant, who had been listening to the French uncomprehendingly, began to speak, but Scottsdale stilled him with a raised hand, gnawing his lip. A short march and they would be at the road. And if they timed it right, they could ambush the truck. He looked up to see Grant looking at him expectantly. Whatever he decided, they needed to escape first.

"First things first, let's get out of here," he said. "Monsieur Beauchene, please show us the way."

Beauchene led them deeper into the kitchen, passing into a storeroom. Beauchene flicked on a switch and a low light bathed the room. "Voila," he said.

In the middle of the room stood the well. It was around five feet across and the stone came up to their knees. Leaning over the edge, Scottsdale inhaled the dank scent. In the dim light, the sides glistened wetly. Running his hands over the stone, he felt the first of the iron rungs hammered into the wall. It was rusty and flaking. He gave it a tug and felt a slight give.

"When did you say these steps were put in?" he asked. "A long time ago," Beauchene replied, shrugging.

"They should hold."

"Can tell it's been raining, sir," Grant observed. "Water level is high."

Scottsdale could hear the water sloshing around and swallowed. The thought of being trapped in the black water made his stomach turn. He gritted his teeth. Only one thing for it.

"I'll go down first," he said. "After me the French, then the rest. We'll have to keep moving when we get to the bottom or we'll run out of room. Everyone clear?" A sea of nods greeted him. "Good. Now, get this bucket out." They hauled out the water bucket and Scottsdale stepped up. The section waited expectantly. He looked over the edge and swallowed. A sudden burst of irritation hit him at his timidity. Decisively, he turned and swung out his leg, scrambling to find the first rung. For a heart stopping moment his leg flailed in space, but his ankle banged painfully into the side and he gratefully found purchase. Very slowly he descended, passing patches of slime that dotted the side.

Gritting his teeth, he carefully lowered himself down until he felt something land gently on him. Looking up, he saw the billowing skirt of Father Curzones' robes. Bits of dirt and drops of water were floating down, disturbed by Curzones' passage and it forced Scottsdale to look back down. Moving as quickly as he could, he saw with some relief the bottom drawing close.

A ledge circled the pool and he carefully stepped onto it. To his right, the water ran into a semi-circular opening that led to the moat. It was only waist high and he grimaced; they would have to crawl. With little time to reflect on this, he edged round and dropped to his knees, peering down the tunnel. The water ran down a narrow channel in the middle but either side was a raised shelf. It was about fifteen feet to the end and he started crawling towards the faint starlight. The tunnel closed over his head, seeming to press down on him and he moved quickly, ignoring the damp seeping into him and the pain from small stones digging into his knees. It would be easy for children but required an uncomfortable crouch for an adult.

At the end of the tunnel he paused. Metal bars were spread across the opening, but years of water had eroded some of the brickwork at either end. And there on the left hand side was the prize. One of the bars had been removed, leaving a gap just big enough for them to squeeze through.

"Who would have thought it," Scottsdale muttered, feeling a surge of elation. Sliding forward, he poked his head outside, feeling the rain on his head. To his right was the corner of the chateau; but immediately to his left was the narrow grass bank that ran between the moat and the wall. They'd have to get wet, but it would do. He scrambled forward, groping until he could feel the wet grass under his hands. With a convulsive heave, he pulled himself onto the bank, shivering as his legs trailed into the frigid water. Getting to his feet, he leant back against the wall, tilting his head to the sky; the rain felt wonderful on his face. Fierce exhilaration flowed through him as he gulped clean air. A crack of thunder rang out and he whooped with joy. He was out, he was escaping, and he was going to rescue the French, get their damn secrets and go home.

Breathing deeply, he looked around. On the other side of the moat the woods were a dark mass stretching away. He shivered at the prospect of wading across. Yet before that challenge, he had to help the rest of the men and he slipped back to the entrance and peered around the corner. Only a few feet away was the pale disc of Father Curzones' face.

"There's a bank just here, Father," he said, pointing under his body. "You'll need to reach across and I'll drag you up. You'll probably get a little wet I'm afraid."

"I don't doubt it, Monsieur," Curzones said and squeezed through the gap with difficulty. With a huge effort, Scottsdale dragged Curzones up the bank until they both lay back panting.

"I know how Noah felt now," Curzones said with a laugh.

"What?"

"Noah! The Ark." Curzones gestured around them. "So much rain!"

Scottsdale laughed. Biblical or not he welcomed the deluge. He moved Curzones further down the bank while the rest of the party appeared. Even at his advancing age Beauchene slipped lithely out, scarcely getting his feet wet.

Sergeant Grant was the last to appear.

"Any problems?" Scottsdale said.

Grant shook his head. "None, sir. I had a quick look round but no sign of anyone other than that truck."

"Good. Now let's get across this moat and into cover." Scottsdale surveyed the moat with loathing. "You first, Sergeant, then the French. I'll bring up the rear." He wanted the men in front, so they wouldn't see him floundering about.

Grant lowered himself into the moat, his face scarcely registering the biting cold as he powerfully forged across, rifle held well above his head. The rest followed, Wilkins letting out a curse as he sank into the water. The rain danced on the surface, rebounding into the men's faces. Packs were kept out of the water as best they could and soon the little party was struggling out on the other side. Grant held a hand out to each man, helping pull people out of the water. Scottsdale was the last out and scrambled up with the helping hand of a grinning Private Pendle. He snapped at them to keep moving and they reassembled in the woods, rinsing out their clothes as best they could. Some found dry clothes from their packs while Curzones rung his skirts out. Scottsdale stomped to the edge of the group. "Bloody water. Bloody country," he muttered furiously to himself, but Davenport overhead.

"Cheer up, sir. We'll be soaked anyway by this rain!" he chirped.

Scottsdale closed his eyes. "Shut up, Corporal," he said and gathered up his gear. He summoned the group. "Time to go," he barked, striding deeper into the woods.

"What should we do with the body, sir?" Grant called out.

"Just bloody leave it," Scottsdale snarled back without slowing his pace and squelched into the wood. The sentry would be missed long before his body was spotted. Scottsdale's anger cooled as he moved, turning to fresh determination. They'd been surrounded, captured and locked up. But now they were free, his enemy was sleeping and all he had to do was turn the men north, go quietly and they could be back in British lines by dawn. But if they did that then they would have failed, Schiller would win, and he'd never see Helene again.

11

"They'll probably get there before us, sir," Grant said cautiously, face creased in a frown. Once they had put some distance between themselves and the chateau, Scottdale had called a halt and relayed his conversation with Beauchene.

"I don't think so." Scottsdale replied. "They were still at the chateau when we left, and they won't be going anywhere fast in this weather."

Scottsdale was earnest in his explanation. He wanted them to understand why they were doing this; he was proposing a potentially futile or even deadly chase when their own line was tantalisingly close. They were bone tired and the wet had soaked into them; each bore the scrapes and scars of the past days. Scottsdale watched gratefully as Curzones handed out the food he'd taken earlier. Yet to his surprise, the men gently refused; it took a moment for realisation to dawn. They'd also taken the chance to liberate several items from the kitchen as they'd waited. Each of them now produced various titbits and Scottsdale smiled; the average Tommy's ability to pilfer food and drink never ceased to amaze him.

His brow creased. Drink. "If I find any of you with booze, I'll take you back to the castle and drown you in the moat myself," he said savagely. McManus studiously avoided his eye.

As the men ate, Scottsdale addressed them. "We've come here to do a job and we've already lost one of ours trying." The men were silent, reminded of the cost of this excursion. "I know we want to get home and we will, I'm sure of that. But the job isn't done yet and according to our friend here we've got a chance to do it right. If we do this, we can end up saving lives," he said forcefully. "Which will make all of this matter. And just as much, I want to stick that bloody German's nose in it." There were a few nods at the mention of Schiller, a man they all loathed. "The road is just up this track. We stop them, get the French and head home." There were a few nods; Scottsdale was satisfied. "Check your weapons and ammunition. We'll move shortly."

Grant came to squat alongside him. Scottsdale could sense his discomfort. "Speak your mind, Sergeant."

"It's a hell of a risk, sir. That garrison will be out and looking for us soon enough."

"I know. But it isn't far to this road. We'll have a look and if they don't come, then we head home."

"We might run out of night if we hang about, sir."

"I'm aware of that, Sergeant," Scottsdale said firmly.

"But we're doing this. It's what we came here for."

"Very well, sir," Grant replied after a brief pause.

"And the French?"

Scottsdale had been contemplating the same question. "Wait here," he said and went to where the Curzones and Beauchene were sitting together, talking quietly. He nodded in greeting. "We're going to be moving soon," he said. "And we must move fast."

"We were just discussing this," Curzones said. "Louis has family south of here. He's going to try and make it across to them."

"There's nothing left for me here now," Beauchene confirmed. "I will go far from here and far from them."

Scottsdale gripped Beauchene's hand tightly. "We owe you a great debt, Monsieur Beauchene, one I can never repay. And I thank you for it."

Beauchene bowed. "It is my pleasure," he said. "Remember; the road is straight through the woods. You'll come out just before the river bridge." With a final embrace of Father Curzones, he set off into the darkness.

Curzones turned to Scottsdale. "I imagine if I returned now, it will be to a waiting party of Germans," he said. "So I shall stay with you."

Scottsdale looked back quizzically. "Are you sure, Father? You can try and get through to the south. It's not going to get any easier here; in fact, I imagine it's only going to get more dangerous."

"Thank you for your concern, Lieutenant, but I cannot abandon my parish. Besides," he added with a grin, "what kind of priest would I be if I turned away from the harder road?"

"Faith is a hard road, Father, isn't it," Scottsdale replied, smiling in return. "In which case, you must be our guest for a little longer."

"Thank you. I will try my best to keep up," Curzones smiled.

"So far, you're doing a fine job, Father," Scottsdale said, and he meant it. The priest was proving resilient and once again Scottsdale had a sense that Curzones had lived a life. "Is there anything you need?"

"Bless you, but I have all I need for now." He eyed Scottsdale. "And you, my son; is there anything I can do for you?"

"I'm not sure what you can do for me right now, Father!"

"You just look so pensive, I wondered what was on your mind."

Scottsdale hesitated. "Many things, Father." Was the thought of Helene clouding his judgement? And was that putting his men's lives at risk? Not that he could ask that of Curzones. "The decisions I make can mean the life of my men. Sometimes, it weighs heavier than others."

"I'm sure it does. It's one thing making a choice that will only impact you – quite another, when it involves other people. You must think back to what you said at dinner – what is the right thing to do?"

"A good question, Father," Scottsdale said. "Perhaps we can discuss another time. I know we cannot afford to lose this war, but that's about it and so, for now, please get ready. We need to get moving." He walked back to Grant, reflecting on Curzones' advice. Running home with a man dead didn't feel right; freeing two people from captivity and helping bring home information that could help win the war did. And even if Major Carter had made clear that Scottsdale's priority was to return home safe, was it right for him to abandon the French to save his men? That didn't feel right, and the thought gave him new determination. For better or worse, they were going to that road.

Setting off into the woods, the darkness closed on them like a glove. Several times Scottsdale heard the stumbles and curses of the men, but he set a fast pace, acutely aware that time was against them. Splashing down the muddy track, he contemplated what to do when they intercepted the truck; if they intercepted it. And how long they should wait; he daren't wait too long before striking out for the British lines as the darkness was their only ally. Glancing up as thunder rumbled overhead, he saw a few patches of night sky breaking through the heavy cloud, allowing a little more light through, and realised the rain was finally beginning to slacken.

The track began to rise gently, and Scottsdale squinted ahead. Either side the trees thinned out and there, raised up to protect from flooding, was the road. Stopping, he raised a hand and conferred with Grant. "I'm going to find this bridge."

"Can't be far if the Frenchie was right, sir."

"That's what I'm hoping." Scottsdale's eyes lighted on Pendle. "Pendle, come with me, we're going to scout the bridge."

Moving at a crouch, they glided up to the road, pausing to listen. The road was in poor condition, pockmarked by potholes that were full of rain water. Scottsdale guessed it was only wide enough for one vehicle to pass. On the other side, the bank sloped gently down to the woods where the path vanished into the darkness. Turning his head, he looked left, to where the road curved away. The horizon was briefly lit by distant guns, but nothing stirred. As he listened intently, an earthy smell of wet grass and mud filled his mouth. Getting to his feet, he beckoned to Pendle and they jogged down the road to their right. A faint hissing noise grew until its source revealed itself – a sullen river made vicious by the recent deluge. Whitecaps dotted the surface and there in front of them was the bridge.

It was a simple stone arch design, wide enough for a single vehicle to pass. Scottsdale walked onto it and leant his hands on the parapet. On the other side was a floodplain. He gnawed his lip. In many ways, it was a good site for the ambush. Yet an attempt to block the bridge was bound to raise suspicion. And he daren't risk firing directly at the truck for fear of hitting the civilians. No, he would need to stop it without arousing suspicion.

Pendle came and stood beside him. "Orders, sir?" he enquired, but Scottsdale was staring at the river. He was looking at a large log that was being carried swiftly downstream by the current. The storm had cut loose a whole array of tree tops, bushes, branches, anything not securely stowed away. Their path through the forest and the road was littered with assorted debris.

He turned to Pendle. "Back to the others," he said. "Time to set you to work, Private."

***

"We need large branches, logs, anything to force the truck to stop." Scottsdale looked around the mud-streaked faces squatting around him. "That's when we strike. We'll be in two groups. My group at the front will take the guards in the cab. Sergeant Grant will lead the rear group and secure the civilians." He turned to Grant, tapping his chest for emphasis. "You have to be fast. Let the truck pass you and once it stops, get as close as you can. Your signal will be my fire. If there's a guard in the back, get your rifle in his face. Yell at him, hit him, shoot him, whatever you want, just frighten the bastard and make sure he doesn't cause us a problem. Questions?"

"How many guards are we anticipating, sir?" Marsh asked.

"At the chateau, I saw three. The driver plus two more. My guess is they'll be one in the back and the others riding up front. But they're guarding two civilians, I can't see there being any more. And remember, they'll be bored, wet and cold. They'll be terrified when we appear."

"What about Father Curzones?" McManus asked.

"He stays here, well back from the road. Worse comes to the worse, he's on his own." He looked around. "No more? Good. Then let's get on with it."

The men foraged around the road and it was Levingston who found the prize – a thick tree branch that had been cut loose by the storm. Grunting with effort, they dragged it into the road, sodden leaves glistening in the rain. Positioning it across a large pothole they scattered a few smaller branches around it. Levingston wiped his hands and stood back. "That'll do it," he said.

"Let's hope so, Private," Scottsdale replied. "Now, we wait. Get to your positions."

Grant and his group hurried off. Scottsdale settled in position, feeling the damp earth beneath him. His eyes fixed on the road. Now they had to wait, still and quiet, for their prey and his mind wandered to the conversation with Curzones. Once again, their lives were at the mercy of his decisions. Simply because of an education and a few months of training, he was given command of men, often better soldiers than he, and they obeyed him unquestionably. He shivered, praying he made more good decisions than bad.

He fought the urge to check his watch constantly, but every minute that eked out was another minute lost in getting back to British lines during darkness. The rain continued, although he sensed that it had lost most of its fury. He watched the treetops swaying in the wind and decided it was getting calmer. Now they just needed the truck to arrive. He gnawed his lip. What if they'd already been and gone? The doubt joined the damp that seeped into him. Yet as he gave in and glanced down at his watch, he froze. Over the rain and wind he heard something else, something man made. He strained to hear. It came again, stronger this time, the faint sound of an engine revving. He breathed in deeply as his heart took off. "This is it," he said. "Get ready."

Pendle and Davenport slid their rifles over the lip and sighted at the barricade. The crank of gears was more distinct now as the driver manoeuvred around the corner. Twin pin pricks of light appeared, growing into the lumbering form of the German truck. It crawled towards them and they held their breath as the headlights flickered over the barricade, exhaling when it came to shuddering halt.

For a long moment, no-one moved. Scottsdale and his party were only twenty yards away. He could see three shapes inside the cab. The driver was talking to the man next to him, gesturing towards the barricade. Scottsdale assumed they were arguing about who would get out. Both stopped speaking as the third man gestured sharply. The door opened, and they stepped gingerly out into the rain, slinging their rifles over their shoulders. Approaching the trunk, one of the men gave it a kick with his boot. Their voices and a short bark of laughter drifted over as they conferred. They turned and trudged back to the truck, leaning their rifles against it and Scottsdale felt a flicker of triumph. Grant and his men should have closed by now and the soldiers were walking back, unarmed. It was the moment Scottsdale had been waiting for.

"Now," he whispered, and two shots rang out. The first soldier was poleaxed, flopping forward over the tree trunk. The other clapped a hand to his shoulder and staggered back, seeking his own rifle but Pendle raised himself, took careful aim and shot him in the back. The soldier slid down the bonnet leaving a trail of blood that was quickly washed away in the rain.

Even as the reports echoed away, Scottsdale was up and running, eyes fixed on the other shape in the cab. That man had thrown open the door at the first shot and fled towards the woods. Scottsdale sent a final shot in his direction to speed him on his way. He shouted back to Davenport. "Stay here, cover the one who ran into the woods!" He was cringing lest he hear mores shots ring out but gave a great sigh of relief as he rushed around to the back of the truck; a German solider lay at Sergeant Grant's feet, bleeding from a gash in his head.

Grant looked at Scottsdale. "He poked his head out and thought about going for his rifle, but I tapped him with this and that calmed him down a bit," he explained, patting his rifle butt. "Then he tried to sit up, so the young lady clobbered him with him his own rifle."

"Really?" Scottsdale asked stupidly, trying to keep the smile from his voice. He looked up and found himself looking into the beaming faces of Fauvelle and Helene. Reflected in Helene's gaze was a similar emotion, of joy and fear and a fierceness that came from the adrenaline of thinking that something had ended but now could begin again.

"Yes," Helene replied. "Quite the most enjoyable thing I've done in a long time."

Scottsdale smiled back, unable to think of more to say. The spell was broken as McManus coughed. Colouring slightly at his own lack of reserve, Scottsdale cleared his throat. "Mademoiselle Dubois, Monsieur Fauvelle. I hope you are unharmed?" he asked formally.

"We are, Lieutenant, we are, and I thank you for it!" Fauvelle replied, climbing down and embracing Scottsdale.

Helene leapt nimbly down. "My thanks too," she smiled, giving Scottsdale a quick kiss on the cheek. Several of the men grinned. "And to all of you!" she added, raising her voice to the men assembled around the truck. "We are truly grateful."

"Can't resist a pretty face, that's our problem," Pendle quipped, and Helene waved her finger at him in mock reproach.

Scottsdale focused his mind. "And your equipment and research?"

Fauvelle reached into the truck and patted the battered suitcase. "Safe and sound, Monsieur. We wouldn't allow Rademacher to take possession of it entirely. He obviously thought it was safe enough with us, but thanks to you and your brave men here we are."

"That was Rademacher in the front?"

"Yes," Helene replied. "Is he dead?"

"No. He took off into the woods when the firing began."

"Surely we should go after him?"

Scottsdale shook his head. "No. We can't afford the time and anyway-"

"You are soldiers and he is a scientist!" Helene interjected. "It would be simple to find him."

Scottsdale was irritated at being cut off so abruptly. "He's long gone, and it doesn't matter how good we are, in this weather in the middle of the night we won't find him."

Unwilling to be denied her revenge, Helene tried a different tack. "And if he warns the garrison?"

The thought gave Scottsdale a momentary pause, but he dismissed it. "When that truck doesn't reach the airfield, someone will come looking anyway. His time will come but for now we need to get moving."

Helene nodded reluctantly, but her face cleared as she saw Father Curzones emerge from the darkness. "I saw you had triumphed again, Monsieur," he said to Scottsdale, "so I risked the journey." He turned to Fauvelle and Helene. "How wonderful to see you both again."

"And you too, Father," Fauvelle said.

"They like to kiss a lot, don't they," Pendle observed as the French greeted each other

"More kisses than you've ever had," Marsh replied, prompting Pendle to reply with an obscene gesture.

Scottsdale tried not to fall prey to the fierce elation he felt. His gamble, so far, had paid off. He walked back to where Davenport stood, peering into the darkness. "Any sign of him?"

"None, sir. Took off like a startled hare. Wouldn't be surprised if he's still running."

Scottsdale gathered his thoughts. Now they would be hunted. It was the early hours of the morning and their escape would soon be discovered. Nonetheless, it would still take time for the truck to be found and the search started. That was their window. For the first time in a while, his mind also turned to the British lines. Griffin has said they'd probably have forty-eight hours before the line withdrew again. Which meant they needed to make it home during the day that had just started. Make it home to a British position under assault, being pursued by a vengeful Schiller. In the darkness, he grinned. A complete balls-up, Carter had called it. It wasn't far wrong. Yet he was filled with an absurd optimism and he summoned Sergeant Grant.

"Right. Let's consider our options," he began, rubbing his hands together. "Take the truck and make a dash for it. Or route march. If we take the latter, what route and how the hell do we know what's facing us. Thoughts?"

Sergeant Grant was succinct. "We take the truck, sir, and we run slap bang into a German patrol. If we travel along the roads, it's just more likely Jerry will be on them."

"Agreed. Meaning we're going to have to march. We've got, what, three hours until dawn?"

"I'd say so, sir."

"And we have to get to the canal in the dark, with the civilians in tow. It's going to be tight." He consulted the map, moving the map reading torch over their proposed route back to the canal. Snapping it shut, he turned to the group. "Father! A word please."

Father Curzones smiled. "A very quick moment, please," he asked and bent down to finish speaking urgently to Fauvelle and Helene. Scottsdale eyed the group. Fauvelle was listening seriously. He was going to find their march tough, but Scottsdale suspected his devotion to Helene would drive him on; if necessary they'd carry him. He smiled as he imagined one of his men trying to carry Helene. No, her spirit and fight would keep her going. His eyes slid over to Curzones, a man quite unlike the inoffensive priests of rural England he'd known.

"Funny bugger for a priest, isn't he," Grant said, seeing Scottsdale's thoughtful gaze.

"Very much so. Why was he the contact for the scientists? Come to think of it, he didn't make much of an effort to leave either."

"I'll keep an eye on him," Grant promised, and Scottsdale nodded as Curzones came over.

"Apologies, Lieutenant. How can I help?" Curzones asked.

"We are heading back to Pont-a-Vendin, Father. We're going to avoid the main roads and I'd be grateful for your local knowledge."

"Happily, of course. I know a few places the Germans have occupied between here and the canal."

"Excellent. Our plan is to get there by dawn and cross over back to the British lines."

"Then we have a long walk ahead!"

"That we do, Father, that we do." Scottsdale turned back to Grant. "I want our best eyes out front."

"McManus,sir,"Grant replied immediately. "Eyes like a bat."

"Like a bat?"

"Yes, sir."

"Well in that case, he's lead, then the French, the men and you in the rear."

"Yes, sir."

"First though, tie that German up and put him in the truck. And get it off the road. Doesn't have to be far, just enough to get it out of the way." Grant barked an order and the truck was slowly wheeled off the road into the woods. It wouldn't bear close scrutiny, but it was all they could do.

Their little group reconvened at the road and Scottsdale looked them over. A battered section of Tommies and in their midst, three French civilians. A motley bunch and he smiled. It felt like an appropriate reflection of the chaos of this campaign. Now all they had to do was slip through German lines, in the dark, while being ruthlessly hunted.

"Let's go home."

12

Schiller stared balefully at the soldier standing rigidly at attention before him. The man's forehead was beaded with sweat and he stared fixedly at a point above Schiller's head. As soon as the alarm had been raised at the airfield, a search of the chateau had found the prisoners missing and the hapless guard tethered in the cell.

"Tell me what happened," Schiller demanded, his voice dangerously low.

The Gefreiter swallowed nervously. "While escorting the prisoners, I was attacked, sir, and they managed to knock me out."

"You let two unarmed prisoners, one of whom was a priest, knock you out!" Schiller exploded.

The guard clenched his jaw. "Yes, sir."

"Two unarmed men," Schiller repeated in disbelief. "I cannot begin to *imagine* the incompetence. You are a disgrace to your uniform."

The guard wisely chose to remain silent. Schiller looked up at the garrison commander, who was standing stiffly to one side.

"I want this man punished, Herr Major. Do you hear me? I want him broken; he is guilty of the grossest dereliction of duty."

"He will be, Herr Hauptsturmführer," the commandant replied. Schiller's authority in this matter came from Berlin and the commandant's only wish was that Schiller would leave and leave soon.

"Good." Schiller looked back at the soldier. "Now get out of my sight." The man saluted hurriedly and left, the commandant following. Schiller leant back and sighed. The anger was an acid inside him. He rubbed his eyes, still puffy from lack of sleep, and tasted the lingering aroma of last night's red wine at the back of his throat. He'd been in a state of furious disbelief ever since being rudely awoken half an hour earlier. The news that not only had the British soldiers escaped, but that they'd managed to free the French scientists as well, was impossible to digest. He massaged his temples. This wasn't what he wanted, to be hunting these civilians; he should be back on the front line, driving the Tommies into the sea.

"Damnit!" he shouted, bringing his fist down on the table. He ignored the papers that fluttered to the floor, rubbing his throbbing hand. The indignity of it burned; to be humiliated by the escape of *his* prisoners. He was incredulous.

A knock at the door brought him back to the present and Rademacher entered. Schiller surveyed him coldly. Rademacher was a civilian, a clerk and, Schiller assumed, a coward. After all, only he had made it out of the ambush alive. Yet he also had powerful backing. For some time, there had been murmurings of strange events at the heart of the SS leadership. Himmler's love of mythology and extravagant ceremony was well known. The Yuletide celebrations of the SS were legendary, and Schiller had embraced the ritual element of his new role with fervour; it gave him a sense of belong to something greater. However, there was an inner circle that aspired to a greater power, an occult view of the world where science, mystery and spirituality mixed. Rademacher had gained entry to this circle through his membership of the *Ahnenerbe,* a group dedicated to proving the existence of a superior race of people from whom modern Germans were descended. It meant that Rademacher had influence and so Schiller had to tread carefully, regardless of his own feelings.

"Hauptsturmführer Schiller," Rademacher said sitting down. He showed no sign of the ordeal he had been through. A patrol from the airfield had discovered him dishevelled but unharmed. Now he carefully crossed his legs, raising an eyebrow inquisitively as he opened a gold cigarette case. Schiller nodded and Rademacher proffered the case. They both lit up and exhaled.

"May I ask of your plan for the recapture of the fugitives?" Rademacher asked. "It is imperative that we do so."

"I am well aware of that."

"Good. It has been a most unfortunate night."

"*Unfortunate* is not the word I would use. Gross incompetence has caused this, but I will put it right."

"And how are you proposing that?"

Schiller gritted his teeth but explained his thinking. Since he'd been woken, he'd been assessing what he would do if he were Scottsdale; and how he would stop him. "They have to get back to British lines, but I don't think they'll go the shortest route from here. That will take them too close to Lens and there's too much activity there for them to be safe. No, they'll go back the way they came."

"Do you know where that is?"

"Not for certain, but there was a report circulated about a sentry who was stabbed the night before last." Schiller rifled among the papers. "Yes, here it is. Near Pont-a-Vendin. They think it was a stray soldier or even a guerrilla fighter, but it ties in with these British soldiers to my mind. It's a quiet sector and from the church is only a few hours. I think that's where they crossed and that's where they're going."

"I hope for your sake, you're right," Rademacher observed. He cleared his throat. "There was one further point

I wanted to make. I am no military man, yet I must ask if it would be prudent to arrange for some reinforcements. This British solider has proven remarkably resourceful."

Schiller's head jerked up. "The military execution of this operation is my responsibility, not yours. My men are assembling now and unless you have anything useful to add I suggest you report to Scharführer Schultz in the courtyard in fifteen minutes." He paused to shrug on his overcoat, straightening his peaked cap. "You ask of my plan. My plan, Herr Doktor, is to hunt them down. To kill Scottsdale and give you your scientists."

***

Scottsdale set a brisk pace; he had no doubt Schiller and Rademacher would be fanatical in their pursuit. Pendle was put in charge of the suitcase. "Don't fucking drop it," Sergeant Grant said curtly as he handed it over. Around them, the night crawled with activity. Distant guns growled and several times the snarl of engines drove them to ground. Father Curzones led them in a wide circle of one town where the Germans were billeted, and it ate into their time. Dawn was their enemy as much as the expected German pursuit. There was refuge in the darkness and every minute they struggled on, that refuge was at risk.

At the front, McManus moved silently until, as they crested a small rise at a line of trees, he raised a hand and dropped to one knee. The rest of the party followed suit as Scottsdale hurried forward at a crouch. The diminutive Irishman motioned him down and they sank to the earth. Cautiously, Scottsdale wriggled after McManus, following his example and removing his helmet. He could feel the wet earth under his fingers as he dragged himself the last few yards to the treeline. Slowly, he moved aside the lower leaves of a tree and whispered to McManus. "What is it?"

McManus didn't answer but simply pointed. It took a moment for Scottsdale to pick out what McManus had somehow noticed. In the hollow beneath them, a German unit was camped. Scottsdale could see dark shapes by the muted light of a small fire. Several vehicles were parked, and improvised shelters had been set up by running tarpaulins between them. He shuddered at the distinctive shape of the black and white *balkenkreuz* painted on the vehicles. The unmistakable outline of several half-tracks was visible, machine guns poking forward over their elongated snouts. Alongside were several smaller armoured cars and Scottsdale realised they had nearly stumbled into an armoured reconnaissance company. He breathed a sigh of relief at McManus's watchfulness. Carefully, he indicated back, and they scrambled back towards the rest of the group.

"Well done, McManus. How did you know they were there?" Scottsdale asked.

"Smelt the smoke, sir," McManus replied.

Taking a wide detour of the hollow, their party ploughed on. Dropping back a few yards, Scottsdale kept time with the French civilians. As tired as the section was, he trusted that they would keep the pace. Yet the civilians weren't trained for this and he was worried. Seeing Fauvelle stumble, he held out a hand to the Frenchman. "Steady there, Monsieur."

Fauvelle looked up gratefully. "Thankyou, Monsieur," he gasped.

"My pleasure. Not far to go now."

"Thank God it has stopped raining at least."

"Truly." Scottsdale looked up. Fauvelle was right. The rain that had so forcefully beat down on them had eased off; it made the going a little more bearable. The storm had cleansed the air, leaving behind a crisper, sharper atmosphere. The clouds had been swept away, and a soft light from the moon guided them as they doggedly ploughed through the fields. By cutting across country, Scottsdale was leading them on the most direct route as well as avoiding the main roads where German patrols would stalk. Yet there was a price to pay; the going was far harder. Sticky mud clung to their clothes and sapped their strength.

Glancing behind, he saw Helene's unmistakable outline. She had tied her skirts around her legs and her body was bent in a determined poise. Catching Scottsdale's eye, her teeth flashed white as she smiled. "A nice night for a country walk!" she said, though Scottsdale sensed her cheerful tone was forced.

"Fantastic exercise," he replied. "We often do this at home."

"Of course you do. Mad dogs and Englishman and all that."

"I thought that was about the midday sun?"

"I think it just means Englishmen have very little sense," Helene said drily.

"Impossible to deny."

"I'm very rarely wrong, Lieutenant."

"I shall bear that in mind, Mademoiselle."

Scottsdale turned back, smiling in the darkness, before guiltily looking around, wary lest his men notice. He shook his head, feeling a surge of energy. Ridiculous, he thought. Turning his mind back to the more serious matter at hand, he called a halt to allow the party to catch their breath. Gratefully they paused, and Scottsdale beckoned to Curzones. It was always worth checking his map reading with local knowledge. "Recognise this area, Father?"

Curzones nodded, catching his breath. "Yes. The stream we passed just now is outside Merlon. We're not far. Perhaps another hour?"

"Good," Scottsdale said, but inwardly he cursed. They were running out of time. "We'll rest here for a minute," he continued. "Any food and water, share it out." He licked cracked lips as he watched their last remaining morsels being parcelled out. The men were eager to share their food with the French civilians, gently pushing back on their refusals. He even saw Marsh, the arch hoarder, sharing out the last of his boiled sweets.

Catching Grant's eye, Scottsdale inclined his head and they moved a few yards away. "The men have taken to our French guests," he remarked.

"That they have. They expect to be in the shit, if you'll pardon the expression, sir; but seeing civilians in the middle of this never feels right."

"No, it doesn't, does it," Scottsdale said reflectively. He paused before turning to the topic that was foremost in his mind. "Speaking of shit; I don't think we're going to make it over the canal by dawn."

"Suspect you're right, sir."

"And if that happens, then we're going to be in a spot of bother."

"We're going to need a hell of a lot of luck, sir."

"Exactly. And it will depend on Schiller too. If he finds us, then our priority has to be getting the French away." "Then it'll be a rare fight, sir," Grant replied.

"Yes, it will. So we have to think about how we narrow the odds."

"I've still got the mines, sir," Grant said, patting his rucksack. "We won't be able to hold for long, but it may be enough to let them get away."

"Good. Anyway, what is it Davenport says? It may never happen. But if it does, let's give the bastards hell."

They moved back to the copse where the group was sheltering. The slumped shoulders and slow breathing of Fauvelle spoke to his fatigue; a fatigue echoed even among the filthy soldiers. They had been moving constantly recently and the accumulated stress and strain was eating into them. Scottsdale straightened his frame. He had to keep driving them. That would be the tonic that galvanised them – the hope of escape.

"Time to get moving," he said. "When we're back I promise you all the rest you need. I'll even buy you all a drink."

Forging ahead, Scottsdale ignored the protest of his body, focusing on the adrenalin as they closed on the British lines. Inch by inch, and despite his own reservations, he was beginning to feel a quiet, desperate optimism that they may make it across the canal. Taking out his map, he tried to find a landmark to pinpoint their location. If he was right, then they would shortly be at the next waypoint, Annay, that lay only a couple of miles from the canal. As he did so, he realised he didn't need the torch; the night was dying, and the blurry outline of northern France was emerging. Indistinct shapes revealed themselves as hedges and trees. Steam rose off the sodden land and Scottsdale inhaled the scent of wet grass. Faintly at first, then more confidently, came the soft sounds of the morning refrain as birds stirred. The land shook off the storm physically, leaves dripping rain and swaying softly after the fury of the night's wind. Yet Scottsdale surveyed the lightening sky with a grimace. They were so close. He gnawed his lip. Assuming the British line held, they could make a dash for the canal. Feeling a sense of renewed confidence, he summoned the group together.

"How's everyone holding up?" he asked.

"Surviving," Father Curzones replied.

"Good, because we're nearly there. We've made better time than I hoped. We're just outside Annay which means we're nearly home but we're losing time and losing light. So we're going to go straight through Annay and onto the canal. No mucking about now, we just need to get across the canal, so we need to pick up the pace for the final push."

There were a few nods of assent and Scottsdale could feel a lightening in their mood. The idea of escape was indeed invigorating them. It was useful, but he raised a hand warningly. "We're not out of the woods yet but we've a fighting chance. Which, frankly, after the last couple of days, feels like a minor miracle. But keep your eyes peeled, the Germans are irritatingly persistent." He turned to McManus.

"Us first again, Private."

"Yes, sir."

"When we get to the village, any movement, any sign of the Germans, shout."

Their party set off at a jog, acutely aware they were becoming more conspicuous. Marsh stumbled in his eagerness, cursing as he nearly fell. Scottsdale felt utterly exposed, his gaze darting around, searching for any hint of danger. They could see further as the day grew, and they wanted to cower from the light. Ahead of them lay Annay, the welcoming brick of the back of the first houses coming up fast. Their fear gave them a breathless speed and they made rapid progress through the outskirts. The houses huddled together, weather beaten and scarred. Little gardens peeked out from each house, some tended, others overgrown. Their group ran down the road, arriving in the village square. Even though they'd seen no sign of the enemy, Scottsdale half expected the crack of a German rifle. Instead, they were met with the curious stares of a couple of villagers. Father Curzones shouted a question at them and they answered shortly before turning away. Scottsdale raised an eyebrow. "Well?"

"They've not seen any Germans, but they weren't eager to talk," Curzones said.

"I could see that. They looked nervous."

"Wouldn't you be, Lieutenant? Most of the people have fled."

"I can think of worse ideas," Scottsdale said and turned back to the section, sharing a quick grin with Helene, whose face was flushed from their efforts. There was a sense that they were nearing the end, and he felt an undercurrent of energy in the group. Helene and Fauvelle were talking animatedly to each other and everyone's pace had picked up. "Not far now, people," he said and jogged to the front, eager to move on while their luck held. The road meandered north out of the village and he could glimpse woods in the distance; this was their target, where they'd encountered the sentry two nights ago. He felt like a different man than the one who'd led their party across the line and he could scarcely believe they were back. Scanning the village for danger, he went over the plan in his head; instead of going through the woods they would go straight down the path that led to the canal. It was exposed but with time running out on them he was prepared to gamble.

120

It was McManus who heard it first. Cocking his head, he frowned and instinctively laid a hand on Scottsdale's arm. Scottsdale paused, feeling the first tendril of alarm. The rest of the party slowed to a halt with him. "What is it?" Scottsdale asked.

"Thought I could hear a motor, sir. Faintly, but something."

Scottsdale swallowed. A motor meant Germans and Germans meant Schiller. "Stay here," he ordered the group. "McManus, with me." They retraced their steps through the quiet streets until Scottsdale held a hand up. He couldn't hear an engine and was feeling the first wash of relief when McManus gestured to their left.

"Dust trail, sir," he said. "A truck coming down the road, I wouldn't wonder."

Scottsdale squinted and in the faint light saw that McManus was right. Down the road that ran into the village from the east was a clear trail; it could only be from a truck or car and if it was motorised, then it was German. He kicked the ground, tasting sick frustration. They were so close. Damn them. He was faced with a choice; to hide or to fight but he instinctively knew what he had to do. They couldn't hope to hide another day, tired and cut off, so they had to fight. He was angry but it didn't change the situation and so he snapped to McManus and they ran back to the others.

"I'm afraid we've got company," Scottsdale said without preamble. "It seems the Germans haven't given up." "Fucking hell," White muttered.

"What are we to do?" Fauvelle asked.

"We've only got one choice," Scottsdale replied. "We're going to attack. Immediately." He paused, taking a deep breath. "Remember why we came here lads; to get something from this mess. Well, this is that something, something important. Our job is to take the Germans away from the civilians, so they and their box of tricks can get away." The men prepared in grim silence, Pendle handing over the suitcase to Fauvelle. "But remember, they don't know we're here, which gives us an advantage." He looked at Sergeant Grant. "Remember when we spoke about narrowing the odds?"

"I do, sir," Grant said. "No time like the present."

"Precisely. So let's do it by killing some of these bastards, ok? Prepare those mines. The rest of you, fall in and wait."

He turned to Davenport. The man was rock steady and that was what was needed now. Gripping his arm, Scottsdale gave him his instructions. "Remember the abandoned farmhouse we came to after the woods? Take the French and go there; don't stop for anything. We're going to hold the Germans up. Understood?"

"Yes, sir. How long should I wait?"

Scottsdale had been thinking of this. Part of him wanted to send the French ahead to the canal but he was reluctant to let them go completely. "Give us an hour. If we're not back, make for the canal."

"And if the worst should happen?" Helene asked softly.

"If the worst happens, then run," Scottsdale replied vehemently. "Run and hide. Listen to Davenport. Get across that canal and if you can't, go south, anywhere away from those bastards over there." He felt an overpowering need to embrace her, to feel her against him just once but he savagely thrust aside the impulse. It laid a further goad to his rising anger; anger at how tired he was, anger at Griffin and anger at the Germans. But just for a moment they had the advantage – he knew the Germans were coming and where they were coming. He had the men and the will to inflict pain and he relished the idea. Looking at the faces of the section, he saw his determination reflected; they were ready too. It was time to stop running.

13

"I want two fire positions, in those two houses." The houses stood at the junction with the road that came from the east. "Aim for the drivers first, follow with grenades. Two groups. Sergeant Grant, your group take the second truck. My group take the lead truck. Questions?" The men were silent, a few nods as they looked intently at Scottsdale. "Good. The key here is to hit hard and move, no hanging about. Fire and manoeuvre. We keep drawing them back towards the square and away from the canal. That's what will give the French the time to get clear." He looked at Grant. "Are we ready at the square?"

"All set, sir," Grant confirmed.

"Good. I want to give them such a bloody nose that they back off," Scottsdale continued. "That's our chance; if we hit them hard enough it will give us a fighting chance of slipping away too." In truth, he wasn't sure how practical a plan that was, but it was all he had. "Now, let's go, quickly now."

They hurried into position, throwing glances towards the growing dust trail that was fast approaching. Scottsdale watched the civilians disappearing before joining the men; he prayed they would be reunited. Sergeant Grant led his group across the road while Scottsdale and his group battered down the door to their house, cautiously entering a living room that overlooked the road. It was a cramped space, tables, chairs and stools squashed together. A large fireplace dominated one wall and a grainy picture of a family posing proudly was propped on a rudimentary mantelpiece. Briefly, he flicked the button on the large wireless set that sat on a table, but no sound came. A circle of black dust surrounded the large coal bucket propped up next a small woodpile. Scottsdale moved through into a small kitchen at the back, pausing briefly to look upstairs; nothing stirred, and he gave the place a cursory look over. At the back was a small kitchen with a view over the garden. He opened the back door which gave out onto a neatly planted patch of vegetables and flowers. At the bottom a path ran back to the road through the village. Glancing back over this shoulder to check where the men were, he quickly took the opportunity to relieve himself, wondering again at the body's reaction to impending combat.

Back inside, he saw the men were making ready, knocking through the front windows and constructing places to site their weapons. Anyone glancing in their direction would be unlikely to see them in the shadows and, if they were seen, Scottsdale hoped it would be too late. Following suit, he settled down and sighted down his rifle, feeling the comforting solidity of the butt against his cheek. Steadying his breathing, his gaze travelled down the road, imagining the trucks coming into view. Lifting his head, he looked across the road, noting that Grant and his men were out of sight. Their signal would be Scottsdale's men opening fire.

They didn't have long to wait. Scottsdale's pulse leapt as a truck crawled into view. Beside him Marsh shifted, cocking the Bren gun that was cradled into his shoulder. Dalton carefully arranged a couple of spare magazines on the floor and then unslung his own rifle. Scottsdale licked his lips and focused on slowing his breathing, ignoring the now familiar taint of nausea and adrenalin that greeted the enemy. No matter how prepared he was, it was always there, clutching at his gut. Yet he had learnt that alongside it was the driving, elemental force of combat that flushed his system and allowed him to operate; the imminent intensity of a life and death struggle, the need to take life to survive, buried the terrible fear. And whilst the time that now ticked by felt endless, he knew, too, that it would later resolve into the smallest of sequences and minutes.

He stared intently down the road as the sickly cough of the engine grew louder. The blunt nose of the truck crawled towards them, a thousand yards away. Scottsdale gritted his teeth; now he wanted it to close quickly so they could act. The faintest tremor shook his hand and he instinctively clenched his fist. He could make out figures in the lead truck, the first targets. Without taking his eyes from it, he gave his final instructions. "Remember, Marsh and I target the driver.

Everyone else on the truck itself."

"Yes, sir," Marsh replied, his voice tight.

Scottsdale shifted to stop his leg shaking and squinted at the truck. It was taking forever. He looked away and back to the truck. Without question, it was slowing to a halt. He felt the first flickering of alarm. "What the hell is he doing?"

***

Schiller tapped his knee repeatedly, craning forward to peer through the dirty windscreen. "Come on, let's get a move on!" he snapped at the driver. He'd torn through the chateau earlier, rousting the men onto the trucks but their progress had felt painfully slow. The trucks were requisitioned, and he chafed at their lack of speed; away from the main arteries it was quieter but also much slower going on the rough roads. They'd stopped to ask several German units if they'd seen or heard any small groups but had only been met with blank looks. The idea that the British would slip through his fingers was tormenting him. Their escape was a personal affront and the mission was becoming less important than the need for him to purge this stain to his competence by recapturing – or killing – Scottsdale.

He had ordered them to use Annay as the base for their search as it was nearby the woods where the dead sentry had been found. They would form a picket line and hope to scoop up the British as they tried to cross, using small parties to flush them out. He had given serious consideration to interrogating the local population, but he didn't have the men to do a proper search. If he had gotten this wrong then the British would escape, but he prayed fervently that in short order they would recapture the French and Scottsdale would be dead.

Rademacher noticed his restlessness. "They can't be far away," he said.

Schiller's instinct was to ignore him, but he relented; there was little point in antagonising a man with Rademacher's connections. "I don't doubt it, but the problem is if I've read this wrong. They could be further away or even crossed over by now."

"It would not go well for either of us if that were the case."

"I understand that all too well, Herr Doktor."

"Good. I have too much riding on this to accept failure. We must end this."

"We will, but I want to make sure this is done right this time."

"I thought you were happy we have enough men to deal with this?"

"I am, but it's not just a question of numbers. A few men can quickly even that up."

Rademacher raised his eyebrows in surprise. "After our previous conversation, I'm surprised at your timidity." He gestured through the windshield. "Regardless, we've almost arrived."

Biting back his anger, Schiller peered forward towards Annay. He frowned. Casualties didn't concern him particularly, but other than the main road this was the only route into Annay, making it a perfect site for an ambush. Moving at speed into unreconnoitred land chafed against his military instincts; he knew how swiftly panic could spread. They'd already suffered casualties and rushing headlong into the village risked further losses they could ill afford. Military good sense didn't end regardless of the rage he felt. "We have to stop," he said aloud, not to anyone specifically but to confirm the decision he had just made.

"Stop?" Rademacher queried.

"Yes." Schiller leant over to the driver. "Stop the truck! Now!" The driver bought the truck to a shuddering halt, shunting them forward and back. Schiller gave him a murderous look before jumping down, cutting off Rademacher's questions with a curt, "Wait here." He strode to the back of the truck where Scharführer Schultz threw up a smart salute.

"Orders, sir?"

Schiller had been considering this. "We need to scout the village, but fast. There's no time for a proper reconnaissance so get a couple of men and send them up the road. Got it?"

Reckoning

Schultz snapped out orders and two men jumped down. Moving gingerly, they set off down the road in short, sharp bursts, pausing in doorways and behind cars for shelter. Schiller watched them, understanding their fear. They were being sent forward, exposed and hemmed in, to trigger a trap. If the enemy were here, they were dead men; if not, they would live. On such a chance the two soldiers now sweated, desperately trying to sense any danger. Schiller felt no pity; this had to be done and done it would be.

The crack of a rifle shattered the morning stillness. Schiller felt a grim satisfaction at being proven correct. "Down from the trucks!" he roared, and the rest of the men leapt down from the trucks. Bullets were zipping past them, but it was at an extreme distance and he roughly yanked one soldier upright who had taken shelter. "Get up!" he roared, pulling the man forward. Looking back to the road, he noted that the two soldiers had nearly reached the junction before they'd been shot down. They lay in the road, arms outstretched, and he surmised that the British were waiting there. "Spread out," he ordered. "Schultz, your men down the road, the rest of you round the flanks." The British may fall back now their trap had been sprung but he felt a fierce exhilaration; they were here, that was all that mattered. He had found them and now he would finish this and bury Lieutenant Arthur Scottsdale.

***

Scottsdale cursed as he saw the two soldiers cautiously moving toward them. He gnawed his lip, considering the idea of falling further back as he was eager to use the slim advantage that surprise gave them. Yet there was a risk in doing so; the Germans could turn right at the junction towards the canal and the civilians and that was unacceptable. Their only job now was to lure the Germans toward them and away from the French. They were the flame and Schiller was the moth that had to be burnt. In doing so, they may well extinguish their own light, but it would have meaning and that gave him heart. So he would trigger the trap and bring the German fury onto them.

"Wilkins, you're on the second soldier," he instructed. "Marsh, when we fire, start targeting those trucks." They nodded, and Scottsdale turned his attention to Sergeant Grant and his group across the road. Now the Germans had sent a reconnaissance party forward, Scottsdale would fire and then pull back immediately; he needed Grant to be right behind him so, carefully, he rose to his feet and went to the window and waved across the road. With relief, he saw Grant materialise. Through a quick mime, Scottsdale managed to convey his plan. With a final thumbs up, Grant disappeared and Scottsdale resumed his kneeling position, looking down the road.

Very carefully he lined up his rifle on the leading German, resting the rifle barrel on the window sill. He gently brushed off the broken glass that fell to the floor with a tinkle.

The sun had risen higher and was sending its warm light into the soldier's face. So much the better, Scottsdale thought. Beside him, Wilkins shifted his weight, his breathing audible. The Germans were closing, only a hundred yards away. In the distance the trucks stood waiting. Everyone was waiting, holding their breath, to find out the judgement on the two men. Scottsdale felt their fear and understood it. Such was the pitiless logic of war; sacrifice two to save more.

He aimed at a point just above the man's belt and briefly thought of Major Carter. God would not save this man today. Gently, he squeezed the trigger, feeling the kick in his shoulder. Several birds were startled and flapped away, squawking their protest. A moment later Wilkins fired too, joined by the chatter of the Bren as Marsh opened up. Scottsdale looked up to see the first German slump to his knees, holding his stomach, before toppling forward, helmet spilling into the road. His comrade across the road joined him, cut down by Wilkins. Down the road, Marsh snapped out bursts at the trucks which, ant like, had sprung into life, men pouring out of them and beginning to hop forward. It was enough. Scottsdale stood and waved to Grant, who emerged and sprinted across the road with his group. Puffs of dirt dotted the road as the Germans returned fire and bullets smacked into the house, but they all made it inside safely across.

Reckoning

"Time to leave, gentlemen," Scottsdale said and led the way into the garden, following the path he'd noted earlier back to the village square. A glance to his left showed the coal scuttle helmets of the German infantry working their way through the fields behind the road and a faint shout went up. Immediately, rifle fire spat towards them but, keeping low, they emerged onto the road and jogged back towards the square which lay off the road. As they neared, Scottsdale slowed and held up his hand, beckoning Grant to him. "Show us the way, Sergeant," Scottsdale said. "And I suggest everyone pay attention, otherwise they'll be losing a leg shortly."

Grant led them forward. He had laid several mines in and around the entrance to the square, marking them with stones which he now removed. If even one of them went off it would give the Germans pause for thought. The square itself was a rough oval shape, with houses crowding around most of it before opening out onto the fields behind Annay. A general store, shabby café and bakery sat alongside the town hall, a faded tricolour lying limp on its front. It seemed deserted, but Scottsdale expected that, and he led them towards one of the larger houses at the far end of the square. It gave a good view of the entrance and at least backed onto the fields that led towards the woods, giving them an outside chance of escape; a chance that would depend on their wits and a lot of luck.

Scottsdale gestured to the door and Marsh nodded, handing off his Bren. He took a breath and crashed a heavy boot into the door which gave readily. Moving inside, it took a moment for their eyes to adjust to the gloom. Levingston had moved furthest when a sudden furious flapping of feathers and alarmed squawks of a pair of chickens assailed him. "Jesus Christ," he swore, waving the animals off. Just as he had gotten control of the chickens, he was faced with a pair of frightened faces. "Civilians, sir," he called out and Scottsdale strode through.

"Get out!" he snarled. He couldn't afford to be polite, the civilian's lives depended on it. "*Allez vite!* Pendle show them the door, now."

"Our chickens, Monsieur," the man said imploringly as he was ushered towards the door.

Looking around, Scottsdale saw Marsh had a firm grip of the birds. "Give the man his chickens."

Marsh shifted. "Seems like we may need them more, sir, if -"

"God dammit, Marsh, don't argue with me!"

Scottsdale shouted and yanked the chickens out of his hand. He ushered the Frenchman out and told him to run fast and far. "Now, let's get this place ready. Levingston, Wilkins, upstairs. If you see any Germans, don't wait, shoot them." He turned to the rest of their group. "Marsh, Dalton, get the Bren sited, rest of you find a vantage point. Go."

Levingston and Wilkins clattered upstairs; the tinkle of glass from broken windows was almost immediately replaced by the sharp report of a rifle. Scottsdale went to the bottom of the stairs, shouting up. "What can you see?" "Coming in through the fields and gardens behind the houses across the road, sir!" Wilkins shouted back. The crack of the rifle rang out again. "Loose order, a platoon looks like. We're keeping their heads down."

Scottsdale went back to the living room. If the Germans were still coming it meant they thought that Scottsdale had the French – and meant the Germans hadn't found them. That part of the plan at least seemed to be working.

A shout sounded from the front and he hurried into the living room. "Company, sir," Pendle said. Scottsdale peered out of the window. He couldn't see anything and raised an inquisitive eyebrow. "Just saw one of 'em pop his head round then withdraw it sharpish," Pendle explained. "And I definitely heard trucks, so I reckon they've brought the rest of the blighters up."

"Good. If you see them, give them hell."

Pendle spat out the window. "Right you are, sir." He paused. "Could murder a brew though."

Scottsdale smiled. "You and I both, Private." Patting him on the shoulder, he conferred with Grant who had found some bread. Scottsdale took the proffered offering. "Thank you, Sergeant. Get whatever you can."

"Will do, sir." Grant scratched his chin. "They don't appear in any hurry, do they?"

Scottsdale had been pondering this too. "No and when I wonder why I don't like any of the answers."

"Nor do I."

"Whatever the reason, we need to be ready. What's out the back?"

"Gardens, sir, either side. Looks like an orchard behind and then fields all the way to the woods."

"That's our fall back then. And we can't wait too long, or they'll surround us. So be ready on my signal. We'll hold them here as long as we can and then we're gone." "Yes, sir," said Grant.

Scottsdale considered their position. His major fear was being surrounded and cut off, but he also knew it wouldn't be easy to do so quickly. They had to keep the Germans focused on them and hurt them when they appeared. But why weren't they already attacking? He wondered if they should keep falling back but a shout came from the front followed a split second later by the crackle of fire.

**

Schiller surveyed the scene, listening to updates from his runners. Kriebs was reporting sporadic fire as his men pushed forward, while Jodel said the road was clear. The enemy had gone to ground in the square, and he grinned. He had them bottled up; this time they wouldn't escape.

He turned to the panting runner. "Tell Kriebs to occupy the houses opposite the square. He's to return fire and keep their heads down." The man saluted and ran off, and Schiller took Jodl by the arm. "Your job will be the most dangerous, Hans, the main assault. Move fast, get close and use your grenades. We'll give you covering fire."

Jodl was easy to warm to, with a face that was never far from a smile. Schiller could see a small shadow pass over even his genial features at the order before he straightened and responded firmly. "Jawohl, Herr Hauptsturmführer. And the civilians?"

Schiller glanced to where Rademacher stood at the truck. "Expendable. Find their equipment, it's in a briefcase attached to the man. If we can capture them all the better but don't place yourself or your men in danger to do so. Signal to begin will be a red flare. Wait for the cover fire, then strike. Now go."

Jodl jogged back to his men and Schiller could see he was relaying the orders. Satisfied, he summoned Schultz. "Take the rest of the men and work round the back. I want to cut off any escape. Clear?"

"Yes, sir. How long do I have to get in position?" "Not long. I can't risk them slipping away, so we will begin the assault to pin them in position. Your job is to get behind them while the fighting is taking place."

"Understood, sir."

Schiller watched Schultz move off; he was the anvil and Jodl the hammer. Soon the British would be crushed, and the scientists would be dead or captured. The end game was approaching, and he welcomed it. As soon as he disposed of this he would return for the final assault and victory in the West. Nodding in satisfaction at the thought, he clamped his helmet on firmly and went to join his men.

Raising his arm, Schiller pointed the flare gun at the sky and pulled the trigger. For a split second everyone, be they German, English or French, watched the vivid smear of red as the flare soared high, fizzing and spitting. Only Schiller, hand pointed above his head, looked forward, waiting for the answering call of his guns. A heartbeat later Kriebs' men opened up a withering covering fire. Bullets began striking the house where the British were holed up, puffs of brick dust leaping up from the front wall. Any remaining glass shattered and from the darkened interior gun barrels flickered in retaliation.

Schiller turned to Jodl. "Now's your time, Jodl!" he shouted, waving the man forward. With a salute, Jodl rousted his men and stormed forward. "A fine sight," Schiller thought as the mass of grey charged forward, war cries echoing out; but at that moment one of the soldiers trod on a mine.

Reckoning

Designed to activate under a man's weight, the steel shod boot of the *Gefreiter* triggered the three-prong fuse that poked a few inches out of the ground. Seconds later the propellant charge initiated, firing the mine roughly four feet into the air. At this height, the scientifically analysed optimum for killing, and less than a further second later, the main charge detonated. Surrounded by up to 350 pieces of shrapnel, metal balls and scrap metal, it spat shards out at high velocity. With a lethal radius of up to twenty metres and a fragmentation pattern of 360 degrees, the impact on the bunched German assault group was devastating. Hundreds of tiny, white hot metal fragments struck flesh at short range. Jodl, exulting in the charge, was a couple of steps behind the man who triggered the mine. Those few seconds meant that he had his face, neck and left side of his body eviscerated. Luckily for his men, he bore a large brunt of the blast, but the wickedly innocuous metal scraps found several more marks, flaying the legs and trunks of more men. Dark blood splashed shockingly over the cobbles and the blast concussion checked the surviving soldiers, who came to a crashing halt, horrified at the sight. Even the fire from the British defences slackened as they stared in awe at the carnage that a single mine had created among the enemy.

Schiller took a moment to respond to the shock. "Cover fire!" he roared, firing his own rifle. Jodl's squad was falling back and Schiller shouted at them. "Keep going! Turn and fight!" But it was ineffectual; the shock of the mine and the chasing fire of the British had broken their spirit and they fled, leaving several of their number on the ground. One man groaned feebly, trying to reach down towards his shattered legs. Schiller cursed. They would have to do this the long way, grinding the British down and he tasted his anger. There would be no prisoners from this, he vowed and stalked away to reorganise the men.

14

"Sweet suffering Christ," Pendle said as the Germans limped away.

"Nasty little bastards," Marsh commented with satisfaction. "They'll have felt that! Just be thankful it wasn't you running over it!"

"Amen," Pendle replied. "Ah – bloody – men."

Scottsdale silently agreed. The effect had been shocking, far better than he hoped. He let that expression hang in his mind for a moment; it had to be as devastating as possible, but did he really hope for it?

The thought was stilled as the momentary lull was shattered by renewed German fire. It came on with a desperate ferocity, as if in affront at the temerity of the British resistance. Bullets smacked into the house, the snarl of machine gun and rifle rending the air. A tempest flooded over them. Enemy infantry worked into the houses along the entrance and from cover poured fire onto the house.

Upstairs, Levingston and Wilkins tried to use the advantage of their position, but they were targeted, hot metal swamping the windows. They ducked down as the sheer weight of fire drove them into cover, able only to occasionally pop up and snipe at the Germans. Downstairs, Marsh was cursing, hammering out short bursts with the Bren. Grant was methodically tracking targets through the smoke and dust but the grey shapes flitting through the square were harder marks to put down. They worked their way around the edges of the square, occupying houses and shops, while others scurried across the open space, using cars for cover. As the enemy infantry drew closer, their fire became more accurate, forcing the men down more frequently. Yet they were also more vulnerable, and Pendle hurled a grenade at a group that were sheltering by a truck; it shattered one end forcing them to duck back which exposed them to McManus' rifle. One man went down, shrieking and holding his leg, before being dragged back into cover.

Scottsdale looked at the men. Their faces were blackened and filthy; the rank stench of cordite filled the air. The noose was closing, and it was only a matter of time before they were overwhelmed. He flinched as bullets spat by, goading his anger. "Keep firing!" he hollered, rising up to fire himself before ducking back to re-load. Yet the Germans were squeezing them in and he feared that they were being surrounded.

Grant caught his eye and scampered over. "They're getting on top, sir!" he shouted.

"I know. Try and keep their heads down. We'll move shortly." He had an idea, a desperate one but it may just work. What they needed was one more distraction. Keeping low, he smashed the table and chairs into smaller pieces and piled it in the middle of the floor. A quick scavenge in a bureau yielded a bundle of papers which he added, along with the curtains that had been torn down. "Sergeant!" he shouted. "Give me a hand!"

Holding out his lighter to the pile, which took to the dry wood and paper immediately. He blew and nurdled it into greater vigour as Grant came over. Scottsdale handed him a taper. "Spread this around. We're burning this house down."

"We're burning the house down, sir?" Grant said in astonishment.

"Yes, Sergeant, burn it down," Scottsdale snarled. "It will cover us." He felt an unjustifiable anger welling up. He desperately wanted this to work and he didn't want to stand around answering questions on it. "Get a move on. As soon as it takes, we're out the door." He stood and hollered up the stairs. "Levingston! Wilkins! Get down here. We're leaving."

An answering shout reassured Scottsdale they were still alive and moments later they clattered downstairs, coughing as the smoke thickened. Levingston was bleeding from a cut on his head.

"Hurt?" Grant enquired.

"Nicked me but I'll manage."

"Get a dressing on it, Sergeant," Scottsdale ordered.

By now the blaze had taken hold on the old, warped wooden stairs and smoke was filling the room. Vivid orange flame crawled up the walls and an intense dry heat buffeted them. Sweat broke out on their foreheads and they crouched low. "Time to go," Scottsdale shouted. "Show the way, Sergeant." Grant led them to the back of the house and opened the back door with a shove. They bundled out into the garden, gulping in air. Scottsdale was third in line and it was the sound of the first gunshot that made him realise he had made a terrible mistake.

***

Schiller seethed. His men were wearing down the British, but the use of the mine enraged him. He was unable to shake the feeling that Scottsdale was one step ahead of him. He could see they were making progress, but he waited impatiently for news of the breakthrough. Surely it was only a matter of time before they were overwhelmed. He looked as Rademacher walked carefully over, hands behind his back. Schiller clenched his fist. Why was the man wearing an overcoat in this weather?

"What was that?" Rademacher asked.

"That was a mine."

"An impressive detonation."

"Impressive isn't the word I would use," Schiller replied acidly.

"I meant no offence," Rademacher responded coolly. "I was merely observing from a practical, a scientific point of view. It was -"

"I don't care what you were observing," Schiller snarled, his frustration boiling over. "Unless you have anything useful to contribute I would advise you to remain with the trucks until we finish this."

Rademacher stared at him for a long moment before replying. "As you wish, Herr Hauptsturmführer," he said. "Just make sure you do finish this."

Schiller watched Rademacher's retreating back and shook his head. The implicit threat hung in the air, but he was too angry to care. He should be back with the rest of the SS Totenkopf division, pushing towards Dunkirk, not running after civilians. They had to finish this so he would be free to rejoin the offensive. Turning back to the square, he frowned. Attuned to the noise of combat, he sensed a definite slackening of fire. He was about to bark an order when he noticed something strange; the house where the enemy had holed up was on fire. Dark smoke was billowing out of the windows, fanned by the outside air and he could glimpse orange flames bubbling up inside. The house was leaking smoke and a mucky pall was wafting across the square. It didn't make sense; had the mine somehow set the house on fire? He snapped his fingers at his runner. "Find Kriebs and ask him what he can see. Hurry." The man scurried off and Schiller gazed at his retreating back. And where the bloody hell was Schultz?

Scharführer Schultz paused to get his bearings, wiping the sweat from his face. Progress had been frustratingly slow as his assault group worked their way behind the buildings that faced onto the square. They'd skirted the dumping ground from the café and bistro, while it had taken more time that he had anticipated to cross over the gardens that stretched out behind each house. Several of them were bordered by high walls and even those with a simple wooden fence usually had a hedge or tough brambles to negotiate. The noise of battle drove him on. He was acutely aware that the plan relied on his group striking while their enemy was focused on the frontal assault. However, after a brief crescendo of noise following the red flare, he noticed a distinct slackening of fire and cursed. It could only mean the other assault group had been beaten back and he urged his group on.

He was so intent on the way forward that it took a moment for his feverish mind to register the new smell; he could smell burning. Looking up, he saw smoke billowing from the windows of the next but one house. Instinctively he knew this was their target. "That's it!" he shouted, and the assault group surged forward with renewed vigour. They had only one more garden to cross but came to a halt as there, spilling out of the burning house and into his gunsights, was the enemy.

"Open fire!" he shouted, but the men were already raising their rifles and a ragged volley crashed out. Out of breath, their aim was largely wild, but Schultz grimaced in satisfaction as one of the leading Tommies slumped to the ground. The others broke sharply away and hurled themselves into the next garden, beginning to return fire. Several of his men hurled grenades and the rest took cover, firing through the smoke towards the enemy. He felt a surge of triumph; one of the Tommies was dead and now he had them cornered. All he had to do was keep them pinned down until the rest of the unit arrived, and this would be over.

***

Scottsdale instinctively shied as the gunshots rang out, a curse torn from him. A heartbeat later Levingston collapsed, arms flung up, a plume of blood arcing from his head to spatter over Scottsdale's horrified face. Levingston passed the threshold between life and death in a split second; one moment a vital, active man, the next a jumbled mess lying on the dirt. Scottsdale hurdled the body, galvanised by shock and realised he was screaming; not only to make himself heard but in real visceral fear. "Break left! Break left!" he hollered, blindly firing towards the dim shapes of the enemy. Behind him, the men had more warning and they fired back, providing much needed cover as there was no going back into the blazing building. Grant barrelled into the garden to their left, jumping the low wall and clearing the way for the others who leapt after him. Bullets fizzed past them, hissing as they sliced through shrubbery. Scottsdale heard a shout – "Grenade!" – warning or command he didn't know but ducked instinctively. It exploded, fountaining dirt into the air and spattering them with mud.

"Oh, Jesus Mary," McManus mumbled as he reloaded with trembling fingers.

"Where the fuck did they come from!" Wilkins shouted.

"Everyone stay calm!" Scottsdale shouted. "Wilkins, Pendle, Dalton, keep their heads down." He hunkered down behind the wall, trying to control his breathing and clear the image of Levingston collapsing in front of him. With a shudder of disgust, he suddenly felt the stickiness on his skin and angrily wiped his sleeve across his face. Another man dead; those fucking Germans. Checking his rifle, he focused on their situation as the squad duelled with the Germans. He had to think. They could try and withdraw further but that was further away from the canal and he wasn't prepared to give up on the idea of escape. They couldn't go back the way they came either. Which meant that they had only option. He beckoned to Sergeant Grant.

"We've got no choice," he shouted. "We have to attack. If we can break through, then we can get into the orchard and out of this damned place. Nothing fancy. Any grenades we've got left, throw and then we charge." "Understood, sir," Grant replied, reloading. "I'll go first."

"No you bloody won't, Sergeant." Scottsdale snapped. It was his duty to be first. "Keep their heads down as long as you can. McManus, Wilkins, you're with me. Sergeant, when we block your line of fire, bring the rest of the men."

"Yes, sir." Grant looked Scottsdale in the eye. "We'll be right behind you."

"Good. Fix bayonets." He looked over the men as they prepared, dull steel clicking into place. Once more he felt a deep swell of affection. They were all flawed, but they were still fighting and still trying, exhausted though they were. "We go hard and once we're amongst them and they'll break," he urged.

"And when we're through, sir?" Grant asked.

Scottsdale pictured the layout of the village. "Out the back of the village and make for the farmhouse."

They assembled behind the wall, grenades ready. Pendle licked his lips and nodded. Scottsdale felt a sudden craving for water. He swallowed and raised his hand, dropping it as his signal. "Now," he said.

Whilst the others popped up to provide covering fire, Pendle and Wilkins hurled their grenades. The pineapple shapes wobbled over, dark blobs against the burgeoning pale blue sky. Scottsdale rose to fire deliberately at the enemy. Reloading, he waited for the impact, bowels tight. The detonations were his signal and he rose up, hurdling the wall; McManus and Wilkins a step behind him. To their left the remainder of the section fired towards the enemy, seeking to keep their heads down. Scottsdale was panting hard; they didn't have far to cross, but every detail was painted in vivid colour. On his right the dry crackle of the burning house as old wood was devoured. A pall of smoke flit across their front, the tang of charcoal catching in the back of his throat. Bursting through the smoke, the snap of bullets fizzing past him ignited his fear but also his anger. A rising tide of adrenalin and hate and joy flooded through his body, wrenching an incoherent cry from him as he closed on the enemy. The ragged breathing of the others told him they were still running behind him; ahead he could see little white flowers around the border of the fence ahead. A coal scuttle helmet lifted into his vision, the stubby barrel of the rifle rising to meet him, but his intense fear turned to jubilation as the German buckled, thrown back, arms wide, by the impact of a bullet. Now the rest of the section rose to follow, joining their battle cries with Scottsdale who had reached the German line.

With wild instinct, Scottsdale hurdled the hedge. Relief at reaching the line, terror at the expectation of death and defiance and anger all melded into a monstrous desire to inflict pain and death on the enemy. He turned to the nearest solider who tried to bring his weapon to bear but in doing so, slipped in the mud and Scottsdale snarled in triumph. Feeling the angry joy at having an enemy at his mercy, his rage flowed through his bayonet thrust. The steel slid wetly into the German's chest, driving him to the ground and Scottsdale stared into his panicked face as he died. A rifle fired shockingly loud in front of him and he registered the searing pain across his arm; he was shouting again, firing his own rifle, madly and inaccurately, feeling an intense relief as the man before him was shot down from behind. Even then the Germans could have rallied but their resolve was shattered, and he could see they were fleeing. The sight of Sergeant Grant and the squad tumbling over the fence, bayonets drawn was enough for them.

"Sergeant, get over to that gap and post a man," Scottsdale panted, indicating where the Germans had disappeared. As Pendle hurried off, Scottsdale squatted down, catching his breath. He looked at the reddened end of his bayonet and grimaced; two bodies lay unmoving beside him. Their faces were twisted in death and he looked away, feeling a mild sense of shame. He was drained, utterly, by those savage few moments. Yet as he looked up he found McManus looking at him curiously.

"A wild one you are, sir," McManus remarked.

"Yeah, and I seem to recall you telling me not to do anything stupid, sir," Marsh added, panting.

Scottsdale hesitated. He sensed it would do no harm for the men to see him in a different light. "Sometimes a little unpleasantness is needed," he said.

"Well, unpleasant for them but not to watch, sir," McManus replied.

Scottsdale straightened. That was enough. "Sergeant Grant, any sign?"

"Not a thing, sir. Licking their wounds."

"That won't last long. Let's get the hell out of here before they come back. We're heading north." North towards safety; to the British lines and to Helene.

***

Hacking their way through the bottom of the garden, their smoke-blackened group made their way into the orchard. Marsh reached for an apple, twisting it off and taking a bite. He angrily threw it away as he tasted the rotten flesh and stomped off after the rest of the section. Scottsdale paused to look back, wary of pursuit. He could see the fire had spread to engulf large parts of the square. A billowing plume of smoke rose into the air, an incongruous dirty smudge against the beautiful blue sky. For a moment he stared at the sky; the blue was so pure. It represented summer and cricket and being outside and warmth and drinks. Yet here it was death's companion, a killing sky. And besmirched by fire, a fire that was destroying not only people's homes but their livelihoods. He felt a twinge of guilt, running a hand over his grimy face, feeling the stubble rasp across his palm. It was necessary, he thought grimly, but he couldn't shake a deeper guilt that had already wormed inside his gut. Another of his men was dead, another one who wouldn't be going home. They all trusted him and obeyed without question, yet if he made the wrong decision, they died. He sighed and turned away. He had to keep moving forward, always forward, lest his cease to function.

Hurrying through the orchard, they came to the farmland that led to the woods. Scottsdale constantly scanned behind them but there was no sign of pursuit. To an extent he wasn't surprised; the fire, the confusion and their swift break out all played into his favour. As a small group he hoped they could slip away although he wasn't banking on it. The Germans would work out where they were headed soon enough. Perhaps if they were lucky, the canal would be reached before then. He smiled mirthlessly; he didn't feel lucky. Patting his pocket, he checked the flare gun Beaufort had given him was still secure. The bastards better be waiting there for him if he needed to use it.

Ahead of him, Pendle cursed as he stumbled and fell to the general amusement of the rest of the men. Scottsdale sensed the laughter was forced, over the top; it was the laughter of men who sought diversion from the reality of what they were going through, of leaving another man behind. He knew, too, it was necessary.

"This bloody muck," Pendle said, brushing himself down.

"Suits you covered in all that shit," Marsh needled him.

"Shut up, Swampy. You stink like a pig most of the time."

"A pig?" Marsh guffawed. "Coming from the bloke on all fours in the mud?"

"Piss off. And what is it with this bloody army; we're always fucking marching somewhere in the mud. My Mum was right, I should have joined the navy."

"Locked up in a tin with a thousand other fellas? Sod that."

"And why aren't we ever on roads, eh, not even on exercise. Answer me that."

"Perhaps you should ask the Lieutenant."

"What does he know, he's only a Lieutenant."

"He knows a damn sight more than you," Grant interjected.

"What I'm saying is, who's in charge, like really in charge, at the top. Because it isn't precisely going well is it?" "And it would be better if you were in charge?" "I ain't paid enough for that job, my friend. But someone, somewhere is making an awful bollocks of our current trip to France."

"Bound to happen," Wilkins agreed. "Sooner we get back to bloody England the better if you ask me."

Wearily, they trudged on, approaching the woods in loose order. Scottsdale called a halt as they closed and gathered them together. "Next stop, the farmhouse. We'll pick up the French there and Corporal Davenport." "Don't suppose we can leave him behind can we, sir," Marsh piped up.

"You'll be left behind if you don't shut up," Grant growled.

"We move fast and head for the canal," Scottsdale continued. The faster we do the better chance of getting across before they catch up. Understood?" He looked around.

"Good, let's move."

***

Schiller paced restlessly, shaking his head. He ignored the heat of the fire that raged around him. He was staring at the body of a German soldier, feeling an intense fury. The sight of Rademacher picking his way toward him fed his pain. He spat on the side of the road, grim faced. It had been the reappearance of a bleeding Schultz who had confirmed the final details for him. Schultz was badly wounded, and Schiller paused for a moment as the man lay panting on the ground, determined to give his report. "They overran us," he said through gritted teeth. "I'm sorry, sir."

Schiller stared down at him. The man had failed him, just like all of them. He turned away, unable to speak, and gestured to the stretcher bearers to take Schultz away. Every day of this was a stain on his honour and his reputation. This wouldn't be the end, he vowed.

"Listen up!" he shouted at the men who were stowing the wounded and collecting their equipment. "We don't stop! You hear me? Until we have these cockroaches. I want them dead!" He paused, breathing heavily. His men looked at him warily. "I want them dead," he repeated under his breath and summoned his NCOs. "We will move out immediately," he declared. Even if it took every man there, he would have his revenge on Scottsdale and the damned priest.

15

Scottsdale felt unaccountably nervous as they neared the farmhouse and the realisation made him feel guilty; he half heartedly tried to tell himself that it was concern for the mission that lengthened his stride, but he knew better. Shaking his head in exasperation, he quickened the pace until they came to the little clearing where the abandoned farmhouse lay. Raising a fist, they squatted down in the trees; nothing stirred saved the rustling of leaves in the gentle breeze. Even the rumble of guns seemed muted. It seemed completely deserted and for a moment he panicked; had they already gone or, worse, been captured? "Pendle," he said quietly. "Go take a look." "Yes, sir," Pendle replied and scurried out across the clearing. Reaching the first building, he flattened himself against the wall and inched towards the main house, ducking under each window. Scottsdale drew in his breath as suddenly the front door suddenly swung open, creaking loudly. Instinctively, Pendle threw up his rifle before sagging in relief as he heard the cheerful tones of Corporal Davenport. "Wouldn't get far as a cat burglar would you, Billy?" Pendle straightened with a grin. "Just making it easy for you, Corp."

"Of course you were," Davenport replied before throwing up a salute as Scottsdale approached at a jog.

"Report?" Scottsdale demanded.

"All quiet, sir. Frogs are inside. Heard the fireworks but I had an inkling you'd be back."

"Good," Scottsdale replied brusquely, already moving past him. He pushed open the door and entered the farmhouse, his eyes taking a moment to acclimatise. The civilians were in line before him and he drank in the sight of Helene, who returned his gaze, smiling quietly.

Davenport had followed him in and continued admiringly. "The lady wouldn't hear of leaving either, sir. Told them right off for even thinking of it," he said.

"I was sure you would come back to us," she said simply.

"It is very important," Scottsdale said slowly, "that we see you and your secrets to safety, Mademoiselle. Very important." Helene smiled back, dipping her head slightly in acknowledgement of the spoken and unspoken truth in his statement.

Father Curzones stepped forward. "Mon Capitaine," he said and gave Scottsdale a resounding kiss on each cheek. "When we heard the noise," he shrugged to demonstrate their fear. "But thanks be to God, you are safe."

"And the Smelly, Father," Grant said.

"The Smelly?"

"The Short-Magazine Lee Enfield Rifle, Father," Scottsdale explained. "We haven't got time to hang around though, the Germans won't give this up. Do you have everything you need?"

"Of course, Monsieur," Fauvelle replied, patting the case.

"Excellent!" Scottsdale said, smiling broadly. "In which case, can I suggest we get the hell out of here. We must keep moving." It felt like an absurd mantra he'd been repeating for days, though it didn't make it any less true. "Sergeant Grant, in rear. McManus, up front. Let's go."

They set off, and once again a sense of optimism began to flow through the group. The men were invigorated by their reunion with the civilians and their pace quickened, aided by the light of day. Though they were running on fumes, their clothes musty from the sweat borne of fear, with the end in sight they felt rejuvenated and girded themselves for the final push. This feeling was part of a subconscious cycle, processed automatically by a mind that was fixated on survival. Only later would they stop and think of men who weren't returning and the wounds to mind and body. For now the way was clear; get across the canal. The uncertainty beyond, of being trapped by the German army, was remote, inconsequential. They would get through the next hurdle, then seek to meet the next. Experience had taught them not to look too far ahead. As the woods closed around them, Scottsdale ordered total silence lest the enemy be lurking within. He gazed up at the sky as a plane flew low overhead; though not given to any particular religious feeling he nonetheless muttered a quick prayer. War made it easy to lose faith, yet perversely in the chaos of battle sometimes the only logical thing to do was to pray.

Helene joined Scottsdale in the middle of their column. They were following the path to the canal and the woods spread thick on either side. It was a dark mass, depths hidden from the sunlight by the dense undergrowth and tall trees.

"It seems we are almost home, Monsieur," Helene said lightly.

"Almost," Scottsdale said smiling; he knew Helene was under no illusions that the danger had passed. "Once we are back in British lines you will be safe and that's the most important thing."

"Even more important than our magic suitcase?" "Now that depends on who you ask. There will be some delighted people when we return with you and your secrets. But to me, yes absolutely."

She smiled, and they walked on in companionable silence for a few steps. "What's London like?"

Scottsdale looked at her in surprise. His world had narrowed to the next hour, the next step forward; the thought of the world beyond was almost unreal. Helene shrugged. "I have to look to the future now," she continued, a hint of bleakness in her tone. "Who knows when I'll be able to come home. Or what will happen in the next months and years. The world has been turned upside down."

"Truly," Scottsdale agreed. "As for London, I've not been back for a while now, but I think you'll like it. It can be a grey old place but it's when we've got our backs to the wall that we're at our best."

"So now really is your time then!"

"Sadly, yes! But either way I look forward to seeing it. Because we have to get you home. I really never thought it would be as bad as this. Everything I've seen here - the butchering of civilians, the brutality, the torture - it can't be allowed. And if getting you and your suitcase back helps then we have to do it; we just have to get you back."

"I would do anything to help defeat them," she replied vehemently. "How do you describe them in English, that word you use?"

"Er, bastards?" Scottsdale replied sheepishly.

"Yes! Bastards," she added in English. It sounded so different in Helene's musical accent. "A good word I think for these people."

"Very apt."

"I just wish we'd killed Rademacher."

"Really?"

"Yes. I cannot forgive him even if I wanted to. He's done a deal with the devil and tries to justify it in the name of progress; progress that led to the death of my father. He deserves to burn in hell."

"His time will come," Scottsdale replied. "For all of them."

She smiled. "Somehow, someday, yes it will."

Their conversation was interrupted by a shout from Sergeant Grant. Panting, he threw up a salute. "Bastard's are coming again, sir. They just don't want to give this up." Scottsdale stood impassive, feeling the surge of nausea as a tight ball in his gut. It was swiftly complemented by anger, which he gave free rein to. Bastards. Bastards. "Where?"

"Not far from the farmhouse, sir. Looks like it's the rest of them."

"How long?"

"Matter of minutes I'd say."

Scottsdale grimaced. They'd already put some distance between themselves and the farmhouse, but it wasn't enough. If Schiller was coming after them he would have to be stopped. He looked over the group, expectantly waiting his orders. It didn't need them all for this final act; the path was narrow and the enemy depleted. Yet he wouldn't now, after all this, ask them to risk sacrificing themselves. He felt he owed them that.

"This is it then," he said forcefully. "No finesse, it's all or nothing now. Sergeant Grant, get everyone to the canal. Find the boats and get across. Or swim. Whatever you do, don't stop and don't look back."

Grant shifted uneasily. "What about you, sir?"

"I'll hold them off from here."

"I'll help, sir," Grant said firmly. "You can't do it by yourself."

Scottsdale's impulse was to argue, but he knew enough of Grant to know it wasn't a debate. In truth, with Grant they stood a far better chance of getting back. "Thank you, Sergeant. Collect up the remaining magazines; we'll need them. Corporal Davenport, you're in charge of the section. We'll make our own way back."

"Just the two of you?" Father Curzones asked.

"It's the way it has to be, Father. But at least I've got one last party trick up my sleeve." He held up the flare gun. "A present from Mr Griffin. When the shooting starts, I'll call in the artillery."

"Thank you for everything," Father Curzones said gravely. "I pray we will be reunited shortly."

"We will," Scottsdale replied firmly. "I'm not dying here; no one else is bloody dying. Now go," he said brusquely, curtailing any further goodbyes. "Be safe." With that he turned on his heel and walked back to Grant, snapping orders to cover the leaden weight he felt inside. "Back to the farmhouse. We just need to hold them up until I call in the artillery. And then we have to move – fast."

"Don't need to worry about that, sir," Grant said fervently.

Scottsdale grinned. "Let's hope they can shoot straight."

They hurriedly moved back up the path to the farmhouse, keeping a careful eye out until the clearing came into view ahead. In the shade lay the farmhouse; it looked deserted and he breathed a sigh of relief. Turning to Grant, he spoke quickly. "Find some cover and when I fire, that's your signal. As soon as it gets hot, I'll fire the flare and then we run like hell."

Grant nodded, and they moved either side of the path to find a suitable position. Leaning back against the broad trunk of an oak, Scottsdale briefly closed his eyes, breathing in the musty odour of the woods as the sun burnt off any lingering moisture from the storm. Shifting his weight to find a more comfortable spot, he checked the Very pistol was to hand. He could scarcely believe he'd ended up here, hiding in a wood in France. Nothing had been as he had expected. Their retreat, the astonishing and terrifying first taste of combat, the helpless pain of watching men under his command die. And he'd been completely unprepared to feel the depth of the wild rage and joy that flowed through him during battle. Theory and imagination were a grotesque facsimile of reality. He felt a pulse of anger as he remembered the German planes attacking terrified refugees. He remembered, too, the dead German sentry; a man like any other, until transformed by his uniform into the embodiment of a brutal regime. A regime that taught men like Schiller, men who tortured priests. The image of Curzones strapped to the altar table came to him. Yet to Schiller that was justifiable, it was necessary – for him, brought up in a broken country, the pain and the terror were regrettable yes, but subservient to a greater good. The clarity that gave to Scottsdale was that they weren't simply fighting Germans, they were fighting Nazis, men committed to a way of thinking that was at odds with the common tenets of moral behaviour. And he also knew that it was just as important to him to fight for the men under his command as it was to defeat that enemy.

Tentatively, he also allowed himself to think, too, of Helene. She was unlike anyone he had known. He was drawn to her compulsively; her energy, her independence, her fierce intelligence and her courage. His heart beat faster at the thrill of the barely acknowledged idea that she also felt something for him. Yet she was a world away from him; French, a refugee and a whole life separating them. Briefly, he toyed with the thought of her returning to Essex with him. It would certainly give the village gossips something to speculate on during their interminable teas. When he thought of Essex, of home, it was with a fierce protectiveness, but he also knew instinctively that he wouldn't be able to slip seamlessly back into that life. Not because it was mundane – that was worth the fight – but because everything had changed in these short few weeks. War was the great leveller and courage didn't have a relationship with class or gender; Lieutenant Berry was proof positive of that. No, too much had changed, and he felt an ache that he was probably going to die before he could live a different life.

A low whistle from Grant brought him back. Peering around the tree his heart jumped; German infantry were slowly spreading out into the far end of the clearing. He briefly wondered if he would be able to pick Schiller out. If nothing else, the man did not lack courage and would be at the forefront of the German party. Regardless, they had to drive the Germans to ground, giving time for the French to flee and for him to fire the flare.

Hidden in the shadows, Scottsdale took careful aim, tracking a short soldier who was at the forefront of the enemy party. Gently squeezing the trigger, he fired, satisfied as the man staggered back, clutching at his shoulder. A heartbeat later, Grant fired too and they both methodically emptied their magazines. It had the desired effect, forcing the Germans into cover. However, the answering fire came for them, snapping into the leaves and branches. The enemy began creeping further forward, using the farmhouse for cover and spreading out into the woods. The weight of fire became increasingly oppressive, hampering their attempts to lay down a substantial suppressing fire. Praying that Griffin was watching, Scottsdale pulled out the Very pistol, shouting to get Grant's attention. Grant nodded and leant out to fire rapidly, giving Scottsdale a second of breathing space. Yet as he stared across the path, Scottsdale felt time slowing. Grant's lean frame was in profile and it captivated him. Rifle raised to shoulder, helmet slightly askew, each recoil minutely clear. How was he not being hit? Around him fell bits of leaf, dark green and ripe from the summer sun. Pellets of wood spun crazily as man met nature, rifle bullet meeting tree. Scottsdale realised that Grant's mouth was open; it took a moment for him to realise he was shouting and to register the words. "Fire the fucking flare, sir! Fire it!" It jolted Scottsdale out of his haze and into action, raising the pistol above his head. The sky was a blue plain of impossible brightness, the silhouette of the highest branches stretching out to the heavens as if imploring their sustenance. And streaking high, the smoky discharge of their final gamble, the flare exploding in the sky.

Muzzy headed, he gazed at the colour staining the sky until the crash of gunfire came roaring back; the Very was struck from his hands and he hurled himself back into cover. The German infantry were darting forward, and he fired wildly. A grenade detonated nearby, kicking up earth, and he and Grant ducked, coughing as smoke washed over them. The enemy were across the clearing and crowding the start of the path. One soul, braver than most, burst forward firing wildly. Grant put him down, but the respite had to be only temporary now; their only hope was the guns. Scottsdale strained to hear the rumble of an artillery strike as he reloaded mechanically, but the only sound was the crack of rifle fire, the guttural cries of German and the whine of bullets that came ever closer. Despairing, he leant out and shot an infantryman who'd crept close. Futile, he thought. Glancing across the path he saw Sergeant Grant bleeding heavily, dark blood snaking down the side of his blackened face. "Futile," he said aloud, acid despair bubbling up. And then he thought of Helene, he thought of the suitcase that could change the world, and he felt a peace. Their sacrifice would be worthwhile, it would have value. He wasn't going to die some shitty death in a shitty forest in a pointless fight that no one save the relatives of the dead would care about. Death would have value and not only that, he would have the satisfaction of knowing he had denied Schiller.

The German fire intensified, reaching a crescendo. Scottsdale and Grant couldn't do anything but flatten themselves to the trees, hugging their bodies close, resigned to death but frantic to live. Scottsdale closed his eyes. He took a deep breath. A shout came from ahead; it was time. This was the enemy's charge, this was his death. Spinning around the tree, that wonderful shot up tree that had saved him, he saw the mass of German infantry coming towards them, no finesse. Some would die but others would get through to stand triumphant over his body, to rifle his pockets and take his trinkets. He raised his rifle and took aim. Time to die. Finger curling round the trigger, he breathed out and squeezed the trigger, just like they taught a young man whom they took from life, moulded and remade into a machine that killed for King and country. And as he fired his defiant round into that dark mass flooding towards him, it exploded into a flash of intense light and vivid orange flame.

***

Reckoning

Groggily, Scottsdale struggled to sit up. He shook his head slowly, trying to clear the ringing from his ears. His head throbbed. Blinking away the mud and leaves that coated his face, he looked around. Shattered tree trunks, branches hanging at cracked angles and shredded foliage still falling softly to the ground greeted him. Where was he? He looked down at his battledress. It was filthy. Wasn't right, he told himself. Must get ready. He frowned. A dark pool of liquid was growing on his chest. Bloody mess. Bloody. Blood. His stunned mind processed slowly. It was his blood and it was dripping down his face onto his chest. Raising a hand to his face he tried to wipe it away. His mouth was so dry. God, he needed water. Water. Canal. The canal. He shook his head again, little droplets of blood springing off his face. Must get back to the canal before the Germans. Germans, where were the –

A second concussion thundered down, exploding deeper in the woods. The guns! He scrambled back into the shelter. "The guns!" he mumbled delightedly. "The bloody guns! Griffin, you beautiful bastard!" Turning his head, he glanced up and froze. Stuck in a branch above him was the precisely severed leg of a German infantryman. He blanched. With an effort of will he tore his gaze away and looked up the path. The farmhouse lay obliterated and smoking. An ethereal smoke lingered, carrying with it the fetid stink of cordite and sulphur. Dimly, he could make out figures up ahead, some lying prone on the ground but others stumbling backwards.

Grant! Where was Grant? Looking over he saw a booted leg sticking out from where Grant had been standing. He felt a rising panic, realising how much he depended on the gruff Sergeant. "Grant!" he shouted hoarsely, swallowing hard and shouting with greater force. "Sergeant Grant!" A surge of relief swept across him as the leg twitched, then the knee raised before the rest of Grant emerged, blinking, to sit up. "Are you hurt?"

Blearily Grant waved a hand, brushing himself down and searching around for his rifle. Forcing himself up, he leant against the tree. "I'll be ok, sir," he replied. "But can I suggest we get the hell out of here?"

Scottsdale grinned. "A fine idea, Sergeant." It took a moment for him to register the deep rumble as another shell tore across the sky. They threw themselves flat and prayed. Nothing, Scottsdale thought, but nothing could be worse than being under artillery fire. There's nothing you can do save huddle yourself into the smallest, tightest ball, every muscle taut, jaw clenched and then feel the aftershocks that signal you are still alive. The impact sounded and immediately they struggled up and started running. Scottsdale glanced back. Behind him the path was completely wreathed in dense smoke, white from the discharge of the shells and dark from the fire laid by the wrecked farmhouse.

A few scattered shots followed them, but their fear lent them speed and they ran on, panting heavily. Reaching the end of the woods, their adrenalin surged as they burst out onto the plain, the gently sloping ground speeding their flight. Scottsdale felt horribly exposed after so long hiding in the dark and he glanced wildly round as they sprinted, pouches and canteen flapping, towards the canal. The sun had risen higher and he caught the familiar summer smell of flowers and grass, even as the sweat poured down his back. Faster, faster. They were so close, eating up the ground, gripped by a panic that they'd come so far only to be cut down so close to their goal. Scottsdale's body was instinctively tensed, waiting for the sharp rebuke of a rifle to cut down their audacity in expecting their journey to end successfully. Come on, come on. He couldn't summon any spit, his lips cracked and bleeding. He'd abandoned any pretence at stealth and laid himself in the uncertain palm of fate; had the Germans from the woods really pulled out? Were the Germans even now recovering and following down the plain, rifle lined up on his back? Please, please. The words spilled out of their own volition even as he struggled for breath. Please, please. The heavy tread of Grant was beside him and yes, there, there was the lip of the canal! It was so close, let my legs hold out, let the gods, anyone's God, stay the hand of the enemy for just that little bit longer.

Both men took the slight incline to the canal at a rush, breathing hard. Scottsdale stopped sharply as he took in the scene over the other side. He could see the remains of his section clambering out of the boats, French scientists and Father Curzones safely in tow. He'd been expecting them to be well over and across by now. And he cursed, because Grant was already on his way down to the water and it meant that Scottsdale was going to have to swim again. Momentarily closing his eyes, he went to take a step forward before pausing, frowning at the sight across the canal. They were waving at him and shouting, something he couldn't hear well enough, his ears still clogged from the concussion of the artillery. Were they welcoming him? And why was Corporal Davenport raising his rifle?

It was the zip of a bullet that jolted him to the realisation that they weren't safe yet. Even then he couldn't quite bring himself to believe it. They'd outrun Schiller, hadn't they? Surely they'd finally shaken off the pursuit? He turned and felt the bitter anger boil inside again. Because Schiller hadn't stopped. The artillery hadn't driven him off. There, limping doggedly onto the plain behind them, was the German. Bleeding, scratched and battered as the rest of them, but coming for them. Even as Scottsdale looked back in appalled stupefaction, Schiller swung up his rifle and sighted, directly at him.

16

Schiller sat up. The artillery strike had been shocking. At the point of overwhelming the enemy they'd been struck down, the concussion stopping them dead. Several men had been tossed aside by the force of the blast. One soldier came to twenty feet behind them; his tunic and left boot were blown clear off his body, but he was otherwise unharmed. Another had lost his leg and lay on the path, face blanched and pallid, lips compressed in pain. Schiller looked down at him. The frightened soldier looked up, desperately seeking some sign of hope, but the pale eyes of Schiller betrayed nothing more than an academic interest as the man's life ebbed away. Blood rose from the soldier's mouth and dribbled onto his chin as he coughed before he slipped, inconsequentially, to death. Another lay holding his shoulder, moaning in pain. Schiller coughed, roughly cuffing his eyes which stung in the smoke. Madness. That this mission had come to this. He looked around, but the remnants of his men were hobbling away. Cowards, he seethed. He'd teach them not to turn tail when he returned. There was no question what had to be done, he had to go on, to continue until he'd ended this. Staggering slightly, he moved down the path, stepping through the smoke, a feverish glint in his eye. Not bothering to conceal himself, he picked up his speed. Instinctively he knew the British had gone; it's what he'd have done.

Emerging from the woods, he snarled in triumph; his quarry was there. His sole focus was on killing Scottsdale, thoughts of the suitcase blotted out by a monstrous desire to kill. It would prove, emphatically and in a way that brooked no argument, that he, Manfred Karsten Schiller, born in Duisburg, raised to restore German honour, to kill his country's enemies, was the superior solider and part of a superior future. He would be shooting at the extreme of his range, but without pausing he slowed, rifle swinging smoothly up in his hands to rest gently against his shoulder, lowering himself to kneel in one fluid motion, breathing evenly to feel the familiar, reassuring rifle stock against his cheek, smell the metal and oil that made the gun alive to him. As he did so he saw that Scottsdale had turned. The moment crystallised in Schiller's mind and he smiled at its perfection. On the cusp of his victory, he saw what this was; a gladiatorial contest between soldiers, one that had stretched him to his very limits. And at this, the final denouement, his enemy had seen him. He would know that the bullet that came to snatch his life away had been delivered by Schiller's hand. With exquisite joy, his finger curled around the trigger, ignoring the fire that was coming towards him. A tranquil smile never left his face as he squeezed gently on the cold metal and a heartbeat later felt the kick, vision obscured for a split second by smoke, before clearing – and yes, yes, there it was; Scottsdale falling down the canal, falling to his death. Realigning his aim, he squeezed off a further few rounds at the figures on the far side of the canal. Satisfied, he turned and scurried back towards the German lines.

***

Scottsdale fell and cried out. Turning from the horrifying sight of Schiller, his foot crept over the lip of the bank, unbalancing him. He rolled painfully to the bottom and came to rest partially in the canal. Cursing, he looked round for his rifle, gratefully scooping it up. He glanced over at the other bank, where there was a clear commotion, but his mind was still focused on Schiller. Getting to his feet, he scrambled cautiously up to the top and peeked over, scanning the horizon, but the plain was empty. He breathed deeply in relief, smelling the grass and dried mud, and leant his head against the bank. Safety. They'd made it. A deep, all embracing sense of fatigue gripped him. Safety. Scarcely credible safety.

Shouting began to penetrate his wall of fatigue. Levering himself up stiffly, he turned. The first thing he saw was a knot of people on the other side of the bank. He frowned; he'd seen enough of war to know when someone was hurt. The next thing he saw was an outstretched leg and his blood froze. He could see a shoe poking out, but it was a woman's shoe, clearly visible. It was twitching. A metallic taste flooded his mouth. There was a man kneeling beside her, red cross visible, applying pressure. Fauvelle stood nearby with Father Curzones' arms around him. He was crying, his distress visible in his convulsing shoulders. Helene. Oh God, please no, not Helene. You miserable bastard God, don't do this, not now, not after this. His hand was shaking, jaw slack. Without thinking he clambered down the bank, plunging into the canal, barely registering the intense cold that failed to numb the panic that propelled his wildly thrashing heart. Grant dove in after him. Over and over in Scottsdale's head a mantra came unbidden; please God, no, not her, please God, no, not her, deeply knowing the futility but refusing to accept what he hadn't yet seen with his own eyes. Rising from the canal and climbing to the knot of people, who looked at him with pitying eyes and it was Father Curzones who tried to intercept him - "Please, Lieutenant" - but Scottsdale brushed him off, never even glancing at him, fixated on getting to Helene, to confirm what he already knew had happened. Marsh moved aside a soldier with a warning look until finally, breathing hard, Scottsdale came to a halt standing over the body - yes, the body. For this was no longer a living, vital person; no longer a breathing, laughing, teasing, enigmatic person but a lifeless, slack shell. Nothing remained of the person who inhabited it. It was impossible, it was offensive, that this had happened; he couldn't accept this. Fixedly, he stared down, automatically noting the details that gave the story of her death. The small, dirty hole that told of the trajectory of the bullet. The blouse, stained dark from the unstoppable blood that poured out of her, fleeing with her life. The bloodied bandages that told of the desperate attempt to staunch the flow and to cheat the crossing guard of his victim. Futility. The futility of life, the futility of war, the futility of love, the futility of trying to take something clean and pure and worthy out of this shitty few days draped in the most glorious of summer weather, hunted and hounded and killed. Caught and killed.

He felt a hand on his shoulder but refused to yield until he realised he was dripping water onto her. Dripping the dirty water onto the bandages, turning them a watery pink. It broke the spell and it was suddenly intolerable. He shrugged off the hand, a nauseating anger rising, a physical thing he could feel climbing up his throat, clawing at his innards, something that needed release. The face of Schiller burned in his mind. Every time he blinked, it was there. The hateful face, the pale eyes, the arrogant sneer. There was a pain in his gut. He leant forward, hand moving towards his stomach, but he caught sight of Father Curzones' concerned face and realised they were all looking at him. He couldn't accept their pity. He didn't want to – no, he mustn't – show the pain. He had to escape, to get away. Then Grant spoke, and it brought him back from the edge.

"Sir? Orders?" The word jolted him, reminded him of his position, his responsibility, of the need to be, in every way, an officer of the British army; unbending, an example to his men. In the instant of this mental readjustment he welcomed it for rescuing him but loathed himself just as much. Straightening, he wiped his hands over his tunic. Staring out over the canal he spoke very deliberately. "Send for a burial party. Father, Monsieur Fauvelle, come with me. Sergeant Grant, take them men, find our positions and wait for me." "Yes, sir." Grant's reply was tinged with relief. Like the men, he'd noticed the affection between his Lieutenant and the Frenchwoman. Indeed, they were quietly proud of him and many ribald comments were shared about it. He turned to the rest of the squad who were looking curiously at their officer. "Right, stop gawping, get your gear," he barked.

There was an immediate response as the men gathered themselves together and moved back through the British position. A silence hung over them, the exhaustion of their ordeal beginning to sink in, and they ignored the shouted questions from the rest of the company.

"Did you see the Lieutenant's face?" Perkins finally proffered. "He looked like hell."

"Not a happy man."

"Shame about the Frenchie."

"A tasty bit of skirt she was," Marsh said crudely.

"Bloody shame. She didn't deserve that." Pendle said. "And I think she liked the Lieutenant too."

"As if you'd know; the only girls who go near you are the brass kind."

"You know what I like about you, Marsh? You've got a face like a bulldog chewing a wasp. It frightens the girls, so they come straight to me."

"You're a berk, you know that."

"Cut it out, the pair of you," Davenport said wearily. "You're both hideous."

"Not like that Frenchie," Wilkins mused. "Fiery, too. Gave the priest hell when he suggested leaving the farm." "A lovely girl," McManus said softly. "Can see why she took the Lieutenant's fancy."

"He did not look well, did he?" Pendle repeated.

"He'll be ok," Grant cut in.

"Well, he has to be, doesn't he, Sarge? Cos if he isn't, then we're all in trouble."

Grant shot Pendle a dark look but he couldn't disagree. Incompetent or damaged officers were a menace. "He's fine," he asserted. "And let that be the end of it." Coming across some open space, Grant ordered a halt. "Stay here and start getting yourselves sorted while I go and find out what's going on. Davenport, you're in charge." "Right you are, Sarge," Davenport said.

Wearily they sat down, groaning as they took off their packs. Pendle sat on a crate and shrugged off his webbing. He reached into his pack and pulled out a can of blanco; he looked at it and back to his gear before throwing it down in disgust. "I'll clean it later," he muttered. Wilkins made a pillow of his hands behind his head and gazed up at the sky while Marsh rummaged around in his pack "I'm starving," Marsh said.

Pendle's head whipped round. "You and me both. What have you got in there?"

"Nothing for you," Marsh said sourly.

"Ah, come on. Can I cadge some spam?"

"Bugger off."

"What have you got?"

"Enough for me. Unless you've anything to trade?"

"Of course I don't! I've been fighting. This bloody war," he exploded. "Sending us out there into the middle of the German army. And now Norm and Taffy dead. Bastards. I'd shoot the bloody lot of them."

Wilkins glanced at Marsh, gesturing towards Pendle but Marsh ignored him. "Ain't life a ball, eh fellas," he said. "Half of Germany a mile away and here we are – hey, what the hell are you doing!"

McManus had walked up behind Marsh, ripping a bar of chocolate out of his hand. Chucking it onto Pendle's chest, he turned back to face Marsh who had struggled to his feet in outrage. "I'm doing what you should have done," McManus said.

"What I...what bloody business is it of yours?" McManus made to move past, but Marsh blocked his path. "I asked you a question," he snarled.

Glancing down at his chest, McManus stepped a little forward. "I heard you."

Marsh looked round in indignation, but Davenport had slowly stood. The rest of the section watched as Davenport pointed at Marsh. "We share what we have, Swampy. There's enough shit going around without us adding to it."

Marsh slowly exhaled and held out his hands placatingly. "Fine," he said. "I was just messing around." Shaking his head, he sat down. "Bloody liberty," he grumbled. "What's an Irishman doing here anyway?" Pendle inclined his head in salute as McManus sat back down. An uncomfortable tension lingered, lying across the group like a blanket on a hot day. Distant sounds of planes and gun fire rumbled on. Marsh turned his head and spat.

Davenport began rummaging around one of the crates, pulling out a pile of papers. Turning one of the pages over, he held it out and chuckled. "Here lads, listen to this. Jerry's been in touch." Affecting an exaggerated German accent, he began to read aloud. "'British Soldiers!' - that's you lot," he said looking up at the squad, face bright with humour – "'Look at this map; it gives your true situation! Your troops are entirely surrounded'- And here's their very nice request –

"Stop Fighting! Put down your arms!'"

"Give us a look at that," Pendle said chuckling. "Honestly, what do they expect? Right-o lads let's all surrender."

"Yep, was thinking the same myself actually. Now I've read this, let's go find Scotty and tell him we want out."

"That's a fine idea, Private Pendle. You should be promoted."

"Actually, can you pass those over?" They looked round quizzically at McManus who was getting up. "Why, what do you need them for?"

"I need something to wipe my arse with." Gathering up the loose leaflets he headed out to the sound of raucous laughter.

***

It would be impossible for Scottsdale to describe what happened after he left the canal. His mind wasn't consciously aware of the decisions he was taking and for once he was grateful for the stultifying bureaucracy of the army; equipment had to be checked, notification of the men's death made, documents initialled, reports written, ammunition and rations drawn. It allowed him to partially shut down, as if he were observing himself from above, while he continued to perform the role of a junior officer in the British Army; here he signs a chit for stores, there he asks for and receives directions to battalion headquarters. No quivering upper lip. Good show, old man.

Father Curzones and Fauvelle trailed behind as he led them to battalion headquarters. Fauvelle was in a state of abject misery and Scottsdale found that it helped to steady him. He wondered what it was it about Fauvelle's evident pain that calmed him; the dishevelled face, the red eyes, shoulders shaking to the rhythm of his sobs. It reminded him of the funeral of his great friend, Geoffrey Deacon. Geoffrey was an exuberant, cheerful character, who'd filled those around him with equal part exasperation and affection. They'd been firm friends since meeting at university. Scottsdale's initial shyness had been an affront to Geoffrey who'd made it his life's work to bring him out of his shell. They'd gone to parties, met girls, and studied together. Scottsdale revered him. Then came the news; Geoffrey had been burnt to death in his Hurricane. Scottsdale was devastated. Yet on that crisp winter's day they'd lowered Geoffrey into the earth, it was the sight of Mrs Deacon, pale and hollowed out by grief that steadied him. He noted this curious fact and continued towards his next task. To find Mr Griffin.

Father Curzones tended to Fauvelle, murmuring soothing words, but kept an eye on Scottsdale. The British soldier was very upright, hands clenched. Everything about him was taut. He saw the way Scottsdale's jaw had set and knew from his experience of living with death that Scottsdale was pushing his grief down. Curzones knew, too, a single wrong word or gesture could release a corrosive anger. With a quiet word to Fauvelle, he cleared his throat and came alongside Scottsdale.

"Lieutenant Scottsdale?" he enquired. There was no reaction. He touched Scottsdale's arm gently. "Lieutenant?"

"Yes, Father?" Scottsdale's voice was flat.

Curzones felt the need to slow him down somehow. "How are you, my son?"

Scottsdale continued walking.

Curzones tried another tack. "Life is cruelty is it not?"

"Life is what it is, Father and being in the middle of a war is hardly the time to be discussing it."

"Can there be a more appropriate time? We are surrounded by death. Surely now we understand what life is for, what is most precious to us and for what cause we sacrifice."

Scottsdale closed his eyes. He was incredibly weary, as though a breath of wind could stop him and turn him round. He knew what Father Curzones was trying, knew it was well meant and knew he would have no part. What he needed was to focus on the immediate tasks in hand and then find somewhere away from anyone else. Lest the embers in his belly ignite.

He sighed and opened his eyes. "When it comes to it, Father – and never forget this – we fight because we're here. Because there's no one else. We fight for the man next to us, we fight for the hope of home and we fight because we have no choice. There's no one else. So it's us."

"You fight for more than that, Lieutenant. You're fighting for what is right!"

"Your God tells you this?" He jerked his head towards the German lines. "The same God that tells the same thing to that lot over there."

"We do not need God to show us what is right. You said so yourself! We have to protect the innocent, to prevent the worst parts of man becoming part of life."

Scottsdale gave a hollow laugh. "Clearly, I need some practice at this protection business. More of my men dead and now -" He stopped abruptly.

"And now?"

The silence stretched out. A motorcycle engine in the distance caught, fired and roared into life. Curzones tried once more. "What happened, it wasn't your-"

"Enough Father, enough! I have no need of this, do you understand? Comfort Maurice if you must. He has need of you and your God, but I do not."

Lengthening his stride, Scottsdale strode on, leaving Curzones looking sadly at him. There was nothing to be done. They're just boys, he thought. And English to boot. They never stood a chance.

17

Schiller stood rigidly in front of the desk. "Yes, Herr Gruppenführer," he said through clenched teeth. Since he'd been summoned that had been the only thing he'd been able to say. Wave after wave of attack on his competence had assaulted him. He burned with humiliation.

"This was a personal priority of the Reichsführer. He is not a man who likes to be disappointed. And nor am I. You had the resources, the men and you let them slip through your fingers. Intolerable."

The mention of Heinrich Himmler, head of the SS, made Schiller wince. He ran an unforgiving organisation where the price of failure was often terminal.

. "My initial reaction was to reassign you to administrative duties pending a full investigation," Gruppenführer Kruger continued remorselessly, and Schiller felt his blood run cold. An investigation followed by demotion or worse. Disgrace.

"However," Kruger said, and paused, looking up. He was a short man with close cropped grey hair. A silver topped cane was propped up alongside the desk, testament to the loss of a leg in the first war not far from where they were today. "Given the current situation, I've been persuaded that we can better use you and the remnants of your men. Perhaps even a chance to redeem yourself."

"I will do whatever is required," Schiller said stiffly. "I should imagine so." Kruger paused to sip his coffee. "You are extremely fortunate that we are having this conversation. Doktor Rademacher has been flown to Berlin, where he will be debriefed. I think it is safe to say he will be going away to think about his failure for a long time." He smiled thinly. "It is not wise to come to Reichsführer Himmler's attention unless you are able to please him."

Schiller had no love of Rademacher but nonetheless felt a twinge of sympathy. He would prefer to charge a tank than displease Himmler.

"The final chapter of this campaign – perhaps even this war – is upon us, Schiller," Kruger continued. "Imagine that. After the slaughter of the Great War, we are on the brink of ending this conflict in weeks! All there is for us now is to push the British into the sea. And for that we need every man."

Schiller awaited the next words in desperate hope. He'd returned to camp still exultant after the death of Scottsdale; the escape of the French scientists had seemed almost inconsequential. He accepted that the mission had failed and that burned his professional pride but in truth, with the end game approaching in the west he felt it would render the failure inconsequential. Yet he'd been thoroughly disabused of the notion after he gave in his report. The summons to this office had followed swiftly, preceded by a notable stiffening in manner of those at headquarters. Eyes that once met his now slid away; a certain reserve was palpable in acquaintances. The dressing down that followed stripped away any lingering sense of achievement he had. What mattered now was whether he was damned to disgrace or whether he'd be given the chance to redeem himself.

Kruger shuffled his papers before leaning forward, hands steeped under his chin. "You will be returning to the Totenkopf division to take part in the final assault. You can expect to be at the forefront of the advance, where the action is the most intense. If you should fall, you will do so with honour. If you should prevail, you will restore your reputation." He paused. "There is no other outcome for you."

Schiller closed his eyes and breathed deep. This was the certainty he craved. It was clear what his duty would be. To drive the Tommies to the sea, to drown them and their French allies in blood and for him to be at the spearpoint of the advance. It was all he wanted. "I am honoured to be part of this momentous time in history. I will not let you down." "I should hope not," Kruger said drily. "Now, to the current situation. The British are surrounded and most of the French armies have capitulated. Boulogne has fallen, and it seems they are going to try and evacuate from the only port left open to them – Dunkirk. An incredibly stupid idea. Nonetheless, we've been held back by headquarters. It's infuriating, but there it is. Apparently, the Luftwaffe have decided they can bomb the British to defeat by themselves." "Aircraft can't win this by themselves," Schiller growled.

"Obviously, but since their bombing of Rotterdam caused the Dutch surrender, their stock has grown. The British and French will be a harder nut to crack and we're going to be needed sooner rather than later." He gestured to a map. "We are squeezing the enemy back on all sides. The end is getting closer, so I expect we'll be called upon shortly, so you need to be ready."

"I will be, sir," Schiller said grimly.

"Good. It goes without saying that this is your last chance, Schiller." Kruger stood, signalling the interview was over. "Back to your unit then. And to your death or the restitution of your reputation."

***

After getting directions from a passing artillery officer, Scottsdale eventually led their group to a small country house on the outskirts of Meurchin. From a distance it resembled any other refined French dwelling but up close the signs of war were evident. Several craters pock marked the garden and one corner of the main building had collapsed. An outhouse lay blackened and various trucks containing signals troops and medical orderlies were scattered through the gardens. Scottsdale's eye was drawn to the flower beds that bordered the drive. They were a riot of colour waving defiantly in the wind even if half of them had been obliterated by bombing.

Feverish activity surrounded the house. Dispatch riders hurried out, faces blackened and lined from exhaustion, as they rode to deliver another hard message to units on the verge of collapse – hold, whatever you do, hold; of utmost importance, strategic imperative etc., etc. Handing over another death sentence. Staff officers milled about. Striding into the main hall, Scottsdale felt an undercurrent of panic; like an over-packed suitcase it threatened to spring out. Grim faces were everywhere. In the corner a bloodied French officer sat weeping quietly. An ashen-faced staff officer nodded robotically as messenger after messenger came in, whispered in his ear and handed over the latest news of German advances.

Scottsdale approached the front desk where a harried corporal simultaneously tried to answer phones while scribbling messages. "Clarke! Clarke, where the bloody hell are you?" he shouted, cradling the phone to his ear. His gaze settled on Scottsdale, taking in the bloodstained smock and drawn face. They all looked like that now. "Be with you in one mo, sir," he said, before speaking rapidly into the phone, signing off with, "Right you are, sir."

As he replaced the receiver a whippet thin Private came racing across the hall, waving a signal. "Got it, Corp," the Private said, handing over the signal triumphantly.

The corporal took it, initialled it and snapped back, "Back to the QM with you lad," and then turned to Scottsdale. "Sorry, sir. What can I do you for?"

"We're looking for a Mr Griffin. Where can we find him?"

The corporal's eyebrow raised ever so slightly. "You'll want to be heading down to the east wing," he replied pointing to their right. "Down that hall, keep going until you hit the staircase, left and it's at the end on the right."

Scottsdale nodded, turned on his heel and strode down the corridor, Curzones and Fauvelle hurrying to keep up. He wanted this over with and was conscious of his rising anger at the thought of seeing Griffin again. They wound their way forward until they found a heavy wooden door. Taking a breath, Scottsdale rapped hard and, after a moment's pause, the laconic voice of Griffin bid them enter.

Griffin was leaning over a table, pen poised while Beaufort held a sheaf of papers. They looked up as Scottsdale entered, Curzones and Fauvelle close behind. Of all the people Scottsdale had seen recently, Griffin looked the least perturbed. Seeing them enter, his face creased into a wide smile and he came out from behind the desk. Beaufort straightened too, a knowing smile on her face.

"Lieutenant Scottsdale!" Griffin exclaimed. "I can't tell you what a pleasure it is to see you!" He turned to Father Curzones. "And, of course, Father Curzones, how are you my friend?" Scottsdale watched in surprise as Griffin and Curzones embraced like old friends, before Griffin turned to Fauvelle. "Monsieur Fauvelle, an honour to meet you." Glancing down, he saw the suitcase clutched tightly in Fauvelle's grip and reached out a hand. "And this is the prize," he said with deep reverence. "May I?"

Taking the case Griffin laid it gently on the desk. The latches clicked loudly, and Griffin raised the lid. He stepped aside and held out his hand in invitation to Beaufort who stepped forward and examined the contents.

"Well?" Griffin demanded. "Are we happy?"

"Badgering me won't make this go any faster," Beaufort murmured as she continued her examination. After a further pause she straightened and removed her glasses.

"We are happy," she said simply.

Griffin smiled delightedly, and Scottsdale thought he was on the brink of bursting into dance. "You've done us a great service, all of you! This" – he tapped the briefcase with an immaculately manicured finger – "this could alter the course of this war, let there be no doubt about this. You should be proud of what you achieved, a mere handful of men and this most gratifying of outcomes!"

"A handful of good men, some of whom who died for this," Scottsdale growled. "Not to mention Monsieur Fauvelle's niece, Helene." It was the first time he'd spoken her name and to his shame he felt his voice thicken.

"Yes, regrettable of course, and Monsieur Fauvelle my condolences for your loss." Griffin's voice had the slightest edge of impatience. "But we've no time to lose," he continued briskly. "We must spirit you and your bag of tricks away with alacrity."

Scottsdale interrupted. "Were you aware of the German party hunting them?"

Griffin straightened and looked at Scottsdale. "Was I aware of a specific threat? No. Was it obvious the Germans would try and find it? Yes. As we spoke about, Lieutenant, it was clear that our enemy would try and recover this as well."

"They had several platoons looking for them." Scottsdale knew there was no profit in this; Griffin neither cared nor desired to know. Yet he continued stubbornly, compelled to make Griffin see, to take some responsibility. That was what he wanted, someone to take responsibility for the deaths of his men and for Helene, to assuage his guilt. It was pointless, but he couldn't stop. "We should have had more men, better information. We could have saved good people from dying."

"Good people die in wars," Beaufort said gently. "You know this."

"That doesn't bloody help." Scottsdale shook off the hand Father Curzones laid on his arm. "Does this sit easy with you both? These people going to their deaths while you play the puppet master?"

"Don't be so naïve, Lieutenant," Griffin snapped. "I haven't got time for this. This is what it takes to win wars."

"I know what it takes," Scottsdale snarled. "I've seen it close up, I've seen the bodies. We were blundering around out there with a psychopathic German on our tails. We should have been warned."

"You've done well, Lieutenant, and I will put this down to stress." Griffin's voice was icy. "You did your duty and you've achieved something significant, take comfort from that. But enough. Don't push me."

Scottsdale closed his eyes, dark red flashes filling his vision. He felt nauseous. The worse part was he knew that nothing could be done now, that is was pointless pursuing this. Griffin wasn't going to give him absolution. He nodded stiffly.

"Good," Griffin said. "Now, to the future. As you may have noticed, there's something of a flap going on. It appears we are going to have to take the whole damn army off with the navy. Perhaps we might see some inter-service cooperation now, rather than bickering over who is the senior service."

"They must be well prepared for this?" Father Curzones enquired.

"Apparently not. It's a giant bugger's muddle out there. Hopefully, it's not too late." He turned to face Scottsdale. "The general idea is going to be to evacuate from Dunkirk, but I'll let

Major Carter fill you in on the relevant details. As for us, Monsieur Fauvelle, nothing as vulgar as a sea voyage I assure you. We shall be leaving forthwith by plane to London." Griffin turned to Curzones, placing his hands on the priest's shoulders. "And finally, my dear Remi. As ever, I am indebted to you. I assume you are returning home?"

"Of course. Now is not the time to leave."

"I have room on that plane for you."

"Thank you, but it is my duty to remain, as you well know."

Griffin smiled broadly back. "I do indeed. There will be much to do when I get back to London and we can begin planning our operations here. You have all you need?" Curzones nodded. "Excellent. Then I must command you to remain safe – you are too valuable to me."

Scottsdale looked from one to the other, recognition dawning. Curzones was no ordinary priest caught up in events. He was one of Griffin's agents. Catching Scottsdale's eye, Curzones smiled apologetically and came over. He gave Scottsdale a swift peck on each cheek. "It would not have helped if you had known."

"A priest and a spy eh, Father? A sinner and a saint."

Curzones smiled. "No, mon ami, that is you. I simply do my part."

"What would God make of that?"

"My God is of the Old Testament." Scottsdale looked at him quizzically and Curzones leant in close to his ear. "So if you find Herr Schiller, I urge you to look to the scriptures to guide you."

"The scriptures?"

"Yes. So sayeth my God: 'It is mine to avenge; I will repay. In due time their foot will slip; their day of disaster is near and their doom rushes on them.'" He patted Scottsdale on the shoulder. "Go with God, Lieutenant. I will pray for you."

"Thank you, Father." Scottsdale was touched and saddened as Curzones and Fauvelle took their leave. There were no words he could summon for Fauvelle other than a muttered apology before Curzones took Fauvelle by the arm and led him out, leaving Scottsdale with Griffin and Beaufort.

"A sinner and a saint? An apt description," Griffin remarked. "The Father there fought in the Great War and was lost, utterly lost for many years after. Found salvation and thankfully for England, found me as well. We've been building networks here since '38 and he is the best of them, of that there is no doubt."

"The Germans tortured him you know?"

Griffin looked up. "I didn't but I can believe it," he said grimly. "They've been trying to counter our networks for nearly as long." He smiled. "Damn difficult business this spying game." Puffing ruminatively on his pipe he eyed Scottsdale. "And what of you, Mr Scottsdale? I rather think you've a talent for this sort of thing."

Scottsdale snorted. "I'd hardly say that."

"Oh, I don't know. Managed to get across the line, locate our friends and get them safe home. Rather a good show actually."

Again, Scottsdale felt his anger rising. It was the blithe dismissal of those who were unimportant to Griffin. Fauvelle was safe, Curzones was safe, they were important, they were safe. But Helene wasn't. Or Levingston. Or White. He shook his head wearily because he also knew that in the end, Griffin was right. It *was* a good show. "I don't think I've got the stomach for this kind of work, Mr Griffin."

"You'll be surprised what you can get used to, Lieutenant," Beaufort said mildly. "Particularly when you realise the stakes."

"Perhaps," Scottsdale said.

"Perhaps, indeed," Griffin said briskly. "There will be a time when I need people like you, Scottsdale. And it won't be long until that day comes. So don't do anything stupid like getting yourself killed in the meantime, there's a good chap."

It was said lightly but there was no mistaking the underlying tone of command. Scottsdale nodded and collected his cap. "I'll do my best."

"I know you will."

Scottsdale left, walking much more slowly this time. Emerging into the sunlight, he fixed his cap firmly onto his head, feeling the crunch of gravel under his boot. Would he help Griffin? For the moment, it felt too raw, that there was a moral cost he was uncertain he could bear. Yet he also knew that his grief for Helene would eventually fade. And Griffin was right that what they had achieved was vital to the war effort. He shook his head. What he wanted now was to rest, to lay his head down and, just for a time, forget those striking brown eyes that stared up accusingly from her dead body on the canal shore.

18

"Good to see you, Scottsdale," Major Carter said warmly, ushering him inside. After leaving Griffin, Scottsdale had been directed to where Carter was waiting to be debriefed. In truth it was the last thing he felt like doing but seeing Carter's obvious relief at having him back had helped. "Sit down and tell me what's been going on," Carter instructed.

Scottsdale composed his thoughts. "It's been a difficult few days, sir. We recovered the technology, but I lost two men killed as well as one of the civilians."

Carter grimaced. "I always knew it was going to be a damned dicey affair. I take it Jerry wanted it too?"

Scottsdale nodded. "Yes, sir. At first it all went smoothly. We met up at the rendezvous but that's when the Germans showed up." He could still picture Sergeant Grant's head appearing as he delivered the news that the Germans had arrived and were hunting them. "They were led by an SS officer, a man called Schiller." Scottsdale had to pause to swallow the rage that threatened to overwhelm him when he mentioned that name. "He'd been tasked with capturing the civilians too and he came in strength, at least a couple of platoons."

"Not the best of odds then," Carter commented.

"We were outgunned, sir, so I tried to hide. But this German tortured the priest who was sheltering the civilians. I still can't believe what he did." The wet slap of Schiller's fist striking flesh echoed in his mind. "Maybe I should have kept quiet, but I couldn't let him continue; besides I thought it was only a matter of time before the priest broke. I know I would have, although now I know the man, I fear I underestimated him."

"One of Griffin's private army then?"

"Yes, sir. Used to be a soldier before becoming a priest. I liked him."

"Interesting fellow. Not many men find God through killing."

"Indeed, sir. Once our position was revealed my options were limited," he continued. "They had too much firepower and there was no way out. That's where we lost Private White to a grenade." He was looking at Major Carter but seeing White's blood spreading across the floor, hearing him choking on his own blood. "It was hopeless, sir. We would have been slaughtered one by one, so I surrendered."

"You did the right thing I'm sure."

"I truly hope so, sir, although I wonder if we'd kept fighting - "

"You'd all have been dead, and no use to anyone," Carter growled. "Don't spend your time second guessing yourself. Only one path that leads to and it ain't pretty. Now go on."

Scottsdale nodded. "Yes, sir. We were taken to a nearby chateau and managed to escape with the help of a local man. Once we were out, we set an ambush and rescued the civilians."

"Not precisely in keeping with my instructions, Lieutenant," Carter growled. "But it's fine work I must say." Scottsdale nodded. "Thank you, sir. Then it was a fight back to our lines. They just didn't want to give up those scientists. Private Levingston was killed in Annay as we fell back. Shot in the head." His decision to go out that door. Unconsciously he raised a hand to his cheek as if to wipe away the stain again. "I thought we were done for to be honest, but Mr Griffin's flare worked, and we got back over the canal. That's where we lost the civilian."

He stopped and stared into space. A dry retelling of horror and fear and anger. A cursory mention of the end of several people's lives. His written report, laboriously pecked out on the typewriter, would be the same. The deaths a footnote.

"Then you've done bloody well," Carter said firmly and stood up to stare out of the window. He radiated energy. "Division are delighted and now we move forward. Always forward, Arthur, you understand? Otherwise you'll end up in knots."

"Yes, sir." He saw that Carter was advising him, in his own way. "Forward."

"Exactly. And that means getting out of this benighted bloody country," Carter continued with relish. "In what apparently came as a shock to our dear commanders and none whatsoever to anyone with an ounce of intelligence, the Frogs and their Belgian cousins are being driven back everywhere. Ever met a Belgian? No? I've met a few, damned odd most of them and difficult to know where you stand with them. And in a war, no bloody use to anyone." Carter looked up at Scottsdale, eyes twinkling. "It's not official policy yet but it's blindingly obvious all roads lead to Dunkirk and a boat home. Regardless, that does not mean that the Frogs are completely useless or, indeed, that we are free from working with potentially incompetent partners. Quite the contrary in fact. First," he said raising a stubby finger, "the French are putting up a bloody good fight near Lille and will take a substantial part of the rearguard at Dunkirk. Decent of them although they should frankly; it's their wicket after all. Secondly, we are now reliant on the Navy to get us home while the flying circus try to protect us. So God help us frankly; who knows what kind of bath tubs we'll end up in getting back to dear old Blighty. Boulogne has fallen, and Calais is invested which leaves Dunkirk as the only satisfactory option for withdrawal. With me so far?" Scottsdale nodded. The man's constant bullishness was invigorating if perhaps more unforgiving than Scottsdale felt strictly fair. "Absolutely, sir."

"Course you are, Scottsdale. Wouldn't give you the time if I didn't think you knew your arse from your elbow. Happily, you seem tolerably competent. So – as I was saying, that in broad strokes is the strategic situation. Which to you and me and any sensible chap is a right bloody mess."

"Hard to argue, sir."

"Try arguing with me my boy and you'll wish you were back in whatever awful shire threw you up screaming for your mother's tit." As he spoke Carter was clearing the debris off his deck while simultaneously unfolding a large ordnance survey map. Finally bringing the recalcitrant object under control he gestured for

Scottsdale to join him. They stared down at the coastline of northern France.

"Now, I mentioned we are part of the canal line. This is Dunkirk here," Carter began, placing a finger on the coast, "which is where we are heading." He slid his finger south. "And this is the Dunkirk corridor. It's bordered to the east by the Ypres-Comines sector, with the Belgians on their left flank extending to the channel." He moved his fingers round the map. "In the south, from Raches all the way round to Gravelines on the coast, via La Bassee, Bethune, St Omer – with our army behind all these canals. Essentially, anyone the other side of the canals is probably going to shoot you."

Scottsdale looked at the map. "That's a long line to defend properly, sir," he commented. "Where do we think the Germans will focus their attack?"

"No idea. We know they've made localised bridgeheads but oddly enough over the last couple of days reports have indicated that they've stood down their armour. It's only been infantry and light AFV activity."

"Seems bloody odd when Dunkirk is only thirty miles away."

"Quite. But whatever the reason it's given us some precious time to get organised. Over the next few days our chaps will fall back along this corridor" – he moved his pencil from La Bassee to Dunkirk – "and once there we've nowhere else to go but home." Carter moved his pencil to an area slightly south-east of Dunkirk and proscribed a gentle circle. "We've flooded this area to hamper their tanks although frankly at this stage it's like gnats biting a giant's arse, won't make a great deal of difference. Nonetheless, this coupled with the canals, has given us some tactical advantages and is helping us slow the Germans. But it can only be slowing them down now – the more men we evacuate, the fewer we have to hold the line."

"A difficult position, sir. How is the Navy planning on getting us home?"

"That is the salient point of course. Normally, I wouldn't rate a naval man's chances of pulling something like this off higher than an American divorcee marrying the King of England – but as we know, stranger things have happened." He tapped his pencil on the map. "The navy chaps are going to have to disembark our army using any means available. Naturally, Jerry is aware of this and is attempting to bomb them back to the Stone Age."

"How many men have they got out like this, sir?"

"No idea. We've already taken off a lot of the HQ staff and other support troops. But we've still got tens of thousands of fighting troops all over the place and every man we save now is vital; every man who can wield a rifle, a bayonet or if needs be a spade, will be needed for when Herr Hitler invades Britain. Equipment is nothing, we can build more or, if our American cousins get off their overfed backsides, buy more. The men are the key you see."

Scottsdale nodded. "What about these beaches, sir? Can we use them?"

"Too shallow for most of the naval ships but rumour has it we're sending over anything that can float to get the men off the beaches and ferry the men out to the waiting big ships. From the sounds of it everyone is taking a hell of a beating, the flier boys and the navy. We, as always, are bearing the brunt of course – but I have decided we are all going to get home, one way or another. Clear?"

"Couldn't agree with you more, sir."

Carter straightened up and lit a cigarette. Exhaling he continued. "Now as for the 2nd Essex. I've already sent several officers and some of the men to embark for home." Carter nodded at Scottsdale's surprise. "Standard practice in situations like this. They'll be needed to form the nucleus of a new 2nd Battalion if we are annihilated."

Scottsdale blinked. The fact they were already planning for such a scenario drove home the seriousness of their situation.

"But let's hope it doesn't come to that shall we?" Carter rubbed his hands together. "As for the rest of us. We are staying attached to 50th Division and current orders are to retire to Fromelles, which is here" - he placed a stubby finger on the map - "and await further orders. It's likely we'll either be holding a temporary defensive line or delivering localised counter attacks."

"Do we have anti-tank support, sir?"

"The Norfolk Yeomanry are attached to the division and I'm trying to wangle some of their chaps, but they go where they are needed most. So for now, you'll be reliant on your own anti-tank rifles. Obviously, I am aware of their limited value against the better armoured Panzers, but we use what we have. We are no longer fighting a battle to win – we are fighting a battle to survive. So, we hold then move back – hold then back. Got it?"

"Crystal, sir."

"Good, because I won't tolerate any cock ups." Carter straightened. "We are being relieved by the 2nd Leicesters this afternoon, so find C Company and prepare the men. We've got to get back to Dunkirk where we'll be directed to our no doubt luxurious berth for our passage home. Problem is to get there we need to head through the world's largest traffic jam while fighting the Germans. Because at this point anyone left on this side of Dunkirk is now the rear-guard. So, congratulations; you are now a member of His Majesty's glorious rear-guard at Dunkirk."

Scottsdale grinned. "Thank you, sir."

"Too right, Scottsdale! One day the poets will write of this in the same way as Agincourt and Waterloo. Who knows, may even get a decent speech out of the new PM. Has a way with words does Mr Churchill." Turning, Carter bellowed loudly. "Badenhoff! Where the bloody hell are you man?"

An impeccably turned out soldier carefully entered the room. He had a serious face and spoke softly. "Yes, sir?"

Seeing Scottsdale's raised eyebrow, Carter continued. "My batman. And yes, I've ordered him to change that infernal name, but he's had the temerity to refuse, haven't you Badenhoff?"

"My name is my name, sir," Badenhoff replied, completely unperturbed.

"Thought they were playing silly buggers with me at HQ when they sent him down. But it transpires that is his actual name. Remarkable isn't it?" Scottsdale nodded in reply. There wasn't much else to add.

"How long have you been with me?" Carter demanded of Badenhoff. "Five, six years?"

"A shade over six, sir."

"And damn lucky for you too."

"Quite so, sir."

"Tolerably competent though I grant you."

"Deep praise indeed, sir," Badenhoff replied with the slightest inclination of his head. Scottsdale had to suppress a smile. It was clear the two men had been together for a long time.

"Enough of your impertinence. Show Lieutenant

Scottsdale to wherever that benighted Scotsman McDonald is and then back here sharpish. All clear?" Scottsdale and Badenhoff nodded in unison. Carter beamed and turned to face Scottsdale. "Look after yourself Scottsdale and remember, speed is of essence now. It all rests on getting to Dunkirk."

***

Threading his way through the battalion positions, Scottsdale was deep in thought despite the exhaustion that clung to him. The familiar refrain of a group of Tommies singing along to the popular song, *"South of the Border,"* floated toward him and the sound gave him comfort; as did the thought of Major Carter.

At the approach of Scottsdale, the men scrambled to their feet. He looked at them, thinking of all the pain and hardship they'd been through, yet also of what they had to come. It was remarkable what men would put up with if the need arose.

"I think we'd all agree it's time to go home," he began. "I know you're tired, and we've lost good men these past weeks. Our job now is to get to Dunkirk and find a boat home. Clear?"

Growls of agreement greeted Scottsdale's words.

"Good. Pack your gear and wait for my orders. Sergeant Grant? With me."

Scottsdale and Grant moved away. "How are they?" Scottsdale asked.

"They'll hold, sir," Grant said carefully. "Everyone could do with a rest."

"We all could. They'll be plenty of time for that when we get back to England."

"They'll be fine until then. For the moment there's too much to do to be thinking about anything else, sir. And I'll keep them busy."

"Good, thank you, Sergeant. We'll be moving to Fromelles where we'll get further orders. For now, try and find some rations. Send Marsh but be quick," Scottsdale raised a finger. "And for god's sake be careful. Use my name with the Quartermaster but now is not the time to be had up by the military police for pilfering a chicken."

Grant looked offended. "They'll be none of that, sir. No MP would get anywhere near the lads."

Scottsdale laughed. "Good. Wait for me here." He strode off to locate Jock and came across him sitting in between some tents sipping, inevitably, on a tea. Seeing Scottsdale, he rose languidly to his feet and smiled. Scottsdale took in his friend, eyes red and sunken, streaked with grime. He imagined he looked the same and stuck out his hand in greeting.

"Jock, good to see you."

"And you Arthur. Was positive Jerry had you this time. Rumours going around you've been off gallivanting around behind enemy lines?"

Scottsdale didn't want to go through the events of the last few days again. He wanted to forget it and forget Helene. He nodded. "Yes, very unpleasant. I thought that was going to be the end of me. Let's just hope there's no more of these jobs to do."

"Well, if there is, just think of the old saying," McDonald replied. "'Ours is not to wonder why, ours is but to do and die.'"

"You've a fine way of cheering a man up."

"Well, how about a cup of tea instead?"

"Much more like it." Scottsdale took the outstretched mug. The tea was sweet and hot, and he sipped gratefully. A couple of seagulls turned lazily on the wind, a reminder of their proximity to the coast and of the barrier they still had to cross to get home. A barrier the Germans had to cross too though, he thought grimly. That was coming next. And what then? The Nazi flag fluttering over Buckingham Palace? SS guards at Parliament? A sudden image of man speaking German in the House of Commons pinged into his mind and he shook his head. It was inconceivable. No, they'd have to stop them on the beaches. Wishing to rid himself of these thoughts he turned to McDonald.

"How have things been here?"

"It was, relatively, quiet for a couple of days. The odd spot of artillery but they've been concentrating farther east. You've arrived in the nick of time I'd say, they've been stepping up their artillery and sending more aggressive patrols. An all-out attack can't be far off. Samways was killed, obliterated by a shell. Barely enough of the man left to bury." Scottsdale tried to picture the hapless Samways but couldn't place him. "Who was Samways?"

"B Company. Ugly as sin. Used to run a boxing gym before the war."

Try as he might, Scottsdale couldn't picture him, and he felt a twinge of guilt. It was just a name to him but behind every name was a mother, father, son or daughter and a shattered life. Yet he had to shrug it off; there was so much death it simply wasn't practical to concern oneself with those who didn't directly impact your own narrow slice of war. A few weeks ago, he'd have chided himself harshly, seeing it as unfeeling but now that concern seemed trivial. "Maybe that's the best way. One moment you're there, the next you find out the answer to one of life's big questions."

"What happens next? The bright lights of heaven for the likes of you and me, I'm sure."

"I wonder, Jock. The things we're doing, how can you be so sure." He thought of the moment he'd driven his bayonet into the German's chest. The raw joy, the exultation. Surely taking any kind of pleasure in this was wrong. Yet, just as in the fight at the canal, he *had* felt joy. Not only that but it had made him more effective, made him a better leader.

"Because what we are doing is, in the end, right," McDonald said firmly. "We're defending ourselves and the world from a rapacious, vicious regime bent on conquest and Lord knows what else. Trust me, I've no great desire to be
here but it is our duty and God will forgive us."

"I hope you're right."

"I don't doubt it. Besides, my family always goes to heaven." He settled back and lit a cigarette. "I was assured of this on the

182

death of my father when I was seven and I've no reason to question that. Nanny was always right."

"Wouldn't wish to question her."

"If you'd met Nanny you may well question the 'her' part but nonetheless, certainly not a woman to be crossed. Frankly, sometimes the Germans seem quite tame by comparison."

Scottsdale chuckled. "Major Carter said you had the plan for getting home?"

McDonald smiled mirthlessly. "Yes, such as it is." He pulled a crate between them and overturned it to make a makeshift table. Undoing a pocket on his battledress he unfolded a map. "This is us," he said jabbing his cigarette at the map. "This is Fromelles, our next waypoint – shall I tell you how you'll know you're going the right way? Head for the bloody great pillar of smoke. That's Dunkirk."

Their conversation stopped as Lieutenant Berry appeared. Scottsdale's anger stirred the moment he heard the man's pompous tones. "Ah ha! The gallant Lieutenant Scottsdale. Well, well. Glad you've decided to return to the fray." His curiously high-pitched voice dripped with sarcasm. "What would we do without you?"

"Oh do be quiet, Berry," McDonald said wearily.

"And the trusty side kick." He bowed ironically. "Haven't you got somewhere else to be?" Scottsdale asked.

"No, Scottsdale, I do not. I'm *far* more curious about this little mission you've been on. Or to be specific that French tart I saw at the canal. Very careless Scottsdale, getting her killed. I love a good Frenchwoman, decadent don't you know."

Scottsdale's body was tense. "You need to be somewhere else, Berry," he growled.

Berry continued, sensing he had managed to hit a nerve. "Perhaps that's why the French are losing? Women dropping draws and men down with clap, what!" He roared with laughter.

"We're losing the war too in case you hadn't noticed," McDonald interjected.

"Don't be so bloody defeatist. It's an officer's duty to lead by example, you should remember that."

183

"Lead by example? I completely agree." Scottsdale was standing now, anger flowing through him. "Lead from the front, Lieutenant Berry, putting yourself in the same danger as your men. Not hiding behind them while they do the dying for you!" He finished with his finger jabbing into Berry's shoulder.

"The hell are you implying, Scottsdale," Berry blustered.

"I saw you at the canal, you miserable bastard. Hiding when they needed you."

"Damn your eyes, that's slander," Berry snarled, leaning in closer. As he did so the distinctive whiff of alcohol swept over them.

"Have you been drinking, Berry?" Scottsdale asked quietly.

"I had a glass of something at lunch," Berry replied dismissively.

"More than a glass by the looks of it. You're a disgrace."

"He's not worth it, Arthur," McDonald said. Scottsdale paused, looking at Berry's sneering face and felt nothing but contempt. He turned away. "That's right Scottsdale. Turn away from your betters. As soon as I'm home I'll be out of this dreadful unit, somewhere I can really be useful. Not playing nursemaid to some bloody Frenchies."

Scottsdale very clearly felt the moment he broke and made no attempt to stop himself. His fist was already closing as Berry stopped speaking. He could taste the anger and he revelled in it. McDonald was right, Berry wasn't worth it, but Scottsdale didn't care. The man revolted him and the thump as his fist landed in Berry's midriff was ecstasy, everything right rolled into a fist, all the pain and rage in him expressed through the purity of righteous violence. Berry staggered back, clutching his stomach and retching. McDonald shot up, a look of shock across his face, laying a placating hand across Scottsdale to prevent him following up. "For God's sake, Arthur."

Berry clambered to his feet. "I'm connected, Scottsdale," he hissed. "I know half of Horse Guards. As soon as we get back I'll have your hide."

"Damn your connections," Scottsdale growled. He didn't care. Berry was a drunk and a coward. The sooner he was gone the better.

"Just stay out of my way while we're still here and try not to get your men killed."

McDonald was straining to hold him back. "Arthur, this isn't the time!"

Scottsdale laughed. For the first time in what felt an age, he felt good. "Get out of here, Berry," he said scornfully.

Berry righted himself. He was trembling, but it was fear as well as fury. "Jumped up little sod," he hissed and limped off.

"That wasn't wise," McDonald admonished him.

"I don't care. That felt good and more importantly, it felt *right*." He exhaled loudly and gestured towards Dunkirk from where a steady plume of black smoke continued to bellow out. It was from the oil tanks the Germans had bombed and now acted as a menacing beacon. "We're the last remnants of the BEF, we're trapped against the coast and surrounded by the overwhelming mass of the German army." Scottsdale turned back to McDonald. "We've got more to worry about than him right now wouldn't you say?"

19

The first British soldier he shot after returning to the SS Totenkopf felt immeasurably significant to Schiller. The Tommy was in a strongpoint that was stubbornly resisting their assault troops. Moving into the line as part of a replacement detail, he found the men under his command wary. After the rapid speed of their advance the resistance in front of them was increasingly bitter as the British fought to hold the line.

"They're directly ahead, sir, set up in a fortified farmhouse," said the senior NCO. "We've assaulted twice but been beaten back."

"Tank support?" Schiller demanded.

"None left, sir. We did have a couple of Mark-IIs but they've been knocked out."

"And the enemy, what is their disposition?" "We've hurt them, sir, and there can't be many left but they're well dug in."

"What of the surrounding ground? Can we bypass and deal with later?"

The NCO shrugged. "They're covering the main road north, sir. We could but it would pose a risk to our armour and transport."

Schiller mused. A weakened enemy awaiting their fate, unlikely to be able to cover all their ground and space for a small team along the flanks. "They must be eliminated," he declared.

"I agree, sir, but we're waiting for the artillery to soften them up."

"Wars aren't won by timidity, Knochlein," Schiller snapped. "Assemble your squad. I will lead a small team under cover of the mortars. We only need enough fire to cover our approach. Send over five salvoes, spaced out. I'll attack when the final salvo is fired. When you hear me, bring the rest of the men. Clear?"

"Yes, sir."

Schiller nodded in satisfaction. "Good. Get the men ready." He turned to look at the NCO who was visibly exhausted. "Don't you see. This is all history. We are part of something never seen before and we *must* keep on until we have driven the British into the sea."

Schiller felt the familiar thrill of being back in combat as they moved stealthily forward towards the farmhouse. Evidence of the previous fighting was everywhere. Several bodies lay alongside the smoking hull of one of the tanks, its gun barrel pointing to the sky. The farmhouse itself was barricaded at the doors and windows. Scorch marks and pockmarks from bullets dotted the wall. A stable adjoining the main house housed the anti-tank gun.

The familiar rumble of mortars sounded, and they threw themselves flat, waiting for the detonations to pass, before rising and sprinting towards an abandoned tank that lay in front of the farmhouse. A shout sounded, and a volley of shots rang out, but the men made it safely. Schiller peered round the tank, ignoring the ping of bullets striking the metal of the tank. Several of his men fired back, keeping the defender's heads down while Schiller slowly raised his rifle. He could just glimpse a shape in the stable and he waited for the man to move again and when he showed himself, shot him through the head.

That was the signal. The squad charged the stable. A cry sounded behind as one of the men was cut down, but the rest convened around the door, flinging grenades inside. The detonations were followed by the cry of wounded men. Schiller was first through the opening. A British soldier appeared; they both fired but Schiller's was the truer aim and the man crumpled. Behind him the rest of the men surged past. A couple of shots sounded before Knochlein appeared, grinning triumphantly. "They've gone, sir, pulled out."

Schiller nodded. Losing the gun had made the position untenable. "Send a runner back to regiment. Tell them we've taken the strongpoint and the road to Estaires is clear but if we're going to go down there we need armoured support."

A low moan sounded from the corner of the room. A British soldier rolled over, his chest a bloody mess. "Please," he gasped.

"Water." Schiller looked at him without pity, taking out his pistol. He took two steps and shot the man through the head. Holstering his weapon, he closed his eyes and breathed deeply. He was on the path to redemption.

***

Scottsdale sat up, yawning hugely. Running a hand over his stubble, he suddenly felt a great urge to be clean shaven. Getting to his feet, he strode outside the house he'd been allocated. Since leaving the canal several days ago, they'd alternately marched or been driven ever further north towards the coast. Once or twice they'd been stopped and readied for localised counter-attack, but each time the familiar order to retreat had reached them. Men had continued to be lost to occasional strafing attacks and the chaos of the roads. Finally, however, they'd arrived at La Doulieu in the early hours and like so many places they'd passed recently it was largely deserted. Each house they entered was a snapshot of a lost life; food and drink ready on the table, a stove still alight, knitting left alongside. People hadn't fled until the last possible moment, but when they had, they'd gone in an instant. Outside, the scars of war were evident; destroyed buildings, cratered roads and deserted cars dotted the area.

Scratching his face, Scottsdale went in search of clean water, but a shout interrupted his search. "Officers to report!" Grimacing, he crammed his cap on and jogged over to the convent that served as battalion headquarters where the rest of the officers had gathered.

"Good morning, gentlemen," Major Carter boomed. "Why a good one I hear you ask? A bloody good question! We are surrounded by the enemy; our backs are to the sea and the food around here is execrable!" There were a few rumbles of laughter. "But that's fine by me. We're a fighting regiment and twenty odd years ago our fathers were killing Germans here and by God, we're going to do the same."

He paused to take out a cigarette, patting his pockets before Captain Revie came forward and proffered a lighter. "Obliged to you, John," Carter said. "Now, just south of here, the 2nd Division has been fighting hard to hold back the Germans. The Norfolks and the Royal Scots in particular have been in the thick of it, and intelligence says that they've come up against several armoured divisions, including the SS Totenkopf, a ruthless bunch of bastards by all accounts. Their sacrifice is keeping the corridor to Dunkirk open so it's absolutely vital work. Today they need our help." Carter moved to a board that displayed a large map of the area.

"We are here," he said, indicating La Doulieu. "And the enemy have had the bad manners to reach as far as Estaires, here. Between us is Vierhourt, which is the main jumping off point for the roads to the coast and into the rear of our forces. We can't allow them to take it." He grinned. "Now, even the dimmest amongst you will have noted that it isn't far from here. They must be stopped and it's up to us to do it."

A muted rumble of conversation broke out at the news. "Gentlemen!" Carter said, raising his arms for quiet. "Specifically, we will occupy the crossroads at Vierhourt, setting up a blocking force and denying it to the enemy." He turned to point at Captain Revie. "John, C Company will lead on this. You'll have a couple of platoons from B Company to make up your numbers. It's incredibly important we do this. If the Germans get through, then they'll roll right up the backsides of the BEF; and I'm sure you'll agree that isn't fun for anyone."

"Is there a chance the Germans will simply bypass the town, sir?" asked an officer, also airing the widespread fear that they would be surrounded and cut off.

"Unlikely. Although they've shown that tactically they want to avoid getting bogged down, they need possession of Vierhourt for their armour. It's the roads, you see. That's their best chance of stopping us getting out at Dunkirk."

McDonald raised a hand. "Who's in the town now, sir?"

"No idea," Carter said brusquely. "There are lost units everywhere, so there may even be some friendly forces around. However, if the enemy are there, we are to expel them. If not, to fortify it."

"Are we expecting tanks, sir?"

"Oh I should think so. Intelligence – if we can grace them with that description – says the 3rd Panzer Division and
SS-Totenkopf are concentrated locally, so yes, absolutely."

"Can we expect any gun support?"

"Yes, we've got some of the Norfolk Yeomanry and their guns. Not as many as I want, but it's better than nothing." Scottsdale and McDonald shared a look. Any antitank guns would be priceless in stopping an armoured German thrust.

Carter's tone became serious. "Listen, this isn't the best party we've ever been invited to. We'll be outnumbered and quite probably out gunned. But it's one I wouldn't miss for all the tea in China."

"Easy for him to say," McDonald muttered to Scottsdale.

"What's that, Jock?" Carter enquired.

"I said I can't wait, sir," McDonald said, raising his voice.

Carter joined in the chuckling. "Spoken like a true Scotsman! We've got an important job to do and I'm sure you'll all be up to the mark." He smacked his palm for emphasis. "The enemy presses forward on every side so we must buy time to withdraw. If it comes to it, I expect every man to fight to the last round. And if that does transpire then the sacrifice will be in the finest traditions of this regiment and the British Army."

The officers absorbed this in silence, considering that message. Scottsdale pictured that summer in La Rochelle before the war; how carefree he'd been and how unimaginable this world was then.

"How long do we have to hold, sir?" Captain Revie asked.

"Best information I have is rest of today and possibly tonight. Ultimately, we're still falling back, but we need to buy some more time."

The briefing broke up and the platoon commanders huddled round Captain Revie. They scanned the only map to hand; during planning it hadn't been considered necessary to provide comprehensive maps of this area. Instead, they had some detailed maps of Belgium and had become increasingly reliant on Michelin maps liberated from hotels to know the local ground.

"Arthur, your boys will lead," Captain Revie instructed. "We'll set up our HQ in the centre and push out defences onto the roads leading into the town. We'll need the gunners for that."

"When are they arriving, sir?"

"Any minute now. You get moving, we'll follow shortly."

Scottsdale and the men clambered into the Bren carriers and set off immediately. A few minutes later the lorries followed, containing the remainder of the company, along with the anti-tank guns. Scottsdale savoured the wind in his face that took away the lingering smell of burning and horse shit. Around them was a flat landscape of farmland, an occasional row of tall cypress trees dissecting the horizon. Everywhere were pillars of smoke that marked a burning tank or village.

They snuck across countryside, away from the major roads but even here the roads were crowded with refugees. Several times they had been forced to a stop until they'd cleared a path through. In one case, a man remonstrated furiously with them until he suddenly broke down, sobbing; it was a deep, anguished noise and the reason for his pain became apparent. Under a sheet in his cart lay a woman and a child, their blank stares mute witness to their fate. Scottsdale stared down, a sudden jagged pain in his stomach as Helene's face came to him. Rage and guilt washed over him, a rising tide that constricted his throat.

"Move the cart, Sergeant, now," he said harshly. He approached the Frenchman. "I'm sorry for your loss, Monsieur." The man waved a hand dismissively. And rightly, Scottsdale thought. There was no cure for that pain. He pushed thoughts of Helene away; he had to lead, not to remember.

A sign told him that Vierhourt was close and he gnawed his lip, considering the situation. He turned to Sergeant Grant, shouting to be heard above the noise of the engine. "When we debus, we'll secure the crossroads and set an outer perimeter."

"I'll give the Boys rifle to Marsh, sir," Grant suggested. "It'll need someone steady. Dalton can take the Bren with Pelham."

"Good," Scottsdale agreed. The Boys rifle was effective against lightly armoured tanks and vehicles, albeit at a close range, and would be a useful ally to the anti-tank guns. "Make sure he's got

191

cover and support as they'll target him." "Understood, sir. We'll give -"

"'Ware aircraft!" Their heads snapped up to scour the sky above and behind them. "Coming in from behind!"

Scottsdale picked out the dark spec in the sky. It had to be German. The only planes they'd seen had seen in weeks were German.

"Everyone off the road!" he roared. "Move! Move! Get into the field and find cover!"

The men scattered. Some went to ground in the ditch along the road, but Scottsdale hauled them up. "Not here, get into the fields!" His heart was pounding, and he looked up as a deep roar swamped them, the plane flying low over their heads. The distinctive glasshouse nose of the Heinkel He-111 swept by, its machine gun chattering. "Down!" Scottsdale shouted, flinging himself to earth, but they weren't the target. The bomber swept on and the plane jumped ever so slightly as two bombs wobbled out of its undercarriage. It was targeting the lorries carrying the rest of the men. The first bomb detonated with a flat crack but fell wide of the road. The lead lorry emerged from the smoke just as the second bomb detonated, and the back of the lorry leapt into the air before thumping back to ground. It veered wildly, tyres screeching before coming to an abrupt halt.

Scottsdale raised himself up, wiping down his battledress. He watched the Heinkel warily as it climbed away towards the east. "Anyone hurt?" he shouted but no answering shout occurred, and he puffed his cheeks in relief. The bomber was probably returning to base and seeing their little convoy had taken a chance to jettison its final payload.

"I am getting royally sick of being fucking bombed," Wilkins said sourly.

"You and me both," Pendle replied.

The lorry was being examined but had escaped serious damage and Scottsdale turned away, eager to get going again. He urged the men up and they clambered back aboard the carriers, setting off as fast as the roads allowed. Closing on Vierhourt fast, he felt the familiar tightening in his gut. "Concentrate now!" he hollered and the soldier manning the vehicle mounted Bren cocked the weapon and crouched low. Before today, Vierhourt was a sleepy place but now its position gave it importance and Scottsdale swallowed. Clusters of houses appeared, and they passed a neatly tended cemetery. He read the sign on the gates as they passed – *Tombes de Guerre de Commonwealth.*

The road narrowed, houses crowding either side. Neat gardens and flower boxes decorated the compact houses, but the closer the they got to the centre, the greater the visible damage. Several houses had been destroyed, probably by bombs, and they had to swerve around piles of rubble several times. Cars caught up in the maelstrom were blackened by fire and a dog bared its teeth at them as it slunk away; it had been tugging at something hidden by a low wall. A dead horse added to the sense of gloom and the men gripped their rifles tight. They trundled on, aiming for the church spire that rose up and marked the centre of most towns. As they did so, the houses became larger, faded orange brick walls marking their boundaries.

Scottsdale tensed as they rolled forward and came to a halt in an open square. He read the sign: *Place de la Mairie.* He wondered who Marie had been. In front of them a squat church sat solidly in the morning sun. A variety of houses, shops and hotels crowded around. A road cut through left and right, while he could see another disappearing off behind the church. This was the crossroads. He looked around. The *Hotel de Ville* was a grand building, resplendent in the sunshine. That would be their HQ but for now his responsibility was to push out checkpoints onto each of the main roads leading to the square. Sergeant Grant came to stand with him, slinging his rifle over his shoulder. "Not a mouse stirring, sir," he observed.

"Thankfully. But I'm sure that won't last long." "Life's rarely that good," Grant agreed.

"So let's get the men busy." He pointed south. "That's where they'll most likely come from."

"Or they'll try and flank us."

"At some point yes, but first they'll try to gain possession like us. Either way, I want checkpoints on each of those roads. How many Brens have we got?"

"Three, sir."

"And four roads. Let's assume that they aren't coming from the north and share out the Brens with the parties on the other roads. We'll have the carriers here until we know where the main assault is from."

"I'll form three parties, sir, and get them going."

"Good. The rest of us can start fortifying the town hall." Scottsdale gnawed his lip. They would be spread painfully thin, but they had to hold.

Grant threw a salute and soon groups of men moved off to take position. In the square, Scottsdale directed the remainder to start building a barricade and fortifying the *Hotel de Ville*; abandoned cars, carts and the chairs and tables from a café were all loaded together to form a defensive line in front of the town hall. Scottsdale paused, laying a hand on the faded brickwork still warm from the summer rays. He imagined Helene enjoying a drink in the sun and winced. And though he wished it didn't, Schiller's face, came to him too. A tremble of rage flickered inside him. Fear too, which never went away, but what he would need shortly was a killing rage.

From the upstairs window of the *Hotel de Ville*, Marsh shifted the Boys anti-tank rifle against his shoulder to a more comfortable position. Its elongated barrel poked forward, ending over five feet from where Marsh lay. The slide mounting and padded butt were designed to help absorb the savage recoil from each 0.55mm round but it was universally disliked for the kick. It needed a strong man to manage and Marsh sighted moodily down the barrel. Behind him Pendle lay stretched out on a large four poster bed.

"Bloody odd this," he said, wriggling around.

"Don't fall asleep on me," Marsh replied sourly.

"Some chance of that. Can't get comfortable on all this at all." Tutting, Pendle sat up and swung his feet onto the floor, leaving dirty mud across the sheets. "It's too soft." Picking up his rifle, he peered out of the window. Distant woods and farmland stretched further off while below he could see men strengthening the

194

barricade. He frowned thoughtfully. "Reminds me a bit of where I'm from round here. Do you know Chelmsford at all?"

"Not really," Marsh replied. "Had a cousin who lived that way though."

"Never mind that," Wilkins interjected. "Why do we keep getting the worst jobs? Chasing Frenchies and now stuck out here."

"Because we're here, that's why," replied Pendle.

Wilkins glanced at him and shook his head, popping a cigarette in his mouth. "Give us a light," he said to Marsh, who also lit up.

Settling himself back behind the Boys, Marsh exhaled through his nose. "What I'd give to be back in Ilford."

"Ilford? Knew lovely girl there once," Pendle said wistfully. "Blonde hair, lovely curves."

"I'm sure she was a rotter," Marsh said.

"Nah, she was lovely, really was. And very generous with her affections. Spent most of our time in bed."

"Sounds like the kind of girl I'd like to know," Wilkins said.

"Oh she was lads. Should have married her!"

Wilkins began to reply but the distinctive sound of a Bren gun cut through the air. They tensed, and Watkins scrambled forward, raising his rifle.

"Oh Christ," Marsh whispered. The Bren sounded again, intermingled with the pop of rifle fire.

"There's the answering fire," Wilkins observed, licking his lips. "Not long now."

Downstairs, Scottsdale waited nervously. "Into positions!" he shouted and strode to the centre of the square, peering anxiously south where the firing had come from. A shout sounded, and he hurried forward with Grant, meeting a panting solider heading towards them.

"Report?" Scottsdale demanded.

"Germans, sir," the private panted.

"I know they're Germans, Phillips – what strength?" Scottsdale said impatiently.

"Couple of armoured cars and motorcycles, sir. Looked like a scouting party. We caught them by surprise and knocked off a couple of the motorcycles before they withdrew."

"Well done. Anything else, report back to me immediately." Scottsdale turned to Grant. "And so it begins. "And so it does, sir."

They were interrupted by a shout and turned to see that the rest of the company were arriving, the trucks pulling up in the square. Thank God, Scottsdale thought to himself, and walked over to Captain Revie, who climbed down from the lead truck.

"Hello, Arthur. Situation?"

"We've just had first contact, sir, a small scouting party from the south. I've set up roadblocks on the main roads in but we're thin on the ground." He indicated the town hall. "I thought this would be our fallback, sir."

"Good." Revie thought for a moment. "Listen, I want you to take the guns and form a strong blocking force on the road from Estaires; that's where we can expect their main thrust from. Catch them before they even get here, so push out and find a good place. Clutton can advise you where to site his guns."

"Clutton, sir?"

"Yes, Lieutenant Clutton is in charge of the anti-tank guns. I want you to hold as long as you can, give them a bloody nose, then fall back. Alright?"

"Yes, sir," Scottsdale replied, his heart sinking a little at the idea of pushing out toward the enemy. At least they would have the protection from the guns. He moved off to gather the men, gazing around Vierhourt. The little *estimanet*, with its table and chairs outside for customers to sip their aperitif in the sun; the imposing town hall, martial tricolour rising lazily in the summer breeze; the butcher's shop with its smiling cartoon pig welcoming custom. Such an ordinary place, he thought. Yet appropriate too. Death, after all, was ordinary. It made no distinction and took them all, one way or another. The only difference now was how quickly it was catching up.

20

"Hello, I'm Clutton, 257 Battery, Norfolk Yeomanry. Although in truth, we can't even muster enough for a troop – that's four guns – I'm afraid." He had sandy hair and an easy going manner. "Glad to have you with us."

"Scottsdale, 2nd Essex. Glad to help and to be honest, the men will be delighted to have some gun support. How effective are they?" he asked as they walked over to where Clutton's 2-pound guns were being prepared.

"Well, a lot depends on how we are set up. Range, angle of attack and all that. But in broad strokes, the light tanks and your general AFVs are pretty easy meat, but anything much bigger and sometimes I feel we may as well be farting at it for all the good it will do. Although we did manage to frighten one crew into bailing out," he mused.

"They look good to an infantryman I can promise you."

"And you to us happily," Clutton smiled. "The problem we have is manoeuvrability. It isn't easy to move just shy of a ton of gun under fire.   Rather inconveniently, the Germans keep bypassing our gun positions you see."

"How rude of them," Scottsdale said drily.

"Very," Clutton agreed cheerfully. "But as I say, a lot depends on the set up. Once we're dug in we can inflict some real damage, especially if they're coming at us. So this place should suit." He stroked the gun barrel affectionately. "And Bessie here has some tricks."

"Bessie?"

"The gun," Clutton explained. "Named them after all the girls who broke my heart. Can't remember why but there you go. We've

197

had Lizzie, Maggie, Gertie and Betty, among others, but now only Bessie and Betty remain. Heartbreakers the lot of them."

"Let's hope they are equally devastating to Germans."

Clutton smiled. "They can be. Rather clever design actually. We've a 360 degree traverse which is handy and a very high rate of fire now that I've whipped this lot into shape. Isn't that right, Greaves?"

A corporal grinned back, revealing a large gap in his front teeth. "We manage, sir."

"That and the fact that these lovelies are known formally as the QF 2 Pounder – which stands for 'quick firing'." Clutton grinned. "So you see Scottsdale, I'm sure we can be useful, but we will need your chaps to see off any infantry."

"Understood. All we need now is a good place for your beauties to do their work."

"Shouldn't be too hard to find," Clutton said. "The key is making sure we aren't seen until they're close."

"Let's head out then. It won't be long before they come. How long until you're ready?"

Clutton looked over to his troop. "Imminently. Just filling up."

Scottsdale saw several jerrycans of petrol. "How much fuel do you have?"

"Plenty actually, one of the few things we aren't short of," Clutton replied. He smiled sadly. "Keep losing guns you see."

Scottsdale nodded. There wasn't much to add. Instead, receiving the signal from Clutton, he ordered their party to set off. They drove towards Estaires. The road stretched arrow straight away from them. As they neared the end of the town, the houses thinned out until there were only a few scattered farms. Scottsdale saw that Clutton was waving to him and gestured quizzically. With an emphatic nod, Clutton indicated he had found his ground and Scottsdale ordered them to halt. Jumping down from the carrier, he walked over to Clutton. "This will do?" he asked.

"Absolutely." They had reached the outskirts of Vierhourt and Scottsdale gazed out. The sun dappled road stretched away, lined by regularly spaced trees swaying gently in the breeze. The road was raised slightly from the surrounding fields. Clutton gestured further out, where woods spread either side of them. "Those woods are terrifically handy," he said enthusiastically. "Should channel them right down our throat, which is where we want them." He turned back and pointed at the last house. It was partially destroyed. "You see here?" he said, indicating the garden. "Our dastardly enemy has destroyed their vegetable patch which has created a lovely dip. It's perfect for our chaps as it gives us defilade. We can set up Bessie here and your lot can provide close support from the house. Over there," he added, turning to point the other side of the road, "looks a good spot for Betty. We can strike the road from both sides. Can I trouble you for some of yours to support Betty?"

Clutton was gesturing towards the treeline, which offered a degree of cover, but Scottsdale frowned as he looked it over. "I'd be worried about your silhouette there, if I'm honest," he observed. "My men can get low, but a gun will stand out."

Clutton smiled delightedly. "We'll make a gunner out of you yet, Scottsdale! Quite so, but we have one final trick available. We carry around some of our own camouflage. Attaches to a bracket on the front of the gun. Once that's up, it will help us blend in with the surrounding shrubbery."

Scottsdale nodded. "Good." He beckoned to Sergeant Grant. "Send a section to cover Betty."

"Betty, sir?"

"The gun, Sergeant."

A section under Corporal Townsend began digging in as Clutton's men manoeuvred the guns into position. Straining and cursing, they finally positioned the guns to Clutton's satisfaction, while the rest of Scottsdale's platoon fortified the house and dug slit trenches in the garden. Gesturing everyone to take position, Scottsdale trotted out in front of them. From the road their position was well concealed, and he returned to Clutton.

"Excellent," Clutton said with satisfaction. "Once they know where we are then it's a whole different ball game. The thing is you can't, happily, see a great deal out of the slit of a tank once they are buttoned down tight. God willing, we can get them close before they find us."

"And hit them hard," Scottsdale said grimly. "Unless we can force them back entirely we'll have to leave Betty and Bessie here. I don't want to be caught trying to lug those back with a couple of panzers breathing down our neck."

Clutton looked pained. "Yes, I dare say you're right." His face cleared at once, however. "We'll just have to push them back then," he added cheerfully before rummaging around in the carriage of the nearest gun, emerging with his steel helmet. He took of his cap, with its distinctive royal cypher that signalled the unit's relationship with King George VI and crammed his helmet on. "Time to get the battle bowler on."

Scottsdale smiled. The time to put his helmet on would have been while they were travelling to the battle, but Clutton was hard to dislike. The guns, even with their limitations, were welcome and from their fixed position he was confident they would be able to hurt any German column approaching. The key would be the timing. Pull back too early and they would throw away their advantage; too late and they would be cut off, surrounded and cut down.

Scottsdale stuck out his hand. "Aim true."

"I always do," Clutton replied. "Opened the bowling you see."

Scottsdale laughed and headed across the road to the house. Grant reported that the men were ready, and Scottsdale settled down to wait. Checking his rifle carefully, he briefly closed his eyes. Before he could stop it, an image of Helene flashed before him. He shook off the thought of her and opened his eyes to gaze down the road. To where the enemy was beginning to stir.

**

Schiller stood erect as feverish activity continued around him. He mused how war could turn the most insignificant place into a pivotal setting for the outcome of a battle. Vierhourt was about to add its name to that list. Their scouts had come back bloody. That meant the British had arrived first and would have to be expelled. Schiller and the men of Infanterie Regiment 1, together with tanks and men from the neighbouring 3rd Panzer Division, had been assigned the task of taking the town. He'd felt a fierce joy as they'd rumbled forward earlier that morning, bumping over the roads and waving at the Luftwaffe who soared above them.

"Soon we'll go and introduce ourselves properly to these Tommies," he shouted out and was rewarded with a few chuckles, although more than one solider stared into space. They had endured several days of brutal fighting and Schiller knew that they had to keep moving to maintain their momentum. He turned to Untersturmführer Kohler, who was gazing pensively towards Vierhourt.

"If they've had time to dig in, this could be difficult, sir. We could use some Stukas or some artillery to soften them up."

"We could always do with Stukas," Schiller said dismissively. "But we have to move quickly, so we'll do this ourselves."

"Of course, sir," Kohler replied hastily. "What are your orders?"

"As soon as the tanks are ready, we'll move off. Usual drill; we support the tanks and take care of any infantry or anti-tank resistance. If we can break them quickly then there's nothing to stop us rolling into the rear of the British Army." Schiller smiled mirthlessly. "That would be a spectacle."

"It would indeed, sir." Kohler paused. "I can't help but think if we hadn't stopped, we could be at Dunkirk by now."

Schiller glanced at his subordinate. The order to halt had left many baffled, although the chance to rest was welcomed too. Yet in their division was a lingering sense of bitterness. After establishing bridgeheads over the canal at Bethune, they'd been forced to withdraw, only to assault the same ground two days later. It had been a costly error.

"Possibly," he allowed, "but it doesn't matter anymore. The division is relying on us. Are the men ready?"

"Yes, sir."

"Good. We'll move shortly."

Schiller checked his watch and tutted before striding over to where the tanks were laagered. The sound of diesel engines and sharp tang of petrol filled the air and he breathed deeply, running his hand over the flank of a Panzerkampfwagen III being made ready. They were truly magnificent beasts, he thought. Finding the company commander, he nodded in greeting. "When will you be ready?"

"Within the hour. We've got a few mechanical issues. What news of the Tommies?"

"Waiting for us," Schiller replied grimly. "A patrol was shot up, so we can expect infantry but there's no sign of any armour."

"Good. Because my orders are to take the town quickly and I'll need you there straight away. If there are antitank guns then we need to destroy them, fast."

"Understood. We'll be close by when the fighting starts. If you can cover, we will close and take the ground." "Excellent. See you in Vierhourt."

Schiller inclined his head and walked off, gazing down the road. A lovely summer's day was in full bloom. He grinned wolfishly. Men would die today; it was a killing day.

***

Scottsdale rubbed his eyes. It wouldn't be long before the assault came. A stillness hung over the position and his stomach rumbled. Rummaging around in his pack, he bit into a biscuit, wincing at the rock-hard consistency. Washing it down with some warm water, he watched as cigarette smoke wafted lazily up from the trench the men had dug in the garden.

"Never saw the appeal myself," Pendle said as Davenport exhaled.

"No better time to start, Billy," Davenport said cheerfully. "Does wonders for hunger and calms the old nerves a treat." He proffered the cigarette to Pendle with a raised eyebrow.

"Nah, I think I'm ok ta."

"Your loss," Davenport replied.

Pendle's stomach growled, and he grimaced. "I'm bloody starving."

"You're always hungry, Billy. Didn't they feed you before the army?"

"They aren't bloody feeding me now, so it makes no bones what happened before." He pointed at Davenport with his bayonet. "You know what the problem is don't you?"

"I've a feeling you're about to tell me."

"It's all those rear echelon spivs. Safe as houses behind the lines *and* they get their dirty paws on the supplies first. We just get the muck that's left."

"Yep, and muck it is too. Here we are getting shot at and they can't even give us any good grub." He shook his head. "Needs to be sorted out that."

"Some chance."

"Never mind," Davenport said with a grin. "We'll just have to slot a couple of Jerrys and get our hands on their sausages."

Pendle sighed. "What a way to get a proper meal."

To Scottsdale, their loose line was pitifully thin; a platoon of tired men with a couple of anti-tank guns and machine guns. Another blow had come when he'd been informed that their supply of high explosive shells for the 2inch mortars had been lost in the chaos of the retreat. Taking off his helmet to scratch his head, he stared up at the bright blue sky. The very worst of weather. Nothing to impede the Luftwaffe as they laid waste to France; soldiers, towns, villages, people, dogs, horses, cattle. Nothing was exempt, nothing spared in the onslaught.

Sergeant Grant approached and saluted. "You look very serious, sir."

"Oh, you know how it is." Scottsdale smiled. "Probably just thinking too much."

"Thinking too much rarely helps these situations, sir."

"As ever, the font of wisdom, Sergeant. How are the men?"

Grant shrugged. "Same old. Tired, hungry. But there's fight in them."

"Glad to hear it, because we're going to need it."

"I've put the transport a little way back, sir," Grant said, gesturing behind them. "And although they lost the HE, we've got plenty of smoke for the mortars. Gurney and Hudson have set it up."

"Good. It'll be needed. The trick is going to be getting back to Vierhourt. We'll need to judge it just right otherwise it will get very unpleasant, very quickly."

"Sounds familiar, sir," Grant replied with a ghost of a smile.

"Truly, Sergeant, truly." Scottsdale's tone turned serious. "I want you on the left flank. Look to me for when we pull back, but the main thing is to keep their infantry off the guns."

"How long are you planning to hold?"

"Depends on what comes down that road, but if we can hurt them and fall back, then we've done our job."

Grant nodded. "In that case, sir, I'll get myself in position." He saluted and moved over the road, leaving Scottsdale to return to the partially destroyed farmhouse. As he did so, he glanced up and his eye was taken by the winking of sun on metal. Shading his eyes, he followed the vapor trails that weaved across the sky until he saw two dark shapes. It was impossible to know but he felt strongly it was a British plane being pursued. It dipped and bobbed but the hunter gracefully followed each attempt at evasion in an ethereal, deadly dance. It was completely silent here, but he wondered how it sounded inside the cockpit; the buffeting of wind, the clanging of bullets striking metal, the ominous cough of an engine mortally struck. That realisation building that your time had come as the acrid black smoke from a plane beginning to die engulfed you. Rising above it, the triumphant tattoo of the enemy's machine gun on your fuselage. Scottsdale stared unblinking until his eyes watered. Bail out, he silently urged, as the plane nosedived. Fire engulfed the cockpit; he prayed the pilot was dead. He felt a sickening sense of shame and rage, unsure why. Was it because it reminded him of Geoffrey Deacon? Or just because it was another sign of the enemy besting them. He turned away, lest his anger betray him to the men whom he knew still looked on him warily.

Well, damn all of them. Damn the Germans, damn Lord Gort and the BEF. Today he was going to fight, fight for Helene, fight because that's what meant something right now, because, even though he knew logically it wouldn't, perhaps he would find some relief in the maelstrom of battle.

Reckoning

***

The runner threw up a salute. "We are moving out at 1300, sir. Please ready your men."

"Understood," replied Schiller, and waved the man off. He checked his watch. Fifteen minutes. "Kohler!"

Kohler hurried over. "Yes, sir?"

"We move out at 1300. Get everyone on the trucks."

Kohler ran back and began issuing orders. The soldiers who had been languishing in the sunshine roused themselves. A last cigarette was smoked, a letter home carefully tucked into a pocket. Helmets were crammed on. Schiller could feel the nervous energy flowing amongst them. It was something they'd been used to these last few, heady weeks. And largely it had been triumphant, their tactics working time and again. Find the enemy, concentrate their armour and attack quickly in overwhelming strength. The rapier thrust had been blunted recently but they had supreme confidence in their high command and their officers. Though their fatigue sapped them, the tonic of victory kept them moving.

The throaty roar of multiple twelve-cylinder engines coughing into life sounded. They ticked over, revving engines growling. Black smoke drifted into the air and tank commanders spoke into their transmitters, asking for final checks. Schiller looked at the tanks as they moved out and clenched his fist. It was time. "Let's go!" he roared.

Their column rumbled forward. They knew that the Luftwaffe ruled the sky and kept their hatches open to allow a breeze in. It was stifling hot inside the tanks and incredibly loud. Once combat was joined and smoke filled the buttoned down tank, it became a dark, humid box that coated the men with sweat and dirt. Yet briefly they were able to roll forward unhindered, only the dust of their convoy to irritate them. The squat shapes lumbered forward, the dull panzergrau colouring blending into the surrounding fields. Their tracks left smears across the ground before they turned onto the road to Vierhourt. In the van were the tanks, followed by the Schutzen, the motorised infantry, in their lorries, together with the men of the SS-Totenkopf. The men swayed in the back of the trucks.

They were being asked for one final effort, to break into the rear of the British as they fled towards Dunkirk; to deliver the coup de grace that could end the war.

21

Scottsdale's head turned. A low hum was growing, and he swallowed dryly. Looking round, he saw that the men had made the connection too. Davenport took a last lingering drag on his cigarette before flicking it away; McManus checked his magazine and reloaded his rifle. Clutton raised his hand in half salute before disappearing out of sight. Across the road, men hunkered down, cocking Bren guns and Boys rifles in preparation. Unmistakably, the rumble of diesel engines and shriek of metal moving against metal was coming closer. Scottsdale's gut tightened. Emerging from the faint haze shimmering in the distance, indistinct shapes firmed into the grey shapes of the enemy. Men shifted. A tightness had settled over the infantrymen that only the sight of enemy armour can provoke. Scottsdale uttered a short prayer and it reminded him of Father Curzones cynical words to him. "Everyone is a believer when the shooting starts."

The pachyderms ground forward, the deep rumble from their guts reaching the British soldiers clearly. A pennant fluttered energetically on one of the leading tanks. Scottsdale hoped Clutton had marked it as it would be the German commander. It was up to Clutton to begin the engagement, yet the tanks rumbled ever closer, and Scottsdale shifted uneasily. He could make out details of individual machines; the shiny scars on the snout of the lead tank, its cannon turning slowly left and right, were clearly visible. Every hatch was battened down now it had closed on the enemy, and it bristled with menace. The convoy stretched out; tanks, lorries and half-tracks in a winding line. He looked down it and swallowed, waiting for Clutton and his guns.

"Fire the bloody gun," Marsh muttered.

The sun glinted off metal. Sweat dripped down

Scottsdale's back and he couldn't control the tick in his leg. He remembered his advice to Clutton; leave it late, make the first rounds count. Now he was living that advice and every second grated as the enemy hove into view. Across the road, Pendle watched, spellbound, as the shrubs and grasses around him trembled at the vibration of the tanks. The antitank gunners, hidden behind the armoured shield of their 2pounder, waited for the command to open fire. Acting as Commander, No.1, Clutton picked out their target, assigning the range, direction and lead required. It was a Panzer Mk-II, one of the quicker but relatively lightly armoured tanks in the German divisions. The number 312 was inscribed on its turret, revealing it as the second tank from the first platoon of the regiment's third Leichte Panzerkompanie and it was now located in the telescopic sight of the gun. The gunner, No.3, squinted through it from his seat on the left side of the gun, traversing the handwheel between his knees, the barrel moving gently as it tracked the tank. The loader, No.2, had already fed an armour piercing shell into the breech from his position on the right side. A tracer fuse allowed the gun commander to spot the trajectory of the round. Clutton stared in rapt attention at their target as it inched forward. The round had to count and so, scarcely breathing, he waited until the final moment before leaning forward and saying, softly but clearly.

"Open fire."

The gun No.3 depressed the left foot pedal and with a sharp crack, the gun recoiled. The round streaked across the open ground, travelling at over 2,600 feet per second and struck the tank. It was critical to penetrate the armour, as the shells were designed to explode only after doing so, and it was why Clutton had left it so late to open fire. Unable to see the British defence, the German column had entered the lethal radius of the 2-Pounder. Clutton's aiming point was not straight on where the strongest armour lay, but from the flank, and the shell sliced through the weaker armour. The driver and loader were riddled with shrapnel as the shell obliterated the gearbox, sending thousands of shards of hot metal ricocheting around the interior. The commander, seated in the turret, screamed in pain as his legs were peppered. The tank veered drunkenly to one side, smoke and flames boiling up from the open wound in its flank. Hauling himself up, the commander threw open an escape hatch and fell out as ammunition inside the tank began to explode.

"Open fire!" Scottsdale shouted, and a larger orchestra of violent noise was unleashed. Bren guns rent the air, joined by the shaper reports of the rifles. "Target the infantry!" he shouted as return fire began to hum around them. Bullets whipped through the long grass and hedges, smacking into the house.

The second tank swerved away, engine pitch rising, but the crew of Bessie was waiting. The gun rocked as the breech recoiled, ejecting the spent cartridge with a waft of white smoke. The gun No.1, observing the strike of the shot, cursed as the round ricocheted away. Their target was a Panzer Mk-III and its heavier armour and surge of speed saved it. Now it turned towards the gun, her position betrayed by the discharge of smoke and tracer. Feverishly, the gun No.1 shouted corrections as the tank halted, rocking back as its gun barrel searched for their position. Scottsdale felt he could hear the sharp cry – *"Fieur!"* – followed a split second later by a spout of flame leaping from the 37mm cannon. Simultaneously the 2-pounder fired, striking the tank. A horrible screech sounded, chunks of grey metal shearing off into the air. Scottsdale looked back towards the gun; the tank's shell had flown over the position, exploding harmlessly behind. Yet the tank came on, heading directly towards the gun position, machine gun firing, intent on snuffing out the danger. Another round flew past the tank harmlessly; the gun No.1 looked up as the tank closed, nose dipping as it went over a rise in the ground. "Aim for the tracks!" he shouted and the No.2 frantically worked the elevating handwheel to shift target.

"Fire!" Greaves shouted, striking the tank which swerved violently and halted.

"Hit it again!" the loader shouted as the panzer, still full of fight, swung its cannon towards their position.

"Come on, come on," Scottsdale muttered but the 2pounder rocked again, the round striking the weak part of the armour where the turret joined the chassis. The cannon immediately stopped moving and moments later the crew bailed out.

"Crew in the open!" Grant shouted.

Pendle tracked a German as he dropped down, his distinctive black uniform stark against the green grass. "Not so fucking brave without a tank between us now are you," he whispered and squeezed the trigger, watching in satisfaction as the man arced his back and fell.

The tanks now spread out either side of the road, exchanging fire with the British line. Scottsdale ducked as a tank shell struck the house, shattering the upstairs bedroom. A cloying smoke lingered above the fields; darker shade bellowing from the burning tank mixing with the lighter shade from the tanks' smoke generators. The German infantry scurried forward, using the ditches for cover. Machine gun and rifle fire slashed through the treeline and thudded into the house. The platoon fired back rapidly, trained to fire, repeat and fire faster than anyone else in the world, continuing a tradition that spanned the Peninsular War and Mons.

Scottsdale reloaded, grimly satisfied. They were holding and had inflicted some damage. He gnawed his lip; judging when to disengage would be the trick now. Levelling his rifle, he rose back up and fired into the maelstrom in front of him, aiming for the indistinct shapes of the infantry. As he did so, two tanks darted forward from the curtain of smoke, much closer to the British lines. They belched fire and he watched in horror as shells exploded in the treeline, exactly where the second gun was sited.

***

Schiller waved the men forward. "Out of the ditches!" he screamed, grabbing the men and hauling them up. "Get up you bastards! Move!" He waded forward, oblivious to the crack of fire that whistled around him; his sleeve twitched at the passage of a bullet. Around him the panzers manoeuvred, firing past the burning carcass of their lead tank. He could see explosions landing in the British positions ahead; a house was on fire, but they had to get further forward and engage the enemy infantry. "Get the machine guns set up!" he shouted and grimaced as men frantically placed their guns, snapping out rapid bursts of fire to provide cover.

As soon as the first shots rang out, the convoy had scattered. The lorries and half-tracks rapidly disgorged their infantry while the panzers spread out into the fields either side of the road. They immediately initiated their smoke generators before engaging the anti-tank guns; working in tandem, lighter tanks to the fore while the heavier tanks provided cover. To their rear, the platoon commander zipped back and forth in his modified Panzer-Mk I, trying to pick out the anti-tank locations and direct his tanks onto them. It was an unceasing ballet glimpsed through fire and smoke; tanks worked in pairs, one pair covering as the other moved, before swapping roles. They swung diagonally across the front, changing speeds and angles to throw off the aim from the gunners, all the while seeking to knock out the main points of enemy resistance.

Hearing the rising cry of revving engines, Schiller looked to his right where two shapes emerged to surge towards the tree line, converging on the enemy anti-tank gun. The sharp spark of tracer flashed out again, striking the lead tank just as it fired, causing it to veer to one side, its own shell landing harmlessly in front of the British line. Yet in the second tank, the commander ordered a halt and screamed the order to fire. The stubby snout of the 20mm Kampfwagenkanone L/55 auto-cannon steadied before belching an explosive shell at high velocity at the gun; it exploded alongside, tossing the gun commander aside, while the loader reeled backwards, bright blood seeping through the fingers clamped to his face. Part of the gun shield was torn away to spit metal shards out and the gun came to rest on its side. A mangled wreck, spattered with blood, replaced a tank killer.

Schiller shouted in triumph, and the men surged forward. He could hear the jingle of equipment and harsh panting of the men behind as he led the charge. "Onwards!" he screamed, glancing to his left where a panzer on the raised road jerked back as it fired, before a shell crashed into its nose. Metal sprayed high into the air. Inside the tank, stacked ammunition caught fire, triggering multiple explosions. The tank rocked savagely as it began to die. Schiller turned back to the treeline, still several hundred yards ahead; the shrubbery was dancing as machine gun fire tore into it and he picked out the dinner plate shaped helmets of the enemy. He raised his rifle but swore as he stumbled on a root, landing on all fours. He growled in anger as something heavy fell on him; a heartbeat later the chatter of a Bren gun reached him, the meaty thud of bullets striking flesh following. The men dropped to the ground, following Schiller into the ditch. Blood stained the grass around them.

"We're pinned down, sir!" Kohler shouted.

"Keep moving!" Schiller said furiously.

The men kept themselves low, firing towards the trees and the house. They moved in short rushes, sprinting a few yards before throwing themselves flat. Smoke gave them some cover but one man was struck, falling in agony to the ground. Glancing ahead, Schiller saw that the gun killing tank had been savaged in return by the British and was limping backwards into the smoke. He cursed savagely; they were being bogged down and the British were still fighting. Turning, he shouted to be heard over the din. "Keep on firing! We have to keep their heads down!"

***

Scottsdale coughed and wiped his sleeve across his streaming eyes. Smoke was leaking from the burning roof and beginning to thicken uncomfortably. He staggered as another crash shook the house. Columns of dust drifted lazily down, illuminated by sunlight shining through a neat row of bullet holes across the front wall. The German fire was making movement difficult. Most of his men were already dug into the garden but the fire meant the reminder had to abandon the house.

"Corporal Davenport!" he shouted, and Davenport appeared, crouching down. "Get everyone into the garden.

Spread out in the trenches. Got it?"

"Yes, sir."

"Good. Get them moving." Scottsdale laid his rifle on the window and fired rapidly towards the German infantry. Beside him Private Bingham fired bursts from the Bren, his assistant, Stewart, calling out targets and ready to change the barrel if it overheated. From the corner of his eye Scottsdale saw the rest of the men leaving the house. They crouched low, inching out into the trenches. At the end of the garden, armour piercing shells spat out as the crew of Bessie, under the energetic supervision of Clutton, loaded and fired in a manic and deadly game of cat and mouse with the panzers. The tanks fired and moved, trying to work their way into a killing shot, but the gun survived, sheltered by its position. The constant smoke offered further relief from the probing panzers and allowed Clutton to track and respond to the most immediate threats, calmly offering corrections to his crew.

With relief Scottsdale saw the men were safely out of the ruined house; it was now their turn. He turned to Bingham. "You first, Private. When I give the word -" The rip of machine gun fire slamming into the house snatched his words away. A stitch of bullets mangled the windowsill, chewing through the wood, spitting misshapen shards out. Bingham flung his hands to his face, falling to the floor; a piercing shriek filled the room as Stewart tried to hold Bingham down, but he was thrashing around. Scottsdale scrambled over too, trying to see the damage but Bingham was bucking wildly. Dark blood was weeping from multiple wounds, through his fingers, down his neck and face.

Desperately, Scottsdale fought to calm him. "Hold still Bingham! Hold still!"

"My eyes, oh Jesus, I can't see!"

On his knees, Scottsdale tried to prise Bingham's hands away from his face. They were slippery with blood and Bingham's fear lent him strength.

"Let me do it, Private! It's the only way to help you!"

Bingham whimpered, and Scottsdale ducked as another patter of bullets lashed the house. "Get a dressing," he snapped at Stewart. Finally, Bingham's hands came free and Scottsdale involuntarily flinched, grateful Bingham couldn't have noticed; his face was riven by the splinters. He moaned, and Scottsdale splashed some water over his face.

"Let's put a bandage on it, Private," he said gently. It was plain Bingham would never see again, even if he survived. "We'll get you bandaged up and get the medics to look after you, ok?"

Bingham sobbed brokenly, panting fast. Shock was setting in and he had an ominous pallor. "Give me a hand," Scottsdale said to Stewart, and they took Bingham by the braces, dragging him outside and laying him flat.

"You're safe here," Scottsdale said. "We'll get you to the medics as soon as we can." He rose, anxious to get back to the line but Bingham gripped him hard.

"Please, sir. Please," Bingham whispered.

Scottsdale looked down at the terrified man; his gut twisted, sick at leaving him there, broken and bloody but there was nothing more he could do. "I have to go but we'll be back for you. Come on, Stewart." He tugged his hand out of Bingham's grasp and scuttled back towards the line, relief and guilt washing over him.

Scottsdale slid into the slit trench, taking in the activity around him. The rattle of machine gun fire and crash of the surviving anti-tank gun continued, their defiance answered by the enemy's cannon and rifle fire. The line seemed stable but, with one gun out of action and more men wounded, they couldn't hold out much longer. Bingham had not been the only man laid out.

"Runner coming, sir!" Scottsdale spun round and saw Private Deighton sprinting towards them. Gun fire swept the road as he swerved towards where Scottsdale was waving. With a final leap, Deighton made it into the trench. "Christ," he said, panting heavily.

"Well?" Scottsdale demanded impatiently.

"Orders, sir. You are to withdraw to the rest of the company."

Scottsdale nodded in relief. "Tell Captain Revie message understood, will commence withdrawal as soon as practical." He gnawed his lip as Deighton once again braved the fire and hared off back down the road.

Now it was a question of timing. Scrambling out of the trench he scuttled on hands and knees to the gun position. It was hardly elegant but infinitely preferable to being shot. He rolled into the old vegetable garden where Clutton continued to direct his team.

"We seem to be in something of a stalemate!" Scottsdale shouted as he peered out towards the fields. "Indeed!" Clutton replied before holding a hand up to Scottsdale and speaking to Greaves. "Keep an eye on that chap on the right flank, he's a chipper bugger." He turned back Scottsdale. "They can't do their usual trick of driving round us because of those woods, so as long as they don't get a lucky ball through, I think we can hold."

"Well, we've got our orders; we're falling back. I want to be ready to start pulling back as soon as we can."

Clutton nodded. "Fine. I wouldn't be surprised if Jerry's planning the same; they prefer to fall back and find another way round in my experience. Won't be easy, though. If they see us pulling off, they'll be up here quicker than a rat up a drainpipe."

"How long do you need? We've got plenty of smoke we can use."

"On a good day, my lads could get the guns back on a trailer tow inside ninety seconds – but this is demonstrably not those conditions. And Betty is placed very awkwardly."

Scottsdale paused. "I'm afraid your other gun has been knocked out."

Clutton blanched. "Ok," he said after a brief pause.

"Just us then. Well, we can get moving pretty sharpish, but I'd appreciate any cover you can give."

"That's the one thing we can do. We'll put down smoke. You pull back first, rest of us will follow."

"I'll get my chaps ready then. When I see your smoke, we'll start packing up."

"Good. I know I don't need to tell you but don't dawdle. Once we reach the trucks we're going to be gone, so make sure you're with us."

"Don't worry. Whatever happens I'm not leaving Bessie to these barbarians."

Scottsdale nodded and moved off. He sent McManus to alert Sergeant Grant on the other side of the road and summoned Gurney and Hudson to him.

"Get the mortar. When I give the word, throw down as much smoke as you can manage. We need it right across the front understand?" They nodded and set up the 2-inch mortar. It was a small, ordinary looking metal tube about 50cm long. Hudson simply propped it up and angled it towards the enemy, using the white line painted down the tube to help his aim. Hudson waited for Gurney to signal he was ready and then dropped the bomb with its distinctive four-finned tail down the firing tube. Hudson controlled the fire by depressing a small trigger lever and now the two fell into their firing rhythm, laying down smoke across their front. Each time, Hudson shifted the angle a few degrees.

Sensing their own fire slackening Scottsdale cupped his hands. "Keep firing! Keep pouring it on!" The enemy would guess they were pulling back but Scottsdale wanted to make sure they didn't press their attack. The fire intensified as the white cloud descended across the fields, obscuring the enemy. Bullets still whipped through the smoke but were largely high and flew harmlessly overhead. Scottsdale saw that Clutton was as good as his word and had immediately begun to prepare the remaining gun for transport. He gnawed his lip, judging his moment, beckoning Davenport to him.

"Leave a Bren crew and start getting the men back in the trucks. Go!"

Davenport called to the closest Bren team to join Scottsdale, and Privates Dalton and Pelham scurried over. They set the Bren up, firing through the smoke while Davenport moved rapidly down the line, stooping to touch men on the back and order them back. Singly and in pairs, the platoon jumped out of the ditches and trenches, keeping low and sprinting back to the trucks. Across the road was a similar story, Sergeant Grant sending men back until it was just the Bren teams and Scottsdale who remained. Scottsdale gazed anxiously forward, drumming his fingers on the stock of his rifle, dreading seeing tanks emerge but finally, with a surge of relief, he ordered the last of his men back. Running at full tilt he took Sergeant Grant's outstretched hand and clambered into the truck, avoiding the wounded laid out on the floor. A chorus of shouts told the driver all he needed to know, and the engine gunned as their small column fled back to Vierhourt.

22

The platoon commanders gathered around Captain Revie with the late afternoon light playing across their haggard faces. Around them lay the pastel-coloured frontages of the cafes that crowded the town square; the unassuming church bathed in the warm light, its modest bell tower poking skyward. A gaggle of birds lifted off, disturbed by the soldiers as they formed blockades along the narrow streets. In ordinary times the tables and chairs would be crowded on such a lovely summer's day, but ordinary times were a distant memory. Instead, scavenging dogs skulked through the wreckage of burnt out cars.

Scottsdale gulped down a mouthful of water, glancing at the other men; a palpable sense of exhaustion hung over them. McDonald was grimacing slightly as he listened, a bead of sweat limping down his unshaven cheek. Berry slouched alongside, twitching every so often at the distant crump of artillery. Since the incident at the canal he and Scottsdale hadn't spoken unless unavoidable in the discharge of their duties.

Captain Revie had adopted a permanent frown over the last few weeks. He spoke rapidly. "This is our redoubt," he said, indicating the town hall. "Each of you is in command of a blocking force on one of the roads that meet here. You're to hold them until relieved or ordered to retire."

"And if we don't get any orders, sir?"

"You heard the Major. We stay until our ammunition runs out."

"Can we expect any reinforcements, sir?" Berry asked.

"No. We won't have any artillery support either. It's just us and whatever comes down that road." Revie smiled bleakly. "We need one final effort gentlemen; to hold this damned place long enough to make a difference. We know how they like to fight so watch for any flanking manoeuvres. The advantage we have is this isn't tank territory; they like space. We can get at them with the Boys and with Clutton's gun. But watch for their infantry."

"Any more information on what we're facing, sir?" McDonald asked.

"Same as before. Elements of the 3rd Panzer and Totenkopf divisions are known to be operating in this area, so most likely they'll be your opposition." He looked sternly at them. "Make them pay for every yard and if you're getting overrun, fall back to the redoubt. Any questions?"

Scottsdale began to speak but stopped abruptly; the whistling of an incoming mortar was followed a spit second later by the crump of detonation. More bombs rained down, and the men scattered. "Spread out!" hollered Scottsdale, waving his arms as he raced away from the square. The glass frontage of a chemist's shop shattered, spreading lethal shards outward. A wave of dust washed over Scottsdale, and he threw himself into the nearest house, a pall of dirt coming with him. Scrambling back to the door on his hand and knees, he caught sight of a solider sprinting across the square, helmet clasped to his head with one hand, the other gripping his rifle. Scottsdale urged him into safety, but a bomb detonated beside him and when the dust cleared the soldier was sitting up groggily, having been flung to one side. Looking down, he started screaming, reaching his hands out imploringly. A bloody stump had replaced his lower leg. His screams reached into Scottsdale's gut before two soldiers emerged and dragged the soldier to safety, leaving a black trail along the ground.

One bomb struck the church, shattering part of the roof, but worse was to come. A great crack rent the air, and Scottsdale's head snapped up. Emerging from a pall of dust was the bell tower but it seemed soft around the edges and it took him a moment to release what was happening. To his rising horror, the tower was buckling, gaining momentum as it toppled sideways, a vast wall of brick and dust crashing down into the square. Scottsdale remembered the soldier posted there and swallowed. In regular intervals came the drawn-out whine of incoming bombs, followed by the crash of masonry. Some of the bombs landed in gardens and fields, others struck homes and shops. A dirty smoke enveloped Vierhourt as it was peppered with iron; men sought what refuge they could in cellars and under stairs. Scottsdale swore bitterly, knowing that this was only the prelude to the main assault. His only wish now was for that assault to begin so he could fight back, rather than helplessly endure this impersonal battering.

Sensing the firing rhythm was slackening, Scottsdale emerged into the sunlight; he had to get back to his platoon. He dodged down the road, darting from doorway to doorway to avoid the strikes that kept coming; at one point he felt the draught of an explosion but with a final surge he made it back to their position.

"Get ready!" he shouted as he ran through the position to his post. "That will just be the warm up, they'll be coming now!"

Mentally, Scottsdale ran over their position. They were covering the same road they'd travelled back on from the confrontation earlier. It led straight into the heart of Vierhourt and the square. A smaller side road led off at right angles before turning back and also ending back at the central square. Lieutenant Berry was positioned there to guard against being flanked. Scottsdale had decided to set up at the junction of these two roads. The junction itself was wide and irregularly shaped; as the main road approached the junction, it curved left and widened considerably, leaving a fifty-yard gap from the buildings on one side to the corner of the junction. The curve also meant that the buildings on the top side of the side road overlapped the junction and had an unimpeded line of sight back down the road. Similarly, the café that marked the corner was taken over and presented a good vantage point to engage any enemy coming up the road. Scottsdale's own position was across the road from the café. He'd also positioned some of the men in the tallest building next door; it contained a dressmaker's shop and the men settled down in the top floor, busy fortifying their positions. Loopholes were created, walls between houses knocked through and furniture scavenged to form solid defences and machine gun nests. They'd also constructed some rudimentary anti-tank obstacles, dragging cars and masonry into the road to form barricades. Even the craters created by the enemy mortar fire would help slow the tanks. And the tanks were the key; should they burst through the roadblocks then the infantry would swarm behind them and Vierhourt would fall.

The thought of tanks made him glance across to Clutton. He was based in a destroyed patisserie that commanded a clear view down the main road. The rubble of the front room provided natural cover and the gunners supplemented the defences with whatever was to hand. Since most of the building was already destroyed, it also made them a little safer from tank shells. Clutton straightened and waved a hand laconically. Scottsdale returned the gesture. He looked around; the men were quiet, flinching as occasional mortar bombs continued to explode. A final meal had been wolfed down and ammunition distributed. Marsh cradled the Boys rifle and the Bren gunners checked their barrels one last time. They knew the assault was imminent, and were tense in anticipation

"All ready, sir," Sergeant Grant reported. "As much ammunition as they can manage, and all the grenades distributed."

Scottsdale nodded. There was nothing else to say. He breathed deeply. Such a wonderful day. A gust of wind swept a paper down the street and he watched it sway and dance in the air. Taking out a cigarette, he bent his head. Just as he moved the cigarette to the flame, he paused. He could hear the familiar noise of engines; the sound of the enemy. His nausea came quickly, followed swiftly by the acid of his anger in his gut. Bastards. He lit the cigarette, inhaling deeply.

"Here we go again," Grant muttered.

Wilkins cleared his throat and spat. "Fucking place."

McManus mouthed the Ave Maria silently. "Pray for us sinners now, and at the hour of our death."

Weapons were checked, a final glance and nod shared among neighbours. Down the road, they caught the first glimpse of the enemy rolling towards them. Scottsdale peered through the binoculars he had inherited from a fellow officer who'd been shot the day before. The tanks were monstrous close up, inching forward, beetle like. Smoke drifted above their dark grey carapaces, while infantry trotted alongside, looking around warily. He focused on the lead tank as it swung onto the road towards them; it had the distinctive stubby howitzer of the Mk-IV and it loomed large in the binocular sights, crabbing menacingly forward, machine guns poking out like mandibles.

Without warning, it stopped and, as Scottsdale saw in minute detail, opened fire. Moments later the whine of the shell reached him, and it crashed down; in seconds their view was obscured by a thick curtain of smoke. Scottsdale surmised that it was a defensive measure to provide cover to the German column; they were taking no chances after their fight on the outskirts. The tanks' machine guns opened up too, spitting fire toward them. They were spaced out, and the lead vehicle edged forward, its cannon firing blindly through the smoke. Alongside, the infantry moved up in bursts, leaping from doorway to doorway, using the smoke as cover. Clutton's team fired back sparingly; they were unlikely to find a knockout blow at this distance and wanted to keep their position concealed as long as possible. One shell struck a house, bringing a section of rubble down on the soldiers following behind. More smoke was fired to settle over the British positions, but gusts of wind partially cleared the air. Bren teams targeted the infantrymen, their chattering rising above the crisper reports of rifles.

"Find the infantry!" Scottsdale roared through the gloom as the smoke covered them.

The heavy machine guns of the German infantry added to the din; a storm of fire flickered through the smoke and dust that was shot through by shafts of light from the sinking sun. The wide road allowed a second tank to bring its machine guns to bear and it fired through the smoke. Fire from both sides was wild, however, aim spoilt by the smoke and Scottsdale was more concerned with the infantrymen that was using the tanks and smoke to cover their advance. They were hunting Clutton and his gun, Bessie now living up to her name as Ordnance QF, Quick Firing, and the lightly armoured tanks were vulnerable as they closed. A Panzer Mk-I, never designed to be in a combat role but pushed forward to fill gaps in the armoured regiments, moved ahead, trying to make a dash for the junction. Armed only with machine guns, its 13mm armour could not withstand the antitank gun. Clutton grinned in satisfaction as it slowed and belched smoke from a rent in its side, quickly veering off the road before grinding to a halt. Hatches opened, and the crew bailed out, running the gauntlet of British fire. The next tank nosed past, shunting its mate aside, its cannon swinging towards the junction. It paused, rocked, and fired. The shell screamed down the road, slamming into a house, spraying brick and glass over the road. Scottsdale and the men sheltering alongside flinched.

"Infantry on the right!" Pendle shouted, and he and Wilkins fired together, seeking the grey figures which ran up the side of the road. They fired rapidly, sending the Germans to ground. Bullets whipped back in vengeful return, forcing them to duck back into cover. Upstairs in the dressmaker's shop, Private Dalton lay flat, absorbing the recoil of the Bren gun. From their elevated vantage point the smoke was thinner, and it enabled them to pick out the most advanced German infantry. A burst of fire threw down several who were closing, forcing others to go to ground. Scottsdale caught glimpses of the enemy entering houses either side of the road. Seeing a man carrying a machine gun, he brought his rifle up but snatched at the shot, cursing as the man disappeared.

Seconds later, an enormous crash sounded. "Christ," Scottsdale said involuntarily, looking across the junction. His heart lurched; the front of the building was ruined, and bright flames were already bubbling up, showing through the smoke that wreathed the house. He caught a glimpse inside, where a pale dust covered everything except for a spray of black splashed across the back wall. It was, he realised, blood. A soldier staggered out into the light, helmet gone. Scottsdale was transfixed. He couldn't take his eyes off the red shoulder flash that spelt out 'Essex' in gold letters. Below it, the rest of the man's arm had been surgically removed by shrapnel.

"Get down!" he roared desperately as the soldier moved into the road. But hearing the voice, the confused soldier instead moved towards it, blood dripping down his face. Immediately, Scottsdale tried to rise, making to go and drag the man into cover but an iron grip sank onto his shoulder.

"Leave him, sir!" exhorted Sergeant Grant.

Scottsdale spun round in fury. "Let go of me," he snarled.

"It's suicide, sir!" Grant replied desperately, hanging onto Scottsdale who was trying to shake him off, but a flurry of machine gun fire threw the soldier down. Scottsdale swore viciously and fired repeatedly, sending his hate to the enemy in the form of a stream of .303 bullets. He seethed, until his magazine clicked, and he ducked back, trying to clear his mind of the dead man.

***

Schiller growled at his men to keep moving. They were covered by dust and exhaust fumes. Smoke spiralled up from the battered town where the enemy waited in the ruins. Schiller was in the van, leading the assault groups who would be supported by engineers from the Pionier Kompanien. Their force had been split; two platoons of tanks and supporting infantry had been sent in a wide arc to try and find another way into Vierhourt but the bulk of the attack would rest with them.

As soon as the first gunfire had sounded, he waved the men forward. "Move! Quickly, now! Muller, Lahm, get the MGs set up!" A flurry of activity broke out, men hurrying forward. They had to gain fire superiority to allow the infantry to close in and overwhelm the British. Behind him came the deeper report of the infantry gun and he grimaced in satisfaction; the 75mm Leichtes Infanteriegeschutz had gone into action. It was a small, two-wheeled light howitzer that added firepower to their assault group. The stubby barrel, like a squashed nose, could maintain a high rate of fire and was light enough to be dragged into place. It was an effective weapon for close combat. The crew quickly set it up, using the range drum to target the junction at a distance of two thousand metres. They loaded high explosive shells, beginning to send down barrages towards the British.

Schiller ducked as machine gun fire spat toward them. He summoned Kohler to his side. "We need to clear the houses and find any anti-tank guns. Take the engineer squads for clearance but use gardens, roofs, whatever it takes to avoid getting pinned down. Clear?"

"Yes, sir," Kohler replied.

"Good. And spread the word; I don't expect the British to surrender. Shoot first and ask questions later."

They scurried forward, bending low. A tank rocked back as it fired towards the British. Running the gauntlet from doorway to doorway, the assault groups steadily advanced but as they closed so the danger from the British increased. Schiller saw one group rush forward, aiming to establish a bridgehead further down the street. Two men were flat, firing their MG-34, the loader feeding the ammunition belt in while the gunner squeezed the trigger, firing rapid bursts. The group hustled forward under this cover. Chips of stone flew from the walls as they were targeted; several men threw themselves into cover, bundling into houses but the braver ones kept going. Schiller clenched his fist, willing them on as they closed to within a few hundred metres of the junction. They sheltered behind a burning tank, panting hard. Schiller watched as the squad leader rose up, swerving round the tank, several men hard on his heels. Yet they were forced into the road by the heat of the tank and the hyena-like chattering of a Bren gun rang out, the gun scything them down into a bloody heap.

Angrily, Schiller fired down the street. His men were occupying the houses and shops one by one, and it afforded them cover. Yet Schiller also knew that shelter could paralyse a man; he had to keep them moving. "Only machine guns to wait!" he roared, entering a house and physically dragging two men up. "Keep going; find a way through to the next house." The men responded, some firing round doorways and windows as others darted up the road to the next house. Where possible, they also worked their way through gardens behind. One squad made substantial progress, crossing several gardens but a withering fire forced them to ground; unable to pinpoint the source of the fire, they had to withdraw.

Schiller glanced out as a tank lumbered past the window. Bullets pinged off its armoured hide, raising small sparks. The tank paused, fired and then continued rumbling forward. "Let's go!" he shouted and ran out, following the tank as it moved slowly down the street. It fired again, and he saw more smoke flooding the junction. With a burst of speed, he sprinted over the road, his men following and throwing themselves into cover, breathing hard.

Schiller poked his head out and assessed their situation. They were still four hundred yards away and the British fire was intense. One tank was on fire; another was moving steadily, trying to pin down the anti-tank gun. A round ricocheted off the tank with a loud clanging, gouging a line along the tank's hide. Methodically, the assault groups worked their way forward, using the combination of smoke, machine gun fire and the tanks to inch up the road. Ahead, an enormous crash sounded, and a vast wall of smoke blossomed up from the junction. Schiller clenched his fist; that was a strike from the field gun. It gave the men heart and they grimly kept on.

"I want a concentrated fire down here," Schiller shouted, gesturing towards the junction with a chopping motion. "Machine gun squads to pin them in place. Get the rest of the men moving forward; use the tanks for cover." He looked forward, seeing the outline of the leading tank as it shifted across the road. It fired but seconds later was struck. Metal shattered, and the tank drunkenly swerved as a red-hot shell punched its way through the armour. The radio operator's head was removed entirely by the shell which exploded seconds later. Hot metal fragments peppered the interior. The driver, sitting at the front, received a lump of metal in his neck and slumped forward. Fire broke out immediately, but the tank kept moving, the driver's grip on the main drive still fixed in place even as his life bled away. The burning tank ran off the road into a house and kept going, ploughing through the front room before finally coming to a halt with its nose pointing out in the garden. Most of the house collapsed around it, releasing a vast wall of dust over the road.

Schiller turned. "After the tank!" he shouted, and they sprinted down to it, flinching as bullets spat around them. The man next to Schiller leapt over the flank of the smouldering tank, only to be struck down by a burst of fire. One moment he was a ball of energy and motion, a heartbeat later he collapsed, like the strings of a puppet being snipped through. Schiller slipped, falling to one knee, before scrambling over the mound of rubble that had been created by the mortally wounded tank. He raised a hand to shield himself from the intense heat, thankful that the smoke pumping out of the tank's flank gave them over.

Most of the house had subsided into the street. Several men sheltered behind what remained of the front wall, firing towards the British lines. The ragged edge of wooden floorboards poked out above them while the creaking and groaning of a dying house echoed around. Gingerly, Schiller picked his way towards the back of the house, careful not to disturb too much. From the cracked window he could see a neat garden. He cautiously moved outside, half expecting the whip of rifle fire. To his right a row of gardens stretched away. They were partially obscured by the drifting smoke and darkly shadowed by the fast-fading sun. At the bottom of the gardens he could see what looked like some sheds and storage buildings. He felt a pulse of excitement. Ducking back into the house, he grabbed Kohler. "I want to get a team around the back. I think there's a way to hook round to the side road."

"They're watching the back, sir," Kohler warned. "Although a small group could get through."

"We will," Schiller confidently. "Get a section together and bring an MG crew."

He checked his rifle. This was their opportunity; find the flank, tear into the enemy and open the way for the tanks.

23

Scottsdale ducked as another shell exploded behind them. Briefly losing sight of Clutton through the curtain of dust and smoke, his heart was in his mouth; the gun was essential if they were to continue to hold. He sagged in relief as the tireless gun sounded, defiantly firing back. Clutton was calmly instructing his crew as they engaged the tanks. The gunner's face was pressed to the telescopic sight. Fire whistled around the position and Scottsdale noticed the loader was lying motionless on the floor, his head thrown back. A small wisp of smoke lazily rose from the neat bullet hole in his forehead.

Turning back to his front, he saw the lead German tank swerve, flames boiling out of its flank. Behind it he could glimpse another tank, its engine revving as it accelerated. Either side of the street, the infantry picked themselves up and ran forward, shouting in fear and desperation. Some went down but the majority stormed forward, using the shell fire to find cover in doorways and houses. Bullets whipped around Scottsdale, small puffs of dust sprouting over the front of the house.

"Cut them down!" he roared.

Scottsdale absorbed the recoil of his rifle against his aching shoulder. The dust swirled around them, shot through by the early evening light. A great, incessant roaring had taken over, inside his head but also in the street; a clamouring metallic flood of noise, the thud of bullets hitting plaster, of wood splintering and metal shearing, men shouting. Bren guns hammed out, barrels glowing hot; Private Dalton's face screwed into a grimace as his body shook. With a click the distinctively shaped curved magazine emptied and Private Pelham swiftly changed the magazine.

Scottsdale glanced over the road as he reloaded, flinching as Private Stewart slumped forward from his position covering the gun crew, clutching at his stomach. He felt a wild anger inside. "We hold! We have to hold!" He was furious, shouting the words over and over. Some of the men would hear him he knew but others could not. He had to be heard! The thought ate at him. Scarcely realising what he was doing, he ran across the junction, shouting as he fired. "We have to hold!"

"Mad bastard!" Pendle shouted.

The passage of a tank shell buffeted Scottsdale, who staggered onto one knee, shunted forcefully out of his daze. Adrenalin flooded through him and he sprinted back to cover, a volley of fire slapping into the wall behind him. Grateful hands pulled him inside.

Sergeant Grant loomed over him. "That was not clever, sir."

"Yes. I suspect you're right, Sergeant," Scottsdale replied, panting. The momentary madness had been a release and now he could concentrate on leading again. He looked up at Grant. There didn't seem anything to add. "Let's get on with it," he said grimly and picked up his rifle.

***

"I'll go first," Schiller instructed urgently. "Then small groups, ones and twos. And stay low." He smacked his palm for emphasis. "We can't be seen, otherwise we'll be dead."

With a final puff of his cheeks, he scurried out into the garden. He ignored the crescendo of firing from the road and concentrated on staying unseen. He wasn't trying to go directly towards the junction, but out and round to join the smaller road that led to it. A small shed afforded some cover and he paused, looking back. He beckoned to the next group and two more men darted over. Schiller tensed, waiting for a shout but no sound came. Turning back, they fought through some shrubs at the bottom of the garden to reveal a rotten looking fence. Beyond was the more solid shape of the back of several large sheds and warehouses, likely the storage of some business. Which meant they would be empty.

"Reus, Muller. Get inside that building."

The soldiers climbed over the wall and shortly after came the tinkling of glass. Reus reappeared and beckoned to Schiller. "We're in, sir," he reported. They climbed over the wall and followed Reus inside. As their eyes became accustomed to gloom, they saw the detritus of farming scattered everywhere. Rusty tractors were parked alongside tools and overalls. Large double doors dominated the far end; shafts of sunlight beamed gently through the glass panels. Shading his eyes, Schiller peered out but could see little. Lifting the locking bar, he slowly eased the door open. Cautiously he emerged into the soft light. They were in a storage yard; abandoned and half dismantled farming machinery dotted the area. To his left, a track led away towards the fields but what caught Schiller's eye was a narrow path to their right. It ran parallel to the road they were fighting down, and he smiled grimly. This was the way in.

"Follow me," he ordered. "Move quietly." He set off, brushing aside the branches that reached across the path. He would have preferred more men, but a smaller force had a greater chance of remaining undetected. The path followed a brick wall that marked the end of the gardens and they ducked low as they passed lest they be spotted. Yet they covered the ground rapidly, and soon reached the end of the path.

Schiller realised they had reached a side road and smiled in triumph. They'd come out on the bend; ahead it continued straight to the centre of Vierhourt and to the right was the junction, a mere two hundred yards away. Schiller could see houses leading down to it and the flickering of fire through the fug. This was the moment to assault. He turned to beckon to the men bunched behind. "Immel, you first-"

The bark of a rifle cut him off and Immel slumped forward, a dark stain blooming on his battle dress. Chips from the wall and the bushes flew as enemy fire poured towards them. Schiller glimpsed movement from a house opposite and realised he'd run into another enemy force. "Into the houses! Over the wall!" he shouted, firing back. Rapidly the men clambered over the wall, one man cut down as he did, before Schiller hauled himself over last, pursued by fire. They landed in the garden of the house on the corner and swiftly reorganised. "In the house, get some fire on them," Schiller ordered. The MG crew ran upstairs, their heavy boots traipsing mud over the carpet. The tinkle of breaking glass was followed a moment later by the chatter of the machine gun. Fire was exchanged at point blank range and all the windows were rapidly shot out. Glancing up, Schiller watched the curtains dancing as they were plucked by bullets. He thought for a moment; they couldn't stay where they were indefinitely but strangely the enemy appeared content to contain them. He smiled mirthlessly. Timidity would be their undoing. If they could storm the houses on the other side of the road then they could turn and attack the junction. It would require some bloody work and some men would die but it had to be done. The sun was getting lower in the sky and he knew they were running out of time.

"Listen to me!" he said, raising his voice. "A last effort! We are going to give them a volley and grenades and charge them. On my signal!" Taking a deep breath, he pulled the pin on a grenade.

***

Lieutenant Berry licked his lips nervously, his upper lip glistening with his sweat. He was crouched down, reloading his pistol with faltering hands. The shout that the enemy was in sight had paralysed him, leading Sergeant Robson to prompt him for the order to open fire. Berry had felt a momentary wild triumph as several Germans fell, but now he found himself sheltering as the Germans returned fire. With a curse, he recalled the conversation with Sergeant Robson earlier that day. Robson was a rangy and quietly proficient soldier and had approached him in the diffident manner that Berry had come to resent. It was Robson's way of suggesting what Berry should be doing. "Permission to speak, sir?"

Berry gritted his teeth. "Granted."

Robson cocked his head. "I was just thinking about the flank, sir, and about the kinds of tricks the Germans get up to."

Berry pursed his lips and breathed in. "Is that right, Sergeant."

"Well, sir, I just think that we should push the platoon forward to the corner houses – rather than back towards the square."

Berry looked up sharply. Damn this man's impudence. Who was the bloody officer here! "Listen to me, Sergeant. Our role is to be a blocking force. We have a defensive line in depth back to the square." Berry paused and softened his tone ever so slightly. "I appreciate your views, but the main objective is defence of the square. And if the enemy does appear in front of us, I'm sure we can deal with them. You understand?"

Robson met Berry's gaze squarely. His expression was entirely neutral, but Berry had the uncomfortable feeling the man was judging him. "Yes, sir, that's clear, thank you, sir. I only ask since we risk giving the Jerries some space to move into if we don't garrison on both sides of the road. Perhaps if we -"

"Enough, Sergeant," Berry snapped. "Get to your post."

Robson's point was now eloquently being proven. Berry's initial triumph had congealed as the Germans had spread into the houses opposite them. He cursed inside. Why hadn't Robson warned him properly? And he hadn't the men to cover everywhere; it wasn't fair.

A sharp cry sounded to his right and he recoiled at the sight of Corporal Mortlake staggering back from the window, gurgling and clutching at his throat. Berry's nausea was rising, and he almost gagged. Dimly, he registered Robson was shouting at him and he stared back, recoiling at the iron grip on his arm.

"They're attacking, sir! What are your orders?" Robson said urgently.

Berry scrambled to his knees and peered outside. He saw a wave of field grey uniforms flooding across the road. Several were hit, but the rest swarmed forward and began dropping grenades through windows, before forcing their way inside. Where had they all come from?

Shakily he stood. "We've no choice, Sergeant," he said, his voice strangely calm. "We should pull back towards the square and join the redoubt."

For once Robson's mask slipped. "Pull back, sir," he asked in disbelief. "We outnumber them, sir. We should attack!"

Now the decision was made in his mind, Berry's confidence returned. "Those are my orders, Sergeant. Please carry them out!"

Robson hesitated, mouth slightly opened as if he wanted to say more, but Berry gave him no choice. He clattered downstairs and shouted at the men to pull back, leaving Sergeant Robson to glance forlornly across to where the remnants of a platoon were being overrun by the Germans.

***

Schiller charged forward, exulting in the sense of movement; movement meant advancing and advancing meant victory. A few scattered shots had met them but, inexplicably, the British were retreating. Grenades went off, and the men piled inside the houses, the futile cries of several soldiers sounding as they were cut down. Yet most of the enemy had fled, and the men were elated, incredulous they'd survived the mad dash. Schiller snapped his fingers. "Where's Kohler?" he asked. "Here, sir," Kohler said, pushing through the remaining men. "Orders?"

"MG here to cover our backs. Anything appears, shoot and don't stop. Rest of you, with me. Down here is the junction. We're going to take that gun and end this. Come on!"

They were pitifully thin on numbers, but they had the advantage of surprise as they crept towards the junction. The remnants of the smoke and the waning light shielded them, and they closed fast. Schiller picked out the thud of from the anti-tank gun and bared his teeth. All the British attention was on the forces attacking in front of them and Schiller and his men took gleeful advantage, almost reaching the junction when they were spotted. Fire began spitting towards them, smacking into the houses, but it was too late; they'd reached the gun and, pausing only to lob grenades, they forced their way inside the patisserie. A British soldier staggered out of the smoke and was shot down, another made a dash out of the front but was caught. A burst of fire and he crumpled to the floor. From upstairs, a grenade dropped down, bouncing from step to step, but, following Schiller's example, they fired through the floor and were rewarded by a shrill cry and the thump of a falling body.

Now they were inside, the enemy was reluctant to shoot for fear of hitting their own men. Turning the corner to the shop front, Schiller saw the prize. A gunner straightened up, his shocked face staring back as Rues shot him down. An officer stood at the gun, calmly sighting along his revolver and firing. A German went down as he closed, before one of Schiller's men fired rapidly into him from point blank range. The officer dropped to his knees, a look of mild surprise across his face, before toppling face first to the ground.

Schiller howled in triumph, adrenalin coursing through him. The way to into Vierhourt was open and he could barely contain himself. Looking to his right, he glimpsed the grey nose of a tank as it manoeuvred around piles of bricks, burnt out cars and tank carcasses towards them. Only a thin line of infantry stood in its way now.

A burst of fire from across the junction forced him to duck. Wiping sweat from his eyes, he breathed in deeply, reigning in his adrenalin to assess their situation. They were desperately short of men and intensely vulnerable to counter attack, most of the men having fallen to the twin assaults. Dragging the body of a corporal towards him he efficiently stripped it of ammunition, parcelling it out to the remaining handful of men. If they could hold a little longer until the tanks reached them then today would be the day they broke open the way to the coast and the annihilation of the British Army.

***

For a moment, the numbing hand of dread fear paralysed Scottsdale, his exhausted mind grappling with the picture he saw. Instinctively his skin crawled at the guttural cries of the triumphant Germans. His eyes were drawn to something glinting in the low sun; it was the gold cipher on a Yeomanry cap badge. Clutton's genial face flashed through his mind and the surge of anger and sorrow for that easy going, efficient soldier galvanised him into action. Glancing to his right, he saw another tank was closing, cautiously negotiating the burned-out hulks in its way. The darting shapes of infantryman followed. He beckoned Grant over. "We're running out of time!" Scottsdale shouted over the din. "We have to knock out the tank and clear that pocket of infantry." Grant nodded, head down as he reloaded his rifle. "What are we going to do with that tank, sir?"

"The Boys rifle is all we've got left and it better work, because if not then we're going to have to stop it ourselves." "Could do with some luck, sir," Grant replied with a faint smile.

"I think we're overdue, Sergeant." Scottsdale grinned back. He gripped Grant by the shoulder. "Go and find Marsh. Tell him to wait for the tank to get close."

"Clear, sir. What about you?"

"We'll keep the heads of those bastards down," Scottsdale replied grimly, nodding towards the far side where the remaining German infantry were hiding. "As soon as that tank is dealt with, we'll clear them out."

Grant nodded and took the stairs two at a time, flinching as bullets snapped through the air. His nostrils flared at the rank smell of cordite and dust that hung heavy in the air. Upstairs, he darted through the hole hacked in the connecting wall only to come to an abrupt halt, horrified at the sight of jumbled figures lying haphazardly across the floor. It took a moment to recall that Marsh was set up in the dressmaker's shop and the scattered figures were mere mannequins.

Muttering a curse, Grant gripped his rifle tighter and forged on. The hammering of machine gun fire ripped away as he threw open the next door, his boots crunching across shattered glass. Inside a solider slumped awkwardly, his breath coming in shallow gulps, a darker trail showing where he'd been dragged. With a sigh of relief, he saw Marsh lying flat, the distinctive shape of the Boys rifle cradled against his shoulder. As he entered the flat crack of the anti-tank rifle sounded and Marsh rocked back under the powerful recoil.

Marsh glanced to his right as Grant crouched next to him. "I've already put a couple on him, but he keeps coming!" "Let him get closer," Grant urged.

Marsh grunted. "All bleeding well for you to say, but he knows where I am now!"

Grant glanced up. The tank has nosing forward and, as if on cue to Marsh's remarks, its main armament swung towards them. A slight pause, Grant holding his breath, then the tank rocked as the shell flew towards them. "Take cover!" Grant shouted but the high explosive shell tore through the shop, enveloping Grant in a huge crash and flinging him against the far wall. Dazed, he struggled to sit up, a dense cloud of smoke and dust washing through the room. He coughed, waving a hand feebly in front his face as he hunted his rifle. The movement caused a shaft of pure pain to lance through his shoulder and he gasped. He felt like a wet towel was wrapped around his head, deadening the noise of firing. Groggily, he dragged himself to where Marsh lay face down. A bright gash of dark red stained the side of his face but he was at least breathing evenly.

With a grimace, Grant rolled Marsh over and picked up the Boys rifle, his heart lurching as he saw the tank looming, its machine gun firing in short bursts. Bullets struck sparks against its hulking front as the Bren gunners desperately tried to halt it. "Not so fast, you bastard," he grunted, snuggling the padded rest into his shoulder. Although the rifle had two distance settings – 300 and 500 yards – British troops had learned the hard way that anything above 300 yards was ineffective and to truly have a chance they needed to be within 100 yards of their target, and in most cases, attacking the weaker side armour. Unlike the explosive force of an anti-tank shell, the rifle relied either on the interior shrapnel effect created by the armour plate shattering or by hitting something vital in the guts of the tank. Ideally a lethal spray of tiny metal fragments would incapacitate the crew sheltering inside. It also meant that the man wielding the rifle had to be lucky – very lucky. Lucky to hit the armour at the right angle to allow the .55 calibre bullet to pierce the plate. And lucky that when the bullet did pierce, it created enough shrapnel to either hit the crew or another vital component of the tank.

As Grant hunched over the rifle, barrel weaving, he tried to ignore the stabbing pain in his side. In front of him, the tank reached one of the makeshift barricades made from the rubble of a partially destroyed building and a variety of carts. The tank, unwilling to ride directly over the obstacle and reveal its vulnerable underbelly, manoeuvred and in doing so presented its flank to Grant. It was only a few moments, but it was the moment that Grant fired, feeling the savage recoil. Frantic fingers worked back the cocking lever and fired another round into the side of the tank. His wide eyes never left the tank which to his stunned disbelief, instead of straightening up to deliver the coup de grace to the beleaguered infantrymen, trundled, almost gently, to a halt. In turning it had exposed its weakly armoured side and the rifle had found the vulnerable engine block, which now hissed and began belching smoke. One of the crew had been cut down and the remaining crewmen bailed out, leaving the tank to smoulder gently in the dying light.

24

Schiller fired across the junction, content to snipe and await the breakthrough. It was getting harder to see clearly as the light failed, but all he had to do was ensure that his final few men were available to provide close support. He could see a tank closing in; darting and ducking behind came the rest of the infantry. Even as he watched the tank paused and its gun swung towards the British position. He couldn't see the impact but the enormous crash from across the road told of him of the impact and he felt like whooping with joy.

"They're dying over there!" he shouted gleefully, uncaring if his men could hear him. Here was the hour of his redemption, to be at the spear point of the German advance, to play a critical part in kicking in the back door of the British Army and turning victory into rout. He sat with his back to the wall, fumbling to reload. Finally, it clicked into place and he looked around. From within the shattered remains of the patisserie, several men were crouching, dust covered and grim. British and German bodies lay scattered around. He smiled mirthlessly. He would enjoy ending the final stubborn resistance in Vierhourt.

A sudden prickle of apprehension flowed through him and he looked up with a frown, trying to pinpoint what it was that prompted it. Then realisation dawned. Where was the familiar sound of tank treads? Or the grinding of metal and gears? Turning, he scrambled back to the entrance and looked out into the road. His heart lurched. Why was the tank stopped? He stared disbelievingly. Move! Why wasn't it moving! He was unable to tear his eyes away. Why had it stopped? It wasn't on fire. The anti-tank gun was dead. There was no reason. Surely it hadn't broken down.

A flash of movement caught his eye on the other side of the tank. His mouth gaped as he realised it was the crew bailing out and, beyond, the infantry falling back. He screwed his fists in absolute fury, rage and frustration boiling over. "Stop running!" he screamed. "Turn and fight, you miserable pieces of shit!" Spittle flecked at his mouth and he found himself raised on his knees, gesticulating wildly towards the tank. One of his men tried to pull him down but Schiller, feeling the hand on his sleeve, turned and cuffed the man away. He was witnessing his redemption being taken from him, at the very point of victory.

"Sir, get down please! What are your orders?"

Schiller felt the exquisiteness of his black anger. Clearly the man was angling for retreat. Damn his cowardice. "My orders? My orders are to fight on!" Schiller turned, eyes blazing. "Gather your weapons. We don't need that tank!" He was screaming, worked to a frenzy by the hate he couldn't control, by the terror of seeing defeat and knowing what would become of him if he failed twice in a brutal, totalitarian system where only the end results mattered. His savage fury cowed the remnants of the squad. Some were fatalistic, brought to the very edge of exhaustion, fighting too hard and seeing too many people - friends, foes, civilians, animals - killed and mutilated. Here perhaps was an end. Some were terrified, seeing in Schiller the impossibility of compromise, but unable in themselves to defy him, so deeply embedded was their obedience to the authority invested him in. And under it all, no one wished to publicly refuse to fight on, no matter how hopeless the mission.

"Now listen to me," Schiller screamed. "This isn't over. One last effort, we can still win this fight." He paused, taking in the men before him. Expendable. Useful. So long as they bent to his will.

***

Scottsdale watched in horror as the shell streaked from the tank. The force of the explosion sent a dust cloud rolling over their position, darkening an already fading landscape. He swallowed as he pictured the men fighting there, trying not to think that Sergeant Grant - dependable, ever present - was dead and that it was his order, his words that had sent him to his death. He shook the thought off; that had to wait.

"Watch for the infantry!" he shouted. He fired into the smoke and the gloom. He briefly wondered if the encroaching dusk might give them a chance to escape but he knew it was hopeless. There was a reason that armies marched in summer and long days to fight was one of them. Even in the last dying embers of the day there was enough light to illuminate their defeat, a defeat that would come against the backdrop of a gorgeous cornucopia of colour: the palest of sky blues, a darker orange shot through with purple as the sun faded away. And there was enough light to see the scattered remnants of the company. Bloody rags and bandages crawled over each body, all covered in a sheen of dust, faces blackened by smoke and cordite. Scottsdale tried not to picture the bodies that the rubble hid, tried not to think of Sergeant Grant and the others he had led to battle but would not take home.

He swore viciously, bitter resignation flowing over him. They'd failed and borne a cost he was uncertain he could bear. Looking round, he beckoned Davenport, feeling a momentary twist of his guts; usually it was Grant's solid frame looking back at him. "We are going to fall back to the square," Scottsdale shouted. "Bren team last! Tell -" he stopped to duck as a flurry of bullets smacked against the wall above his head - "tell Brookes and Gartner to start getting the men down from the higher floors. Don't mess about, get back to the square."

"But, sir -" Davenport began before Scottsdale cut him off.

"Make sure the wounded go first."

"Sir!" Davenport insisted. "The Germans are falling back!"

Scottsdale's head snapped back. "What?"

"They're falling back, sir," Davenport repeated. Scottsdale looked out. Seeing the panzer, he half turned back to Davenport, but it dawned on him that something was missing. Movement. The tank had stopped. Why had the tank stopped? Wait, there was movement. His heart lurched but he realised he was watching the German infantry dodging as they fell back.

"Happy bloody days," Scottsdale murmured wonderingly. How was this possible.

"Sorry, sir?" Davenport leant forward, trying to catch Scottsdale's words.

"I said happy fucking days, Private!" he roared triumphantly, feeling the adrenalin surge through him, invigorating every part of him. He raised his rifle. "Pour it on them boys!" he shouted. "Send the bastards home with an Essex goodbye!" Scottsdale felt an equal sense of wonderment and bitter regret. The Bren ripped out again, the sound more confident, more victorious it seemed. Infantrymen grinned through blackened faces, the euphoria beginning to seep through the British position. Wilkins tracked a German infantryman, felt the kick in his shoulder and bared his teeth in satisfaction as his mark slumped down.

"How the hell are we still alive?" Wilkins shouted.   "Luck of the Irish!" Davenport shouted back, nodding towards McManus.

Scottsdale slumped back, suddenly exhausted, drained by the fight and his grief. It seemed impossible there was still some of his men left; some but many others dead. Grant and the others. And Helene. His anger ate into his fatigue and he welcomed it; the day wasn't done yet. There was one final nest of the enemy to clear out. He took

Davenport by the shoulder. "Last task. Clear the bastards out across the junction. I want suppressing fire followed by grenades and then we're going to go over there and show them the bayonet."

"Yes, sir," Davenport said grimly and proffered his canteen. Gratefully Scottsdale took a swig. As he wiped his mouth, he saw a shape materialising out of the darkness. Unmistakably, the broad figure limping forward was Sergeant Grant. He felt a surge of relief but carefully smothered his instinctive smile as Sergeant Grant drew up before him.

"Hello, Sergeant."

"Hello, sir," Grant replied. The side of his head was a mess of dirt, his hair matted with blood. A rough bandage was wrapped around his upper arm and parts of his battle dress were burnt and torn. "Got held up by a tank."

"Tricky. Seems you managed to deal with it though. That was useful."

"Marsh put a few down on it with the Boys rifle until he was hit. I got lucky."

"How is Marsh?"

"Alive but he'll have a rare sore head tomorrow, sir. I can't imagine it will improve his humour I'm afraid."

"Terrible times, Sergeant, terrible times." Scottsdale suddenly laughed out loud and clapped Grant on the shoulder. Grant smiled back, holding the look for a long moment, more words unnecessary, before Scottsdale turned back to the men sheltering around him. "We're not done yet!" he said, raising his voice. "We're going to clear the last of those bastards out over there. Sergeant, you're to stay here and make sure none of that lot returns," he added, gesturing back down the road.

"I should come with you, sir," Grant replied.

"You're in no fit state, Sergeant."

"Sir, if I can -"

"Shut up, Sergeant. Stay out of bloody trouble for once and that's an order. Wait until you see us in possession and then we can reconvene."

Grant nodded. "Yes, sir."

Scottsdale looked round as men huddled round him in the ruins; more came clattering down from upstairs, others materialising, hopping over broken masonry. In the darker recesses it was harder to make out faces as the afternoon surrendered to evening. Yet that offered relief; he wouldn't be able to see the faces that were missing. Raising his voice, he spoke forcefully. "We've got one more job to do! Now I'm not asking you to keep fighting because it will help our army escape, though God knows that's important enough. I'm not asking you to fight for our country or for glory, or any of that nonsense; I'm not asking because it's your duty either. I'm asking you to fight on because it's right!"

He felt his own rage and grief and pain and swallowed. "I'm asking you to fight for the man next to you and for the men who haven't made it. I'm asking you to go over there to kick seven shades of shit out of them because they deserve it! They deserve to suffer!" He panted, breathing hard, feeling his energy and anger flowing through him as he heard the answering growls of

241

agreement from the shadows. "We're going to go over there and show them some steel. They'll run and if they don't they'll die where they stand!" He breathed in. The usual smell of summer, of grass and flowers, had been obliterated by the smoke and diesel fumes of the shattered town. Above was a blaze of colour while below was grey, mechanical. Men hunkered down in dark recesses and corners as lethal metal rent the air. Animals fled; only men endured. They girded themselves for the final assault. Bolts were worked back on rifles, grenades carefully stacked. Everyone was thirsty, crack lipped. Sweat had dried to a hard crust that stained clothes, ingrained deeply. All their puffy, red eyes were trained toward the enemy, waiting for the moment of release.

Scottsdale raised a hand and looked around. The fading sunlight glinted off a bayonet. He took a deep breath.

And then dropped his arm.

***

The brief lull over Vierhourt was shattered a split second after Scottsdale's signal. A thunder of rifles, machine guns and pistols washed over the junction. The men's focus had narrowed to the most precise point. They forgot everything about why they were there. They forgot even that they were no longer in England. All that mattered was the enemy; to silence them would end the day, would stop the fighting and, at least in that moment, provide a measure of solace for friends who had fallen in the fight. It was the only thing that mattered and so they poured forth their fire, deadly lead streaking molten hot through the air to pepper the frontage of the German redoubt.

"Runners ready!" he roared. He could see little answering activity from the patisserie. He turned to Sergeant Grant who had taken his usual position alongside. "When you see my signal, close up with us."

"Yes, sir."

Scottsdale glanced at Grant with a small smile; it was time to end the fight for Vierhourt.

"Essex! On me!" Leaping over the low wall, he surged across the junction. In doing so he staggered slightly, nearly tripping over broken concrete. He snarled in anger, affronted at the check on his progress. He sprinted on, feeling his empty water bottle flapping against his hip. Alongside came the runners, spread out across the road, converging towards the ruins of the patisserie. A surge of release, of rage and joy, flowed through him. He wanted the enemy then, he wanted to see them die. And in that moment grey helmets rose above the shattered brick, rifles raised, blossoming orange flame. For a heartbeat his eyes shut instinctively but then he found the grenade, pulled the pin and flung it. Some of the runners had fallen but enough were through. Scottsdale was confronted by the low wall of the patisserie. Without pausing, he leapt threw the shattered remnants of a window, coming to rest in a half crouch. Before he had time to take his bearings, a German soldier swung his rifle towards Scottsdale's head. Desperately throwing up an arm to ward it off, Scottsdale gasped in pain as the rifle crashed onto him, driving him to the ground. The soldier stood over him, rifle raised above his head, a snarl etched into his face. Before he could bring the weapon down, Scottsdale swept up his own rifle and thrust upward, fourteen inches of steel sliding into the man's groin. The German cried out in agony, dropping his rifle, just as another Essex man swept through, impaling the German on his own bayonet. Scottsdale scrambled up as the man collapsed. Noise crowded in on him; the hoarse shouts of men fighting, sharp reports of rifles and, unrecognised at first but increasingly clear, his own desperate shouts of rage and fear. A shot rang out and another man following Scottsdale through the window jack knifed, falling face first.

He looked around; a nightmarish scene played out. Among the carcass of the shop, knots of men were struggling together, locked in a desperate combat. Their shapes were indistinct in the half light, only their guttural cries betraying their nation. Occasional flashes as rifles discharged froze images briefly. McManus was methodically bayoneting a German who was pinioned against a stone oven, a steady stream of Gaelic issuing forth as his ancestors lived through him once more. A German was screaming as he strangled Pendle, only for Davenport to take two quick steps, put

243

his rifle to the German's head and pull the trigger. The man slumped to one side, pulse of black blood squirting out, covering a cursing Pendle.

A shout caught Scottsdale's attention and he turned to see a soldier approach a doorway before being flung back. Around him the final German soldiers were throwing up their hands in surrender. Yet there was a final knot of resistance and Scottsdale instinctively moved towards it.

"Davenport!" he said. "Secure this room and signal to Grant. The rest of you, to me." Cautiously, they approached the doorway. Scottsdale nodded at the men lined up alongside him. "Get a grenade in there."

Dalton and Wilkins lobbed grenades through the door. As he did so, several shots rang out and the men ducked before the explosion ripped out, smoke billowing through the door. Scottsdale spoke clearly in the silence that followed.

"If there is anyone alive in there, surrender now." He licked his lips as they strained to hear any answering voice. Yet suddenly, baffling, Scottsdale could hear sound of laughter. The men looked at each other, puzzled, even angry. They wanted this to end, not this final act of insanity. And it was an anger that echoed in Scottsdale. What was fucking funny about this? He was seething and took up his rifle. Yet just as he was about to move, a voice rang out, and it froze him cold; it reached inside and took hold of his rawest nerve and laughingly twisted it.

"My God, Lieutenant, how on earth are you still alive?"

Scottsdale was moving before he consciously chose to. Any consideration of danger was absent. There was simply a burning need to see if it really was the man who'd been the source of such unfettered misery. His attempts to bury the memory of Helene, to simply survive the trauma, were undone in one split second of that scathing voice. It had been necessary, too, to bury thoughts of Schiller; thinking of the retribution the man deserved ate into him like an acid, and he had pushed the thoughts away. Yet now the box was sprung open, the acid was leaking inside him and he pushed his way forward; rage, disbelief, fear all jostled for position.

Shafts of faint sunlight cut through the smoke wreathed room. Scottsdale waved a hand to clear it and stopped abruptly. Schiller lay on the floor, propped against a wall. He had one hand pressed into his stomach, which glistened wetly. A faint trickle of blood trailed from one corner of his mouth. Two bodies lay motionless beside him.

Scottsdale felt a thundering in his head; he was unable to speak, thick with the need to hurt. In his wildest imagining, he did not think they would meet again on the crowded battle field of northern France. His men had followed him inside and were arrayed in a semi-circle behind him, rifles raised, but he raised a trembling arm to hold them.

For a long moment, no one spoke before Schiller stirred. "I could have sworn I killed you," he said in disbelief.

Scottsdale stared at Schiller. His rage swept over him in waves, its energy electrifying his fingertips.

"I was sure…at the canal…" Schiller continued, before he suddenly exploded. "You ruined everything! Everything!" "I did my duty," Scottsdale said tightly.

"And I mine."

"Your duty was torture and murder?"

"I would do it all again for my country."

"Then you regret nothing? You stand by all of it?"

"Sir," Grant said warningly, but Scottsdale ignored him.

"You don't regret any of it?" Scottsdale shouted. "Answer me you bastard! Justify it to me, justify the deaths!" He couldn't invoke her name, but Scottsdale felt clearly that she was very much with him; that she would bear witness to this man's death, a death he was intent on administering.

"You don't understand -"

"I understand!" Scottsdale roared. "I understand what you are! And you have to pay for what you did!" Scottsdale loomed over Schiller, while his men looked on nervously.

Schiller laughed hoarsely. "Again with this bleating, Lieutenant? I do what is necessary. You're too weak to see that."

"Killing and hurting the innocent isn't strong!"

"No one is an innocent; you are with us or against us."

"What kind of person can you be," he said, an edge of despair in his voice, "to believe this. There can be only one end for you; you cannot live." Scottsdale felt the warmth of that certainty, a deliciousness of the restraints falling from him. He would end this monstrosity himself.

Schiller hauled himself painfully to his feet. "Perhaps you finally begin to see what you need to do. But your lesson comes too late." He suddenly reached into his pocket and pulled out a pistol, but he was weak, and Scottsdale knocked it away with his rifle, following up by driving the butt into Schiller's gut, who sank to one knee, crying out in agony.

A great crashing wave of hate washed over Scottsdale. Schiller looked disbelievingly down at his stomach and then, more slowly, back to Scottsdale. And Scottsdale finally, in agonising joy, saw fear. And he wanted to savour it, to wallow in it; to beat Schiller, make him feel just one part of the pain he had inflicted. He wanted to hear him break, to cry and to say, yes, what I did was wrong. To admit his guilt and accept his sentence.

Yet the man's fear held a mirror up to how others had felt when Schiller had been in control. Scottsdale's fist was ready; he desperately wanted to punish but in that flash of empathy he already knew he couldn't do it. God, how he wanted to, but if he took the life of a scared, unarmed man, he would just become the very thing he loathed.

He hung his head, breathing deeply. "Damn you, Schiller," he said in a low voice. "She deserved everything. And you took it all away." He turned away. "Tie him up, Corporal," he said to Davenport. "The rest of you, out, now." The men shuffled out as Grant waited for Scottsdale. "The right thing, sir," he said softly.

"Yes," Scottsdale replied bleakly. "Remarkable how shit that often feels."

Grant began to speak but a cry sounded from behind and they whirled round. Davenport was staggering away from Schiller who now turned, Davenport's rifle in hand, and rushed at them, the bayonet lunging towards Scottsdale. Scottsdale raised his own rifle, but Grant shoved him hard out of the way. Schiller kept going, his face a snarl of hate, the bayonet arrowing towards Grant's chest but Grant parried the thrust expertly. Dropping one hand off his rifle, he drew back a granite fist and smashed it into Schiller's face. The German staggered back, arms spread wide and Scottsdale was moving, fast. With a great shout he lunged, burying his bayonet deep into Schiller's belly. Legs pumping, he ran Schiller across the room and against the far wall, an incoherent cry wrenched from him, until he ended up inches from Schiller's face, watching as the man's life ebbed away.

He stepped back and dropped his rifle, leaning forward with his hands on his knees, sucking in air. Grant started forward, but Scottsdale held out a hand to stop him. He felt sick and inordinately weary. A vivid image of Helene's smiling face came to him and he tried to smile. A wellspring of emotion began bubbling up within him, threatening to overwhelm as his throat constricted. Yet the men crowded back into the room and the iron grip of army discipline began to reclaim him. He straightened, determined to remain whole and functioning in front of his men. His grief would come later, privately.

"Sergeant," he said shakily. "See to the wounded. Strip the Germans of anything useful. We need to find Captain Revie."

25

"Put a rocket up them, gentlemen! Don't stop until you see England!" The urgency in Major Carter's voice clear.

Scottsdale nodded. "Don't worry, sir, we'll keep on them."

"I should bloody hope so, Scottsdale, otherwise you'll feel my boot connecting with your arse; that or it'll be getting tickled by a panzer!" He grinned broadly. "They say the devil makes work for idle hands so there must have been some truly indolent bastards around to land us in this particular pile of excrement." He raised his voice, so the nearby men could hear him. "But you're not idle, are you? Or at least you'd better not be unless you want to get stuck here! Well, do you? No ale and no-one speaking a word of English! Time for us to go home!" A few grins met his words and Carter turned back to the officers.

"Godspeed gentlemen. Don't hang about as things are going to move quickly now. The Belgians surrendered yesterday, and our pocket is being squeezed. Your action was one of many that have been taking place to buy us time. We've being turning towns into strongpoints all along the corridor; Cassel, Wormhout, Hazebrouck and others but they're all falling one by one. With Calais and Boulogne captured, Dunkirk is the only show in town and it won't be open for long."

"What's the plan for evacuation, sir?" McDonald asked.

"We'll be taken off from the harbour. Look out for the Navy liaison officers and whatever happens, don't stop." He surveyed the column of men trudging toward the coast. "Never thought I would see such a black day. Now it's up to us to make sure it doesn't get any worse." He threw up a salute and gestured to the driver who accelerated, beeping his horn to clear a path.

Scottsdale took a deep breath. Over the heads of the men trooping forward was an ever-present beacon of black smoke; it was from the destroyed oil depots at Dunkirk and its taint spread over the coastal plain, catching in their throats. They were marching directly into the maelstrom where salvation lay, and all around was chaos.

Salvation in chaos. Appropriate enough, he reflected grimly. As evening had settled over Vierhourt they had been ordered back again, beginning their final journey to Dunkirk. The Germans had assaulted the town from different directions, hurling themselves desperately at the defenders but not breaking through. Tanks and armoured vehicles had been beaten back, sometimes at point blank range, men desperately fighting house to house. The carrier platoon that formed a mobile reserve had been virtually annihilated plugging gaps in the perimeter; it was on one such raid that Captain Revie had been severely wounded. Scottsdale breathed a deep sigh of relief when he saw McDonald limping towards him in the evening gloom. Part of him had hoped for news of Lieutenant Berry's death but only briefly; it was an unworthy thought. The man was alive and though Scottsdale sensed the surliness of the men under his command, there was nothing to be done until they returned to England. Scottsdale was determined to have Berry removed but it would wait. The most important thing was that they had done what they'd been ordered; bought time for the BEF to fall back. Each rearguard action was a plug in the collapsing dyke that was the allied front as it folded back on itself towards Dunkirk.

Before they could think of rest, they'd set off again, this time to Watou, arriving in the early hours. Yet despite his enveloping fatigue, Scottsdale had been unable to sleep. Instead he had watched as the night sky was lit up by occasional bursts of brilliant white from flares and the reflected orange glare from towns that were on fire. Just for that one night he'd felt strangely safe amongst the carnage. Perhaps he was too drained to care. Resolutely, he sought to forget Manfred Schiller. He was not troubled by the man's death, but he wanted to erase him. Instead, he dwelt on Helene, hearing her laugh, picturing her rolling her eyes in exasperation. Finally, the ache that thinking of her prompted in him made him push thoughts of her away. His job now was to focus on bringing them home safe. He stared up into the sky until the crackle of small arms fire and growl of artillery lulled him asleep.

"Get them together, Sergeant," Scottsdale said, rejoining the platoon.

"Come on you lot!" Grant barked. "On your feet unless you fancy swimming home," he said, kicking Pendle's feet. For just a second Scottsdale pictured himself pitched overboard into the channel and blanched.

"Right, gentlemen," he said wearily, surveying them in the early morning light. They were filthy and bloody. Each had made their own additions scavenged along the way to their official kit. McManus kissed his rosary beads while Davenport surreptitiously patted his own lucky charm; a scrap of a mortar round that had failed to explode at the River Dyl. Helmets were dented and worn in whatever manner was most comfortable. Yet their weapons were clean, and they had the hard look of men who had seen combat and learned the means of survival.

"Gentlemen," he repeated. "An expression not a description I think it's fair to say," he said drily. There were a few answering chuckles from the men. "We're going home, I'm pleased to say. The Navy are going to take us off at Dunkirk."

"Now we're in trouble, boys," Pendle chirped. "The Navy are in charge."

"Thank you, Private," Scottsdale said. "But right now they're our best friends. We're moving in five minutes. Where possible we follow the roads but if we need to we will cut across country. But I've no desire to get cut off from battalion; our days of gallivanting are done."

"Excellent decision, sir," Davenport piped up.

"Yes, I do occasionally have them, Corporal," Scottsdale replied. "Now, I want to be hitting the perimeter at Dunkirk by lunch. I don't want to stop for long. Shit and eat if you must but be quick. Now is not the time to get lost, clear?"

With a collective muttered groan, the section mustered, swinging on kit and slinging rifles. "Christ," said Marsh, wincing as he stood up, a hand to his bandaged head. "This fucking war," he added viciously.

Wilkins stretched. "I'm not sure I can walk, let alone run, if Jerry catches up."

They moved out, sliding into the shuffle of tired men. The roads were desperately congested with civilians and soldiers of all descriptions, all moving north, all seeking shelter. Slowly, they carved a way towards the coast, asleep on their feet. As they got closer more fields were flooded to thwart enemy tanks, adding another layer of torture; tired men were forced off the road into the freezing cold to avoid air attack and to skirt cratered roads. A shuffling line would quickly scatter as the Luftwaffe came on; trucks halted, and men jumped out, joining those leaping into the fields and ditches. Some were lucky, but many more were struck by cannon fire and bomb. After one hit and run attack, a supply lorry had run off the road. Desperate men rushed it, ignoring the furious reprimands of officers. Biscuits, boiled bacon, corned beef, all were carried off in triumph by ravenous soldiers. Largely unit cohesion remained in place but there were groups of soldiers wandering back without any firm control. Like the whole army, they scavenged what they could, and Scottsdale stared speculatively at the truck before beckoning to Grant.

"I'm going for a comfort break, Sergeant. Be gone a few minutes I should say." He paused. He could not directly tell Grant to loot army property. "Keep the men occupied, understood?"

"Crystal clear, sir," Grant said and grabbed Marsh.

As he relieved himself, Scottsdale reflected on how far his attitude to army and personal property had come in a few short weeks. He shrugged. A man could change a lot in a few weeks of war and he was pleased to see Grant back with their prizes, including a bottle of brandy that he had secreted under his coat. Carefully, he showed it to Scottsdale.

"Thought this may come in handy, sir."

Scottsdale hesitated but only for a second; damn the army. "Thank you, Sergeant."

Grant chivvied the men into moving out again.

Scottsdale hitched up his rifle and set off at the front. The sun inched higher and just as slowly they fought their way through the seething mass of men, horses, trucks and civilians. There was a constant sound of revving engines which grated, made worse by the churned-up dust that coated them. Mounds of horse manure added to the rank odour that was in stark contrast to the glory of the surrounding countryside. Either side of the road lay the blackened carcasses of abandoned vehicles, nose to tail; some had been deliberately disabled by retreating soldiers, others the victims of the incessant raids of the Luftwaffe. In one field scores of trucks, cars, motor cycles, tractors and guns were stacked together and set ablaze. Ammunition that was no longer needed was thrown into the maelstrom. Men staggered on, swaying with fatigue, coughing in the rank air. The walking wounded limped forward, the pull of home driving them on. Some were carried in wheelbarrows by their mates. Beeping horns and shouting sounded incessantly.

Furious dispatch riders recklessly wound their way through the clogged roads, desperate to deliver the order that would stop a regiment or a battalion and redirect them to join the defence.

"Poor bastards," Davenport muttered as they passed by one such group that was manning an outpost.

"Better them than us," Marsh replied, but they all lowered their gaze as they passed the unfortunate men, feeling the shame of their escape while others remained behind.

Scottsdale watched a butterfly dancing crazily alongside the remains of a light tank. He recalled its name; a painted lady. It was also the nickname given to the prostitutes that were readily available in many towns. He watched until it landed on something dark; a soldier's boot sticking out from under a blanket, part of a row of bodies laid out beside the road. He looked away and straightened, feeling the familiar dull ache in his lower back.

Coming around a bend in the road the normally taciturn McManus swore softly. Scottsdale saw the cause of McManus' distress; a squad of French artillerymen, with their curiously shaped helmets, was weeping as they lined up their horses and shot them in the head, one by one. Anything that couldn't be taken with them was destroyed. British soldiers were methodically working

252

their way down a row of cars and lorries, emptying engines of oil and water and running them until the belched smoke and seized up. Tyres were slashed, windscreens smashed, and petrol tanks holed.

Scottsdale surveyed the destruction as he walked forward with McDonald. "It's incredible how much material we're leaving," McDonald observed. "There won't be a lorry or anti-tank gun left in England at this rate."

"The world's largest scrapyard," Scottsdale mused. "Thank God for the channel."

"Truly. It stopped Napoleon and now it's going to stop Hitler."

McDonald glanced at Scottsdale. "Do you really think so? We're leaving most of our equipment and half our army here. It's going to be a damn close-run thing if they do invade."

Scottsdale shrugged. "Well, it's either that or surrender isn't it. And they will come. So we'd better hope the Navy and the brylcreem boys make a better fist of it than we have."

McDonald nodded soberly. "We really have made a total mess of this haven't we. Best get home and start barricading the doors."

As they spoke, they crested a small rise and looked down towards what was once the pretty seaside town of Dunkirk. Scottsdale checked his watch.

"Midday, Wednesday 29th May 1940. The 2nd Essex arrives at Dunkirk." Grimly they surveyed the scene. A huge black cloud from the blazing oil tanks hung low over the town. Half of the Dunkirk was burning, set on fire by incendiaries. Ruined buildings were everywhere. The roar of planes, the crack of artillery and rattle of machine-guns made an unearthly discord of sound to welcome them. A trail of blackened and twisted metal lined the roads that were chockfull of soldiers marching down to the sea. To the east, Scottsdale saw the long queues of men dotted across the wide beaches. Everywhere he looked there were soldiers, ants crawling over the town. Even as they watched, a bombing raid was taking place, German planes swooping on the harbour. Fountains of water shot up, but a destroyer appeared through the spray, desperately making for England. Ships of all sizes dotted the sea. He swallowed;

the idea of being sunk and being deposited in the Channel appalled him.

"What a shambles," he sighed. "Come on, let's go and find a boat."

A naval liaison officer directed them towards the harbour. The roads were strewn with debris, bricks and masonry. They negotiated craters, passing the corpses of horses and overturned cars, lorries ablaze on either side. Houses were alight, walls sagging and through it all the constant roar of the raging oil depot fire. With horror Scottsdale saw cohesion breaking down in places. A man staggered past, holding out thirty gold rings on a string that he'd looted from a destroyed jewellery shop. Scottsdale's anger nearly boiled over, but the man fled before Scottsdale could grab him. Another had a marble clock strapped to his back, while others were laden with what they had scavenged in the ruins. Dead bodies, civilian and military, lay unburied everywhere. A loose horse galloped wildly past, its flank wet with blood, its white eyes stark. Scottsdale saw an officer, breathing rapidly, walking up and down brandishing his revolver; every time he saw a solider smoking he would run up and shout loudly: "Light discipline! Put out that cigarette!", even though it was the middle of the day. He repeated this for a few minutes before finally sinking to the ground crying.

Before Scottsdale could help, the wail of air raid sirens went off, followed moments later by the pop of anti-aircraft guns. Taking their cue from the other soldiers, they sprinted for shelter, following some soldiers diving into a doorway where they found themselves at the top of the stairs leading to a cellar bar.

"In here, Pendle!" Grant shouted.

"Thanks, Sarge," Pendle said breathlessly.

"Not a good time to piss, Private."

"Agreed, Sarge. Agreed."

The thump of bombs reverberated through the cellar. It was drenched in British and French soldiers. Pendle made a move towards the bar but a growl from Grant stilled him. Judging by the smell, Scottsdale doubted they'd be anything left anyway. Many of the soldiers were flat out on the floor or tables. Several were comatose from drink and the smell of rum was heavy in the air.

Others were simply exhausted. Scottsdale went to sit next to a French soldier who was staring into space, apparently watching the world go by. He gave a slight pressure to move the man further along the bench. A flicker of irritation stirred as the man didn't react.

"Come on, Monsieur," he said but stopped as the man slowly topped over to one side. He was already dead. Grant dragged the corpse away and sat down in its place. Both men lit cigarettes and leant their heads back, adding to the fug that hung over the bar. From around the corner a piano suddenly cut through the noise and Scottsdale couldn't help but smile. The mournful sound of "There'll Always Be An England" sounded a poignantly defiant note until an enormous crash bought a flood of dust and parts of the ceiling down on them, bringing the music to an abrupt halt.

Scottsdale stared at the ceiling, exhaling deeply, listening to the rhythmic thump of bombs falling. His men were collapsed in various places around him, eyes closed, trying to get comfortable. His own eyes started to close but a voice penetrated his muzzy head; it was a runner from the regiment. Raising a hand he waved, and the man came forward.

"What have you got for me?"

"Hello, sir. We're to assemble on the mole for embarkation tomorrow morning. Report at 0530. Until then, billet where you can."

Scottsdale turned to Grant. "We'll stay here then unless otherwise ordered. Tell the men to get some shut eye." He stopped as a loud crash sounded. The men barely flinched. "Tomorrow, we're going home." And with that, he leant back and closed his eyes. He was exhausted beyond measure. Tomorrow they were going home. Thank God.

***

London, August 31st 1940

London had changed an awful lot since he'd shipped across to France in the autumn of 1939, Scottsdale reflected as he strolled in the late summer sunshine. Barrage balloons now dotted the sky, windows were covered in tape and sandbags were piled up against the entrances to government buildings. Most strikingly was the impact of the intensifying German air assault as they turned their focus from bombing airfields and shipping toward London; here and there a cordoned off house or row of houses that had been reduced to rubble. Yesterday morning he'd emerged to find a London bus nose first in an almighty crater.

Passing a newspaper boy shouting his wares on the corner, his eye was caught by the headline on the boy's sandwich board. '53 Cheers for the RAF!' it screamed. Fishing out a penny, he took the paper, jumping onto a bus and beginning to read. The Air Ministry was reporting a great victory for the RAF over the marauding enemy bombers. Scottsdale, like many others, took the figures with a dose of salt, but was still comforted. Throughout the summer they'd suffered as the German air assault intensified, the RAF fighting their desperate duel in the skies above southern England. The news that France had signed an armistice and was out of the war had followed swiftly after Dunkirk; an invasion had felt inevitable. The time Scottsdale had spent working with the Local Defence Volunteers, who had recently been renamed as the Home Guard, had not inspired confidence. Yet the weeks ticked by and the Germans hadn't appeared on the plains of Kent; though the fear of invasion remained, there was a growing sense that every week was a week to be better prepared.

Flicking through the pages, he tutted at another advert from the Ministry of Information and its Silent Column campaign. It showed a finger being held to a woman's lips with the words 'Keep it to yourself and make others do the same.' The constant focus from the Ministry on careless talk and the risk of spies seemed designed to generate suspicion and panic; it implied that everyone was a spy and the people didn't have an ounce of intelligence regarding discussing military secrets. He'd even heard of people being prosecuted for defeatist talk and that sounded uncomfortably like the very type of tyranny they were fighting. Scottsdale rolled his eyes and sighed.

Reckoning

The months since their return had been discomfiting. Sailing out of Dunkirk harbour on HMS Whitehall, attacked and bombed one final time, he'd felt an overwhelming sense of regret and fatigue. Many good men, men whom he had commanded, wouldn't be making the short journey home. They lay where they fell, among the civilians caught up in the conflict and the animals sacrificed to support it. Sadly, inevitably, it felt a little easier to think of them each day. Back in England it had taken several weeks to piece the battalion back together; men appeared from as far afield as Aberdeen, washed all over the country during the chaos of the evacuation and subsequent embarkation in England. A brief reunion with his parents had followed; uncomfortable in his own bed on the first night of his disembarkation leave, he'd felt an overwhelming guilt. His parents hadn't wanted to pry too much; they had always opposed his desire to join the army and they were mainly relieved he was alive. He was grateful, but it felt so incongruous, sitting down to a special dinner – the meat had been saved up – while he pictured those left behind. Helene was still too painful to discuss with anyone; he was unsure if he'd ever be able to speak of her.

Over it all hung the thought that the Germans were on the brink of invasion. Training programmes were put together with an emphasis on tank hunting, mine laying and repelling parachute defence. And so Scottsdale was kept very busy. It suited him, not giving him time to dwell on what had happened. Yet as he had sat down with McDonald the day before, he also had a sense of pride and gratitude. Sharing a whisky, their conversation, at first irreverent, had turned to their experiences in France.

"You know, I was worried whether the men would follow me," Scottsdale had confessed. "I was – am – so grateful they did." He sipped his drink. "Not sure I'd have wanted to pile in behind me if I'm honest."

"Well I certainly wouldn't," McDonald replied cheerily. "But then they do, don't they? And some of them are really rather dreadful," he added slightly sheepishly. "But they fight brilliantly. I remember we shot up a motorcycle recce. I asked for a volunteer to paddle over the canal to see if there was anything useful to nab in the bike. Quick as flash, Jennings and Cook, two of the biggest rogues you are likely to meet, popped up and went over."

Scottsdale smiled. "Amazing what the war does to people isn't it."

"And what's it done to you, old chap?"

"A hell of a question, Jock, but I've been thinking recently and to be honest, as silly as it sounds saying it out loud, I was almost looking forward to it."

"Oh?"

"Yes, I just had this feeling – and I'm trying to avoid sounding dramatic here – but what exactly was the point of everything. I wasn't connecting with the life that was stretching out before me. It made me incredibly restless, but it also felt like I was the only one questioning it." He paused to sip his whiskey. "And doubt can be a prison, you know. Life would be so much easier without it."

"A little bit of doubt is healthy," McDonald observed. "And I wouldn't say everyone thinks the same. We're all individuals at the end of the day."

"I know, but we seem to end up in the same place, the steady job, the right girl, golf on Sunday. That's what was expected of me and it's…I want to avoid the word patronising, as it's better than that; it's not a lack of imagination either. But it's suffocating, and I've never connected with it; and what I can't work out is if something inside me is wrong or is trying to save me for something else, something bigger. But that's the most insufferable arrogance isn't it? To think you're somehow bigger than what's around you. I've no evidence to support that."

"I think everyone questions what's around them; we all wonder if this is it, for want of a better expression." McDonald gestured vaguely.

"Maybe, Jock, but it doesn't seem to change anything."

"Well, perhaps there's a reason for that? Perhaps, ultimately, we end up in similar places because it's what's right for us. Isn't that what people's experience is for, to guide those who come after?"

"Of course. But I struggle to accept they're right; or of at least pretending to." Scottsdale paused for a long time. "Thank God for the war," he finally said bleakly.

"Christ, Arthur," McDonald sputtered. "You don't mean that."

"I hate myself for saying it. I can't stop thinking of the men I've lost and how they died. Legs blown off, shot in the face, lacerated by shrapnel. Dying in agony, screaming for their mothers, utter terror. How can anything so terrifying be so exhilarating? And the terrible things we've had to do to stand up for what is ultimately right. Do you remember talking about death and what comes next?"

"Heaven and forgiveness? I do, and I stand by what I said."

"I still wonder. Perhaps the trick is not letting yourself drown in it, to know where the line is. Because once you cross that line, I think we're all capable of anything."

"Yes, we are," McDonald said simply. "Of good and bad. And war shows us both."

"It does, Jock," Scottsdale agreed. "And it takes a terrible toll, but even with all that, I know this was the meaning I needed. I hate it, because it's obscene and I know just how awful it can be, but sometimes I think the war saved me."

He winced as he recalled their conversation. But he couldn't avoid the truth in what he had said. And if he was honest, that was a large part of the reason he was walking down The Strand that Saturday morning. The summons he received had come as a something of a shock. He touched his inside pocket where the note resided and felt the same flutter of excitement as when he first read it.

Lieutenant Scottsdale,

Trust you are recovered from your exertions. I would request you call on me at my offices at 40 The Strand. I believe there are things to discuss which will be of mutual interest to us. Ungentlemanly Warfare is expanding. Interesting story.

Yours
P.G. Griffin

A small smile crossed his face as he arrived; right next door to The Savoy. How typical of Griffin, he thought. He wondered what the man wanted and what his cryptic remark had meant? He wasn't sure, but straightening his uniform, he entered the ordinary looking door, looking for something out of the ordinary.

Epilogue

London, August 7th 1940

"I understand, Prime Minister, but this is the only option we have. I mean that, sir. There's no other way."

The bulky figure leaned forward through the cigar smoke. "I'm yet to be entirely convinced, Sir Henry," Churchill growled. "Damn it, one doesn't drop drawers after the first drink. We need to keep something in hand." "It's a chance we must take, sir," Sir Henry Tizard said firmly. He had been replaying this argument with the Prime Minister and various sceptical advisors for months and he wasn't about to be swayed. Tizard, an ex-Oxford fellow and chairman of the Aeronautical Research Committee, knew that the fall of France had strengthened his hand. "They've the productive capacity that we cannot match while we fight. And this technology will change the course of the war, I guarantee it."

"A bold claim, Sir Henry," Churchill replied, taking a large swig of brandy. "I like bold claims. But you better make damned sure you're right." He cleared his throat loudly. "Tell me the plan again."

Tizard adjusted his wire frame spectacles and consulted his notes. He already knew the contents by heart, but it was part of his ritual, honed after years of teaching. "I will head up what, for security reasons, we are calling the British Technical and Scientific Mission, Prime Minister. And as such, I will go first, ahead of the main group to lay the groundwork."

"Go on."

"I will be going via Ottawa to speak with the Canadians before continuing to Washington, where I shall meet the rest of the mission."

261

"Yes, I wanted to speak to you about that," Churchill said leaning forward. "It's essential that we select people who can get across the real situation here. At every opportunity I want them to impress upon the Americans how perilous our situation is."

Tizard shuffled his papers. "I think you'll be satisfied, Prime Minister. Our mission has been selected for both their scientific understanding and their understanding of the operational sphere-"

"The 'operational sphere'? You mean the battlefield." "I do, Prime Minister. And our mission has ample experience of it. Brigadier Wallace, our Army man, was one of the last men off the beaches at Dunkirk. He's also an MC from the first war. Captain Faulkner, representing the Navy, has served in the Atlantic and the Norwegian campaigns. And Group Captain Pearce was part of the raid on the *Scharnhorst* in Norway. I could go on."

"Excellent," Churchill growled. "Tell them from me, any chance to impress on the Americans the situation in the field, they must seize it."

"Understood, Prime Minister."

"And the information we are sharing; nothing is held back?"

"Nothing, sir. We've included only the most advanced projects; yet with an eye to operational use. We are swapping knowledge for industrial capacity, so the sooner they can begin production the better."

"Makes sense," Churchill said through teeth clamped on a cigar.

"We have gathered together the latest blueprints and information on subjects as diverse as rockets, explosives, superchargers, gyroscopic gunsights, submarine detection devices, self-sealing fuel tanks, and even what we have on jet propulsion and atomic fusion."

"Certainly sounds impressive, Sir Henry."

"It is, Prime Minister," Sir Henry replied. "Including the jewel in the crown; a working prototype of the latest cavity magnetron."

"And what is that when it's at home?"

"It's revolutionary, Prime Minister, and will give us a whole new range of ground, shipboard and airborne radars, the performance of which will be far, far beyond any that currently exist. It could give us the vital edge to win the war. And with American industrial support, we can get it mass produced and operational in months."

"Now that sounds like the kind of thing that can make a difference, Sir Henry. Proves the old adage that wars are won by brains as much as brawn."

"In this case, Prime Minister, a little of both. I'm informed that the prototype we have was made possible by the sacrifice of agents in the field."

Churchill nodded gravely. "Then I raise my glass to them," he said, holding his glass to the light. "Godspeed, Sir

Henry. Go and change the war."

Historical Note

In August 1940, as Britain battled for its survival and the Battle of Britain raged overhead, a small group of men boarded an ocean liner in Liverpool. Their destination was America and their mission was to prove pivotal in turning the course of the war, giving the Allies the ultimate ability to harness the latest technological secrets to the cause of defeating the Axis powers.

Officially, this was known as the British Technical and Scientific Mission, and its job was to share Britain's latest technology secrets in exchange for access to America's industrial capacity. Unofficially it was known as the Tizard Mission, after its leader, Sir Henry Tizard. Perhaps surprisingly in hindsight, there was resistance to this plan even at the highest levels of government. However, at that time it was still far from certain when – and if – America would join the war, and if they did, would it be against Germany and Japan, or just Japan?

Necessarily, it was therefore a risk but one that the British government, wilting under the German onslaught in the West, was forced to make and with spectacularly successful results. The key technology was the cavity magnetron, arguably one of the most important technology breakthroughs of the war, that led to the development of far more effective radar (and still helps your microwave work today). In fact, it was so important a development that the official historian of the US Office of Scientific Research and Development, James Phinney Baxter III, wrote: "When the members of the Tizard Mission brought the cavity magnetron to America in 1940, they carried the most valuable cargo ever brought to our shores."

I was drawn to the story for a number of reasons. Firstly, of all the major events taking place in 1940 that had such an impact on the outcome of the war, this remained, relatively, less well known.

I thus weaved the story about radar technology and Tizard's mission into the much better known story of the Battle for France and the British Expeditionary Force's retreat and eventual rescue at Dunkirk – to do so, I have had to take some liberties with some of the timelines and personalities around the technology development (the technology was safely in British government hands before Dunkirk, but shifting it back made the story work). Secondly, it was a truly international effort. Though Randall and Boot at Birmingham are rightly recognised for their work on the cavity magnetron, between the wars science was international, with advances made by various scientists and each one built upon by the next. My French characters are a testament to this fact. Finally, I was always drawn to the idea of the "Suitcase That Changed The World", which is how the contents of the Tizard Mission have been described.

When I thought of how I would have Scottsdale come to be caught up in the rescue of the French scientists, I immediately thought of Special Operations Executive – but in May 1940 that organisation did not exist. Instead, there were three existing secret departments, including a propaganda organisation known as Department EH (after Electra House, its headquarters), Section D itself which was formed under the auspices of MI6 and what would become MI(R), from the War Office, that conducted research into guerrilla warfare. Section D and MI(R) would eventually merge but it felt right that Scottsdale would be drafted into the under resourced Section D to work for the elusive Mr Griffin and Miss Beaufort. There has been a real surge in interest in the secret side of war in recent years, and – as popularised by Giles Milton's *Ministry of Ungentlemanly Warfare* – it is a concept that really caught the imagination.

The second requirement was to select a unit that fought in the retreat to Dunkirk. Being from Essex, there was really no doubt that Scottsdale would be from The Essex Regiment and I am indebted to Col. T.A. Martin's excellent history, *The Essex Regiment*, that covers this period in the history of the regiment. I have been faithful to the 2nd Battalion's movements but by necessity have made up both the village of and engagement at Vierhourt. While the movements are accurate as possible, all the characters are invented.

Similarly, the dastardly Schiller is fictional, but I have tried to faithfully follow the *SS-Totenkpf* movements and give a flavour of their brutality, most notoriously seen in the Le Paradis massacre of the Royal Norfolks on 27th May. As someone who had not studied Dunkirk in the greatest of detail before writing this book, I found it fascinating to dig into the details. There are copious books on the campaign, but I found Hugh Sebag-Montiofore's *Dunkirk – Fight To The Last Man* excellent, a detailed account of the BEF's retreat to Dunkirk. It contains copious notes and references/sources, perfect for those looking to immerse themselves in the campaign at a detailed level, along with vivid personal accounts.

This is Scottsdale and Grant's first taste of combat and, indeed, exposure to Mr Griffin and Miss Beaufort from Section D. However, with five more years of conflict ahead, it won't be the long before Scottsdale and Grant will be needed to fight the King's enemies once again. You can keep up to date by subscribing at www.timothyoliver.co.uk – and if you enjoyed this book and found it via Amazon please share a review to help others find it!

Tim Oliver

September 2019

Printed in Great Britain
by Amazon